STARFIRE

STARFIRE

Julian Jay Savarin

This first world edition published in Great Britain 2000 by
SEVERN HOUSE PUBLISHERS LTD of
9–15 High Street, Sutton, Surrey SM1 1DF.
This first world edition published in the USA 2000 by
SEVERN HOUSE PUBLISHERS INC of
595 Madison Avenue, New York, N.Y. 10022.

British Library Cataloguing in Publication Data

Savarin,   Julian
  Starfire
  1.   Suspense fiction
  I.   Title
  823.9'14 [F]

ISBN 0-7278-5582-4

Typeset by Palimpsest Book Production Ltd.,
Polmont, Stirlingshire, Scotland.
Printed and bound in Great Britain by
MPG Books Ltd, Bodmin, Cornwall.

For Mike and Alison
Friends indeed

Opening Gambits

Autumn, 1996.

G eneral Kurinin spoke coldly.
    "There will be *no* expansion of NATO. It will *not* be countenanced . . . whatever the deal the sick man makes with the West. They can sign as many papers as they want. And as for their planned landing exercises in the Crimea with our former Ukrainian comrades, this will have serious repercussions in the years to come which they cannot as yet foresee.

"Besides," he added dangerously, "the Crimea will be returned to us, where it belongs." No one in the room was in any doubt that he meant every word.

December, 1996.

The surveillance satellite, on a routine orbit that took it over the Baltic, spotted the sliver of a structure that should not have been there. An Aurora mission was launched to check that it was not just a smear on the photograph. The advanced aircraft, cloaked in its mantle of stealth technology, streaked high on its reconnaissance mission, its cameras taking high-resolution shots of the area, its pilot secure in the knowledge that any prying sensors would be blind to his presence.

He was wrong.

In the Pentagon, Major-General Abraham Bowmaker, USAF studied one of the Aurora's high-res photos. The structure was clearly to be seen. It had been caught from directly above and from several oblique angles. It was narrower at the top than at the bottom; one face was concave, curving down and outwards to form the wide base; the opposite face was perpendicular, like the sheer surface of a rock wall. It looked as tall as a ten-storey building.

"I'll be damned," Bowmaker remarked softly. "A phase-array radar that's not supposed to be there. Someone's been cheating in the arms reduction business. Someone else will have to spoil *that* little game . . . and I think I know just the people to do it."

March, 1997. Underground complex, Special Research Unit, 2,000 kilometres north-east of Moscow.

"The West has had its Helsinki meeting," Kurinin began. "They are still adamant about NATO expansion, and we are just as adamant that it won't happen. Their intended manoeuvres with the Ukraine in the Black Sea are provocative, to say the least. They are moving into uncharted waters, without heed of the possible consequences both in the short *and* the long term.

"If they are looking for a nightmare, they will find it. I said as much to you last year. Nothing has occurred to make me think differently. If anything, they are courting the nightmare even more closely. Many of our former comrades down there in the south are extremely unhappy with the developing situation. When the time comes, we shall have valuable support from them. They do not like at all what has happened to our once-powerful Union. The man from Bukta, or Basmanovo, or wherever the hell it is he comes from, will have plenty to answer for."

"What can you expect from a Kazakh?" someone remarked sourly.

The contemptuous comment was a geographical liberty; the two villages in question were in the Urals, about 300 kilometres north of the Kazakhstan border.

Kurinin paused to look at his assembled companions. Despite the fact that they were his close colleagues, his eyes displayed an iciness that sent involuntary chills down their spines. His mouth was clamped so tightly shut a pulse could clearly be seen beating along his jawline.

"I will not tolerate such comments," he said in a hard voice. "There are no Kazakhs here today, but we have many on our side. One of the best fighter pilots I've ever known was a Kazakh who had risen to colonel and was due to command a frontal aviation regiment with the rank of general when he was killed on a special mission. I think very highly of the Kazakhs. They too want the restoration of our strength. They are excellent combat troops; some of you have served with them. Our movement consists of people from all over the old Union and I will not allow ethnic rivalry to infect what we are trying to do. *Is that clear?*"

No one spoke. The silence was telling. They had committed

themselves a long time ago and were not about to go up against Kurinin. Just under two years before, one of the founders of the movement had become greedy for power and had begun his own agenda. He was now dead, as were most of his followers. The remainder were still in hiding all over the world, living in constant fear, waiting for the inevitable.

Both cheered and disturbed by the general's uncompromising hostility towards the West, they were careful not to attract any part of that hostility towards themselves. They also chose to comfort themselves with the knowledge that he was a selfless champion of the Motherland. If anyone could bring her back to her rightful position in the world and save her from further disintegration, it was the man standing before them. He would restore her pride and they would support him in that endeavour. It was the reason they had taken time away from their respective units and come to this place. It was the reason they had hitched their stars to his. This was not the time to try to cut loose.

Kurinin's audience was made up of eleven men from various branches of the armed forces including the border guard regiments. Each of these senior officers mourned the dissolution of the old Soviet system, but not because they sought the return of the old political structures. Like Kurinin, they desired a much leaner, more efficient and more powerful Union of the original countries. They yearned for a return to global strength. Their fears about the catastrophic fragmentation of the armed forces – an inevitable result of the break-up of the old system – were very real. Most of them had elected to remain within Russian units rather than move to those of the newly independent states. The others had allowed themselves to be absorbed into the national forces, but their allegiance remained with the former, combined system, and they were working for its re-establishment.

They considered the national forces to be virtually useless. The brushfire wars in Armenia, Azerbaijan, Chechnya and Georgia had all served to confirm the pointlessness of separation. With no unifying system to hold regional tensions in check, the festering conflicts would continue. The winner could only be the West. This, they knew, was what Kurinin had long ago realised. He was determined to reverse the trend, and they would back him all the way.

During the old days the war in Chechnya would never have occurred; or would not have been allowed to drag on. There would have been a swift pulverising blow, rather than this continuous attrition which only produced more and more dead bodies. Those bodies had grieving parents who increasingly blamed the government and the whole business was unsettling the nation. Every time it seemed as if the shooting had finally stopped, it erupted once more. It was a malignant cancer leaking its poison into the body of the nation. The assembled officers were particularly aware of the frustrations and tensions within the armed forces themselves. Already, soldiers were killing each other or taking their own lives. Many, including serving officers, had turned to criminal activities.

The hopes of those at the meeting were pinned upon Kurinin. He was, their very presence confirmed, the one individual they believed could make a difference in these very dangerous times.

"Ethnic, sectarian and religious conflicts," Kurinin told them, "are the banes of progress. Like unchecked nationalism, they destroy entire nations. It should be unnecessary for me to point this out to you. It's all over the news: from Africa and Europe to the Middle and Far East; from the South American states to our own conflicts among the republics. And they will continue.

"Personally, I hate rabid nationalism. When I was a very young KGB cadet, I had an instructor who had made his way through the ranks; not well-educated, but very wise indeed. 'There are only two things you can do when confronted with a nationalist,' he once said to me. 'Either find yourself a very high window and jump out; that way, you'll escape the misery he is about to bring on the nation. Or better still, push *him* out.'" Kurinin gave a fleeting grim smile. "He was a very hard man. He pushed a few people out of windows in his time.

"These conflicts are the things which make up the tide we must turn back," he went on as the smile vanished, "while we rebuild our country. If we do not, we shall allow the Motherland to become a capitalist vassal and the chaos which is already upon us will seem like a golden age.

"Criminality will become the norm, rather than the current rampant aberration. The criminal warlords will be back from the confines of history to plague us and will control whole regions, and even entire states. The West will sit back, feeling pleased with itself. There are times when I feel tempted to simply walk away because eventually this criminality will spill into the smug West itself. It would be fittingly ironic; but we would still be the loser.

"So that is not the answer. We should learn from what we have seen in recent years and resolve not to repeat those mistakes which ensure that the West remains the only winner. I know that like me the victory of the West sticks in your throat. There are those who believe our decline has been a very cleverly orchestrated campaign by the West to win the Cold War without having fired a shot. I do not totally agree with this, but there is no doubt that they have been quick to seize the opportunities given to them by our problems and have sought to manipulate the situation to their advantage. In the old days, they would never have dared to propose manoeuvres on our very doorstep. Imagine the situation if we chose to hold air, land and sea manoeuvres around *Cuba!*"

The expressions on the faces of the assembled senior officers telegraphed very clearly what they all thought.

"Another missile crisis," one commented drily. "Just like that time with Kennedy."

"Precisely," Kurinin agreed. "But they won't be allowed to get away with it. We have the memories of elephants. We shall respond appropriately, and in due course. When we met last autumn," he went on, "there were some remarkable developments that I chose not to reveal at the time. I did not consider it necessary. But . . . things have changed. Dramatically."

Only one man in the audience, standing diffidently in a corner, was below general rank. Kurinin now turned towards him.

"Allow me to introduce Colonel Doctor Yuri Vasilevich Abilev," he said. "The colonel has been working in a particular area of research for a number of years and has some quite astonishing news for us. The Comrade Doctor will later be showing you some truly remarkable work."

Abilev respectfully drew himself to attention before relaxing into the at-ease stance after a barely perceptible nod from Kurinin.

Kurinin rarely used the old salutation. Just as with the other outdated Party trappings that had been consigned to the past, he preferred to keep it in the background. Addressing Abilev publicly by the old title, however, was his way of indicating to the others the high regard in which he held the military scientist. They would thus listen to the colonel with due respect, despite being his superiors by at least two ranks; which was exactly as Kurinin intended.

Besides, Abilev's revelations would astound them.

November base, the Moray coast, Scotland. Same day.

"This gives me a hard-on," Caroline said softly as she passed a

5

stroking hand along the trailing edge of the Starfire's sleek, delta wing. "I still can't believe the boss is letting me fly it."

McCann was having difficulty with some of her words.

"Um," he began. "You can't have a hard-on. I mean you're . . . you're a woman."

She paused to look sideways at him, a mischievous smile at the corner of her mouth. "Great observation, Elmer Lee. Why can't I have a hard-on?"

"Well . . ." he commenced helplessly.

"Think about it," she cut in, still smiling at him. "Think very hard about it."

He thought about it.

McCann, Kansas *City* dude as he was at pains to tell anyone who would listen and not Kansas, *Kansas*, blushed to the roots of a head of hair that was really corn-coloured.

"Oh!" he said. "Ah . . ."

She tapped at his forehead with the tips of her fingers. "Ding ding! Penny dropped?"

"Ah . . ." he said again.

She grinned. "Wait till I tell Karen Lomax."

"Oh, no! Don't. I mean . . . hell, she'd kill me!"

"You know how it is with women," she went on, inspecting her nails closely. "We talk to each other about our blokes all the time. In fine detail."

"You wouldn't!"

She stopped inspecting her nails. "What's it worth?"

"Um . . . ah . . . I'll fly with you when the boss lets you take the ship for a—"

"The best nav on the unit offering to fly with little old me? Why, Elmer Lee, I'm very flattered."

"I'd go through hell rather than let you tell Karen—"

"Are you saying I'm a lousy flyer?"

"No!" McCann denied weakly. "What I mean . . ." He paused suddenly, comprehension dawning. "You suckered me!"

"Elmer Lee, Elmer Lee. You're such a sweetie."

"You wanted me to take the flight all along!"

She tapped at his forehead again. "Ding ding!"

"And you fixed it with Mark? And the boss?"

The grin was back. The fingers moved.

He took a step backwards. "Don't do that. You suckered me," he repeated, aggrieved.

She patted the Starfire's wing. "Don't you want to fly it?"

6

"Hell, yes!" he replied.

"Well then," she said. She patted the wing once more and walked away, smiling.

He shook his head slowly as he followed her out of the camouflaged, EMP-proof, blast-hardened aircraft shelter.

The unit's aircraft shelters were built to withstand not only proximity blasts and direct hits, but also to protect sensitive electronic equipment within from electromagnetic pulses. All November aircraft, without exception, also carried onboard protection for their own systems. Every shelter on the base had been covered with turf in such a way that it looked like a natural mound with grass, weeds, and even shrubs growing upon it. Positioned haphazardly so as to display no discernible pattern or sequence, they sometimes looked like patches of flower-rich meadow, depending on the season.

"I sure fell for that one," McCann muttered ruefully as he trailed after Caroline Hamilton-Jones, an RAF flight lieutenant and, so far, the November unit's first and only female pilot.

The Special Research Unit, same moment in time.

While the embarrassed McCann was catching up with Caroline, General Kurinin continued to hold his audience's attention. Above their heads, in complete contrast to the warm bright day at November One, the Siberian winter still held the land fast in its icy grip. A fierce wind, unheard by the assembled officers, howled down from the Arctic.

"One of the West's most dangerous achievements," Kurinin said to them, "has been the establishment of a multinational unit with elite personnel and the very best in equipment. You could almost call them a modern version of the Praetorian Guard. But they are not to be seen as the modern equivalent of the political toy soldiers of some effete and corrupt emperor. I refer only to their quality and their apparent freedom from normal service constraints. These are truly elite people and perhaps can be more accurately described as firefighters.

"As you know, some of our own specialised units have crossed swords with them on various occasions. Though it pains me to admit it, they have consistently succeeded in getting the better of us. If we do not admit this fact to ourselves, we cannot hope to improve our tactics and so achieve our goal: their total destruction, by *any* means possible. My own nightmare is that they may finally succeed in proving conclusively to their own people the viability of their programme, and so pave the way for a rash of similar units.

"Western Europe continues to suffer from bouts of petty nationalism. Even the British are facing this disease. We have the condition ourselves and have suffered its effects. However, it is in our interests that such disputes within western Europe continue and any input we can apply to help them along will be to our advantage. A bickering Europe is a divided one – see the mess they have made of Yugoslavia – and a divided Europe is a weak one. Plenty of scope for us. The worst possible outcome, from our point of view, would be a sudden attack of pragmatism where they begin to act in concert. Believe me, my friends, a securely interlocked western Europe would be frighteningly powerful."

"They'll never do it," a Belorussian general said dismissively. "They'll be too busy trying to score points off each other. It's the thirties all over again."

"Don't be too sure," Kurinin cautioned. "People like the man who commands that special unit in Britain are a danger. He is a visionary. Worse, a visionary warrior with intellect and, from our point of view, a very dangerous man indeed. He is inimical to everything we intend to do.

"Against all the insular instincts of his own people, he has managed to establish his force. He and that force are our prime targets. Destroy them, and we shall deal a severe blow to the West, even though they seem quite unaware of the true value of the asset he is trying to give them. That is also in our favour." Kurinin paused. "United we stand, divided we fall. That is as true as it ever was. Let us be the ones who are united, while the western Europeans accentuate their own divisions. And we'll do everything we can to help them," he added with grim humour.

He paused once more, taking his time. "Then there is one other."

They waited.

"There is an agent who works with them," he told them quietly. "Note I said *'with'* not *'for'*. This agent, I am quite certain, is Russian—"

"What?" The chorus of interrupting voices did not want to believe it.

Kurinin patiently waited for the uproar to die down.

"She has many names," he continued, "and many disguises . . . She is a formidable operative and one of our high-priority targets. I can tell you no more than that. Now, let us see what the colonel has for us."

November Base.

McCann was still trailing some distance from Caroline Hamilton-Jones, his mind on his continuing embarrassment. He was thus totally unaware of someone behind him, hurrying to catch up.

"Hard-on," he muttered to himself as he remembered their conversation. "Hell, I knew that. Hey, Caroline!" he cried. "Wait up!"

As he was about to trot off after her, his follower drew level.

"Hi," the new voice said. "I'm Jack Brodie. You're McCann, right?"

McCann paused, looked across to where Caroline had stopped to wait for him, then turned with some impatience to the newcomer. He saw a slim man in US Navy uniform a little taller than he was.

"I'm McCann . . ." he replied neutrally, then stared pointedly at the man's rank. ". . . Ensign. And what are you?"

Brodie gave an easy grin. "I'm an RIO radar intercept officer . . . in the back seat . . ."

"Yes, yes. Even the air force knows what an RIO is," McCann interrupted sarcastically.

Brodie should have sensed the warning, but he ploughed on. "I was on Turkeys . . . you know, Tomcats . . ."

"I'm so happy·for you."

"People call me Freebie, on account I'm good at getting freebies."

"You here on a freebie, Ensign Brodie? If so, tough shit. You've got to be good to get into this outfit."

"I'm good."

McCann stared at him. "That's for the boss to decide."

Brodie's grin slipped a little. He glanced over to where Caroline was still waiting. "So she's a pilot, huh?"

"One of the best."

Brodie shook his head slowly. "Women fighter pilots. You won't get me flying with them. We got a few in the navy. Pains in the ass. Still, this one looks good in uniform. Real nice ass on her. Is she hot, or what?"

McCann's round impish face had taken on an expression that should have stopped Brodie in his tracks, even at this late stage. "If I hear you talk like that about this lady just one more time, I'll have your *cojones* for fritters! You got that, buddy?"

Two figures in flying gear were approaching Caroline. They paused for a quick chat, then came on. Cottingham and Stockmann, on their way to their aircraft, one of the unit's enhanced Super Tornadoes, the ASV(E). Cottingham, a USAF captain, was the pilot and Stockmann, US Marines, the backseater. This was not their usual pairing but it was unit policy to swap crews for training missions to make for a smooth transfer should casualties make this necessary.

They paused once more, with the sort of smiles for McCann they would normally reserve for a familiar itch.

"What gives, Elmer Lee?" Cottingham began. "You're looking like you haven't been to the john in a month."

They stared at Brodie blankly.

"It must have dawned on you," Stockmann said to him, "that we outrank you. Forget how to salute, *Ensign*?"

"No, sir!" Brodie snapped off a hasty salute.

Stockmann returned it with a wave of his hand and glanced at McCann's thunderous expression. "So what gives?"

"All I said," Brodie piped up, "was that she had a nice ass." He nodded in the direction of the patiently-waiting Caroline. "Then he said he'd have my *cojones* for fritters. He always talk like that? They an item, or what?"

Cottingham stared at Brodie with baleful eyes.

Hank Stockmann III bared teeth like gleaming tombstones. "You're new here, Ensign."

"Yes."

"Captain. I'm a captain. You say 'Yes sir, *Captain*'."

Brodie swallowed. His eyes darted furtively at each of them. "Yessir, Captain."

"*Captain* McCann always talks like that. The Brits sometimes have a hard time with him but hell, he's American . . ."

"I'm . . . I'm American."

"Hey, Brodie! So you are. And guess what? So am I! Isn't that great? And so is this stalwart pilot next to me who's glaring at you like you're a tick on a cow's backside. He, is *Captain* Cottingham to you. And if we hear you *ever* again say anything disrespectful about the lady, we'll *barbecue* your *cojones*. Five by five?"

"Er . . . five by five . . . er Captains."

"Good." Stockmann walked on.

Cottingham remained long enough to place a powerful arm about Brodie's shoulders. It was not difficult to imagine Cottingham in full pro-football gear, bearing down upon a hapless opponent. Cottingham had never played football, but he was menacing enough to make Brodie wince as the arm tightened.

"Ensign Brodie," Cottingham began softly. "A word about the Brits. They have strange habits. For instance, they don't give people normal ranks like the rest of us mortals. The lady over there is called a flight *lef*tenant, but they spell it like *loo*tenant, with an 'l-i-e-u'. This makes her a captain too. Not your day, is it?"

"No . . . no, sir."

"Also, if I catch you talking about her ass again, I won't just barbecue your manhood, I'll bite all three off first." The arm squeezed tighter. "Are we agreed here?"

"We . . . we are . . . agreed, Captain, sir!"

"There you go, Ensign. Who said we couldn't get on with the navy?" Cottingham moved his arm away from Brodie's shoulders. "Must fly," he said, poker-faced. "Plane to catch."

"And I've got a lady waiting," McCann said.

"These guys are nuts!" Brodie said to himself when he was alone once more. He realised he was shaking slightly. He stared alternately at them as they walked away from him, going in opposite directions. "Nuts!"

Caroline looked at McCann curiously as he came up. "What was that all about?"

"He said you had a nice ass."

"So? Don't I?"

"Sure, but that's not his business."

She smiled at him. "You are such a sweetie, Elmer Lee."

"Um . . . you promise not to tell Karen about . . . you know . . . back there by the plane."

"My word is my bond, Elmer Lee."

"Good enough for me."

One

W ing Commander Christopher Tarquin Jason, MA, DFC, RAF,
and object of General Kurinin's ire, sat at his desk studying
the records of Ensign John Duncan Brodie, known as Jack Brodie.
Sitting in a comfortable chair next to the desk was one of his deputy
commanders, Teniente Colonello Mario da Vinci of the AMI, the
Italian Air Force.

Jason looked up. "Well, Mario? What do you think? Will Brodie
make it?"

The lieutenant-colonel, a lean impeccably turned-out man, gave
a tiny shrug. Da Vinci was fastidious in virtually everything he
did. His flying was faultless; his attire was faultless; his manners
were faultless. He was also ruthless, both as a flyer and as a
commander.

Neither man was aware of McCann's little spat with the most
recent arrival for potential aircrew duties at the November base.

"Brodie is a good backseater," da Vinci began quietly. "He would
not have made it this far, otherwise."

"But?"

Da Vinci chose his words carefully. "It would seem that he has a
difficulty with female pilots. Of course, there are none in Zero Two
squadron . . ."

Jason waited.

"He was overheard talking to one of the newer pilots on Zero
Two," da Vinci went on carefully in his lilting English. "He asked
if it was true that we had a female pilot on the unit. When the man
answered in the affirmative, Brodie was very uncomplimentary."

Jason's eyes looked dangerous. "He was, was he?"

"According to my information, Brodie was very graphic in
expressing his lack of enthusiasm for them. Apparently, he was
crewing a Tomcat that missed a trap one bad night, and crashed
into the sea. The pilot was a woman. They both ejected safely, but
he blamed her for the accident. Did so in his report. Mishandling of
engine power settings. Not enough left in reserve for a bolter. That

12

was why they went in." Da Vinci pointed to the file on Jason's desk. "It's in there; although it is in correct military language. Nothing to show that he was *personally* motivated. If I did not know of his conversation, I would not have guessed from what is written down how he truly feels."

"You mean he stuck the knife in, but kept it all above board."

"That is my opinion."

"I see," Jason said. He shut the file. "I'll study that section carefully. His flying assessments are excellent. His capabilities appear to be far above those required for the basic rank of Ensign. According to his former commander, he's virtually due to be made up to lieutenant junior grade; and he seems to be barely out of his teens. He's certainly not wasting any time. A good man who will go far, by all accounts. I'm hard with my selection procedures, but I like to be fair. If a candidate's good enough, I'll give him or her the chance to make the grade as ground or aircrew, whatever their branch of service."

"The US Navy put him up for selection," da Vinci pointed out cautiously.

"As do many other NATO units. Feather in their caps to have someone sent here."

"We also get those they want to get rid of . . . the ones who are difficult, for one reason or another."

"If you're talking about people like McCann, we do seem to have our fair share of those," Jason admitted. "But you will agree that the ones who have made it through our selection process and training are the very best you could possibly find anywhere; even our reigning champion pain in the neck, McCann."

Da Vinci permitted himself another tiny smile. "Just my point, sir. McCann sometimes makes you want to pull your hair out strand by strand, or scream into the night, or run into a wall with your head—"

"Why, Mario . . . such passion!"

"Blame my Italian parents," da Vinci said mildly.

"So what's the point you're driving at?"

"McCann and Brodie. On the surface, Brodie *might* seem to be just another McCann . . ."

"For which, God help us!"

"My feelings too, sir. Like McCann, Brodie has problems with his pilots. With McCann, it's majors . . ."

"And Brodie, female pilots."

Da Vinci nodded. "But there is a big difference."

"Which is?"

"McCann is not mean. I think Brodie – if I may borrow from Major Carlizzi's New Yorker way of saying things – can be a mean sonofabitch when he puts his mind to it. As you've said, he should be a lieutenant . . ." Da Vinci gave the barest hint of a shrug that spoke volumes.

Jason stared at his subordinate, saying nothing for some moments. "We can all be mean."

"There's meanness, and then there's meanness," da Vinci said. "It knows no boundaries," he went on, emphasising the point he was really making. "I am thinking of something nasty. I think there is nastiness in that accident report."

"Are you telling me, Mario, you consider that Brodie has an attitude problem that could be dangerous to his colleagues in the air?"

"In my opinion," the Italian colonel said firmly.

Jason was again silent. Long moments passed. He stood up, and began to slowly pace the room.

"It's quite ironic," he began. "Brodie is a very ancient name around here on the Moray coast; some say the most ancient of the Scottish tribes. Shame if he does not come up to scratch. The November Programme, Mario," he went on, "is itself a maverick. There are many who would dearly love to shut us down, and not all of them are our potential adversaries from beyond these shores, as you know. So it's small wonder that we sometimes get candidates who are mavericks in their own right, whatever the reason.

"Sometimes they're sent here because their units want someone else to have the problem; sometimes it's in the hope that they'll bring us down. But sometimes we get the real gems. Luckily for us, we appear to have more gems, even among those who may loosely be described as mavericks." Jason gave a brief chuckle. "General Bowmaker once even called me a maverick. Not like you, eh, Mario?"

"That depends on your definition of maverick, sir."

Jason gave him a curious look. "You're the epitome of military correctness. I can't imagine you otherwise."

Da Vinci gave a rueful shake of his head. "I am afraid that even I have got a skeleton. There is a general back in Italy who is very glad I am here and not there."

Jason regarded him with increased curiosity. "What are you trying to tell me, Mario?"

"There is a woman who has been my close friend from childhood.

Our families even expected we would marry when we got older. But, as can so often happen, our lives went different ways. We did not always stay in touch but we never lost that special sense of friendship. Imagine my surprise when, one day, she arrived at my old unit as the wife of the commanding general. One night I was on duty and I received a call from her. She was crying and wanted me to go to the house."

Da Vinci gave one of his shrugs and Jason continued to watch him silently.

"My common sense told me not to go," da Vinci continued, "but my memories of the young girl I used to know made me do the emotional thing. I went to the general's house. The general was not there when I arrived, but Cicca – that is the name by which I have always called her – was there, alone. Sir, she had been beaten, very badly, and by the general. It was also not the first time.

"At his other units she had said nothing. He used to do this even before he was a general, from the first year of their marriage. She said nothing for all that time and never wrote to me about it, although she always knew how to find me. That night I discovered that she had always kept in touch with my family but made them promise not to let me know.

"I tried to comfort her as we talked. Then the general returned. He was very angry when he saw me and ordered me out of the house. I am very sorry to say, sir, I disobeyed. Cicca came to stand between us when he threatened to bring me up before a court martial for disobeying a superior officer. I don't know what she thought she could do. This made the general even more angry. He hit Cicca . . . with his *fist*. For a moment I lost my reason and risked my career. I hit him."

"My God!" an astonished Jason exclaimed. "*You?*"

"Me, sir. So you see, I am not so perfect. The general could not bring me up on charges because, of course, I would have said why I hit him. We both wanted to keep our careers. We agreed to say nothing about it, and nothing appeared in any files. He never hit Cicca again. When I learned I had been selected for the November Programme the general was only too glad to sign the authorisation. What I did was a crazy thing; but if I could go back to that night, I would do it again."

"And I would hold your jacket," Jason told him calmly.

Da Vinci was surprised. "Thank you, sir."

"Thank *you* for telling me." Jason gave a fleeting smile. "I'll try to remember not to hit any women in your presence."

Da Vinci's own smile was sheepish. "That is my only transgression of military discipline."

"It will be our secret, Mario."

"Thank you, sir," da Vinci repeated. "And what shall we do about Brodie?"

"I think I know how to give him his biggest test," Jason said ominously. "The outcome will decide whether he stays with us or packs his bags. When he's been through the standard ASV conversion, we'll schedule an introduction to the ASV(E)."

"Only half our Zero Two complement are E versions, and their slots are all fully booked for weeks ahead. The rest are standard ASVs."

"I've got the answer to that. Give him the usual ASV backseat procedures work-up in the simulator. That should test his mettle. When he's completed that to your satisfaction, follow it up with ten hours of hard-working air time with the pilot instructors. If he proves to be proficient in the back seat by then, give him the simulator conversion to the E, until you feel he's ready for an actual flight. Then I'd like both you and Dieter Helm to see me with a status report. Provided you both agree he's up to it, we'll schedule the ASV(E) flight."

"And the pilot?"

"Zero One should have a slot available. Caroline's the newest member. She'll do rather nicely, don't you think?"

"Uh-oh," da Vinci said.

"If he has got a problem," Jason remarked uncompromisingly, "the sooner we find out the better it will be all round. And I shall want *all* cockpit conversation recorded. Comments?"

"I wouldn't dare, sir." Da Vinci had risen to his feet.

"I'm not being especially hard on him."

"I know you're not."

The Special Research Unit, east of the Urals.

Five hours eastwards from November One, the Arctic wind howled across the vast marshes of the West Siberian Plain to slam itself dementedly against the eastern flank of the mountain range. On hitting the mountains it changed course violently southwards; the cold fury of its breath was felt as far as the northern borders of Iran.

The low-lying surface buildings of the underground complex had been designed with the fierceness of the wind well in mind; their roofs were streamlined to near aerofoil perfection and the wind rushed past them with hardly any turbulence. Tucked behind the protective arm of a high curving outcrop of the mountains, the immediate area was a haven of relative calm. Even so, great billows of whipped and drifting snow surged past in the near distance. There was nothing within the vicinity of the buildings overtly military. There were no runways of any kind, either for long or short take-off aircraft. There wasn't even a helipad to be seen.

Two uniformed soldiers stood at one of the large heavily armoured windows of the main security annex, thankful to be in the warm. Each wore a pistol at his belt. One was a battle-hardened sergeant.

He looked at his younger companion, a conscript. "Well, Daminov? What do you expect to see out there? Yankees coming to feed you hamburgers?" He laughed coarsely.

Feodor Daminov did not rise to the bait. With an intellectual capacity far greater than anything the sergeant could hope to possess, he was accustomed to the crude teasing. The sergeant, however, had formidable cunning. He seemed able to feel only contempt for conscripts, but Daminov was prepared to put up with that.

All Daminov wanted was for his term of service to end before they sent him to Chechnya. He wanted out of this wilderness – seemingly at the edge of the known world – but not if it meant going to Chechnya. If he could just wait out his service without having to face that, he could stand the sergeant's stupid jokes for as long as it took. Besides, the accommodation was luxurious compared to normal army billets. Despite the inhospitable climate, it was almost a holiday posting.

To compensate for the tedium of the enforced isolation, some of the most beautiful women soldiers he'd ever seen – conscripts and officers – were among the site personnel, and a welcome distraction. And as for the food, it was almost like eating in a Western restaurant. He'd never been to a Western restaurant nor to any of the fancy ones in Moscow, but he could let his imagination run riot. Even the sergeant couldn't reach him in there.

Not for the first time, Daminov found himself wondering about this establishment, which had clearly had vast sums spent on its creation.

"I couldn't believe the number of brass hats that came in yesterday," he now said to the sergeant. "The only time you see so many in one place is at the May Day parade."

The sergeant went perfectly still. "Daminov," he said at last, "keep control of that imagination of yours. You were sent up here because someone, somewhere, considered you a good soldier, even for a conscript, and despite that violin of yours. So concentrate on doing your duty. You didn't see any brass hats, did you?" The sergeant's eyes bored into his.

"No, Sergeant Melev. I didn't see any brass hats."

"If I hear any mention of them again, you'll be doing more outside patrols than there are days in the year. And playing violin for the colonel won't save you. You'll play the wretched thing to keep him out of my hair and *still* go on patrol duty."

"Yes, Sergeant."

"You never saw brass hats," the sergeant repeated.

"I never saw brass hats."

The sergeant jabbed a finger at the glass, indicating the raging storm outside. "Keep thinking of that shit out there when that over-educated brain of yours wants to make your tongue wag."

"Yes, Sergeant."

"Don't be too smart for your own good."

"No, Sergeant."

"I prefer soldiers who don't think, and do as they're told."

"Yes, Sergeant."

"That's the trouble these days. Too much education."

"Yes, Sergeant."

"Now I'm off to check on the other sorry specimens, to make sure they're not slacking; or the captain will be checking on *me*. If he thinks he needs to check up on me, it annoys him. It annoys me too, and I take that annoyance out on anyone below me in rank. Watch out for the incoming patrol and warn me on your radio when you spot them."

"Yes, Sergeant."

The sergeant grunted at him, then began moving away to commence his inspection rounds of the duty guard unit. He paused, turning round.

"And keep your mind, and your dick, off the women. That's officers' meat."

"Yes, Sergeant."

As the sergeant marched off, Daminov remembered his waiting girlfriend 2,000 kilometres away in Moscow and thought wryly it was OK for the sergeant to talk. The sergeant's wife had accompanied him to this back of beyond. She was also a soldier. Daminov thought she was uglier than the sergeant.

And that was saying something.

But sergeants could be beautiful too, and there was one who would look like an angel if only she smiled a bit. Daminov felt a twinge of guilt. He had a faithful girlfriend back in Moscow. What was he doing lusting after the female sergeant in the documents section? Anyway, she was a senior rank and, as his sergeant had just said, all the good-looking ones went for the officers. Her boss was a looker too; a captain called Lirionova. His fellow soldiers in the guard unit always talked about those two; everyone agreed they were the best-looking of the lot.

"Lirionova," one of them had said when they'd first heard her name. "Aah . . . Liri! She can empty *my* pistol anytime!"

"Which way?" had come a lewd query through the loud laughter that had followed. "As if she'd waste the time."

"Any way she likes! From above or from below!"

"You've been up here too long. Your mind's living in fantasy."

"Bet she serviced somebody well to make it to captain," the first soldier had gone on, refusing to drop it and shamelessly defaming the object of his lust. "That's not fantasy. Bet she got her promotions quickly too. That's not fantasy either. They say she was a sergeant not so long ago."

"If I were you, I wouldn't shoot my mouth off," a third soldier had cautioned. "She'd better not hear you saying those things. However much you'd like the chance to get your dirty hands on her, she's still a captain *and* she reports directly to General Kurinin."

"You're not me. And who told *you*, anyway?"

"I know who told him," someone else had joined in. "It's that little mechanic from Arkhangelsk who works on the APC engines. She's got a friend in the documents section."

"Women," the first soldier had grumbled. "They never stop yapping."

"Better not make her pregnant, Filenko!" a new voice had then warned the one with the girlfriend from Archangel amid more laughter. "Or it will be the penal battalion for you. Probably for her too. They tell me they have female warders the size of houses who love nothing more than squeezing soft flesh. Your little mechanic has plenty of—"

"Shut up, Arkady Pavlovitch. You're only jealous!"

"Jealous! *Me?* Hah!"

Daminov recalled the incident, a vaguely humorous expression upon his face, as he stared out at the ghostly whiteness that swirled in the early gloom of the day. At this northern latitude – though a good 200 kilometres below the Arctic Circle – daylight did not hang around, even in March. The storm had only served to hasten the onset of darkness.

It was, he thought, almost like being on another planet.

Several levels beneath where Daminov was exercising his imagination, Lieutenant-Colonel Abilev was about to have his moment of scientific glory.

The small auditorium's tiered seats were arranged in a semicircle. The number of people had increased by one: Captain Lirionova, sitting next to Kurinin. Abilev was on the low podium, looking almost sheepishly back at the attentive eyes trained upon him. He was a small man in a uniform that looked as if it could do with a good press and had an air of extreme vunerability. But Abilev was a man of suprises. Unusually for someone who was officially seen as a military scientist, he was a combat veteran with more medals than many of the generals present. A man of high intelligence, there was a steely resolve within him that was belied by his outwardly diffident air.

He was also in overall command of the research unit and the colonel whose liking for the violin so disgusted Sergeant Melev. But the most surprising thing about Abilev was his manner of speaking. When he opened his mouth to do so it was in a voice so deep that those hearing it for the first time – irrespective of rank – tended to gape at him. Many a person had looked elsewhere to check where the sound was coming from. Then they would look more closely at his medal ribbons, and would be prepared to believe anything. If he could win those medals, their eyes seemed to say, then the voice really belonged to him.

A skeletal headset carrying an earphone and dynamic throat mike assembly was clamped to his thinning grey hair. Behind him, a latticed blind was drawing open from the centre to reveal a large white screen. As the blind moved he opened his mouth to speak, but Kurinin interrupted him.

"Colonel . . ."

"Yes, General?"

The deep boom of the voice caught some of his audience unawares. Like so many others before them, some glanced behind to search out the banks of speakers which they clearly believed had amplified Abilev's speech, only to look slightly confused when they could see none.

"Try to remember we're not holders of doctorates in molecular biology or its related sciences. Keep it simple."

"Yes, sir. But I'll need to give an introductory—"

"Just try not to confuse us. Keep to the basics."

"I'll try," Abilev promised, clearly unhappy with short cuts. He gave what sounded like a sigh of resignation and launched into his presentation.

"Comrade Generals," he began, eyeing Kurinin warily, "the march of science is a wonderful thing. We've all heard about the cloning of animals – even humans some would have us believe." He smiled weakly, as if hinting that perhaps human clones were not as rare as people might think. "Or the genetic manipulation of plants. We've seen the large tomato, the giant pumpkin and, of course, the famous Western sheep clone, star of newspapers and TV." He paused as if waiting for at least some chuckles.

The generals looked stonily back at him.

He cleared his throat and hurried on. "Today, I'll be showing you what can be done in the field of plant biology. The manipulation of plant DNA is not a new activity of course. Cultivators did it the very first time they grafted say . . . fruit from the same or different species. I could give you many examples—"

"Colonel, please . . ." Kurinin said warningly.

"Sir." Abilev made a visible effort to truncate his lecture. "To move on. I could tell you about recombinant DNA, mutagenesis, injected viruses used as vectors, gene-coated tungsten beads that are fired into cells with particle guns, reporter genes . . ." He glanced at Kurinin who was staring hard at him. ". . . but I'll keep it short. By injecting nanocomputers into their DNA, we have been able to modify the genetic structure of plants in a manner that has enabled us to greatly augment their natural sensors. You could say that we have created a type of cybernetic organism. Our methods have managed to give these plants the vastly enhanced ability to sense movement, heat and sound, to create a radar-like sensitivity—"

"*What?*" someone exclaimed.

He had them now, he thought with satisfaction.

"We can, Comrade Generals," he told them, "make infrared, radar, acoustic and pseudo-optical sensors out of plants."

"Impossible!" an admiral snapped. "A plant cannot see!"

"With respect, Admiral," Abilev said, "plants do. Perhaps not in the way you or I can; but they sense, they are mobile, they can 'hear' . . ." He paused. "We have examples, as I shall be able to demonstrate later."

He spoke softly into the mike. The lights dimmed and images of plant cells appeared on the screen.

"First," he went on, "a short example of how we carried out our work. It's taken a very long time, but we have found a few solutions."

He spoke again into the mike. The screen was now filled by a single cell. This continued to be magnified until the boundaries of the cell disappeared off-screen, and still the magnification continued. Then it stopped. A circular device, clearly not organic, had come into view.

"Our nanocomputer," he said, "deep within the cell. At the moment you cannot see what it's doing. We'll increase magnification."

The nanocomputer grew bigger until magnification was again halted. Movement was clearly visible.

"Now see what's happening."

There was a collective gasp from the assembled senior officers. The nanocomputer was *interacting* with the cell. Slender translucent arms were detaching themselves from it to swim away and attach themselves to a new host, where the process repeated itself.

"They are renewing themselves and modifying the plant as they do so. You could almost say we have infected the plant with a virus that is busily rewriting and modifying its files. It will be a very different plant to the one we started with. This particular example has infrared properties. Placed in a darkened room and connected to the appropriate monitors, we can see what the plant 'sees'. Just imagine it, Comrade Generals. An innocuous plant in any room can be the ultimate undetectable surveillance unit.

"We all know of camouflaged sensors dropped behind enemy lines: an acoustic unit that looks like a fern until you get close enough to see it's made of metal or plastic; fake trees to hide an antenna; a sensor that looks like a stone buried just beneath the surface. But imagine a situation where assault troops, making their way under the cover of darkness through a wood and believing they're safe, are really under *constant* surveillance the moment they enter. *Every tree is watching them, listening, pinpointing them all the way!*"

Abilev paused again, trying very hard not to look triumphant and not succeeding.

They were all staring at him except Kurinin and Lirionova who'd already known what to expect.

"Or further imagine," he went on into their stunned silence, "an aircraft like a Tornado, flying fast and low between high ground to avoid radar but in fact passing a specially cultivated hill or mountain, or moving along a valley floor *being seen all the way* and tracked into the jaws of a pre-positioned SAM battery or a waiting fighter ambush. And the crew would have *no* idea whatsoever that they were being tracked. The bio-sensors are passive. Therefore they do not warn of their presence and there is no defence against them. Who can tell by looking at a patch of ground that it's 'sensitive'?

"This is not as crazy as it sounds. Plants already possess these sensors. All we've done is augment and harness them. The sensitive plant reacts to touch, or just movement at close proximity. Blow on one and it will react as if you've touched it. Imagine this to be the slipstream of a passing jet and . . ." He stopped, having made his point.

"And you've got working examples?" a Ukrainian general asked.

"We have better than that, General. We've got various examples here as I've said but, better still, we've already got a fully cultivated site. Ten hectares of meadow. That meadow is a combined radar, infrared, acoustic and optical bio-sensor. Our first field prototype. We shall soon be able to do the same to a patch of forest."

They were staring at him in amazement.

"Where is this meadow?" someone asked.

"In the Baltics."

Another stunned silence greeted this.

"Exactly where in the Baltics?" a Baltic-born Russian general demanded.

Abilev looked at Kurinin.

"For the moment," Kurinin said smoothly to his fellow generals, "we prefer to keep the location secret until all tests have been completed. However, we do have the live examples to show you; if the colonel is finished here. Colonel?"

"I'm finished, General. But if there are questions . . ."

"They can be asked in the trials laboratory. You may take us there, Colonel."

"Yes, General."

Abilev spoke into his mike. The screen behind him went blank, the lights brightened and the latticed blind drew itself across as they filed out.

Two

The trials laboratory was a further two levels down. It was an almost cavernous high-ceilinged place, well-lit, and ventilated with filtered air. There were several spacious enclosed booths housing plants of various species and, in some of them, personnel in white full-body environmental suits were busily conducting experiments. They paid only cursory attention to the high-level visitors, concentrating instead upon their work.

A work surface of generous width formed a vast u-shaped desk along three walls of the lab. A neat row of monitors for computer terminals covered most of it and at each terminal people were hard at work on their keyboards.

Before entering, the visitors had been issued with calf-length fabric overboots in white and special area security tags. They now walked uncertainly behind Abilev like a group of students trooping after their lecturer. Kurinin and Lirionova strolled after them.

One of the computer screens was much larger than any of the others. Abilev stopped before it.

A woman in her mid thirties, wearing the long white coat of the laboratory worker everywhere, looked round as they approached but did not rise to her feet. A roundish face with an unexpectedly strong nose was framed by gleaming neck-length black hair. The true colour of her eyes was masked by faintly tinted thick-rimmed spectacles. Her lips looked soft, daringly close to being inviting; and there were pronounced indentations at the corners of her mouth as if she smiled often. Her expression seemed to hint that she found life amusing.

"Are we ready, Doctor?" he said to her.

"Yes, Colonel."

Now on his home ground, Abilev appeared to have subtly grown in stature so that the senior officers – with the exception of Kurinin – were now the ones who seemed diffident.

He turned to them. "Doctor Olga Vasilyeva, our civilian genius. She has worked closely with me on this project. Much of the development owes its existence to her excellent work."

She smiled at them as they nodded respectfully at her. "The Colonel is being modest, but I thank him for the compliment." She looked away to begin tapping at her keyboard. "Now, gentlemen, a little demonstration." She stopped, then leaned back in her chair as the programme began to run.

They had shuffled round so that they could all have a good view of the large monitor.

On screen, a computer animation of a finely-gridded square appeared. From one side of the square, four different-coloured ribbons streamed, to terminate in an underground control station. Next, a plant appeared and its roots began to grow. As the roots touched the grid, they began to merge with it, before continuing into the ground. But something was happening within the grid itself. Pulses came from the plant, passed through the grid then along the ribbons to the control station. Commands came from the station, retracing the route taken by the pulses. Soon a traffic of pulses was going both ways.

"What you're seeing," Olga Vasilyeva was saying, sensing their astonishment, "is a transfer of information from the plant to the control centre, and a transmission of commands from the centre back to the plant itself. The gridded mesh enables us to communicate with the subject. Each of the transmission channels relates to a different sensory function – infrared, acoustic, pseudoptic – in this case radar. Please note I did not say pseudop*tronic* . . ."

"But this is not possible!" one of the generals, a Georgian pilot, exclaimed. "A plant cannot display a radar picture."

"Perhaps I should explain further," she responded mildly. "In the strictest terms, the plant itself is not producing the radar. The various computer programs convert what the plant 'sees' and 'hears', into the required sensor mode. The pictures are synthetic but they are in real time. We have a working example to show you.

"You'll also note," she went on, "that the roots do not go beyond the boundaries of the mesh. No plants within a particular grid will send roots beyond it. They are inhibited and cannot cross that boundary."

"You are confirming what the colonel has told us?" one of the admirals asked, still clearly a sceptic. "That you can really cultivate an area with these . . . sensor plants, making a patch of ground a multi-sensor antenna?"

"Yes. But don't look so surprised, Admiral, or so sceptical. When you're out walking, all around are nature's sensors. We haven't invented them. We've simply taken what is already there, enhanced it, and translated that into a language, or image if you prefer, that we can interpret. It's been going on from the moment life appeared on this planet.

"People record whale sounds and attempt to construct a language, or make music out of them. The Western hippies used to attach weak-voltage electrodes to plants to create a kind of plant *son et lumière* for their amusement. To give us what you see, we've taken that several stages further."

She picked something up from the work surface and passed it over. One of the officers took it, inspected it unsure of what to look for, and passed it on. It was a small gridded square that seemed to be made of plastic.

"That small section of material," she told them as it passed from one to the other, "looks just like a piece of plastic to you. It isn't; it's organic. It looks inert but, when triggered by contact with a plant, it responds and begins to merge. It's a growth accelerator that boosts feeding and, most importantly, it is also the plant's interface with us."

The admiral wanted more assurance. "What about vulnerability? Once the site has been discovered, an attack with defoliants would soon destroy it."

"We have thought about that," she said, "though discovery is most unlikely. If you who see the evidence cannot believe it, why should a potential enemy even imagine such a thing exists? But to answer your question: those plants which are used as sensors have also been modified to resist all known defoliants. They can protect themselves. They break down the toxins, convert them into food and use that as an energy supply. An attack will cause some damage but the area will recover quickly. The defoliant will simply be feeding it. Eco-friendly."

"What about fire? A napalm-type attack, for example."

"Have you heard of the fireweed, Admiral? Fire makes it thrive. And we all know that burning enriches the soil. Again, there is a . . . program, if you like, in the plant's genetic code that will make it recover. The only way to terminate it would be to feed the wrong program into its system via the nanocomputers; like a lethal virus, for example. Or, of course, bomb it out of existence; but that can happen to any sensor array, SAM, or radar site.

"We haven't created an invulnerable system, gentlemen; just one that is virtually impossible to detect and also extremely resilient. What SAM or radar site do you know that's self-repairing? We have simply found another way to harness nature."

Olga Vasilyeva smiled again at the senior officers. She seemed, like Abilev before her, to find humour in something only she knew about.

"I can see that the only way to make you believe what's on that screen," she went on, "is to give you the live demonstration." She looked at Abilev. "Would you like to give it, Colonel?"

"You're doing fine, Olga. Take us to the chamber."

She tapped a key to end the program she'd been running.

"Very well. Please follow me everyone."

It was only when she stood up and began to walk that the visitors noticed her slightly awkward gait.

She gave her right thigh a light pat. "Anti-personnel mine," she told them briskly in answer to their curious stares, "two years ago. Lost it below the knee. And please don't look so embarrassed. I was in Angola studying plant life. Even though that war has been officially over for years, plenty of mines are still around. One of ours, as it turned out. Ironic.

"Perhaps mines should be given operationally-limited lifespans after deployment; after which they would become inert when the fighting's all over. It's a simple thing to do." She gave a soft chuckle. "But of course people will always cheat. You cannot trust anyone these days."

There were a few embarrassed coughs as they tried to come to terms with the light-hearted way she was treating her disability.

"As a pilot," she said to the Georgian cheerfully, moving away from the subject of her leg, "what would you think if I were to tell you that, not so far into the future, the combat pilot will be in a true interface with his aircraft? I don't mean simple voice commands and linked helmet sighting systems. I mean *real* interfacing."

He was closest to her and keeping pace.

His brow furrowed briefly as he glanced at her. "Joined to it? As one complete unit?"

She nodded. "As one; almost in symbiosis. The pilot will have a helmet that will truly make him part of his aircraft. When he puts that helmet on, he will *be* the aircraft. He will see what the aircraft sees, hear it all around him, feel it as an extension of his own self. Instead of looking at a display, he will be in the display. What do you think of that?" she repeated.

"Do you mean see on the display the image of an air target that is a hundred kilometres away? It sounds incredible."

"I mean a lot more, and it's not as incredible as you may think. He will be *near* the target, looking at it as if from just a few metres. He can be as far or as near as he wants to be. The helmet sensing system will give the pilot total situation awareness, in the truest sense. He won't be looking at displays. He will be looking at the sky about him, as if he was outside the aircraft.

"He will have three hundred and sixty-degree vision, and data fusion will give him instantaneous access to all sensor modes in a single scan, should the combat or navigational environment require it. He will be able to see his targets at any magnification that has been built into the avionics. He will see his target and any approaching threat simultaneously, without necessarily needing to turn his head to look. He will manoeuvre instinctively.

"I'll explain further. When you go through a doorway you don't pause to measure the distance on either side before entering. Your eyes assess, and you simply position yourself automatically in a manner that will let you through without bumping into the door frame. You're not even aware of having made all the precise calculations that will get you through. You simply do it. That's how the pilot in that helmet will react."

They were all listening to her as they walked, not certain they should believe what she was saying.

"I can sense your uncertainty, gentlemen," she said drily. "This isn't magic. Nature has already beaten us to it. As with the plant, we shall merely be enhancing something that is already there. The helmet, the aircraft systems and the aircraft itself will be amplifying the natural senses of the pilot. All we're doing is giving mother nature a boost. It will still be up to the pilot's skill to win the fight."

"Taking this to its logical conclusion," the Georgian general eventually began, "am I to assume that one day there could be 'organic' aircraft?"

"Why not?" As far as she was concerned it was perfectly feasible. "We're certainly moving in that direction. By 'we', I mean the scientific community."

The admiral had manoeuvred his way forward. "So the West is even now working on a helmet system like this?" he asked.

"I would be very surprised if they were not."

"And are we?"

"Possibly."

"This is science fiction."

"Science fiction, Admiral," Olga Vasilyeva said, "comes from our imaginings. What we can imagine we can eventually make real and so turn fiction into fact."

"Enhancing the basic human being," the Georgian said.

"Yes."

"You enhance him, give him a longer reach, give him eyes that see over great distances and in the dark. But," the Georgian continued thoughtfully, "when it comes down to it, despite all the technology, it is still one man facing another with a spear in his hand."

"It was ever thus, General. And here we are, gentlemen."

The chamber was a large internal greenhouse reached via a heavy steel door nearly a foot thick at the far end of the laboratory. There was a high gallery, rather like the control tower on the island of an aircraft carrier, with its entire forward section taken up by a banked console stacked with monitoring equipment. Several visual display units were filled with rows of digits scrolling, vertically on some, horizontally on others. Other VDUs showed computer-enhanced images while yet more displayed real-time computer-generated pictures of what seemed like a pair of empty rooms. There was an operator at each VDU.

At a lower level, three metres below the gallery, were two fully-enclosed sub-chambers. In each, a plant about two metres in height stood in splendid isolation in the bed of soil that formed the floor. Nothing else could be seen. There were no electrical cables trailing across the earthen floors to betray any possible connections with the plants.

"Can you all see properly?" Olga Vasilyeva enquired as the generals moved around to select their vantage points.

She waited as they moved around some more until they were all satisfied.

"Gentlemen," she continued. "You're looking at two plants which are identical in every way except one: different transmission of data. The one on the left uses light as the transmission medium. The other, standard electronic data transfer. As the proposed systems will be static, we're using buried cables and fibre optics for data transfer. We set this up when we were searching for the most secure communication system against degradation or destruction by electro-magnetic pulse.

"We wanted a system that was secure from future dedicated pulse weapons as well as pulses from the detonation of a nuclear device. Hardening your electronics against EMP attack is one way but it may not always maintain their integrity. Fibre optics – the system used for the plant on the left – are immune to this kind of attack. We tried secure datalink for the plant on the right but discovered that even a light burst of EMP severely degraded transmission sufficiently to make it virtually useless. The demonstration will show you."

She moved to a large keypad with six rows of black and red buttons, arranged in columns of six.

"Take a hard look at both chambers while the lights are still on," she instructed the generals. "You will see that there are no cameras and no microphones of any kind. Everything you see and hear will come from the plants. The pictures of empty rooms on the VDUs are these two chambers from the viewpoint of the plants."

One of the generals said what the others were already thinking. "*These* pictures?"

"Yes. The computers have taken the pseudoptic signals and converted them into the visual images you see. The plants are 'looking' at their respective chambers at three hundred and sixty degrees. You could not sneak up behind them. Their leaves, their stems, their branches, are live sensors; which of course they are in any normal plant."

"Quite astonishing!"

"It is nature that is astonishing," she reminded them. "Some plants – not these – are mobile, if not in the time-movement scale we normally associate with ambulatory motion. But some are more energetic than others. Take our friend *chlamydomonas*, a microscopic unicell form of algae. This plant – and that is what it is – has two filaments we call flagella which it waves about enabling it to swim. I suppose you could stretch a scientific point and call it a plant-animal, though this would be basically incorrect.

"It actually has a light sensor, a red spot that enables it to detect sunlight. It uses this sensor to orientate itself in order to absorb the greatest quantity of light and so manufacture its food. So the sensor, in effect, also helps it to navigate. All this in something you cannot see with the naked eye. Under the microscope it looks like a green legless beetle."

As they listened to her, their eyes kept darting to the plants in the chambers and the VDUs, switching from one subject to the other as if trying to decide which to watch at any given moment.

"When the lights go out," Olga Vasilyeva continued, "the rooms will immediately darken. We'll then switch sensor modes and you'll see a change to infrared and radar images of the chambers. Two of our colleagues – one to each chamber – will enter through short darkened access points. They'll be wearing night-vision visors so that they can see where they're going. The visors are equipped with headphones. Those are the only aids they'll be carrying, considerably less than a combat soldier on patrol. As you'll see, our organic sentries will still find them. Has everyone had a good look?"

Grunts of assent told her they had.

"I shall now turn off the lights."

She tapped at a key on the pad. The lights in the chambers died suddenly. The abrupt darkness was tempered by the glow from the gallery lighting. The dark twilight was immediately repeated on the VDU pictures. She hit another key and a heavy black shutter, wide enough to span the entire gallery, slid down until the two chambers were completely hidden.

"The chambers are now in total darkness," she told them. "Now take a look at the monitors. You will see that they have temporarily gone blank. For the moment, the plants are 'blind' but they can still 'hear' with their acoustic sensors. Now watch as sensor fusion commences. You'll also note that the plants can 'look' in all directions at once."

Even as they watched, perceptible views of the chambers began to emerge; again from the points of view of the plants. Then a vivid thermal image of a human shape entered each chamber. They watched as the figures moved around, their footsteps clearly heard as they walked across the soil.

There were unrestrained gasps from the assembled visitors.

"This is *really* happening?" someone asked.

"It is," she replied calmly.

"I still can't believe it!"

"Gentlemen," she said, "you're looking at the future. We'll wait till our colleagues have left the chambers then we'll give each room a burst of EMP."

The two figures walked about the chambers for a minute or so, never going out of the "hearing" or the "view" of the plants.

"You can leave now," she said into a goosenecked microphone that was attached to the console.

The two figures left the chambers.

She turned to one of the operators. "All right. Give each a burst."

The monitors linked to the plant on the right suffered white-outs, flashing intermittently with sharp buzzing sounds, before going out completely. The plant on the left was still sending its signals as clearly as ever.

"Stop the bursts," she ordered.

The affected monitors remained blank.

"That is what will happen in an EMP environment," she said to the generals.

"Even with hardening?" the Georgian asked.

"That will depend upon the level of shielding. Our cables in the chamber are undergound, but they were still affected."

"Were they hardened?"

"Minimally. We're increasing hardening by degrees to see at what level reasonable protection can be achieved. However, we all know that the hardened percentage of current in-service equipment is minimal if not practically non-existent." She pointed at the blank screens. "This is the likely result on the battlefield. That goes for all non-hardened, electronically-based transmissions and equipment."

"And your field unit in the Baltics," the Belorussian said. "This uses the light . . . er . . . optic transmissions?"

"Yes," she replied. "Again, nature has come to our rescue. This time in the shape of *Lampyridae*; or, more specifically, *Luciola Lusitanica*. Firefly, to you."

"The *firefly?*"

"The humble firefly," she confirmed with one of her smiles. "Cold light. No heat trace. The firefly, like other light-producing animals, does so chemically. *Lusitanica* mixes its luciferin protein with the luciferaze enzyme and combines the lot with oxygen. Oxidisation produces the light.

"We can replicate the compounds. We have taken the firefly gene, introduced it to the plants and, in conjunction with the nanocomputers, manufactured a boosted light source which is used as a conduit for data. This is further augmented by the high-powered computers at the receiving station. The whole process is proofed against detection, eavesdropping and of course EMP."

"But what about your cell-sized computers?" the Georgian asked. "They are electronic surely, and must be EMP vulnerable."

"They are no longer strictly electronic. They are themselves cyborgs, but more organic than cyber unit. As well as giving new properties to the plant, they have also been evolved into something different. The plant's immunity to EMP has been given to them and they are easily able to defend themselves against these pulses. That is why the plant on the left continues to give uninterrupted data."

"Quite, quite astonishing!" the pilot remarked, visibly impressed and making no attempt to hide it. "Such complexity! I believe I speak for all of us when I say you are indeed a genius, Doctor."

The others nodded their mute agreement, staring at her in open wonder.

"Thank you, gentlemen," she said, then went on deprecatingly, "but the principle is itself relatively simple. The complexity is in its execution. And the genius belongs to all of us who work here. But this is nothing compared to what could be done when we eventually succeed in constructing a coherent quantum computer."

The Georgian stared at her. "What *is* a quantum computer?"

"Ah, General," she said, "it would take more time than we've got to explain it all, and then some more. But try to imagine a glass of liquid as a computer more powerful than anything you know, with *each molecule* doing its own computation. Such a system would make our nanos in the plants look like a hobbled man trying to win the Olympic one hundred metres. The theory is naturally far more complex, but that's the basic premise. Confusingly, it will be a very simple thing to do once we have got it right."

"You are serious about this?"

"I do not joke about science, General. The world scientific community is working in this field. The race has been on for some time."

The astounded Georgian turned to Kurinin. "This is a remarkable place, Feliks," he said, semaphoring with his hands to encompass the gallery. "And I don't mean just this section. I am thinking of this entire research unit. Remarkable. Quite remarkable. Worth the money. I am truly impressed."

Kurinin, who had deliberately chosen to remain in the background while Olga Vasilyeva carried out the demonstration, had a look of benign satisfaction upon his face.

"I thought you would be," he said mildly.

"This is far more than we expected. Your cyberplants put us well ahead of anything in the West."

"And to remain there we must maintain tight security." He looked at each of them as he spoke. "They must continue to believe they are calling all the shots. There are those in the Motherland who believe the West is waging an undeclared war, and winning it. I do not totally subscribe to that view. However, I do not dismiss it out of hand. Such sentiments will be of great use to us at the right time. But, for now, tight security is a prime requirement."

Their expressions said it all. They understood.

"But the doctors have something even more startling to show you," he added. "Colonel," he addressed Abilev, "may we now see the fish we have caught?"

Abilev nodded to another of the operators whose fingers then made a brief flurry at his keyboard.

A video came onscreen. It was of a futuristic high-flying aircraft of unrecognisable design.

"What is it?" one of the generals asked. "One of ours?"

"One of theirs," Kurinin replied. "Stealth-proof – but, as you can see, we still caught it."

"How?"

"The protoype field unit," Kurinin told them, allowing himself a small measure of triumph.

"Did we shoot it down?"

"No. That was not the intention; and we have not as yet added defensive armament to the system. There is still plenty of test work to be done before full integration becomes possible. However, we do have contingency plans in place. If an emergency arises we can call up defensive units, both on the ground and in the air."

"But what was that aircraft doing?"

"Swallowing whole the bait we prepared and laid out for it."

At various points along the sides of the research unit's above-ground building complex were security blisters looking like giant fixed examples of aircraft gun turrets but without the guns. Each was continuously manned, normally by a paired team. The exception to this rule was the blister attached to the main security annex. Its armoured exit led to the operations centre for the entire complex.

The blister currently occupied by Daminov was the senior NCO's station and, like all the other security troopers, Daminov did rotating shifts with the sergeant.

Daminov was always pleased when Melev went on his rounds, relishing the temporary freedom from the rough NCO's jibes. While Abilev and Olga Vasilyeva were engaged in astonishing the generals several levels beneath his feet, Daminov continued to watch the still-raging storm from the secure warmth of his position.

Because of the way the upper parts of the complex had been constructed, Daminov's waist was actually at ground level. The positioning of the blisters – designed to act as observation platforms – gave excellent and unbreachable cover. In the unlikely event of an assault from outside, all he had to do was duck while armoured shutters slammed down over the glass panes.

He would then head for the exit and into a corridor that was in fact a raised walkway. At several points, stairs led down to the operations room where the defence of the unit would be co-ordinated. Every one of the above-ground buildings in the complex had lightweight sensor-equipped turret assemblies mounting quadruple 30 mm cannon, which were retractable through the roof. These were fired from within the complex, making each building essentially a multi-gunned, static tank. The guns had a 360-degree rotation capability, a 180-degree arc of travel from any compass point, and could engage both air and ground targets. There were also retractable missile batteries which again could engage targets both in the air and on the ground.

As he looked out at the storm, Daminov found himself wondering once more about the considerable amount of money that must have gone into the place. From where did they think an attack was going to come? he wondered absently. An assault force of American marines? Way out here, deep in the heart of Siberia?

The thought made him smile in disbelief. It was more likely that the defensive screen was against possible attack by fellow countrymen. Everything was so knife-edged these days that if . . . or perhaps *when* trouble came – given the constant shifting of positions and loyalties of politicians and the military – an attacking force trying to take the complex could easily contain people he'd served with or had met during training. Or it could be armed civilians; the assault on the parliament building was still vivid in his memory. It could all happen so very easily, given the state of the country.

Daminov wondered which side he'd be on in the event of a new revolution. He didn't want to contemplate this profoundly disturbing possibility and longed for the end of his shift so that he could get back to his violin. The sergeant could sneer all he liked.

"Barbarian," he muttered.

"What was that?"

Daminov glanced round, startled. He hadn't heard the sergeant come in. The bastard could move so quietly when he wanted to.

"Khachaturian," Daminov said, thinking quickly. "I said Khacha-turian, Sergeant. I was thinking about his Violin Sonata. I was just reminding myself he wrote that when he was twenty-nine, in 1932."

Melev had come round to face Daminov, eyes baleful. "What the shit do I care about a fucking Armenian scribbler making funny squiggles on a piece of paper? When you're on duty, Daminov, you think about your duty! *Not poncy music!*"

"Yes, Sergeant!"

"I've told you before; you should play the fucking balalaika like any red-blooded music maker not that poncy Tsarist violin. The Tsarists got the bad habit from the decadent West. In the time of Napoleon, they hated being fucking Russian so fucking much, they spoke fucking *French!*"

Melev put his own slant upon his limited grasp of history, but he was voicing the kind of thoughts that Daminov knew many people felt. The Tsars had long gone but in these uncertain times the West was a good monster to blame. But the West had also made its own monster of the old Soviet regime. Old habits took a long time to die. There was a reluctance on both sides to let go.

"Yes, Sergeant," he now responded to Melev's rant.

Daminov was keeping an eye on the storm outside. Even though Melev was bawling him out he didn't want to miss the moment when the patrol hove into view. Although the sensors would have picked up the amphibious armoured personnel carriers long before, Melev would still yell at him for not spotting them immediately.

He thought he'd seen movement.

"Er . . . Sergeant."

"*What!*"

"The patrol. It's coming in."

Melev turned to look. Three APCs in winter camouflage seemed to materialise out of the gloom like mechanical ghosts. They came on, line abreast.

"Who's patrol leader?"

Daminov was quite aware that Melev knew well enough. This was just another little trick to catch him out.

"Lieutenant Fedrov."

"That little ponce!" Melev snarled contemptuously. "Some officer! Got his rank easy. Not like the captain, who came through the ranks. He was my sergeant once. Kicked me in the arse when I gave him too much lip, then boxed me round the face for good measure. Then later he bought me a stiff vodka to show there was no hard feelings. Now that's a real officer."

"Yes, Sergeant," Daminov agreed diplomatically.

The captain was a bruiser of a man, an excellent soldier when sober. As a human being, he stank. Which was probably why Melev practically idolised him. They were two of a kind. Both highly skilled veterans, both nasty when the vodka ruled.

Daminov had once spotted them drinking together in the combined ranks' bar. They had drunk more vodka in one evening than he could have drunk in a week of hard trying. When they walked, neither swayed. It was only when he'd looked into their eyes that he'd seen the murderous fury stirring in there.

Daminov shivered slightly as he remembered. He had thought at the time just how much he would have hated coming up against those two in battle. They weren't soldiers in the purest sense. They were killers in uniform.

"Killers in uniform," Melev remarked suddenly, so accurately voicing Daminov's thoughts that the trooper could not restrain the start this caused.

Daminov glanced warily at his sergeant, wondering if he'd actually spoken his thoughts for Melev to hear.

But the sergeant was not looking at him.

"Killers in uniform," Melev repeated. "That's what a real soldier should be. You're not a killer are you, Daminov? You've never killed anyone. I have. Plenty. So has the captain."

Daminov decided to keep his mouth shut.

The APCs were closer now, still keeping perfect formation.

"Look at that poncing formation," Melev growled disparagingly. "What's he doing? A wet-behind-the-ears recruit could do better!"

It was no secret that Melev despised Lieutenant Fedrov, who had committed the enormous sin of graduating from university before entering the army. The lieutenant was a very clever man with sharp instincts. He knew how to handle Melev, how not to be upset by the sergeant's frequent bouts of insubordination. This infuriated Melev, who would have preferred Fedrov to yell at him or hit him, as the captain had once done. In a strange way, Melev would have respected Fedrov more but Fedrov had refused to play the game. Though it was never mentioned aloud, everyone knew the captain's sympathies were with the sergeant. Lieutenant Fedrov didn't seem to mind.

The APCs now went smoothly into line ahead as they prepared to enter the complex.

But Melev was still not satisfied. "Ragged!" he snapped. "Ragged! I'd show him how, if he was a trooper in my charge." The fact that he could not vent his spleen upon his superior officer infuriated him. "All you officer ponces get up my nose," he added tightly, including Daminov in the blanket condemnation.

"I'm . . . I'm not an officer, Sergeant," Daminov reminded him tentatively.

"You're worse. You act like one! You and your fucking violin. Now take the captain; *he's* an officer *and* a trooper. A man's man. But I don't expect Moscow ponces like you to understand that."

"No, Sergeant." Daminov kept his eyes on the armoured vehicles.

The APCs were almost at the complex.

Without warning, a section of the ground suddenly slanted downwards. As the snow-covered steel ramp lowered, the three APCs rumbled down it with barely a change of pace. Soon they were off the ramp and it raised itself back into position. It had been smoothly done.

"I suppose he thinks he should get a pat on the back for that," Melev growled.

Daminov said nothing.

The whirling snow immediately settled, covering with a new blanket the recent tracks made by the incoming vehicles.

"Patrol secure," Daminov said into his radio to the control centre.

It was as if the APCs had never been.

Three

The storm had gone, and a picture postcard stillness lay upon the Siberian landscape. This was shattered by the lowering of the ramp and the exit of three APCs from their lair on roving patrol. They would replace the patrol that had taken station from Fedrov's group the previous evening and had stayed out in the wastes throughout the night, despite the storm.

By the time the ramp was back in position, the APCs were already well away into the distance. The change in weather had brought with it high streaks of thin cloud, giving the day a fresh-looking brightness.

Then new sounds invaded the stillness. One of the buildings was a recessed hangar. Its roof opened and a helicopter lifted out. Three others followed, each heading off in a different direction. The generals and admirals were leaving to rejoin their various units.

Daminov was not on duty. He sat alone by a window in the near-empty other ranks' mess watching the helicopters depart, their noises muted by the thickness of the glass; but the vibration of their rotors could still be felt through the building.

The previous evening, he'd been summoned by the colonel to give an impromptu concert to an audience of general officers and a few staff officers. He'd chosen a mixed programme of Russian and Western composers selected from three centuries, including the twentieth. Two of the chosen composers would have annoyed Melev, had the sergeant been among the invited: Khachaturian and Tchaikovsky.

But it had gone down well with the audience who had applauded warmly. One of the admirals, a music buff, had even come up to personally congratulate him on his skill with the violin. The admiral had told him he played the piano and enjoyed the sparse compositions of Eric Satie.

Had he been there to hear that, Daminov now thought drily, the sergeant would have had his prejudices about Tsarist officers confirmed.

"I hear you gave the generals a big show last night," a woman's voice said. "Captain Lirionova told me."

He had seen the captain in the front row, sitting next to General Kurinin himself. Next to her had been Lieutenant-Colonel Abilev.

Daminov looked up and sprang to his feet. "Sergeant Konstantinova!"

"Sit down, Daminov! I'm not an officer, nor a brute like that sergeant of yours."

"Er, yes . . . er . . ." He sat back down slowly, staring at her as she put her laden tray down on the table.

She smiled at him as she too sat down, dropping her normally serious expression, becoming beautiful and, he thought, quite sexy.

"What are you staring at?"

"You. You're . . . beautiful . . . Sergeant."

"Am I? I thought everyone in this place considered me a sourface. I know that's what they call me. Sourface."

"Not everyone."

"They do!"

"Some," he admitted reluctanctly.

"And you?" She began to eat.

"I never thought it."

"The perceptive man," she said, speaking between mouthfuls. "You look beyond the obvious?"

"I would . . . like to think so."

"You've got a girlfriend in Moscow."

"Yes." No point denying it. She would have seen his documents.

"Do you miss her?"

"Very much."

"We must all make sacrifices if we are to rebuild the Motherland." It did not seem like just another repeated slogan; she sounded as if she really believed it.

He nodded.

"And how would you go about that?" she enquired.

"I'm here, Sergeant."

"No need to be so formal while we're having breakfast. And relax. I'm not conducting a loyalty investigation. While we are at breakfast, my name is Lyudmilla. Or Milla, if you prefer."

"Yes, Serg— All right."

"That's better. So, do you like it here, Feodor?"

She'd know his name from his files.

"I'd rather be here than in some waterlogged tent," he answered. "Or a leaky barrack room in a hellhole of a regimental camp . . . or somewhere like Chechnya."

"Wouldn't we all," she said with another quick smile.

She was a tall woman with hair that was as dark as the night and violet eyes. High cheekbones and skin the colour of pale honey made her spectacular when she smiled. He wished she did so more often.

Kazakh blood in there somewhere, he thought.

"Where did you learn to play the violin as well as everyone says you do?" she asked.

"My mother," he replied. "She always wanted to be a concert soloist but spoiled things for herself with the authorities when she was a young girl. She argued with her tutor who she thought was teaching her badly."

Milla raised a dark eyebrow. "Sounds precocious. Not smart during those days."

"It was certainly bad for her. They threw her out. But she was right about the tutor."

"I'm sure she was. Those who can't, teach. Or so the saying goes. But it wasn't wise."

"No."

"So she taught you?"

Daminov nodded. "Yes. But she did have it in her to be a soloist. They blocked the opportunities."

"You speak educated Russian. When your service is over, would you like to become a concert performer?"

"I'm not sure I'm good enough. My mother is better."

"From what I've heard people say, you are good enough. Your mother gave you what was taken from her. Perhaps I can hear you play some time?"

He could not believe his luck. She wanted to be with him! The violin had its uses, after all. Officers' meat? What officers' meat? Think about *that*, Sergeant Barbarian Melev.

"Yes! Yes, of course!" Daminov said eagerly. "I'd like that . . . Milla."

"Then it's settled. I'll let you know."

"Yes. Yes!"

"There's just one thing." She had finished eating and stood up, looking down at him.

"Which is?"

"I will not be having an affair with you. I will not have an affair with anyone in this place."

He was almost relieved. The temptation had been removed. He would not be risking a betrayal of his girlfriend.

"All . . . right."

"You look relieved and disappointed. Which is it?"

He gave a sheepish smile. "Both . . . I think."

"Good. You are honest. I like that in a man. Your girlfriend is a lucky woman. Not lovers, but we shall be friends. Yes?"

Again, he nodded. "Yes, Milla. Friends."

"Good," she repeated. "And now I am Sergeant Konstantinova once more."

He stood up. "Yes, Sergeant."

She picked up her tray. "I'm really looking forward to hearing you play."

"Yes, Sergeant," he repeated as she walked away.

He sat down again, thoughtfully, and wondered whether he had not in fact just been investigated.

The last of the visiting helicopters was getting ready for lift-off, thirty minutes after the others had gone; but its engines had not yet been started.

Kurinin and Lirionova, in greatcoats and winter headgear, were standing some distance from it in the hangar, deep in conversation. There were more helicopters in the huge building – some of them gunships – with people working on them; but the two intelligence officers were well out of anyone else's earshot.

The aircraft would be taking Kurinin to an airbase some 300 kilometres away where he would board his flight to Moscow.

Already waiting in the military executive Mil Mi-8 was the overall commander of the destination base and its satellite units in the area. He was the Georgian general.

"I'm sorry we've not had time for a more detailed conference," Kurinin was saying. "As you can see, I was continually engaged with our guests."

"I understand, General."

Puffs of exhaled breath punctuated their speech as the chill of the outside came in through the open hanger roof.

He smiled at her. "Are you coping with your new command?"

"I am. But this is greatly due to the help I'm getting from Sergeant Konstantinova."

"So she is a good NCO?"

"The best, and very knowledgeable. An expert with computers."

"She comes highly recommended. I had to prise her from her unit in Leningrad." Kurinin only called the city St Petersburg when talking to foreigners.

"I was worried at first," Lirionova said.

"Why?"

"She was here before me. She would naturally have expected promotion, and the command."

"Has she indicated any resentment?"

Lirionova shook her head. "No, sir. She's been the best second-in-command I could wish for. May I suggest something, sir?"

"Suggest it."

"Perhaps she could be made a lieutenant. It would be good to have two officers heading the section."

Kurinin looked closely at her. "She has become a friend and you would feel better if she were an officer."

"It would help. She's certainly qualified."

"I'll give it some thought."

"Thank you, sir."

"Anything else? Anything on a security level to cause concern?"

"No, General. Motivation is high."

"Good. Keep up the work. Come down to Moscow with a status report. We can discuss many things then, including your sergeant's promotion . . . and perhaps yours. I shall send for you."

"Mine, General?"

Kurinin was enigmatic. "Something tells me it won't be too long before you become a major."

She beamed. "Thank you, sir!" She gave a smart salute just as the helicopter pilot began to start his engines. "See you in Moscow, General."

Kurinin returned the salute. "In Moscow." He nodded, then turned to make his way towards the helicopter.

She remained where she was, watching as he climbed aboard. She had not lowered and secured the ear protectors of her fur hat and, as a precaution, she now put a hand to it to keep it in place as the rotors gathered speed.

The Mi-8 rose through the roof and headed westwards.

When she returned to her section, Lirionova suppressed her own excitement and called her sergeant into her small office.

"I told the general, Milla," she said as soon as Konstantinova had entered.

"You *what*?"

"I told him you should be a lieutenant."

"Are you crazy? You don't tell generals anything. They tell you!"

Lirionova smiled. "I didn't tell him as such. I suggested."

"And?"

"He said he'd think about it. That usually means he'll do it."

"You know him that well, do you?"

"Not so long ago I was a sergeant too. And then, after I became an officer, I did some work for him and it pleased him."

"But your promotion was rapid?"

"I know what people think," Lirionova said. "But he really is pleased with my work. People think I go to bed with him."

"I didn't say you did."

"I know. But people think it."

"To hell with them!"

"So? Would you like to be a lieutenant?"

"Better pay for a start."

"At least we actually do get paid. Not like some army units."

Konstantinova looked at the captain for long seconds. "Considering the money that's been spent here . . ."

"Which is no concern of ours."

"Which is no concern of ours," Konstantinova agreed.

"Have you found any weak links in our chain of personnel?" Lirionova continued, switching subjects.

"There are a few grumblers, but that comes with any unit. They're all motivated. Nothing to worry about, despite their being stuck out here. This is luxury compared to what they could have expected at an average base."

"Even our local intellectual?"

"You mean the musician? Daminov?"

Lirionova nodded. "He really did play well last night. Strange to find someone like him up here."

"He thinks a lot but he's a good soldier, despite what Melev may like to believe."

Lirionova gave an expressive shudder. "I know we're supposed to consider people like Melev an asset to our fighting forces but he's a very nasty creature."

"What about his captain?"

"Ah yes. Captain Igor Viktorovich Urikov. Nastier still. But, as the general would say, we need them; especially out here. By the way, will you be fine for the firing range this evening?"

"Still trying to teach me to shoot? I've passed my tests. I'm good enough."

"If you're going to be a lieutenant, you've got to be better than just good. Besides, I've got a challenge from Urikov. He says that his worst soldier can shoot better than the best woman in this place."

Konstantinova stared at her but said nothing.

"What could I do?" Lirionova demanded innocently. "I couldn't let that pass."

"If you're depending on me, you've already lost."

"You're doing fine," Lirionova insisted. "The two of us can do it."

"You hope."

"We can also have Olga Vasilyeva, if we want. She can be our secret weapon. She's a fantastic shot, I've been told."

"The doctor? She's not military. We can't ask her."

"Urikov said the best woman. He didn't say she had to be military. Olga needed to be a good shot, considering all the dangerous places she used to go to. Did you know she should really have died in Africa?"

"No."

"She met an American out there, a botanist. It was he who spotted the mine. He pushed her away and caught the full blast. She lost a leg, but he died. There were rumours that they had become lovers but there is no confirmation of this in her files. No one observed them expressing more than would have been expected of scientific colleagues."

"It could mean they were smart enough to arrange their moments of privacy. He did give his life for her. Greater love hath no man . . . Have you asked her a direct question about it?"

Lirionova shook her head. "No."

"Doesn't the general think she may have been compromised? Especially considering the work she's doing? There are botanists and 'botanists' . . . if you get my meaning."

"I know exactly what you're saying, and the general would have considered that. She might well have enjoyed a physical relationship out there with her American but I think she's given us solid proof of where her true loyalties lie. She would never have discussed her work with him. The general must think the same way or he would not have backed all this. General Kurinin is a very careful man; his strategies are long term. He would have checked her out minutely. I've done some of the work on her. She's clean."

Konstantinova nodded slowly. "Perhaps you're right. She's certainly given us an incredible system."

"And it's just what we need."

*   *   *

The journey back to Moscow took four and a half hours and, having crossed two time zones going westwards, it was eleven o'clock when Kurinin strode across the highly polished floor of his gleaming opulent office.

He was followed by a smartly attired lieutenant-colonel carrying the inevitable thin folder beneath an arm. The lieutenant-colonel, Gregor Levchuk, shut the tall heavy door behind them. It moved silently and made a satisfyingly solid click as it closed.

Kurinin hung up his hat and coat then took his seat behind his huge desk. "Well, Gregor? The world still on its axis?"

"Welcome back, sir. The world was still rotating happily when I last looked." Levchuk placed the file on the desk.

Despite the difference in rank they spoke to each other like old friends; as indeed they were. Gregor Levchuk was also Kurinin's right-hand man.

Kurinin looked at him searchingly. "Gregor, every time I see you, you look smarter. And I've been looking at you for years. You're better turned out than many of the Western officers we see at embassy functions."

Levchuk grinned. "They already think we're down and out. Why confirm their prejudices by wearing a shoddy uniform?"

"I know another lieutenant-colonel who appears to think differently," Kurinin said, remembering Abilev.

"So how did it go up there?"

"Brilliantly. I tell you, Gregor, they've got something very special in that place. It was worth setting up the research unit. You must make the next trip. See for yourself. Nothing I can tell you will do justice to it."

"And the generals?"

"Very impressed, and solidly with us."

"Including the two from Belarus?"

"Even more so, as you would expect."

"Did they say much? The Belorussians, I mean."

"One did. The other just watched and listened most of the time. Could be because he was junior in rank." Kurinin drew the file towards him. "This the information on her whereabouts?"

Levchuk nodded.

Kurinin opened the file and began to read the reports while Levchuk stood patiently waiting.

The general finished his reading and shut the file slowly.

"Buenos Aires, Argentina," he said.

"That's what our people on the ground report."

"Why Argentina? Is there any trouble brewing with the Malvinas or Falklands – as the British call them – that we don't know about?"

"It's relatively quiet down there."

"It won't necessarily remain so," Kurinin said darkly. "Where there's the possibility of mineral rights and fishing stocks to be exploited, trouble will not be far behind. If she's down there . . . Let's see . . ." He opened the file again. "She was spotted a week ago but not seen after that. She could be anywhere on the planet, Gregor."

"She could," Levchuk agreed. "But we did intercept that coded burst to one of their satellites, coming out of there three days after she was seen. That was from—"

"Puerto Deseado," Kurinin finished as he checked the file again. "Yes. I've got it. That's nearly two thousand kilometres down the coast, south of Buenos Aires! What's she after down there? A secret naval installation? Always assuming, of course, it was her message."

"Who else could it have been? *We* had no one down there."

"Had?"

"I've asked our people to check on it."

Kurinin gave a tight smile. "The ever-thorough Gregor." He shut the file and leaned back in his richly upholstered swivel chair, hands on the armrests, as if about to get to his feet. But he remained seated.

"She's going to be very difficult to catch, Gregor. In addition to everything else she has going for her, she has Russian cunning. We work in the shadows, but it would seem that we ourselves are being shadowed. So just who the hell is this woman? Who . . . and what . . . is she really working for? Are they Russian? Are they Westerners? Are they Russians *and* Westerners working together? Who are these people?"

Levchuk could give no answers to any of those questions.

"A dangerous woman, Gregor," Kurinin uttered softly. A familiar chill had come into his eyes. "Dangerous to what we plan to achieve. I mean to have her scalp one day. I *will* have her scalp," he added for emphasis.

Levchuk still said nothing.

"Our adversary is an exceptional and highly skilled woman," Kurinin said. "It will take someone very special to catch her."

"Any particular person in mind?" Levchuk enquired.

"Yes, though she does not as yet know it."

"*She?*"

"To catch a thief, Gregor. What better than another woman? We'll give her the appropriate training to enable her to carry out the assignment successfully."

"When will this person undergo training, General?"

"In due course. And we must do so thoroughly. She is, after all, going to be an assassin."

Kurinin's fingers tapped briefly on his desk.

"And I'll tell you something else, Gregor," he continued balefully. "It doesn't matter how many of those damned pieces of paper gets signed with NATO, or what deals are agreed. The situation here is too volatile for such deals to remain permanent. Our strategic plans allow for that.

"I seem to remember that Stalin signed a pact with Hitler, and we all know how that ended. We were allies with the West. We know how that ended too. Why should this be any different? After all, we had a union with the republics. Now we've got basket cases on our borders.

"Lessons of history, Gregor. I never ignore history. Unfortunately, too many people in the world at large seem quite happy to do so. The capacity for stupidity in our fellow man seems infinite. We're not going to sit meekly by and let them push eastwards. We're not going to have them come at us, pushing us further and further back.

"*We* won't stand for it; and in the end neither will our people. There is a great wellspring of resentment over the proposed NATO expansion among the people. The West seems incapable of understanding the fire it's playing with. Their actions could precipitate a civil war in our country. We must never allow that to happen; at least, not unless it can be utilised to our advantage."

"And their special unit in Scotland?" Levchuk queried mildly. The prospect of an uncontrollable civil war filled him with horror. A *controlled* one . . . now that was completely different.

"Can you imagine those aircrews being free to prowl the airspace of the former republics?" Kurinin said in a hard voice. "They would be at our very borders!" The thought of it made him go pale with suppressed fury. "We do not let up on the task of eventually destroying them. I told the generals that the success of such a unit would only pave the way for more.

"The proposed agreements with NATO would eventually have them swarming from the Baltics to the Black Sea, penning us in. It is our task to ensure matters never reach that stage. *Our* task, Gregor. Remember that. Always. However," Kurinin went on thoughtfully, "this flawed rapprochement with NATO may well work in our favour. It will make it simpler to insert our people." He leaned back in his chair and allowed himself the faintest of smiles.

Levchuk looked back at him silently. He too could have been smiling.

November base, the same day.

The woman on Kurinin's hit list was also on Major Chuck Morton's mind. It was not his fault that fate had decreed he should fall in love with a woman he was able to see at haphazardly infrequent intervals. The worst of it, he thought, was that he'd spent several months with her and had kept quiet about how he'd truly felt.

Lost opportunities, he now found himself thinking with some chagrin. *But I didn't know then what she was.*

A fighter pilot in the US Air Force, he had been grounded for running out of fuel in an F-16, despite what everyone agreed had been a subsequently perfect execution of a deadstick landing. But in the end it hadn't mattered in the slightest that he'd saved the tax-payers an expensive jet. Bad fuel management was bad airmanship; a serious enough miscalculation by a rookie, but unforgiveable by a major.

Punishment had been as swift as it had been brutal. He had been lucky not to have lost his newly-won major's rank as well. They must have felt some sympathy – there but for the grace of God, perhaps – for on posting him to a dead end job in the Pentagon they had left him with his golden oakleaves. But the pay-off had been a permanent grounding.

That was when fate had stepped in.

She had been assigned to him in his buried cubbyhole of an office, the extent of his new command. Then, one day, she had spotted an anomaly on a passed-over satellite photograph. That had in turn generated a special mission involving the November squadrons.

The mission had been so successful he'd been rewarded with a return to flying, though not back to his beloved F-16s. Instead, he'd been given a posting to the November unit flying one of the most advanced aircraft in service; a turnaround in his fortunes that had made him an extremely happy man indeed. There was only one cloud on his otherwise perfect horizon: the woman he knew as Mac. More correctly, the fact that he could not see her as much as he would like to.

Even though he now had one November combat mission under

his belt, he was well aware he was still very much the new boy. The standards of the unit were exceedingly high, and many aspiring candidates had been washed out. He'd seen at least two pilots he'd known before – from Stateside squadrons – flunked out of the training; and they had been the top men of their respective units. There were no passengers in this the most elite flying outfit around.

It was with these thoughts troubling his mind that Morton looked at the door before him.

WING COMMANDER C.T. JASON
Officer Commanding

He read the golden lettering on the mahogany plaque with trepidation, patted his uniform needlessly, adjusted his cap and knocked.

"Come in!"

He opened the door, entered, shut it behind him and came to attention. He snapped off a razor-sharp salute.

"Major Morton reporting as ordered, sir!"

"At ease, Major."

"Sir!" Morton relaxed, but only just.

"All right, Chuck. Take off the hat and sit down. And don't look so worried, man. You haven't blotted your copybook."

"Sir." Morton removed his cap and went to the leatherbound straight-backed chair in front of Jason's desk.

While the wing commander's office on the virtually new and expensive November base seemed reasonably well-appointed and comfortable, in comparison with the baroque elegance of Kurinin's Moscow office suite, it was positively utilitarian.

Jason reached into a drawer and took out a plain white envelope.

"This is for you," he said, shutting the drawer and leaning across the desk with the envelope.

Morton reached forward to take it. "Thank you, sir."

Major Charles Morton, was all that was written on it. There were no postmarks. He felt his heart skip a beat.

He turned it over slowly. No return address.

"You know where it comes from, don't you?" Jason asked.

Morton nodded. "I think I know *who* from, sir, but not where from."

"Indeed. As usual, I can't tell you the means by which it got here and, quite frankly, I haven't a clue where it came from originally."

"I'd like to read it privately, sir."

"Of course."

"Hell of a thing, sir, not knowing at any one time where the woman you love happens to be."

"I do sympathise, but it's her job. You know that."

"Sure I do, sir. Thing is, all those months I spent with her, I wasted them."

"*Carpe diem*, Major," Jason said. "Seize the day. So many of us do not, from time to time, during the course of our lives." He sounded as if he counted himself among those who had not. "Lieutenant-Colonel MacAllister, as we must call her, is many things and has many identities: US Marine, USAF major, and others besides."

"And Russian, sir."

"That too."

"Even though I know . . . well, I think I know her . . . it's hard to think we've got a Russian colonel working for us."

"Not *for* us, Major. *With* us would be more appropriate. Whoever she's actually working *for*, will remain a mystery."

"Yes, sir."

"Though we tend to believe we make a conscious choice about those we fall in love with, Major Morton, the reality is quite different. It hits you at the most unexpected times and sometimes it's not even the person you would originally have thought. That's the beauty and the pain of it."

"What if it's a mistake, sir? What if I'm wrong to even keep thinking about her?"

"Do you believe it to be?"

"No, sir."

"There you are. As long as it does not prevent you from performing your duties at the level that is expected of you, I'd advise you to enjoy what you've got."

"Thank you, sir."

"And that's the end of my role as agony uncle. Good day, Major."

Morton got smartly to his feet. "Sir!" He put on his cap, saluted, and turned to go.

"And Major . . ."

Morton paused. "Sir?"

Jason pointed to the envelope. "Hope it's good news."

"Thank you, sir."

Four

The sleek Tornado ASV(E) – sometimes, among its many other names, called the ASV Echo – was at the threshold of the wide main runway that stretched towards the Moray Firth. The day was bright with very little wind and high wispy cloud cover.

Caroline had applied herself single-mindedly towards achieving her goal. She had successfully passed through the screening and initial flying training on the little single-engined propeller-driven Bulldog with its fixed landing gear. She had progressed to the high-performance turbo-prop Tucano which was so powerful a trainer it carried ejection seats. She had gone on to her first jet, the Hawk T1, before moving up to the advanced weapons training version of the same aircraft – the T1A – learning to use it as a fighting machine, going one-on-one in air combat manoeuvring with fellow students and instructors. She had watched as some of her male colleagues had fallen by the wayside; and still she had progressed.

She had then been sent to the Tri-national Tornado Training Establishment, getting in among the really heavy metal and her first twin-engined jet. From the IDS – the ground attack variant of the Tornado – she had been streamed for the standard ADV interceptor version. Then had come the opportunity she had been praying for: a promise that had been made when she had been about to embark upon that monumental change in her career.

If she performed well, Jason had promised, he would give her a shot at trying for the November squadrons.

As she had first been on the November base as a fighter controller, she had worked very hard to ensure she would reach a standard that would make the wing commander honour his promise. He had not let her down. It had been at his recommendation – against the more traditional voices who were still very much opposed to having women in any cockpit, never mind fighters – that she'd been put forward for aircrew training in the first place. He had therefore taken a continuing interest in her progress even when a flight with Caroline had nearly cost him his life.

He'd been flying in the back seat of a her Hawk when an assassination attempt had been made against him. She had crash-landed the terminally damaged Hawk and, though Jason had been severely hurt, it had been confirmed that only her flying skills had saved both their lives. Jason had suffered broken legs and still bore the faint filigree of scars upon his face against which his visor had been shattered; though these were gradually fading. The opponents of women in fighter cockpits had tried to use the crash to ground her but Jason, even during the pain of his convalescence, had not withdrawn his support of her.

Jason had been solidly backed by the Air Vice-Marshal, though she still suspected that Thurson was himself not altogether happy with the idea of women fighter pilots. But the senior officer's belief in Jason was such that he was unwavering in his support of his own former student pilot.

She had then been called for selection to November One and had received her first taste of the phenomenally powerful Super Tornado ASV – the Air Superiority Variant – with its substantial modifications and high-tech display systems and equipment. She had learned to keep pace with the powerful beast which at times seemed to be running away from her. But she had persevered, and was then moved on to the ASV(E), the ultimate enhanced version of the aircraft.

As she held the ASV(E) at the threshold, she reflected upon how far she had managed to get since those first tentative steps towards her dream of being at the controls. She had always wanted to be a fighter pilot, even when she'd been a fighter controller, even when the opportunities for women in the front seat had been scarcer than snow on a baking hot day.

The standard ADV crews had dubbed their mount the flick knife. The November crews had gone one better; the ASV was the superflick and the ASV(E) the super-superflick. There were also ribald variations of the nickname, one of which she tended to use.

Today she was flying with McCann as navigator, as a work-up towards their first flight in one of the pair of November One's newest acquisitions, the spanking new Starfire.

"Okaayy," McCann was saying from the back seat. "We're ready to get this super-superdick off the ground . . . er . . . Sorry, Caroline. I kinda forgot, you know, er . . ."

"It's all right, Elmer Lee. Don't change because of me. I'm a big girl, and I do know what a dick is. And besides, that's my pet name for it too."

"Yeah, sure, but I hope they don't get to hear this conversation down in Operations."

"You're on cockpit frequency."

"Sure, but now it's on the CVR."

McCann was thinking of the minidisk drive of the cockpit voice recorder.

"Thunder Zero One!" came a sharp voice from the control tower. "Are you ready to take off or is this a Sunday stroll?"

"Thunder Zero One requesting permission to take off," McCann replied briskly. "Some people," he added under his breath. "Shame Karen's not on ATC duty."

"I heard that!" the tower retorted. "Zero-One clear to take off. QFE 1013, wind is zero knots."

"Roger," Caroline replied. "QFE is 1013, wind zero."

She reached for the rotary knob on the left-hand side of the up-front panel beneath the head-up display and dialled in the required airfield pressure. Irrespective of the runway height above sea level, altitude would read zero while they were on the ground and when they had landed from the sortie. Over on the top right-hand quadrant of the wide-angle head-up display, the glowing green-dotted circle of the radar height was showing three zeroes at its centre.

In the back, McCann had called up the HUD repeater on one of his multi-function displays. He would see exactly the same symbology that Caroline would see on her head-up display.

"Let's get this baby airborne," McCann said. "Gee," he added, "I always wanted to say that."

"Shut it, McCann," Caroline said as she pushed the twin throttles smoothly but firmly forwards.

"Hey, you're beginning to sound like a pilot. Bad habit."

She smiled in her mask and made no response. McCann would always be McCann. Stopping a charging rhino with bare hands would be far easier than trying to change him.

The ASV(E) leapt fowards, a baying hound unleashed. Its tremendous power no longer held any fears for her. She was in control. She shoved the throttles hard into the stops, giving full combat thrust. The Tornado did what seemed like the impossible and gathered even more speed. The runway streamed into a blur. Outside, the powerful engines split the air with their tearing roar. Inside, only a muted sibilance filled the cockpit accompanied by the indefinable sense of a controlled powerhouse surrounding the vulnerable human beings within.

She swiftly reached forward and to her left on the instrument panel for the short stalk with the little white serrated wheel at its end. There was a small upright catch on the top. She pushed at the catch and lifted the wheel assembly.

"Gear travelling . . ." McCann advised her, watching the three lights of the repeated gear indicator. The greens blinked out, three reds came on briefly before going out as well. ". . . and locked. Let's make like a rocket."

"Going up," she confirmed, and eased firmly back on the stick.

With afterburners roaring, the Tornado stood on its fiery tail and fled for the heavens, going straight up.

"You really love this, don't you?" he said to her.

"Ooh yes!" she said.

Jack Brodie, in flying gear, had seen the take-off. Hair plastered to a scalp made damp from a recent flight, he stood outside the hardened aircraft shelter, helmet held upside down against his body, comms cable, oxygen mask and tubing dropped into it. He was looking up at the fast-dwindling aircraft.

The instructor pilot with whom he'd just made the flight came out of the HAS to join him. The pilot, a Frenchman called Marcel Gireaud and a major, glanced up at the virtually clear blue above him. The sound of the Tornado's passage still ripped at the bowl of the sky.

"You would like to fly in one of those?" Gireaud asked.

"And how, Major! That is some ship."

"There is a system here," Gireaud told him. "All new candidates are converted first—"

"I know, sir. On the standard Tornado ADV, which we've just been using. Then it's the ASV. But there's only one squadron that right now gets to fly the ASV(E). Am I right?"

"You're right," Gireaud answered, looking neutrally at Brodie and giving no indication of whether the interruption had annoyed him. "The ASV(E)s are with Zero One squadron. Zero Two and the newly forming Zero Three will have the ASVs. The ASV is a fantastic ship . . . far superior in every way to the training ADVs. You have seen for yourself. They are very different aeroplanes. Yes?"

"Yeah, Major. I know." Brodie was still looking up at the sky, even though the ASV(E) of Caroline and McCann had long since disappeared, its sounds gradually fading away. "But I'd like to get on Zero One."

"I think," Gireaud began carefully, "that is up to the boss. And, if I may add, Zero One is the very best of the November squadrons who are themselves better than anything, anywhere. You have a big mountain to climb, Ensign Brodie."

"I'll climb it, Major. I'll climb it."

Gireaud gave him a philosophical look. "I wish you luck."

"Luck is good, Major, sir." Brodie waggled the fingers of his free hand, still without looking down. "But so's the magic fingers."

Gireaud gave a fleeting smile. "I will say this for you, Mister Brodie: you have confidence. Do not make it *over*confidence. I will see you at debriefing, if you are going to stand there staring at the sky."

"Can I come along in a while, Major?"

"Five minutes," Gireaud said, moving on.

"Sure, sir."

Shaking his head, the French major walked towards the training squadron building.

At last, Brodie looked down and began to follow, to see Carlo Carlizzi approaching. Carlizzi was also a major, but from the AMI, the Italian air force. Carlizzi was a backseater and one of the senior back-seat instructors. He spoke English perfectly; with the accents of a New Yorker.

He stopped when he got to Brodie. "Ensign Brodie."

"Yes, sir, Major?"

"I just spoke to Major Gireaud. He says you've got the stuff to be one of the best here. This fits with my own impressions."

"Thank you, sir."

"As I came up I saw you looking upstairs. You saw that take-off?"

"Yes, sir! That's one hell of a ship."

"And the pilot?" Carlizzi was looking closely at him.

"Shit hot, sir! That was a hot take-off by any standards. Who was the guy, sir? What's his name?"

"The eleven hundred hours slot? It's a she."

"A *she*?" Brodie's astonishment was as real as it could get. "A tits machine," he went on to himself in a voice that was not exactly full of enthusiasm. "So who is it?" he enquired.

But Carlizzi had also heard the comment.

"I have a little knowledge of the US Navy," Carlizzi said in a suddenly cold voice, "having done an exchange tour of duty. I always thought a tits machine meant a hot classic plane like the Crusader or the F-4 Phantom. The Tornado ASV(E)'s a hot ship but a very new plane. Perhaps you could clarify, Ensign."

"What I mean, sir, is that there's a pair of tits flying it, if you know what I mean." Brodie was clearly thinking he was speaking to Carlizzi man to man.

But Carlizzi's eyes matched the coldness in his voice. "That," he said in razored-edged tones, "was Flight Lieutenant Hamilton-Jones. Yeah. That's who it was. Our very own Caroline . . . the only female frontseater we've got, and we all think she's a hot *pilot*. You got that, Ensign? You watch your goddammed attitude and your mouth!" Carlizzi walked on.

Brodie gaped after him. "Er . . . yes, sir."

Carlizzi did not look back.

Caroline and McCann were transiting high over Scotland, heading south-east for the North Sea ACMI range.

The air combat manoeuvring instrumentation range was as near as they could get to the blood-pounding intense adrenalin rush of actual air combat without getting shot down if they made bad decisions or came up against a better opponent. It was the way to learn from your own stupid mistakes without getting killed for your trouble.

McCann was a veteran of real combat and ACMI dogfights. He'd been shot at. He'd been wounded and had come so close to dying that everyone – including the medical officer on the spot – had thought him dead. But he had come awake again, despite having been in what had seemed like the nap of naps. Now he was treated like some kind of precious mascot by just about everyone on the base. It was a situation he found most agreeable. McCann would not have been McCann otherwise. The words *low profile* and McCann were lifelong enemies.

During the course of her training, Caroline had been schooled in the art of fighting in the air but the usual route would have seen her posted to a standard operational squadron where she would have continued to upgrade her proficiency through constant training operations. Making it to November One, however, was a different ball game altogether.

She had been put through the unforgivingly rigorous programme of November training, been given countless hours of realistic simulator sorties and had flown several checkflights with the senior instructors; but this was her first time on the range with the ASV(E) and with McCann in the back seat.

In preparation for their forthcoming flight in the Starfire, they had flown sim sorties together in order to get the feel of each other's working routines and had also done some checkflights in the standard ASV. But although she felt in control of the powerful aircraft as they hurtled towards their destination, she also knew she would have to be at total ease with herself before she could hope to use it to the best advantage. The coming fight would lay any deficiencies bare, and she would have to learn from the experience so that she could do better next time.

"Go left, one-five-zero," McCann said, calling in a course correction.

"Left, one-five-zero," she acknowledged, making a slight alteration in heading with the slightest of left stick pressures.

The aircraft was so responsive it would be easy to fall into the trap of over-banking and wallowing all over the place in a desperate series of compensatory corrections. That would put her into the dreaded realm of PIOs – pilot-induced oscillations – that haunted every baby pilot; but she was no longer a baby pilot. The wing commander had overwhelmingly displayed his confidence in her.

She was a November pilot now. PIOs were not for her.

The Special Research Unit, east of the Urals.

Lirionova and Milla Konstantinova were in the unit firing range practising for the forthcoming contest with Urikov's team. As yet, they had no indication of who their opponents would be.

"I wouldn't put it past that bastard to put up his best shots," Lirionova said grimly, "just to rub our faces in it. I'd even bet he'll be one of the contestants."

"But he said he'd be using his worst men," Milla protested.

"Believe that when you see it. Urikov dare not lose. How would it look before his men? He'll do anything to win, even if it means going back on his original challenge."

"So he'll put up Melev as well?"

"It's what I'd expect." Lirionova checked the small monitor near her shooting position. It showed a silhouette of the human figure at which she'd just fired six 9mm rounds from her KLIN machine pistol. She was using the full-length thirty-round magazine, so there were plenty left. The computer had placed holes where her shots had struck the pop-up target at the far end of the range.

Urikov's challenge involved the use of three weapons: the Makarov automatic pistol all the military personnel carried as a sidearm, the KLIN and, finally, the AK105 assault rifle. The 105, direct descendant of the ubiquitous world-famous AK47, was a lightweight advanced version with black plastic stock and forebody in place of the more familiar wood. It was not for export and was kept specifically for use by the national forces.

Both Lirionova and Milla handled it well but Lirionova was not happy with her companion's shooting prowess.

On the occasions that she had seen the guard captain, Urikov had looked at her with a barely concealed smirk. His body language had clearly indicated that he thought it absurd she had even dared consider going up against his men. No one was in any doubt that he intended to comprehensively humiliate the women.

Milla was looking at Lirionova's target on her own monitor.

"That's great shooting, Liri," she said. "If that had been a real person, he'd be dead."

"Not good enough. Too wide a spread. Urikov will put his own group *inside* that."

"And I'm not doing so well, am I?"

"To tell you the honest truth, Milla, no. Oh you're shooting well enough to pass the proficiency test . . ."

"At the lowest level," Konstantinova interrupted drily.

"Better coming from you than from me. So what do we do? We can't let that pig win. I want to see his face when a bunch of women beat him and his oh-so-tough soldiers."

"What about our secret weapon? Is she still interested?"

Lirionova looked towards the closed door of the shooting range. It could be opened – either from the outside or the inside – only with a swipe card.

"She sounded quite intrigued," she replied, "and said she'd come today. She should have been here by now, but perhaps she can't spare the time from the lab."

Just then, the door was pushed open and Olga Vasilyeva stood there, her stance slightly awkward because of the artificial leg.

She smiled at them as she entered. "I nearly didn't make it. We've been testing various plants to see which were likely to be most compatible with the process, and one sub-species reacted violently to the injected DNA. It was almost like a human body rejecting a transplanted organ. It got quite sick. We were quite amazed by the similarity."

"What will happen now?" Konstantinova asked.

"I'm afraid it won't recover," Olga said. "The damage was too severe. Now tell me, what do I have to do?"

Lirionova gave her the details of the challenge.

Olga nodded slowly when Lirionova had finished. "Pistol, machine pistol and assault rifle, all at pop-up targets at different ranges and different locations."

"That's it," Lirionova confirmed.

The combination of a movable target butt and target silhouettes of varying sizes enabled ranges of up to 500 metres to be simulated with remarkable fidelity. Scopes were usually used for the extreme ranges but, for the contest, long ranges would not be included. It was all to be with open sights.

Lirionova set up the close-range shoot for the pistol. She handed one of the practice Makarovs to the doctor. Olga checked the weapon with a speed that spoke of practised familiarity. Even as they watched, expecting her to take her time about bracing and sighting, she spread her legs slightly, brought the weapon up two-handedly and fired off a salvo that was so rapid the explosions blended into each other. It was as if a single, long drawn-out shot had been fired.

It was all over in what seemed like the blink of an eye.

They stood open mouthed, staring at her while she remained unmoving, then turned towards the target she had just annihilated, the gun now pointing downwards. Then she cocked and re-cocked the pistol several times to ensure it was empty.

Lirionova looked at the monitor. There was just the one big hole in the chest of the image. The readouts showed that every round had gone through. She was astonished.

When Olga Vasilyeva held out the Makarov to exchange it for the KLIN, Lirionova handed her the machine pistol with something approaching reverence.

"You've got a thirty-shot magazine," Lirionova said, still hardly daring to believe what she'd just seen. "There will be six targets, five shots each. Any more or less in any target will fail that stage. Are you ready?"

"I'm ready. Start the targets."

The range was increased and the target sizes made correspondingly smaller. Then they began to pop up at irregular intervals and in different locations.

The doctor was blindingly fast.

Six precise bursts spat out of the KLIN and then it was all over. Lirionova and Konstantinova checked their monitors. Olga Vasilyeva didn't even bother to look.

Six targets were without heads.

Lirionova was staring at her. "Where did you learn to shoot like that?"

Olga ensured the machine pistol was made safe before handing it back. It was the turn of the assault rifle.

"I'm not at my best," she told them, astonishing them even further. She glanced at Lirionova with a ghostly smile. "I can see by the look on your face that it's the security captain who's just asked that question."

A wordless Konstantinova handed her the loaded AK105.

"Set the targets," the doctor said to Lirionova, eyes on a distant point. "I learned in Angola. He taught me."

"The *American?*" Lirionova could not help it.

The doctor's smile was now wistful. "You would have read my files, of course. Don't worry, Captain. He was not a spy. If anything, I learned more from him than he learned from me. About twenty-five years before we met he was in Vietnam, a very scared boy barely out of his teens. In fact, I think he was only just twenty in that last terrible year of the pull-out.

"He learned to shoot – *really* shoot – in the field. He needed to in order to survive. He told me that while the destruction was going on around him and he pressed himself into the ground as best he could for cover, he found himself staring at the plants as they were ripped apart by the bullets, grenades, bombs and shells of both sides. Every time there was a lull, he would pick up the shattered foliage and study it. He began to wonder how long it would take the plants and trees to recover. It was the beginning of his interest in botany.

"His buddies, seeing his behaviour, began to think he was suffering from acute trauma, certain he was losing his mind. In fact it was keeping him sane. While they could only look forward to the next firefight, wondering who was going to be the next casualty, he found a kind of peace with his plants.

"At the end of the war, he returned to college and studied botany. Once he'd got his degree he began to travel, going to all the rainforests he could find. I think he was getting the war out of his system. He went to the Amazon, the rainforest of Dominica in the Caribbean, Malaysia, Thailand, Queensland in Australia and of course places like Angola and the Ruwenzori in Africa. Then he began to notice something about what he was doing. Some of the places – like those in Africa – were also active or recently active war zones.

"He'd been to the Ruwenzori and had moved on to Angola, where we met. Sometimes we travelled without guards. That was when he taught me how to shoot properly; for self-defence. He had forgotten none of the survival skills he had learned in Vietnam, so he passed some of those on to me. We became lovers, as I'm sure you've already suspected, Captain."

The doctor paused. They had listened to her in enthralled silence. Lirionova gave a slight cough.

"He used to tell me," Olga Vasilyeva continued softly, not looking at them, "that I had the most beautiful legs he had ever seen. There are millions of beautiful women with legs that are far more beautiful, but it pleased me to hear him say that. He used to kiss them and kiss them and kiss them . . ."

Her voice faded as she remembered. She paused, recalling in her mind a time that had been happy for her.

Then she seemed to shrug herself back into the present. "His next destination was Borneo and he asked me to go with him. Naturally, I could not. I had my work, which he knew nothing of. But many of the things he told me about the recovery of plants after being damaged by gunfire have helped in the work we're doing here."

"Do you wish you had agreed to go with him to Borneo?" Lirionova enquired softly. "This is not the security captain asking."

"We're interested as friends," Milla Konstantinova added gently. "And as women."

"It hardly matters," the doctor said, still not looking at them. There was a profound sadness in her voice. "Saying yes would have made no difference in the end. He would still have died. The landmine, you see. It happened before he was due to leave."

She brought the rifle up and fired. Twelve rounds at six targets. She hit every one, two bullets each.

En route *to the North Sea ACMI range, the same moment in time.*

The enhanced air superiority variant of the Tornado F3 – also designated F3S(E) – was of even greater potency than its earlier variant the ASV, which was itself far ahead of the original ADV Tornado that had spawned it. The November unit's policy of continually upgrading its operational aircraft meant that eventually all November squadrons would be flying the enhanced variant.

Wings swept back to the maximum sixty-seven degrees it streaked towards the ACMI range, its air superiority grey colour making it seem ghostly as it flitted through the high wisps of cloud. It could do tricks with its colour and was able to undergo a polychromatic metamorphosis so comprehensive that even the low-visibility, pale blue four-pointed NATO insignia on its wings and tail fin seemed to vanish.

It shared this capability with all the November aircraft, except for the standard ADVs used for basic conversion training. The trick was in the special paint containing "intelligent" crystals which, when electrically excited, could be made to change colour within a seemingly infinite range. This capability could be automatically initiated through the aircraft's various sensors, or via a dedicated programmable keypad in the rear cockpit operated by the backseater. The aircraft could thus become almost invisible against a wide range of backgrounds; very useful in any fight requiring visual acquisition. This capability was regarded as an extra weapon by the aircrew.

The ASV Echo's augmented engines, more fuel-efficient, now boasted a vast thirty-eight per cent increase in power over those of the original ADV Tornado which, although a front-line aircraft with RAF units, was strictly for training purposes at the November base. The ASV(E) was a longer aircraft, with the judiciously expanded area of its variable sweep wings enabling it to maintain its unrivalled superiority in high-speed flying at ultra-low level. Its tailerons were also greater in area, with dog-tooth leading edges. A more comprehensive use of lighter but stronger composite and radar-absorbent materials had substantially reduced its all-up weight. The old-style canopy had given way to a big clamshell that fitted snugly to the new single-piece windscreen, allowing its crew to enjoy an outstanding, all-round visual capability.

The flat underbelly – today missile-free on Caroline and McCann's aircraft but normally carrying four extreme long-range Skyray Bs in their recessed housings – was itself a lifting device. Added to this, the leading edge extensions which reached out from the wing roots to sleekly narrow to a point just beneath and ahead of the windscreen, helped to give the potent aircraft phenomenal agility.

A wide-angle holographic HUD that automatically varied the intensity of its glowing green symbology presented the pilot with all the priority information necessary at any given time. At night or in poor lighting conditions, an infrared window could be superimposed upon the head-up display, offering detailed vision in the dark of the night.

The ASV Echo's gun was very different from that of the original F3 Tornado. On the first ASVs the orignal gun had been replaced by a six-barrelled unit of 20mm calibre. This had now been supplanted by a variable speed system, with the calibre increased to 30mm. It was a deadly, extremely accurate, reliable weapon.

But the only weapon carried for the day's ACMI mission was the air-to-air, missile-like airborne instrumentation pod, carried on one of the short-range missile stations beneath a wing. The finless pod with its long proboscis would monitor all the dynamics of the aircraft's performance plus all weapons data so that the information gathered would be faithfully reproduced as if real missiles and guns had been fired. The opposing aircraft would be similarly equipped and on the operations screen on the ground all nuances of the fight – including a generated visual of what each pilot would see through their HUDs – would be displayed. Bad moves as well as good would be shown in all their pleasing, and embarrassing, glory.

Caroline could sense the powerhouse under her control. On full afterburner, nearly 47,000 pounds of thrust could hurl it at speeds approaching mach 2.6 at altitude; and its thrust-to-weight ratio was close to 1.9 to 1, far exceeding unity. Whenever she shoved the twin throttles against the wall and into full burner, those engines seemed to be pushing themselves through the air with no weight to carry. Theoretically, she could stand the aircraft on its tail and it would keep climbing until the engines could no longer breathe and the wings no longer bite in the high thin air on the dark edge of space.

"This is a slippery, agile aircraft, powerful and light on the controls," she remembered Jason saying to her when he'd informed her he was prepared to confirm her suitability to fly it. "She'll accelerate like the brown stuff off a shovel, and her fly-by-wire control system is multiple-redundant with a self-repairing capability. This means in the event of damage sustained she'll do her best to get you home.

"She's extremely dangerous to an opponent in a turning fight and will take the battle to all levels from lo-lo to hi-hi. In the hands of a good pilot, she's lethal; in the hands of someone with the talent I expect of a November pilot, she's murderous, or should be. An aircraft that is so formidable requires that you stay ahead of it all the time. Know what you're doing. Never allow yourself to get behind the power curve. Do that, and we may one day end up attempting to dig you, and your unfortunate backseater, from inside the Godforsaken crater you made when you hit terra firma."

As she did a quick scan of her displays she vividly remembered his words of caution.

She had taken them to heart.

Five

"**H**eads up," she heard McCann's voice saying in her ear. "We're approaching the combat zone and I'm going to give us some private conversation before the fun begins."

"No CVR?"

"Nope. But not long enough to get them thinking about it down the Hole."

The Hole was everyone's slang for the Operations Centre, the hub of the November base's operational monitoring activities.

"We're supposed to be totally voice recordable, Elmer Lee, so that the fight can be thoroughly analysed."

"Quit complaining! I'm trying to give you some help here."

"But how can you cut out the recorder without anyone noticing?"

"Got me a gizmo from that guy in Engineering who made me the mobile phone killer. Remember that neat piece of kit?"

"I do, and I asked you to lend it to me for when I travel by train. I don't want to have to listen to people shouting their boring conversations. You never did lend it."

"Uh . . . ah . . . OK. Next time."

"And by the way, that 'gizmo' you just told me about is an unauthorised mod."

"It's a tiny stand-alone unit that goes into my music CD channel. It goes into nothing else and doesn't mess with anything except make the recorder deaf for a short while."

"I'm still not sure . . . but all right. So what's this help you're going to give me?"

"First thing. This is going to be a knife fight. No missile engagements. So we're visual and we're going guns. I want you to react when I call it. Don't think, just do it. Got that?"

"Yes," Caroline confirmed.

She had great respect for McCann's abilities and had no problem deferring to his greater experience. The McCann everyone tolerated like a friendly itch on the ground was a completely different being in the air. This was where the real Elmer Lee came into his own, displaying the skill that made him the best nav on the unit.

Only Wolfie Flacht, Axel Hohendorf's backseater, came remotely close. The November unit's top combat crews were the pilot and nav pairings of RAF man Mark Selby and McCann, and Hohendorf and Flacht. Hohendorf and Flacht – like the senior deputy commander, Dieter Helm – were from Germany's *Marineflieger*. They were followed by the Italian Air Force's Nico Bagni and the US Marines' Hank Stockmann, and the US Air Force's Cottingham whose backseater was Denmark's Lars Christiansen. These four crews were November's best and most combat experienced.

"OK," McCann continued. "So who are our opponents today for this great furball in the sky?"

"Not much of a furball; just the two kites in our slot."

"You'll think you're in a furball," McCann predicted. "So? Any idea who's out there waiting to pounce?"

"They kept it from us, as you know."

"They can keep nothing from Mrs McCann's cute offspring."

"Is this what they call the pilot's curse? The geezer in the back seat with a high opinion of himself?"

"Hey, hey, hey, pretty-pretty. I'm the *friendly* guy in back. You want my help or not?"

"Want."

"OK. So Mark's in London getting to know his lady love Kim Mannon even better . . . as if they could get any closer, and Axel's in Germany, carousing with Mark's neat sister Morven, showing off his new Porsche Carrera. Me? I'll stick with my good old American iron, my Corvette—"

"Carousing?"

"Carousing, shmarousing, whatever . . . and Nico's been given permission to go off to Italy to see his darling Bianca, to try and persuade her to give up her very successful fashion design business to marry him. Hah! Some hope. She knows what a fighter jock's pay is like. Couldn't buy one of her creations with—"

"Elmer Lee . . ."

"OK. So I'm exaggerating. But think about this: who else is left to give us a really hard time today?"

"Oh no. Not the boss."

"Not the boss. He's going to be down the Hole, watching for our bad moves and listening to us sweat."

"Gireaud and Carlizzi?"

"Nope. Not even warm."

"Not Chuck Morton."

"Nah. We can take Chuck easy."

"He did get an Su-27 on that last mission."

"Yeah, but Carlizzi was holding his hand."

"Colonel da Vinci?"

"Getting warm, but still keep trying."

"A really hard time, you said. That can only mean . . ."

"Nightmare time! Yes! Our resident Knight Templar, *Fregatten-kapitän* Dieter Helm, scourge of junior pilots everywhere and all-round sadist in the air, step forward! You're on the Elmer Lee and Caroline show! We who are about to get reamed – but not if we can help it – salute you! How do you feel?" he added to her, almost as an afterthought.

"Sick."

"And so you should. This guy is going to fight hard and cause you some real pain. It will be as G-intensive as he can make it and remember this bird of ours can go beyond positive ten. We're talking serious torture here. He'll turn hard and tight to get into your circle, forcing you to go even tighter, until you'll want to cry with all that G squeezing at you – even with our wonderful pressure-breathing outfits – so that you'll think your lungs are going to be somewhere by your knees."

"My *lungs*? Are you talking about my lungs, or do you mean my 'lungs'?"

"Whatever," McCann said quickly.

"Don't ever change, Elmer Lee," she muttered to herself tolerantly. She knew exactly what he'd been referring to.

"Say what?" he enquired, having merely heard the murmur.

"Just some woman talk. You were saying?"

"Um . . . yeah. I don't want to worry you, but he's going to be real mean . . . and it's really going to hurt."

"So you've already hinted."

"Oh, have I?"

"Yes! And thanks for nothing, Elmer Lee," Caroline went on grimly. "Does it get any worse?"

"It does. The backseater's Wolfie Flacht."

"Ooh shit."

"Shit is right, and lots of it. But have no fear, McCann's here. I'm going to look after you. Just do it when I call it, and do it goddammned fast. The guy is going to be out to ream your ass. We may not get him, but we're sure as hell going to make him sweat for his cookies. He hates that, especially if he thinks he should have taken you with one of his sucker tricks. The more he has to work, the more he's likely to lose his cool."

"He never loses his cool."

"Hey, we can pray for rain."

"Commander Helm," Caroline said unenthusiastically. "I really needed that."

"Be positive."

"I am positive. I know he's positively going to murder me out there."

"No he's not. Just be sharp on my calls. Helm doesn't know *we* know he's out there. All is not fair in love and war, so that's a bonus. OK?"

"OK."

"Cool. Now we're switching back to legal. The recorder will be coming on again, and they're also going to hear us down the Hole."

"Roger."

McCann cut off the interrupt from the cockpit voice recorder channel. The CVR was back on line.

Down in the Operations Centre, Jason was watching the huge screen which displayed the positions of the opposing aircraft.

The system had been upgraded so that the original wireframe images of combatant aircraft were now displayed as solid 3D models, with their wingtip trails shown as a white ribbon edged in red and green to indicate left and right wingtip. Whatever their manoeuvres the ribbons twisted, turned and looped, accurately following the aircraft across the virtual sky.

As they moved, all relevant data was displayed next to each: callsigns, current altitudes, speeds and headings. Radar searches were shown as a spreading series of yellow dashes; infrared as red dots, and optical as a transparent cone. Even the camouflaging heat-augmented crystal-enhanced system was represented. Called the Chameleon by just about everyone, when employed, the screen would show a "dissolve" of the aircraft using it and a faint silhouette would replace the 3D image. For the current fight, McCann and Caroline in Thunder Zero-One were depicted as having the blue aircraft, while Helm and Flacht in Thunder Zero-Two were orange.

Mario da Vinci was also in the Ops Centre. He stood next to Jason, eyes on the screen.

"Do you think she will do well?" he asked.

"She should at least give a good account," Jason said. "And

McCann's with her. Although God alone knows whether that will be a help or a hindrance."

"Helm is tough. He will not spare her."

"I would not expect him to. She must be given no favours. She has got this far on her own merit. If she's to remain with us, she's got to be able to take it. I see her as a *pilot*, not as a *female* pilot for whom allowances must be made. She would not thank me for treating her in such a manner."

"Not everyone thinks as you do."

"Here? Or in the units of other services?"

Da Vinci replied in a roundabout way. "Here, everyone wishes her to succeed. Except perhaps Brodie."

"Ah yes. Brodie."

"Ookaayy!" McCann was saying to Caroline. "Showtime! He's going to try to bounce us so keep your eyes wide open and your legs crossed."

"Bit difficult in here," she shot back in the same spirit. "Crossing my legs, I mean."

"You get my drift."

"Yes, Elmer Lee. I do get your drift." But she was doing rapid scans of the sky and her displays. "Helmet sight on."

The target acquisition arrow in the helmet symbology, seemingly positioned upon the sky ahead of her visor, remained centred within the gun steering circle. It would become animated when the target came within sensor range and begin to search it out by first extending itself then pointing in the required direction.

"I'm going to start making life difficult for them," McCann said. "I'm going for Chameleon."

"Go for it."

"Roger that." McCann tapped at the Chameleon keypad. "We're now turning into a nice shade of blue-grey. From altitude, we look like we're part of the sea and from sea level, well hell, we've just disappeared."

"It's a really weird feeling," she said. "Here we are sitting in something solid, yet to anyone watching we've turned invisible."

"Let's just hope the hard man's wondering where we've got to, if he's already on to us. But I keep thinking of Wolfie Flacht in that back seat. That guy's got some nasty surprises up his sleeve. Bad habits he picked up from Axel."

"Nothing to fear, McCann's here. That's what you told me."

"And I mean it, pretty-pretty."

*   *   *

Down in the Hole, Jason and da Vinci had listened in on the conversation and had watched as Thunder Zero-One had gone into dissolve.

Jason had cast a long-suffering glance at the ceiling on hearing McCann's part in the conversation. Around the centre the operators were trying hard to hide their smiles. They all liked to be on duty when McCann was up. His voice recordings entertained them.

"Oh Lord," Jason murmured to his deputy. "He's at it again."

"But he has also made the first move. A wise precaution, as the combat calls for short-range scans only. It is good to take the initiative before getting into scan range. Helm will not like that." Da Vinci sounded pleased.

"All right, Caroline," McCann said crisply. "Head for the deck."

"Going down," she responded immediately.

She was not going to argue. Elmer Lee knew what he was doing. She flung the ASV(E) onto its back and, wings still swept, headed seawards.

"Start the pull-out at fifteen thousand," he went on, "but keep descending. Bring the power back as you do. I want you at sea level with wings spread. OK?"

"Wings spread at sea level. Roger." The acquisition arrow was still not excited. "Was that a proposition?" she queried lightly.

"You kidding?" he responded similarly. "Karen would kill me!"

"I'll tell her you didn't really mean it."

"Yeah." But McCann's attention was out of the cockpit as his head moved this way and that, hunting out a possible ambush by Thunder Zero-Two.

He watched nonchalantly as the Tornado plunged towards the cold grey of the sea. She had good control he mused as she began the pull-out smoothly, continuing downhill and easing back on the power. The sea was approaching with alarming rapidity, but he maintained his clinical observation of the descent.

Then the nose began to rise even as the aircraft continued to lose height. The wings, on auto-manoeuvre, had begun to spread as the ASV(E) lost speed. Still they continued downwards.

At a hundred feet they levelled out, wings fully spread. It had been impressively done. McCann thought she had handled the potent aircraft with superb skill.

"Will a hundred feet do?" she asked.

"On the button. Stay down here for a while. Let's give them something to think about."

Thunder Zero-Two was powering in at 30,000 feet.

"Have you got them yet?" Helm enquired, speaking in German.

"Nothing as yet, *Herr Fregattenkapitän*," Flacht replied in the same language.

"Flacht."

"*Kapitän?*"

"You wouldn't be thinking of trying to help your friends out, would you?" the senior deputy commander asked in a hard voice.

"I would not!" Flacht protested.

"But you would like them to win, perhaps?"

"I am neutral, *Herr Kapitän*," Flacht lied smoothly. "May the best man, or woman, win. I'm not going to make it easy for them."

But he did consider that perhaps if he were just a little slow in spotting something . . . He didn't want to actually help Caroline, as a win under such conditions would cause her assessors to arrive at the wrong conclusion. She had to win – if she managed it at all – in a manner that did not give a false reading of her true prowess. A win made easy could kill her – and her backseater – in a real fight. On the other hand, in a first fight with a master like Helm there was nothing wrong with a little judicious "encouragement".

Too devastating a defeat could be just as catastrophic as a "nudged" win; for losing too comprehensively could easily dent her self-confidence and subsequently make her dangerous in the cockpit. It was a wafer-thin line between covert help and encouragement, he decided.

Suddenly, his train of thought was rudely interrupted by the Tornado abruptly flipping onto its back. Helm was going down.

"I've spotted nothing," Flacht said. "Why are we going down?"

"McCann's in there somewhere," Helm replied firmly, switching to his American-accented English. "That little runt is sneaky. I know he'd just love to take me with a crazy move of his. He hates pilots of the rank of major and above."

And he is convinced, Flacht thought, *that you hate small backseaters from Kansas City, Missouri.*

Helm was referring to the fact that McCann, before he'd been shifted to the back seat, had once been an aspiring fighter pilot. After a hair-raising landing in an F-15, the US Air Force decided enough was enough and offered him a chance to leave or go into the back seat. The hope had been that he would have refused such a perceived humiliation and would have said thanks but no thanks.

Unfortunately for his superiors, he had wanted to remain flying so much he'd accepted; and promptly evolved into a backseater of outstanding ability. But, as with anything to do with McCann, there was a price to pay. He began to have serious disagreements in the air with his pilots, most of whom, for reasons no one could as yet fathom, turned out to be majors. Moreover, McCann always seemed to be right. It had therefore been with some relief that McCann's superiors had agreed to transfer him to November One. Some even insisted that the entire high command of the US Air Force had wept for joy. No one had *seen* that happen, but some believed it.

"Let's have the Chameleon," Helm ordered.

"Chameleon on."

In the Hole, Jason watched as Thunder Zero-Two went into dissolve. There were now two ghostly silhouettes sniffing each other out.

"This should prove interesting," Jason remarked softly.

The two aircraft were still out of short-range sensor scan but were jockeying for the best position prior to that first contact. It was as if two fighters, armed only with knives, had been placed in a darkened room. Each knew the other was there, and each would be groping around for an advantage before the inevitable clash. Pre-fight positioning – a vital advantage – would depend upon who had best read the other's intentions.

"So both are going to open the fight at low level," da Vinci said, watching as Zero-Two's dissolved silhouette headed at high speed for the sea.

"Ah yes. But will Zero-One remain there?"

The two aircraft were drawing inexorably closer to each other. The Ops Centre personnel had fallen silent, each wondering which of the two aircraft would get the first advantage.

"Fight will soon be joined," da Vinci said. "Then we shall know."

"Lose sight, lose the fight," McCann said to Caroline. "You're about to have the hottest one hundred and eighty seconds of your life. If you don't get him in those three minutes, or he doesn't get you, it's a draw. But he'll probably get you."

"Well, thanks! What happened to have no fear?"

"Still there. Keeping you on your toes, is all."

"So you've spotted them? Helmet sight's giving me nothing."

"I've got zilch, but I can feel them. They're close all right. Probably on Chameleon too, if Helm or Wolfie's on the ball. They're still out of sensor range."

"So they're doing what we are? Dancing just out of range then coming in for a fast kill?"

"That's the one. Aah . . ."

McCann had been doing his constant search and had looked behind. He thought he'd spotted an indistinct shape in the distance, coming down but going away from them. Visibility was excellent, as far as the eye could see. The first break, perhaps. It could have been a seabird, of course. On the other hand . . .

"You've seen something? But the helmet sight's not—"

"Go, go, go, go! Don't think! Burners in, and make like a rocket!"

Despite being taken by surprise she did not hesitate. She slammed the throttles forward. The ASV(E) gathered speed in a surging rush. The wings began to sweep as she reefed it into a steep climb, groaning and grunting as the G forces hit her. Then they relaxed as the Tornado settled out of the pull-up and hurtled for altitude.

"We were too low," McCann said quickly as they shot upwards. "They didn't spot us and are heading away. Unless they've turned they're still extending as we climb. Get ready to haul over, roll one-eighty and get after them. To do this right you've got to make the inversion fast and tight. It will hurt but only for a moment. You'll have them on the helmet sight soon after. But don't count on their staying there. Once they realise we've got in first, old Knight Templar's going to come at you like a bear with his butt on fire."

"Don't you mean with a sore head?"

"I mean butt on fire. He's not going to be a happy man. First advantage to you, pretty-pretty."

"You spotted him."

"Hey, it's the team."

"Okay, teammate, we're going upside down."

Caroline hauled the stick towards her, cutting the burners to bleed speed and tighten the turn, straining once more against the G. The pressure-breathing suit was doing its best, giving her tolerance for higher G than would have been possible with just speed jeans. The Tornado pulled onto its back, spreading its wings to mid-sweep for a better bite at the air as it performed a tight half-loop. She rolled upright, and was now heading in the direction McCann had indicated. She shoved the throttles forward. The burners spat out their twin-tongued trail of flame. The wings began to sweep once more and the hunter tore after its prey.

Almost immediately the helmet sight got excited.

"I've got them!" she squealed, scarcely daring to believe it. "We've got them first!"

"Getting them suckered first is one thing. Zapping them . . . now there's a thing. He's not going to sit still for you. Your head is now in the hornets' nest. Stand by for stings. But you can still fox him. OK. He's turned. He knows we're here. I've got him on optical. Patched to you. Check your left display."

She darted a quick glance. There was Zero-Two in a hard bank, streaming vortices and heading their way. Superimposed around the edges of the display were the read-out values of heading, speed, closure rate, angle of approach and altitude.

"My God!" she said. "He looks mean."

"He is, and he's after you. Don't sit there admiring him! He's going to try for a head-to-head. He knows this is going to scare the shit out of you. He hopes. But you're not, are you?"

Silence.

"Are you!"

"No."

"That's what I want to hear. Get ready to counter. When I call it, *do* it."

"Roger."

"You're going to break left. He'll counter, but you're not going left at all. You'll continue the roll through one-eighty to pull right, level out and pull into a climb going like the world's meanest dog wants a bite of you . . . which is better than what's *really* after you. Do it all in one continuous motion. *No* hesitation. You got that?"

"Got it."

"OK. Wait for my call." McCann looked out and saw the indistinct speck hurtling towards them, shifting visual aspect as it approached. "Gawd. These ships of ours do look mean."

Bip.

"He's trying for a shot! *Go, go, go!*"

It all happened in the most fleeting of seconds. Doing as he'd advised, Caroline snapped the ASV(E) into a sharp roll to the left and saw the other aircraft beginning to counter, exactly as McCann had predicted. Remembering his insistence on the fluidity of the manoeuvre, she hid her intentions beautifully, continued the roll, levelled her wings and pulled into the climb all in a single motion.

It worked!

"Don't start congratulating yourself!" McCann's voice came rapidly at her as they tore upwards, his words seeming to run into each other. "He knows what you've done and is already countering your next move. He expects you to pull over the top and come back down to catch him cockpit up and turning into your gun. So right now he'll cockpit *down*, pulling downhill . . . but not for long. He'll be planning to pull up and cut into your loop. While you think you're going to find him waiting he's underneath, waiting for you to give him a nice descending belly shot as you look for him."

"So now what?"

"Keep going."

"What?"

"Go to forty thou. He's not going to expect something so crazy. With missiles up, a straight climb like that's a sure way to a quick barbecue. But we're guns today. He's got to come after you. Keep tracking your head. Give the helmet sight something to eat."

"He's over to the right. Coming up."

Something indistinct appeared to be floating in and out of vision in the climb.

"I've got him," McCann said. "They're still in Chameleon. This is where you get to practise your recovery technique. Cut power, bring the boards out. Disengage SPILS."

"Do *what?*"

He'd told her to temporarily deprive them of the spin prevention and incidence limiting system. In short, remove from use the one thing that enabled her to fly the aircraft at the limit without fear of spinning out of the sky.

"You're going into a spin. You've got the altitude. Plenty of time to recover. He's never going to expect that move. Have you got the balls for it?"

"I've got the balls," she said firmly.

"OK. To make this work, you got to recover *quickly*, get flying speed up and go after the sucker while he's still wondering if you're out of control. Got it?"

"Got it. All's not fair in love and war."

"Now you're cooking."

Helm could not believe it. He had just arrived at 35,000 feet when the Tornado of Caroline and McCann went tumbling past, the Chameleon making it look for all the world like some visual quick-change artist among undersea creatures.

"My God!" he shouted. "She's lost control! Emergency channel, Flacht. Hurry!"

Flacht quickly selected the channel. "Open," he said.

"Thunder Zero-One!" Helm called. "Zero-One!"

There was no reply.

Flacht was more sanguine about the whole affair. He was certain that Caroline could pull out of the spin. If she couldn't, she had no right being in the front seat of such an aircraft. There had been no distress call from Zero-One. Unless something catastrophic had occurred and both crew members were out of it, Flacht's instincts told him that McCann was up to something.

In which case, he thought, he was going to keep his mouth shut. He reasoned that if McCann had indeed created a window of opportunity then the wily backseater and Caroline were about to pull a fast one. They had totally psyched out Helm, who had certainly not expected this. Flacht decided that he was not breaking any rules by saying nothing. After all, they could really be in a serious situation and were even now trying to work it out as they tumbled towards the sea.

He remained clinically impassive and awaited further developments.

"Thunder Zero-One!" Helm was still calling. "Pull out! Pull Out!"

In Operations, everyone watched the screen silently as the falling image of Zero-One passed 30,000 feet. Unlike Zero-Two they'd heard the conversation between McCann and Caroline and were hoping that she could in fact pull out in time.

Jason watched expressionlessly. If this did not work, he would lose one very expensive aircraft, the unit's best navigator and November's first and highly promising female fighter pilot. All in all, a triple disaster of monumental proportions. He was already seeing the headlines: FEMALE FIGHTER PILOT FROM SECRET BASE KILLED IN SMASH. Undoubtedly in great fat searing letters in the tabloids to grab the eye, with a hastily cobbled-together history of Caroline's very personal life tagged on for good measure. They would hunt out anything to do with sex and play it for all it was worth; find ex-lovers, "friends" to tell all. They would also try to create a mythical triangle which would include McCann and Karen Lomax, hinting – though not actually *saying* – that perhaps there had been a quarrel in the cockpit. Lovers' tiff. There would then rapidly follow copious quantities of newsprint about the wisdom of putting women in fighter cockpits.

Someone, somewhere, would find a man who'd been the pimply-faced kid who had first kissed her; and an ex-boyfriend – university, perhaps – would come blinking into the light to talk about that time on holiday; and a school friend would remember how Caroline had been kind, bossy, single-minded and so on. Tick whichever description suited the article.

Then the whole November concept would be laid bare for public consumption. People would crawl out of the woodwork to give "personal" and "expert" insights; and to make uninformed judgements. Perhaps Caroline had crashed because it had been that time of the month, they would say; adding triumphantly that it was well known that women's decision making was suspect during those times. Definitely unsuitable for fighter cockpits. There would be those who would further say she should have been a wife and mother, not hurling several tons of high-tech war machine across the sky. It would go on and on.

It was as ludicrous as it was insulting. Caroline had got where she was because she was good. She had beaten many men to make it. She had fulfilled just one exceedingly tough criterion: she had to be good enough. Being a woman was incidental.

And yet, and yet.

Jason shut his eyes briefly as he thought of the possible nightmare scenario. *If this doesn't work, McCann,* he thought grimly, *I swear I'll come looking for you in the afterlife, just for the pleasure of throttling you.*

Da Vinci was looking at him. "Are you all right, sir?" the lieutenant-colonel enquired softly.

Jason nodded.

"They have plenty of time to pull out," da Vinci said, gauging Jason's thoughts with some accuracy.

"They'd better," Jason said.

He looked at the screen. Had they really fallen only another thousand feet?

"OK," McCann was saying calmly as the world churned about him. "You've spooked the Knight Templar. Time for our surprise. Any time you're ready."

"Roger," Caroline acknowledged, hoping she sounded calm.

The Tornado was falling in a left-hand spin. She knew the procedure and it was easy enough. In-spin aileron, stick fully back. The wings were spread fully forward, appreciably slowing down rotational speed. She had the stick over to the left and held firmly back; and waited.

After about two further turns the aircraft steadied in a shallow dive. She quickly centred the controls, re-engaged SPILS, shoved the throttles forward and, as the ASV Echo responded with seeming glee and began to sweep its wings, she heard McCann's exultant cry.

"Go git him!" the Kansas City pixie crowed. "You'll get just this one chance!"

She hauled the super-superflick into a tight G-intensive climbing turn. Again it hurt. She groaned and strained against the G-forces that punished her. But the helmet sight had caught and firmly locked onto an unsuspecting Zero-Two. On the HUD, the gun "snake", a long line of glowing green dots, was floating within the long U-shaped funnel the crews liked to call the test tube. The bright diamond was firmly fixed in the middle of the circular gun-ranging pipper. Pipper and diamond were drawn inexorably down the tube.

A fleeting chance. Helm was recovering rapidly from his astonishment. He'd be out of there in the blink of an eye.

Then the tone sounded, loud and triumphant.

Had this been a real shoot, Zero-Two would have been straddled with a barrage of massive rounds of very high explosive from the ASV(E)'s multi-barrelled rotary cannon.

Caroline had just nabbed the Knight Templar.

"Yeeharr!" McCann yelled. "You did it, Caroline! You got him! Boy, is he going to hate that! One pretty sick commander."

Caroline found she was shaking. Her entire body felt damp.

"We, Elmer Lee. We did it. I couldn't have without you. Thanks for showing that to me."

"Teammates," he said happily. "Teammates."

"Knock it off! Knock if off!" came Helm's voice on their headphones, signalling the end of that round.

"Roger," Caroline answered, feeling exhilarated. She'd actually beaten the Knight Templar!

"Does he sound pissed off, or what?" McCann said to her gleefully. "But don't think it's over," he went on. "The guy's going to be out to teach you a hard lesson; and he's not going to fall for the same trick twice."

"Got any more?"

"Maybe," McCann said mysteriously.

Six

The pent-up atmosphere in Ops was released with a great shout of *"Yes!"* when Thunder Zero-One pulled out of the spin. However, that was nothing compared to the yell that followed when Caroline and McCann very comprehensively suckered Zero-Two into the killing zone of their gun, and the orange aircraft depicted on the screen had been unceremoniously surrounded by a coffin-shaped pulse of light.

As the noise settled back to the normal murmur of background sounds, people were now surreptitiously glancing Jason's way to check if he disapproved of their uninhibited display of solidarity with Caroline.

Jason kept his eyes firmly on the screen. His expression gave nothing away.

"That was a neat trick they pulled," da Vinci observed mildly. "It would have caught me out too."

"It was," Jason admitted, still keeping his attention on the large screen. "And, for our sins, McCann's passing his bad habits on to Caroline."

"But it worked, first time . . . and that is what matters. In a real shoot it would have been a certain kill. But Helm will not fall for that trick a second time."

"I agree," Jason said. "And Commander Helm will not be a very happy man, having been caught out for all to see. But he can't fault McCann and Caroline. All is not fair, after all, in love and war."

Da Vinci glanced at the wing commander. There was definitely the barest hint of a smile.

In Zero-Two, Helm was furious.

"I thought they were in trouble!" he said tightly to Flacht. Commendably, he did not bawl out McCann and Caroline.

"An honest assumption, *Herr Kapitän*," Flacht said with diplomatic neutrality. Privately, he thought it was superb, worthy of one of Hohendorf's own ploys.

"Well," Helm grated, "the gloves are now off. She wants a fight? Let's give her a real one!"

"Ready for the next round," Flacht confirmed.

"Fight's on!" Helm barked at the other aircraft.

"Uh-oh," McCann said to Caroline. "Hear the tone of that voice? That's a man out for blood. This is where the real pain begins. Stand by to do a real workout. He'll be playing hardball and you're not going to get time to think. You'll be pounds lighter when we're done here."

"One way of getting slim, I suppose," she said as she hauled the Tornado into a screaming climb.

"I'd like to hear what you say about that when we're back on the ground. You might just have a different point of view by then. You never had a workout teacher like this guy."

McCann was looking through the top of the canopy as he spoke. Something flitted on the edge of his vision.

"Break the climb!" he shouted. *"Come hard! On the canopy! On the canopy! Jesus! Do it. Do it!"*

He grunted and strained as Caroline responded to his directions with alacrity. She had moved just in time. Like an angry shark, the sleekly menacing presence of Zero-Two sliced past, deprived at the very last moment of a gun solution.

They were lucky on that occasion.

They fought a further five rounds, of three minutes' duration each; a hundred and eighty seconds of punishing torture per session, but still wildly exhilarating. Those fifteen minutes were the toughest Caroline had experienced in her entire life; but she threw the ASV Echo about with increasing confidence, making the very air her arena. Helm, in Zero-Two, continued to push her to the limits of her skill and endurance, never giving her the slightest quarter.

In response to McCann's shouted directions, she hurled and whirled the roaring Tornado about the sky, feeling the relentless punishment of the forces of gravity as they seemed to be trying to squeeze the very essence out of her.

Despite the best efforts of the full-body anti-G suit with its pressure-breathing vest, she still wanted to sob with the pain of it. And again, despite the liquid conditioning of the suit, her skin felt as if rivers of perspiration were bursting out of her pores. She felt hot and cold at the same time, and her helmeted head sometimes appeared to have glued itself to the ejection seat headrest. Her arms became heavy, fighting the press of G as she worked to keep Helm's implacable aircraft off her six. But the suit helped her withstand far more G than she normally could with just the far more widely-used lower-body speed jeans, as McCann liked to call them.

As she hauled into the tighter and tighter turns; rolled canopy-down to pull away and reverse direction to try and get the Chameleon-happy Zero-Two into gun range; racked into a tight, G-intensive climb before rolling ninety degrees in the climb, pulling over the top, rolling ninety again and hauling on the stick to come charging tightly back, she could hear the rasp of her breathing, reminding her crazily of someone in an iron lung.

And still Helm pushed.

He was relentless. But she was determined not to give in. Never once did she call "Knock it off!" which would have instantly terminated any one of the contests. He was not giving quarter and she was not going to plead for it. Even McCann once felt moved to ask if she wanted a respite.

"No!" she had squeezed out between straining grunts. "Never!"

And so it had gone on.

Then, at last, Helm called "Knock it off!" and it was all over. Of the five rounds, Helm had managed only two kills, and one of those had been sufficiently fleeting to have it marked down in Ops as a damaging shot. The computers calculated they might have made it back to base, or ejected *en route*; so no coffin.

The remaining three rounds had ended inconclusively, with Caroline just managing to keep out of Helm's gunsight, even though she'd never once been able to catch him out again. It was an astonishing display of tenacity on her part.

"Well done," came Helm's voice on her headphones.

"Thank you, Zero-Two," she responded with relief, controlling the urge to take huge gulps of oxygen.

"You have the lead back to base."

"Roger," she said. "I have the lead."

"Good stuff there, pretty-pretty," McCann said to her. "This is surely going to get you assigned to our squadron."

"I couldn't have done it without you, Elmer Lee."

"Sure you could." But he was smiling broadly.

"And Elmer Lee?"

"Yo."

"This is not a good way to get slim."

"No kidding."

Elmer Lee grinned hugely in his mask.

Caroline watched as Zero-Two, now back to its basic paint scheme of air superiority grey tinged with the faintest blue, slid neatly into position on her right wing. The air combat, for all its physical toll, had left her on a high. She had actually got the Knight Templar! Even though it had been just the once, it had been once enough. She'd done it, and it had all been fully witnessed. Nothing could change that.

"Elmer Lee."

"Yo."

"Despite all the sweat and the pain that really gave me a hard-on."

"There you go. And that, by the way," he went on, "was just recorded by the CVR."

"Was it? Oh well . . . too bad. I'll just have to live with it."

And Elmer Lee beamed.

Wings fully swept, the two ASV Echoes made a high fast transit back to base.

"Let's do this with panache," Caroline said to McCann when they were twenty miles out from base. "A high fast overhead pass, continued down to a low one along the runway and into the break. What do you think?"

"Should set a few hairs on fire. What about the Knight Templar?" McCann glanced over his shoulder to where Zero-Two was keeping perfect station.

"I've got the lead all the way to touchdown. He's got to follow, unless I release him."

"This should be fun. OK. Your call."

"Right. Get us clearance and we'll do it."

McCann talked to November who confirmed the circuit was clear and they could do the intended approach.

"Roger," Caroline said when she heard, then called the other aircraft. "Zero-Two, on me."

She shoved the throttles forward. The burners came on and spearing tails of flame torched out of the nozzles. The ASV Echo leapt away, swept wings superheating the moist air, creating a streaming vertical halo about the aircraft just ahead of the tail, making it seem as if the Tornado was permanently emerging out of a living gossamer cocoon.

Although taken by surprise, Helm's reactions were swift. Zero-Two lagged behind for the most fleeting of moments. Soon it was seamlessly back in position, its own halo matching the lead machine's. In this formation the two aircraft tore through the air high above the runway, their engines a screaming rasp that seemed to cause the very earth to vibrate with their passage.

Still in formation they turned onto a reciprocal course to run parallel with the runway, descending as they did so. As they went lower, the halos shifted shape and changed into tortured vortices that billowed off the LERXs, and trailed from the wingtips.

From the ground, it was quite spectacular to watch as the pair turned once more, this time lining up for the centreline.

The two aircraft came thundering low over the main runway, wings still fully swept. Then the leader snapped crisply into a sharp left bank, climbing slightly and bleeding speed off as the wings began to spread. The wingman followed suit scant moments later, fanning out to take up station slightly displaced behind the leader.

Engines began giving a high-pitched whistle as throttles were eased back. Flaps and slats were deployed, generating lift as the speed dropped further. Wheels began to lower. Continuing in formation, they again flew parallel to the runway until it was time to make the final turn that would position them accurately, for the second time, with the centreline.

They landed in formation. Clamshell buckets slammed with a sharp whistle across engine nozzles as thrust reversers came on with a billowing roar.

A giant fart McCann tended to call the effect irreverently.

The two ASV Echoes decelerated so rapidly that the eye was deceived into believing they had come to a halt almost at the moment of touchdown. There was a sudden muting of the bellow as thrust-reverse was cancelled. Buckets unclamped themselves and the two aircraft began to taxi off the runway towards their respective shelters.

The news of the fight had spread around November base like wildfire and quite a few people had come out to watch the approach and landing.

There were three main schools of thought on the base regarding female fighter pilots; and one other. There were many who backed Caroline unreservedly. Many because there were as many women as men in this camp. The second, mainly men, were neutral; it mattered little to them one way or the other. As long as they are good enough, was the attitude of this group. The third, predominantly men but with a good sprinkling of women, were totally against it; but as November personnel they kept such thoughts to themselves and were even prepared to give Caroline her due. Everyone considered

her an excellent pilot and many of those who watched the approach
and landing considered it very smartly and stylishly done.

Then there was the fourth. Only one person inhabited that camp.
Jack Brodie. As far as he was concerned, women fighter pilots were
poison. They poisoned the system. Short cuts, he was certain, were
taken to get them into the cockpit.

"Only so it will look good," he said to himself. "To be goddamned
politically correct. Then under-qualified female jocks can try to kill
backseaters like me. Well, they can buy the farm if they want, but
they can leave me the hell out of it."

They wanted to be treated like everyone else, he mused, until
they screwed up. Then they didn't want to be treated like everyone
else. They wanted special treatment. If you said they had to take the
heat for fouling up, suddenly everyone was on your case. You were
victimising them because they were women.

With these bitter thoughts, the memory of the missed trap on the
carrier and the subsequent ejection running through his mind, Brodie
watched as the Tornadoes taxied along the perimeter. Like everyone
else, he'd heard about Caroline's kill. She had actually taken on the
tough senior deputy commander and had won at least once, doing
so in spectacular style.

"Big deal," he muttered. "She'd never have done it by herself.
There was a man there in the back seat to hold her goddamned
hand."

It never occurred to him to think that, while McCann may have
indeed suggested the idea, only a skilled and confident pilot could
have deliberately employed the potentially lethal manoeuvre, swiftly
regained control and then been quick enough to surprise someone of
Helm's calibre in order to secure the kill. She was the captain of
the aircraft; she could have refused McCann's suggestion if she'd
wanted to.

There were plenty of people like Brodie who would continue to
pursue a particular course of action even while knowing it to be
wrong, losing all sight of the inherent truth of the matter without
realising it. They were the grief-bringers. Brodie's tragedy was that
he was genuinely unaware of this condition within himself.

"There was style in that approach," a familiar voice said.

He'd been standing on his own outside the headquarters of the
operational conversion unit where all the newly posted-in aircrew
got their first introduction to the November style of flying.

He glanced to his right and came to attention. "Major Gireaud,
sir!"

"At ease, Ensign. You've been with us long enough now to know we are more relaxed here. She flies well, does she not, Mr Brodie?" the former Mirage pilot continued. "And after what has happened on the ACMI range, it appears she has all the qualities we require here at November. Dangerous at close-in fighting. That is very good."

"She was lucky, sir."

"Of course she was lucky, Ensign. In our business, it is not enough just to be very good at what we do. Sometimes it can be better to have the luck. You had the luck, Mr Brodie, when your Tomcat went over the side. You were able to eject. I have seen a man go off a carrier, but he did not have your luck. There was no time for him to eject.

"We watched him release his harness as the aircraft began to go under. Ah, we thought as we moved away from him, he will raise the canopy and swim out. Unfortunately, the canopy had jammed. We saw him banging on that canopy as he went under the water.

"Unless you have seen it for yourself, you can have no idea how terrible it is to watch someone go like that. In our job things can sometimes go wrong. It goes, as you would say, with the territory. But it can never be easy to see a man you have been talking to only some minutes before go down in that way.

"The search and rescue helicopter was airborne almost as soon as his plane hit. But . . . it could not save him. Sometimes I still see him, his head moving from side to side, his hands banging desperately at that canopy. Luck, Mr Brodie? We all need it from time to time."

A silence fell between them after the French major's little speech, then Gireaud said, "You are an excellent backseater, Mr Brodie."

"Thank you, sir," Brodie responded with some surprise to the unexpected praise, not quite certain why Gireaud had chosen that precise moment to say so.

"And now," the major continued, "I am going over to Zero One squadron to congratulate Caroline for a mission well done. I had the pleasure of giving her a check flight when she first came here to the OCU. You are coming? I can give you a lift."

"Er . . . I'll catch her later."

Gireaud's look gave nothing away. "As you wish."

McCann and Caroline were walking away from the HAS in their flying kit, helmets in hand, *en route* to squadron debrief. Having come out of their shelter first, they did not see the similarly attired Helm and Flacht emerge from another, two structures away and some distance behind them.

"Captain McCann! Flight Lieutenant Hamilton-Jones!"

"Oh hell," McCann remarked softly to Caroline. "Our master's voice. Wonder what he's going to say about the approach." He came to a halt and turned round, the epitome of innocence, to await his nemesis.

Caroline had done likewise, looking warily expectant.

Helm bore purposefully down upon them with Flacht trailing slightly behind him. The best thing that could have been said about the expression on Flacht's face was that it was no expression; but his eyes were lively.

Helm did indeed look as if the plumed casque of a crusader knight belonged upon his head. It was not difficult to imagine the chain mail and the white surplice with the red cross upon it – belted at the middle to carry the scabbard for the heavy broadsword – clothing his solid frame.

The sharp planes of his face were accentuated by the powerful square jaw and the neatly cropped head of fine blond hair. The pale blue of his eyes had once been colourfully described by an unfortunate on the receiving end of a stare as boiled ice. When asked to explain, that individual had said he wanted to convey the impression of something that was simultaneously hot and cold.

Helm stopped before them, his posture challenging. Flacht prudently halted a few paces behind.

The senior deputy commander stared unnervingly at them for long moments.

"I suppose," he began at last to McCann, "that stunt was your smart idea?"

"Yeeees, sir . . ."

"I was captain of the aircraft, sir," Caroline said quickly. "The final responsibility was mine."

The hot and cold eyes surveyed her clinically. "Are you Mr McCann, Miss Hamilton-Jones?"

"No, sir, but . . ."

"Then please wait."

"But sir!"

"Flight Lieutenant Hamilton-Jones, you will *wait!*"

"Sir!"

"Well, Captain McCann?"

"I figured it was a good move, sir," Elmer Lee replied. "I knew she could handle the spin. Sure as hell worked though, didn't it, Commander?" McCann did not look away.

More agonising seconds followed. Then, abruptly, Helm broke into an unexpected grin.

"It worked," he agreed as they stared back at him, astonished and not a little relieved. "At first, I was furious . . . but really with myself. In combat, it is the unexpected that can give you the advantage you need. You played one, and you got the kill. I would not advise doing that too often, however. You get the one chance to misjudge the pre-spin height, and it is no chance at all."

He turned to Caroline.

"And now, Flight Lieutenant, your turn. Well done. That was an excellent display of fighting. You were determined and never gave up, even when it was apparent you would not get me again. It can mean the difference between becoming the opponent's breakfast and survival. Survival is a win over the enemy.

"However, a little advice. If in a real situation you find yourself against an opponent where both of you are defensive, watch your fuel. Running out of fuel first is a *win* for the enemy. He can either take his time to gun you down or, if you're over his territory, simply leave you there to fall out of the sky for his buddies on the ground to pick up. That is assuming you have the time to eject.

"Either way, it is bad news for you." He gripped Caroline's shoulder briefly. "But you did good work out there. The wing commander is impressed. He was waiting in the HAS when we returned. Now let us go off to debriefing. He will be there to give you his compliments."

"Thank you, sir," she said, looking very pleased.

"This means you buy the drinks in the mess."

She grinned. "A pleasure, sir!"

"And Mr McCann."

"Yes, sir, Commander?"

"Do not give this young woman too many of your bad habits. Please."

It sounded like a plea from the heart.

"I'll do my best, sir."

"Somehow, I am not sure this should make me happy."

As they resumed their journey McCann joined Flacht, leaving Caroline to walk on ahead with Helm.

Nothing was said about the approach.

Flacht gave McCann a surreptitious thumbs up. "I didn't really think you were in trouble out there," he admitted quietly, keeping a wary eye on Helm and slowing his pace slightly to allow the commander and Caroline to open up the distance. "That SPILS trick is one of Axel's too."

"Yeah. I know. Heard him talking about it once to some guy from the Dutch Air Force. Never seen him use it though. You?"

"We've practised it. But we have not yet used it on anyone. Have you tried it with Mark?"

"Nope. Today was the first time ever."

Flacht stared at him. "Do you mean . . . Elmer Lee! What if it hadn't worked for Caroline?"

McCann was unrepentant. "It did though, didn't it?"

"You could both have been killed if she had made a mistake. You should have warned her."

"Nope. That would have made her nervous, which would have scared the shits out of me. As it was, because she felt I was not worried, she reacted instinctively. Hell of pilot."

Flacht shook his head slowly. "Aahh, Elmer Lee . . . Try to remember we do not all have your nine lives."

"You didn't tell Helm though, did you?" McCann countered. "That it could have been a trick?"

"How could I? I might have been mistaken and he would not have been pleased." Flacht grinned suddenly. "Anyway, in a real fight, the adversary would not have known for sure. And we do try to make things as real as possible."

"Wolfie," McCann began approvingly, "you can be devious, even when you may not quite agree with what I might do."

"I have got company in this, I think. The deviousness, I mean."

"Oh yeah," Elmer Lee said happily.

The four of them had put away their gear and were now in their flying overalls in the squadron briefing room. During the debrief the entire fight was replayed at one of the squadron terminals, which had itself received the download from the Ops Centre.

Jason stood to one side, watching as Helm went step by step through each manoeuvre with Caroline, pointing out stages where she could have improved her positioning in order to make a successful acquisition possible.

Because Helm had fought so hard, any chances that had become available to Caroline had been very few and far between. The fact that, in spite of his efforts, he had eventually succeeded in managing a bare two chances – with only one of those a real kill – said much about her own performance.

"To be quite honest with you," he now told her, "seeing these replays in full detail like this confirms the tough fight you gave me. Again, this is good work you have done today, Caroline."

"Thank you, sir."

"Neat approach too," Helm added with a thin smile.

"And I concur," Jason put in, going up to them. "The approach and the work out there. Now gentlemen, if you are all finished here, I would like a private word with the young lady."

Helm nodded at Flacht and McCann, and all three left the room.

Jason pointed at the screen as the others went out. "Very little to improve upon. You've come a long way, Caroline. *We* have come a long way and I'm very proud of you indeed. I have never regretted recommending you for flying duties. Not only have you achieved the high standard required in the service generally, you have also made it here to November and can justly rank yourself among the very best. Officially, you are now a member of Zero One squadron. But that does not mean you can rest on your laurels."

She had been sitting before the terminal. She now stood up, looking both relieved and pleased as she turned to face him. She had long hoped for the posting to Zero One.

"Thank you, boss," she said quietly. "And I promise I'll never rest on my laurels."

"I'm sure you won't."

"Your backing has meant a great deal to me," Caroline went on, ". . . especially during the times when I did ask myself whether I really wanted this." She looked at the fine pattern of almost invisible scars on his face. "After the crash—"

"That was not a crash, it was a well-executed emergency landing. And I know you began to doubt yourself then. But there was no need. As I've just said, you're here. Sufficient proof, if you needed any, of your own capabilities."

Jason paused. He'd been leaning against the briefing desk, out-stretched legs crossed loosely by the ankles. He reached down, almost absently, to briefly rub one of his shins. Despite having made a startlingly rapid recovery to flying status, he still touched the legs from time to time, as if to remind himself they were whole again.

Noting the action, Caroline was instantly solicitous. "Are the legs all right, sir?"

"In perfect condition," he assured her. "I've got into the habit of doing that. I must stop it."

"It's understandable, boss. And in a way it makes you more . . . accessible."

"I'm not certain I want to be too accessible, as you've charmingly put it; but I'll take your word for it. Now, young lady, as you're officially on the squadron strength, you'll be needing a permanent backseater."

She gave a rueful smile. "I shall. I can't keep poaching people forever."

"And I can't assign McCann to you, despite the fact that you worked so well today. It would mean splitting one of my top teams and Mark Selby would never forgive me. However, we do have to find you a navigator of the right calibre, and as soon as possible."

"Anyone in mind, sir?"

"I do, as a matter of fact. He's one of the most promising of the new intakes we've had for some time; streets ahead of the other candidates and, according to his instructors, operationally ready."

Caroline gave Jason a probing look. "Why do I get the feeling there's a 'but' lurking in there somewhere, sir?"

"Check him out," Jason told her smoothly. "I shall go strictly by your recommendations."

"You're giving me final sanction?"

"I am."

She continued to look at him as if expecting more. "I see."

"I'll not force any of my crews into a team that cannot totally depend on each other," Jason continued. "Bad for the team, bad for me and bad for the November project. As the pilot of the aircraft, you *should* have the final say."

"I still think there's a 'but' in there waiting to ambush me, sir."

"Keep an open mind," the wing commander said neutrally. "If this pairing does work, I shall have another top team."

"And if it doesn't?"

"I'll make certain you get a backseater who deserves a seat with you. If necessary, I'll even give you Carlo."

"Major Carlizzi? Sir, he's one of the senior instructors and he already moonlights with Chuck Morton."

"Morton's breaking in his newly assigned nav, so Carlizzi's free to go into a new seat. Would you work with him?"

"Easily, boss. Carlo's a diamond of a nav. So what's the name of the backseater I've got to break in?"

"Brodie," Jason said.

Seven

"*Brodie?*" a shocked McCann exclaimed when Caroline later told him in the squadron crew room, after Jason had gone. Flacht and Helm had also left. "Is the boss *nuts*?" He was at the coffee bar, getting some from the filter machine.

"Speaking from experience?"

She was reclining on one of the sofas, part of the standard issue furnishings of the room, idly glancing through a pile of aviation magazines. Like the chairs that were scattered about the place, it was upholstered in pale blue.

"Don't joke about this, Caroline. *Brodie? The* Ensign Brodie?"

"Repeat the name again. The rest of the world didn't quite hear." They were alone in the crew room.

"Caroline, Caroline, this is serious business. Coffee? Or tea?"

"You make terrible tea. But you're American so it can't be helped. Coffee, please. What's wrong with Brodie?"

"And you Brits make lousy coffee," McCann retorted, pouring out two cups. "What's right with him?"

"People used to say that about you," she pointed out.

"Still do, but I'm cute. Milk? Sugar?"

"A modest man too. No milk. No sugar."

"How can you drink that stuff."

He moved out from behind the counter bringing the mugs with him. Each bore a stylised version of the four-pointed NATO star on its circle. The top and bottom points were elongated and, at the top of the circle on either side of the point, were the figures 0 and 1. On one side of the mug in golden script, was the legend: *Kansas City Dude.*

"Must get you a mug with your own special name," he said as he put the mugs down on a low table. He pulled up a chair and sat down opposite. "How about Iron Maiden?"

"Sounds painful."

"OK," McCann conceded. "But Maiden is good. You just need something cool to go with it."

Caroline had stopped sifting through the magazines. "You'll think of something. Thanks," she went on as she picked up her mug then added accusingly, "and you've got milk *and* sugar in yours."

"Sugar is energy. The milk's half-fat. C'mon, Caroline. That guy is bad news."

"Back to Brodie, are we?" She drank some of the coffee and made a sound of approval. "Good coffee."

"The machine knows what it's doing."

"Why is Brodie bad news?"

"Um . . . he kept going on about your . . . ass."

"Which he said was nice, according to you."

"Well yes, but—"

"I can't refuse to fly with him because he likes my bum. And besides, it's the boss's orders."

"I guess," McCann said unhappily. "Just you watch yourself up there."

"Elmer Lee," Caroline said with a fondness reserved for people she really liked, "I can look after myself. He'll be in the back seat, trussed up like a chicken. Even if he were the world's smoothest lounge lizard, there's not much he can do to me from there."

"Don't count on it," McCann said gloomily, wanting to tell her more but refraining from doing so. The boss must have his reasons for assigning Brodie as nav to Caroline, he decided. "They'd better be good ones," he added to himself.

"What did you say?" Caroline demanded, looking at him curiously.

"Talking to myself."

She leaned across to tap at his forehead with her knuckles. "Ding ding! Wake up in there, Elmer Lee. When did you say Karen was coming over?"

"I didn't. Would you believe my luck? She's just had to take over a duty slot from someone's who's gone sick."

"Poor Elmer Lee. Never mind. You'll see her in the mess tonight. She'll be there for the drinks party. She said she would come if I did well today. And I did, thanks to you."

"Yeah," McCann said.

But his mind was on Brodie. He didn't know what the boss was playing at, but a man like Brodie was like a leopard.

The spots didn't change.

The entire complement of Zero One aircrew – with the exception of those who were on standby duty and Selby, Hohendorf and Bagni who were still away – turned up at the mess to celebrate Caroline's official inclusion into squadron membership. Jason and his two deputies, and Caroline's former instructors, as invited guests, were there too. She had been congratulated by just about everyone.

She now looked at the throng and said to McCann, "I didn't think the squadron had so many people."

"We don't. We seem to have gotten ourselves some unofficial guests."

"They must have heard I'm buying," she said drily. "I dread to think of the size of my mess bill."

"Don't worry. We're all going to share."

"Who's 'we'?"

"The top boys, of course."

"Thanks, Elmer Lee, but you don't have to."

"Of course we do. You're our special new squadron buddy, *and* one of the November originals; you were here when this whole thing began."

"Is Brodie here? I thought he might be among the 'unofficials'. If he's going to be my backseater, this would be as good a time as any to properly introduce ourselves."

McCann shot her an unenthusiastic glance. "He's not here. You didn't invite him, did you?"

She shook her head. "No. I thought it best not to until the roster was officially done."

"Wise move. Ah, here's Karen. Now we can have the toast."

"A toast?" Caroline said warily. "What toast?"

"We've got to give you a toast."

"Oh no . . ."

"Oh yeah."

The slim elfin shape of Karen Lomax, also a flight lieutenant, made her way through the crowd to them. The auburn hair which she tended to wear in a single braid when on duty was coiled and secured at the back of her head in the way he knew so well. The unruly wisps that seemed to escape to curl softly at the base of her neck were there as usual.

They reminded McCann of the first time he'd set eyes upon her. After a somewhat embarrassing remark – inadvertently broadcast over the airwaves during a take-off – he'd been ordered to apologise to her upon landing from the training mission.

"Byee Mummee!" he'd said in his unsual exuberant way, only to be sternly admonished by her for his unauthorised departure from the normal procedures.

"God, I love it when she talks dirty," he'd said to Selby, switching to cockpit frequency just too late to save himself.

Not only had she heard but so had the wing commander, inbound from a training exercise with a newly arrived pilot as wingman. The senior air traffic controller's furious protest had served to underscore Jason's own decision to order McCann to make the necessary apologies. He'd been given the further punishment of being assigned the job of air duty officer in the control tower for a week. Aircrew looked upon that particular duty with all the enthusiasm of a visit to the dentist.

He had gone to the tower to make his apology and the first person he'd seen had been Karen Lomax, then a flying officer and the controller to whom he'd made his unwitting broadcast. Except that he'd been unaware of her identity at the time. All he'd seen had been the back of her head, the graceful neck and the wisps of hair.

Then she had turned, blushing when she realised who he was. He'd looked into what had seemed to him the shyest eyes on earth. The blushes and the eyes smote the Kansas City dude on the spot; never mind the fact that she was already being wooed by one of the hardest men around, Geordie Pearce, an engineer officer and rugby player of fearsome brutality.

But McCann would not have been McCann if he had not gone in where highly astute angels would have chosen to make a wide detour. Pearce was now out of the running but the engineer officer had not taken defeat lightly. Only service discipline continued to prevent him from turning McCann into hamburger meat.

Elmer Lee beamed his welcome at Karen. "Here's your glass," he said to her, handing her a champagne flute. "*A toast!*" he shouted, raising his own glass. "*A toast!*"

Conversations petered out as people turned to look, then they too began to raise their glasses.

"To our newest and most excellent fighter jock," he announced. "Ladies and gentlemen, oil your engines in honour of Flight Lieutenant Caroline Hamilton-Jones!"

"*To Caroline!*" they chorused, and proceeded to empty their glasses which they then promptly held out for replenishment.

"Speech!" someone else yelled.

"Speech, speech!" went the cry as this was taken up.

"Gonna have to, Caroline," McCann told her, grinning.

"I'll get you for this," she whispered fiercely. "You know how."

He glanced at Karen Lomax then back to Caroline. "You wouldn't."

"I'll think about it."

"Wouldn't what?" Karen asked.

"Ah," McCann said. "Ah . . ."

"Just a little lesson I've got to teach him," Caroline said sweetly.

"Speech, speech, speech!" the voices continued to demand.

"You'll have to do it," Karen advised her.

"She's going to do it!" McCann shouted.

"Yayyy!" came the reponse. Then everyone fell silent.

"I hate speeches," she began, "so I'll make this as short as I can. I wish Mark Selby, Axel Hohendorf and Nico Bagni were here tonight, but they can buy *me* the drinks when they get back!"

Laughter greeted this.

"Becoming a fighter pilot," she went on, "is a dream that has meant a great deal to me. I was here when November was being built, as some of you know, as a fighter controller; but what I really wanted was to be a pilot. The boss knew that and supported me, even though women fighter pilots were not exactly a welcome idea in the service and, as we all know, deep down, are still not.

"I was even crazy enough to want to return as a November pilot. I never really expected to get here but I knew I had to try. The boss continued to back me all the way so it's thanks to him that I've made it, and of course to Elmer Lee for helping me get at least one kill on the Knight Templar today. It was a good feeling, Commander," she said to Helm, who raised his glass to her with a twitch of a smile. "It still is. And thank you all for welcoming me so warmly."

"*Yayyy!*" they all shouted when she'd finished. Then went on, "*Boss, boss, boss, boss . . . !*"

"All right you shower!" Jason said loudly. He raised a hand to silence them. "Like Caroline, I'll keep it short. Anyway, judging by your shiny faces, you'll stop listening within a few seconds."

There were loud chuckles.

"Therefore," he continued, "I'll just say to Caroline that she has handsomely exceeded all my own ambitious expectations and that Zero One will benefit enormously from her presence. Here's to Caroline."

"*To Caroline!*" came the shout.

"Now don't say we don't love you," McCann said to her.

"I'd never say that," she said.

"You look happy."

"I am." Then she looked down into her glass.

McCann stared at her, then at Karen Lomax.

What? he mouthed silently.

Karen looked closely at Caroline. "I know what it is. Leave her with me."

She took Caroline out of the bar and into the ante-room. Jason and the other two senior officers came up to McCann.

"Trouble?" Jason asked.

"Don't know, boss," he replied. "I asked if she was happy. She said yes, then went kind of quiet all of a sudden."

Jason stared thoughtfully for some moments in the direction that the two women had gone. "I think I know," he remarked softly.

"I don't understand, sir."

"Neil Ferris," Jason said.

"Ahh," McCann said, a world of sympathy in his voice. "Tough on her, sir."

It was also clear that both Helm and da Vinci understood precisely what had so suddenly altered Caroline's mood.

Caroline had been in love with Neil Ferris, a backseater who had been in the WSO's seat of an F-111 of the Royal Australian Air Force and one of the founding crews of the November project. He'd been backseater to a young pilot, Richard Palmer, when, engaged in hard-turning air combat manoeuvres over the mountains, Palmer had suffered G-induced loss of consciousness.

Ferris had been quick in diagnosing G-loc and had activated the command eject system but the seats had fired both crew members into a mountainside, killing them instantly. Part of Caroline's determination to be a pilot had been fuelled by the tragedy. It had been her way of saluting Ferris. Now that she had finally made it onto November's premier squadron, Ferris's old unit, the memories had come flooding back and had overwhelmed her emotionally.

"She's remembering Neil," Jason was saying. "Leave her be. She'll be fine with Karen."

"Yes, sir."

"Well, Captain. Thank you for inviting us. We senior men have our responsibilities and will leave the stage to you youngsters."

"You're not old, sir," McCann said with his usual recklessness. It had popped out, seemingly of its own volition.

"Thank you, Mr McCann, but you're trying hard to change that, aren't you?"

McCann frowned. "Sir?"

"I'd stop digging, if I were you, Captain," Jason said, straightfaced, as he looked about him. "I sincerely hope no one here is flying tomorrow," he went on. "On second thoughts, I think Zero One should stand down for the day. Patrol duties can be covered by Zero Two. Let's leave the field, gentlemen."

"Night, boss. Commander, Colonel."

"Goodnight, Mr McCann. Good show here tonight. Give Caroline my regards. Tell her if she needs to see me she's welcome to do so at any time."

"Yes, sir. I will."

"Thank you, Captain."

Helm favoured McCann with an expressionless stare, then both deputy commanders nodded at him, and followed Jason out.

Cottingham entered the ante-room. The place was empty, save for Caroline and Karen Lomax, sitting together in black leather armchairs. Caroline was sitting with her head back, eyes closed.

He went up to them. "How's she doing?" he asked quietly.

Karen looked up at him. "She's fine." She glanced at Caroline, who had not opened her eyes. "Look . . . would you mind sitting with her for a moment? I'm just popping out to have a word with Elmer Lee."

"I don't mind at all. It will be a pleasure."

"All right. I shan't be long."

"Take your time."

She smiled at him and stood up. "Thanks."

"No problem."

Cottingham sat down as she left.

Then Caroline sat up, opened her eyes and looked at him. The eyes seemed moist. "I'm really OK."

"Sure. Hey, we all know you're tough. You proved it today by reaming the Knight Templar. Nothing wrong with some company though, is there?"

She smiled a little sadly. "Nothing at all."

"He must have been a great guy," Cottingham said.

"He was."

A silence fell between them.

"Do you—"

"What's your—"

They had spoken together. They stopped, smiling awkwardly.

"You first," he said.

"I was only about to say," she began after a slight hesitation, "that I actually don't know your first name. I know I've been away from here for a while but everyone seems to call you Cottingham, and even the name on your wings patch just says Cottingham. You do have another name, don't you? Or do I have to bribe someone to look in your files?"

"If you knew my name, you'd know why."

"It can't be that bad. I have a middle name I've been hiding for years. I'll tell you, if you tell me yours."

"A bribe."

"Of course."

He sighed. "You really want me to tell you this?"

"As McCann would say, yup."

"Oh, what the hell. OK. It's Augustus. There. I told you it was terrible. My mother had a Caesar complex. Probably thought the name would make me tough and powerful."

"She chose well. You are tough, and you fly one of the most powerful fighters around."

"I don't think she was thinking of fighter planes that day. The only fighters she was thinking of were those in the fancy school my parents sent me to. There weren't many black boys in that school."

"I still think Augustus Cottingham sounds imposing."

"And I still think it's hell to carry around."

"There must be a nickname your family called you."

"My mother always, *always* called me Augustus. Maybe that's why I don't use it; I hated it so much. I love my ma but I can't take that name. She even used to call me her little Caesar. Can you believe it." Cottingham laughed. "And I don't even look like the guy in the film."

That brought a chuckle from her. "What about your father?"

"What about him?"

"What did he call you?"

"Gus. He always did. Drove my mother crazy. He made his money the hard way. My mother's parents already had it when he married her. I think there were times when she thought he could be a bit too rough at the edges for her taste."

"So why don't you use Gus? Gus Cottingham would look good on the patch."

"Never thought of it. Perhaps because I didn't want anyone calling me Gus except my father."

"You admire him," she said perceptively.

"Yeah. He's a great guy."

"I'll call you Gus," she said. "Would you mind?"

He looked at her for some moments, eyes widening as if he'd just been surprised by something that had previously escaped his attention.

"No," he said.

"Oh, good."

"But it doesn't go on the patch."

"Fair enough."

"Now tell me yours. That was the deal."

She grinned at him. "I don't know you well enough."

"Unfair!"

"Of course."

"This means I'll have to get to know you better."

"Looks like it."

"And it's only so I can get to hear that name."

"Of course."

McCann and Karen Lomax were approaching the ante-room when they heard laughter from within.

"What's going on?" he said, hurrying forward.

They poked their heads round the door to see Cottingham and Caroline laughing.

"What's going on?" he repeated in a whisper to Karen.

She hauled him back. "Leave them."

"But . . ."

She sighed. "Honestly, Elmer Lee. Sometimes . . . Does she look gloomy to you?"

"No."

"Why were we coming here?"

"To cheer her up."

"I'll repeat the first question."

"All right. I get the message. So you think there's something going on there?"

"Do you want to ask them?"

"Nope."

"I thought not. Let's go back to the bar. There's still some champagne left."

The Special Research Unit, east of the Urals. One week later, 1500 hours local.

Many people had crammed into the observation area of the range to watch the contest. Urikov had wasted no time in letting everyone know that the upstart women were heading for a comprehensive defeat, and a humiliation of such magnitude for even daring to make the challenge that Captain Lirionova's stupidity would do her career no good at all. As expected, Sergeant Melev was in the team but surprisingly Urikov had decided not to enter.

"He's so sure he'll beat us," Lirionova said to Konstantinova, "he can't even be bothered to cheat by loading the odds in his favour by being in the team himself."

"Be thankful for small mercies!" Konstantinova said. "I'm nervous enough as it is. Without Urikov, we've at least got a chance to wipe the smiles off their faces. I still can't believe how good Olga is and I'm worried it could have been a one-off. They'll never let us forget if we lose this. I'm also the worst we've got. But there's you and Olga. I wish she'd hurry and get here, though."

Olga Vasilyeva was running late, making them both anxious.

"She'll be here," Lirionova said. "She was late last time, remember? Perhaps something in the lab delayed her."

"Are you saying that to comfort me? Or you?"

"Both."

They looked towards the spectators, most of whom were Urikov's off-duty soldiers. Daminov had been put on duty. Konstantinova was relieved by that. He'd said that he supported the women but, for all the understandable reasons, could not have done so openly. Melev would have made his life hell.

Sitting a little away from Urikov's men were the supporters of Lirionova's team, both military and civilian, officers and non-commissioned. Many of the research unit personnel appeared to take the contest seriously. They saw it as a diversion from the daily routine. Many were also daring to hope that Urikov would be beaten.

Urikov, in his capacity as one of the judges, came up to Lirionova. His mean eyes surveyed her rudely.

"Why don't you give up gracefully, Captain?" he began. "You know you only made this ridiculous challenge out of pride. I've included Sergeant Melev because I didn't want to make it too easy for you. But my two soldiers are the very worst shooters among my men." He grinned nastily. "Of course, I mean that relatively. Even as bad as they are, they are far better than the ordinary soldier." He glanced around theatrically. "And where's your other team member, the good doctor? Couldn't you do better? She should stick to playing with her plants. Guns are for grown-ups."

"She'll be here," Lirionova said coldly.

"Must be that leg of hers. It's holding her up." A strange sound came out of him. It was a giggle. "It's holding her up! A good joke, eh?"

Melev and the soldiers smirked.

The other judge was one of Abilev's medical staff, a captain called Simirenko. He glared at Urikov for making the joke about Olga Vasilyeva.

The mean eyes glared right back at him. "You don't like my sense of humour, Captain?"

"Keep personalities out of it," Simirenko snapped.

Urikov turned to Melev and the two soldiers and silently mimicked the medical captain's words. The enlisted men grinned.

"You're an officer, Captain Urikov. Behave like one."

It was not a smart thing to say.

Urikov turned the full baleful glare of his eyes upon the medical man. "You wouldn't be trying to tell me about my manners, would you?" he asked, voice soft with danger. "I'm not your kind of officer. I didn't get a degree with a commission tagged on to it; I'm a soldier, and I came up the soldier's way.

"I may not have the manners you like and I eat roughly like an ordinary soldier but I'll tell you this . . . I *am* an ordinary soldier, and if people carrying guns ever come knocking on this place you won't be worrying about my table manners. You'll be hoping I can fucking shoot straight and fast." He looked at the two women. "And if you don't like me using *that* word, that's your problem. Now where's that damn doctor? I want to get this over and done. I've got better things to do."

"Russian women have an honourable history," Lirionova said cuttingly, "both in the military and out of it. You should at least give us some respect."

"Listen, *Captain*, don't give me any bullshit about history. This is not the Revolution or the Great Patriotic War. This is a changed world and in it are three kinds of people: patriots, conscripts and well-paid professionals. When you get well-paid professionals who are also patriots then you've got an army worth talking about."

Urikov brought his face close to hers, forcing her to take a step backwards. Her expression was one of distaste.

"I hate the fucking West," Urikov went on, "but I'll say one thing for them . . . they worked that one out long ago. And they pay their people. We are paid better than the average soldier but not nearly enough for you to give me lectures about history. Now go and find that damned doctor and let's start this thing."

Over in the spectators' gallery, Urikov's soldiers watched his treatment of Lirionova with glee. They couldn't hear what was being said but they knew their captain well enough to read his body posture and imagine the conversation. The captain was psyching-out his opponents. The fact that he was also a judge and should be neutral cut little ice with them.

"The damned doctor is here," Olga Vasilyeva's voice said from behind Urikov.

He turned, inspecting her as if she were a bug about to be squashed, and said, "Leg held you up, did it?"

She did not rise to the bait. "I've got things to do. Let's get on with it."

Urikov's certainty wavered fleetingly. His expression of open contempt changed to one of cold watchfulness. It was the watchfulness of a wild beast accustomed to being the predator, being forced to reassess the strengths of a potential victim.

"As the challenge is mine," an immensely relieved Lirionova now said to Urikov, "I can choose who shoots first."

"Be my guest." Urikov's certainty of winning was back.

"Each of your men goes first."

He stared at her, attempting to gauge her motives. "It won't do you any good."

"Not afraid, are you?"

He drew himself up to his full height, which was impressive. "You'll regret that remark." He turned to his sergeant. "Melev, you and the men shoot first."

"Yes, Captain." Melev glanced slyly at Lirionova.

"And you'd better win," Urikov growled. There was an implicit threat in the words.

"Of course we'll win, Captain." Melev turned to the troopers. "You're first, Kirillov. Vladimirov goes next; then it's me. Pistol, machine pistol, rifle. I want no misses." He looked at Lirionova. "Kirillov is the worst shot I've ever seen; but he'll beat you . . . Captain." The pause was just long enough to convey the thinly-hidden contempt without making it too blatant for the other officers present to ignore.

"Get ready, Kirillov," Urikov snapped. "Pistol."

Kirillov, the supposedly terrible shot, took up position.

"In your own time," the troopers' captain said.

Kirillov fired. For a bad shot he was remarkably accurate.

Melev gave a sneering smile, deliberately not looking at the women. But it was obvious it had been meant for them.

"Machine pistol."

Kirillov fired the weapon like a man who'd been born with it in his hands.

"Rifle," said Urikov.

Again, Kirillov's shooting was good enough to worry anyone less than a first class shot.

"Stand down!" Melev ordered. He turned to his captain, awaiting the next command.

Urikov looked at Lirionova. "Your turn, I believe."

"Sergeant Konstantinova," she said, "please take up your position."

Milla did so.

"Pistol," the second judge, Simirenko, said. "In your own time."

Konstantinova fired. It was a passable performance but it came nowhere near beating Kirillov.

The soldiers were beginning to smile openly.

"Machine pistol," Simirenko called.

Again, Konstantinova though good, was still roundly beaten.

"Rifle."

It was the same story. Konstantinova looked at Lirionova apologetically.

"It's all right, Milla," Lirionova said.

"You can still leave with some dignity," Urikov said to her, pretending cold detachment but really enjoying making her pay.

"This isn't finished yet," she retorted.

"Suit yourself. Sergeant!"

"Captain?"

"The next man."

"Sir! All right, Vladimirov," Melev went on to the next soldier. "Take position."

"Pistol!" Urikov snapped.

If anything, Vladimirov was better. He beat Kirillov with all three weapons.

Then it was Lirionova's turn. She wiped the smiles off the faces of her tormentors. With all three weapons, she beat Vladimirov's score.

Urikov could not believe it. He glared at the unfortunate soldier, but his most bilious stare was reserved for Melev.

"You'd better not fail me, Sergeant."

Melev did not flinch. "I never fail you, Captain."

Urikov nodded curtly. "Pistol!"

Melev's shooting was astounding. He trounced the scores of all who had gone before. There was an atmosphere in the place that suggested it was all over. The idea that the doctor with the artificial leg could do any better was hilarious. Even those who supported the women – not knowing of the doctor's prowess – seemed to be already admitting the brave attempt had failed.

"Do you still want to go on with this?" Urikov was saying to Olga Vasilyeva. He even managed to sound less brutal.

"I came here to shoot," she said firmly. "I shall shoot."

"Your choice," he said bitingly, looking at her as he would someone who had completely lost all common sense. He glanced at his fellow judge then stood to one side.

Simirenko looked as if he wished she would not go on. "Pistol," he said.

Even the way he spoke suggested he had already accepted defeat for the women and was only going through the motions.

But things were about to change dramatically.

The first indication of what was to come began to filter into the consciousness of those watching, as a result of the way she took up her position. Urikov, a combat veteran of specialist missions, recognised the manner of her stance despite the handicap of the artificial leg. As if time had begun to stretch, he watched as each individual shell casing flew away from the pistol as each precise shot was fired. The speed of her shooting was such that it was all over by the time his mind had switched back to normal.

He stared at her open-mouthed. There was no denying the astonishing score. There was a neat hole in the target, and the computers indicated that all rounds had gone through it.

Simirenko was grinning in happy disbelief. "Machine pistol!" he shouted.

Olga picked up the KLIN and surpassed the demonstration she had previously given to Lirionova and Milla, doing so with even more controlled speed.

Urikov didn't want to believe the evidence of his own eyes. Melev was beginning to look sick. The contemptuous soldiers in the gallery had fallen into a stupor brought on by the turn of events.

"Rifle!" said the grinning Simirenko.

Olga picked up the AK and proceeded to destroy all Urikov's preconceptions. When she had finished, Urikov looked devastated.

"Who the hell are you?" he demanded hoarsely.

"Just a doctor," she said. "Let this be a lesson, Captain. Never underestimate your opponent. As a combat veteran, I would have thought you already knew that."

He turned his back on her and stomped off, leaving Melev and the two soldiers to pick up the pieces of his battered pride.

"A bad loser," she said to her happy female companions. She looked at Melev. "Are you a bad loser too, Sergeant?"

"I am not pleased," Melev admitted frankly. "I don't know who taught you to shoot like that but it is the best I have seen anywhere."

"Why thank you, Sergeant."

"It doesn't mean that I like you three any better for what you have done here today. But I will not pretend you are not good. That was combat shooting of a special kind, Doctor. My captain feels he has been made to look a fool before his men; that he was set up. That is not a good thing." Melev turned to the soldiers. "Let us leave this place."

In the gallery, Urikov's soldiers trooped off, each feeling personally humiliated. The fact that they had been so recently looking forward to the humiliation of the women had been wiped from their minds.

Eight

The Siberian winter continued its reluctance to give in to the coming of spring, and proved it with a fresh fall of snow. It was five days after the crushing defeat of Urikov's shooting team and Lirionova had received a summons to Moscow, from Kurinin. Placing Konstantinova in charge of the section, she left the very next morning, boarding a helicopter to the nearest airbase where a flight was laid on to get her to Moscow.

She arrived at midday and was ushered straight in to Kurinin.

"Ah, Captain Lirionova!" He greeted her warmly, rising from his desk and coming forward to meet her.

She saluted.

He waved a hand in response, then gave her a brief hug. "Please. Take off your hat and sit down." He indicated the gleaming leather of the chair that had been drawn up for her before the desk.

When she had done so he went back to the desk and leaned against it facing her, polished boots stretched out before him.

"Have you had anything to eat?"

"Breakfast and a drink of tea on the plane, General."

"Then you'll be ready for lunch. I am having it brought to my private duty quarters. We will eat there and continue the discussion. But first I want to thank you for the report you sent me on your little shooting contest. You will be surprised at what we have turned up."

"I don't understand, General."

Kurinin smiled. "My dear, in our line of work, sometimes the most innocuous of things can lead to bigger, much more interesting ones. Your contest with that warrior oaf Urikov has opened a line of inquiry we would never have discovered. You have a knack for discovering things, Liri. I well remember the work you did for me when one of our closest people tried to make a bid for power on his own.

"You saved two of our cities from nuclear devastation. The man was prepared to incinerate his own people to get what he wanted.

106

What he could have brought us instead was a full-scale nuclear war. Through your excellent work with our computers you also discovered the existence of an organisation that appears to be supra-national and certainly manipulative.

"We still don't know how long it has been in existence nor are we any clearer about its real motives, since it hides itself very well. However, I have decided to take certain steps, one of which is to elminate someone whom I believe to be one of their key operatives. That is the main reason you are here today."

Kurinin reached behind him to pick up a file that was purple in colour. He opened it and thumbed through the pages. He looked up from the file.

"You reported an interesting comment made by Sergeant Melev after he had witnessed Doctor Vasilyeva's quite remarkable talent with weapons. Combat shooting of a special kind, you report him as having said."

"Yes, sir. Those were his words."

"And accurate. It was indeed a special kind of combat shooting." Kurinin turned back to the file and flipped through a few more pages. "Kevin James Hendersen," he read aloud. "Captain, US Special Forces." He closed the file with a snap and put it down. "One of their youngest captains," he continued to Lirionova. "Probably the youngest in modern times. Barely out of his teens. A man of very special skills for one so young. His capabilities make me wish he'd been one of ours," Kurinin went on drily. "The war in Vietnam certainly did traumatise him. Afterwards he became a scientist. Plants."

Lirionova was staring at him. "Doctor Vasilyeva's American?"

"The very same."

"But the name in the original file—"

"Is Peter Henry Truitt. Whoever's name it is, it certainly wasn't his. As Kevin James Hendersen however, the identity of the doctor's weapons instructor begins to make sense. It is reasonable to conclude he was the man who taught her to shoot the way she has recently demonstrated."

"With respect, General, you're not suggesting that she—"

"I'm suggesting nothing, but I am keeping my options wide open."

"But sir, her entire history is in our files. And she is giving our country an incredible breakthrough. We've always suspected she had an affair with him . . ."

"The details of which she recently gave you."

"Yes, General. But she did so quite openly, even telling us – as I said in the report – how they used to evade the bodyguards."

"Indeed. But sometimes it isn't what is said that is important but what is left unsaid. We have been trying to know more about her selfless American ever since she returned, but of course we were looking for someone called Truitt.

"I'll concede he must have truly fallen in love with her, for him to have done what he did; but that does not take away the fact that a highly skilled US member of the Special Forces was closely involved with one of our most brilliant scientists, who just happens to be working in a highly secret line of research.

"Further, it turns out that this person is also working in plant biology. I was already uneasy about her involvement with this American but, as Truitt, he was more of an irritation. In the old days he would never have managed to get so close to her, assuming she would have been allowed out of the country in the first place. It wasn't until you informed me of the results of the shooting contest that we began looking elsewhere."

"But she never told him anything about her work," Lirionova said. "It seems he did most of the talking about his."

"If he was innocent of subterfuge, it would fit with the identity of a tree-hugging scientist who talked to impress the woman with whom he had fallen in love. But this theory is blown apart when you begin to learn about the man's history. He told her just enough of the truth to make his story believeable. Yes, he was a soldier. Yes, he was deeply affected by his experiences in combat and yes, he apparently did choose to devote his energies to the ecological sciences. An ordinary soldier wanting to atone. And it worked . . . until he began to fall in love.

"When that happened, he began to worry more about her than about the mission he'd been assigned. His first and only mistake was to teach her how to defend herself. When they dangerously began to go off on their own – presumably to consummate their affair – he felt that if they ran into trouble she had to know how to defend herself. It had become too personal. I suspect he dreaded what could happen to her if he were either killed or severely wounded. This was not a man who believed that an overtly neutral foreigner was safe in any of those war zones. He wasn't about to take chances with her life or her personal safety. Rape has always been present in war.

"Because of this love he felt for her he did the one thing that he should not have. He gave her an unusual expertise. And it would have remained undiscovered but for the boastful Urikov and your refusal to be intimidated." Kurinin smiled at her. "You are a radar yourself. Whatever drove you to stand up to Urikov's quite stupid challenge has worked spectacularly for us. Without that challenge, we would never have discovered just how well our doctor can shoot. Her distaste for the brutal captain – and her liking for you and Sergeant Konstantinova – made her respond when you asked her to join your team. Thugs like Urikov always have their uses sometimes in unexpected ways."

"I never imagined how far this would go," Lirionova said in an apologetic tone.

"Don't apologise. The outcome is very helpful to us."

"Even so, General. I expected some reasonable shooting from her; but I still thought I was the best in our team."

"Which leads me to something else you reported she said and I quote: 'Never underestimate your opponent.' Then she made a point of the fact that, as a combat veteran, Urikov should have known that. Her words? Her opinion? Or something she picked up from Hendersen?"

"Doctor Vasilyeva's a highly intelligent woman. It's the kind of comment I would expect from her."

"Possibly. Unfortunately, we cannot ignore Hendersen's presence in all this. I grant you she may well have said the same thing had she never met Hendersen; but she would never have been able to shoot Urikov's team into oblivion had she not met her American. We cannot escape that fact.

"I believe the man we must now call Hendersen – before he began to fall in love – talked the way he did to disarm her natural reticence to discuss her own work. But a man as smart as that would have listened to what she was saying in return, even if no mention was ever made of the work she was engaged upon. Little remarks which to the uninitiated would have no real meaning out of context would send recognition signals to someone who knew what he was looking for."

"But in what way, sir?"

"Let us make an assumption," Kurinin said. "For example, here are words I've selected at random, used by Doctor Vasilyeva when she was explaining some things to me, and remember she was not talking to a fellow scientist: luciferase, mutagenesis, catalytic enzyme. I am not saying she used any of these in conversation with Hendersen yet I find it difficult to accept that even during the most routine of discussions none of these – or similar words – came up during their many talks. It would be like having a discussion about music composition without ever mentioning keys, or note values, or tempo instructions, or time signatures; even if you were composing a piece you wanted no one to know about. It would be a conversation devoid of meaning."

"So you believe he may have picked up key words over a long period and put them into a recognisable pattern like a puzzle?"

"I think he did better than that. I think he already knew what he was looking for, well before he met her. I think our self-sacrificing romantic hero of a captain or very possibly a colonel – if, as I suspect, he was still in service – trailed round the world until he found his assigned objective. He asked her to accompany him to Borneo, didn't he? South-East Asia can be particularly romantic, if you're going to the right destination in the company of someone you love. And after Borneo . . ." Kurinin paused deliberately.

Lirionova knew what he was driving at. "She would not have gone."

"We'll never know. The mine saw to that. But I do wonder what would have transpired, had she gone. Would he have persuaded her to go to America with him? And there, my dear Major, is the cunundrum. Just how much did Mr Hendersen know? And, more to the point, did he have time to convey this knowledge to his masters, whoever they may be?"

"Sir, you said major . . ."

"So I did." Kurinin looked at her with a rare warm smile. "You no doubt think I've made a mistake." He reached once more behind him, picked up a sheet of paper and handed it to her. "As of today, you have been advanced to major and your Sergeant Konstantinova is now a lieutenant."

As she read the promulgation, a light flush appeared on her cheeks. "I'm . . . I . . . Thank you, General." She returned the promotion order. "Urikov will be livid," she continued with the ghost of a smile. "One can only guess what he'll make of it."

"If you have any problems with him," Kurinin said in a hard voice, "let me know. He has only himself to blame if he feels his macho pride has been dented. Further, I certainly do not want to discover that the commander of the security troops at such a highly sensitive unit is beginning to show signs of instability. I can soon find him a less comfortable posting like UN liaison in the Congo, with that neanderthal sergeant of his for company. The two of them can have a nice African holiday."

"I'll bear that in mind," she said, enjoying the vision of Urikov and Melev out there in that particular cauldron of human insanity.

"This will go via the usual channels to Colonel Abilev," Kurinin went on as he placed the promulgation order back on the desk. "You've both earned your promotions; but with them come new responsibilities."

She nodded. "I understand."

"They are not the ones you may be thinking," he said. "I'm sending you for advanced specialist training, Major, after which you will be given a very special mission. Are you prepared to do that?"

"Yes, sir."

"You don't know what I am proposing."

"I will do as the General orders."

"Excellent, Liri," Kurinin said. "I'm pleased to see that I did make the right choice."

"And when do I start, General?"

"Not immediately, but you will not have long to wait. When we're finished here in Moscow, return to the research unit and wait till you hear from me. You are to discuss this with no one, not even with Konstantinova. She'll be taking over from you when you do leave."

"Her own command at last."

"As you suggested when we last spoke. However, she is only to know – at the appropriate time – that you're being posted out. In the meantime keep an unobtrusive eye on the doctor."

"Yes, sir. May I know what the mission is to be?"

Kurinin studied her silently. Several seconds passed. "You will be trained to hunt down and eliminate a particular operative; the one I mentioned earlier. You will be given further details prior to, during, and at the end of your training. You will go anywhere in the world, as necessary, in order to carry out this task. Do you still wish to do it?"

"Yes, sir."

Kurinin regarded her with great satisfaction and nodded approvingly. "Now, time for our lunch. We have plenty to discuss."

The Pentagon, the same day. 1300 local.

The high-resolution photograph of the phase-array radar that Major-General Bowmaker had looked at had been followed a day later by a card that appeared among the papers on his desk. Like so many of the mysterious notes, cards, photos and messages that came his way, there was no clue to how it had got there. The card had carried a single message: WAIT.

So he'd waited to see what would come next.

Now he was looking at another card which had fallen out of a file that had come to him from the Joint Chiefs. The contents of the file had nothing to do with the single word on the card: NOVEMBER.

He turned the plain white card over. There was nothing on the back; no indication, as usual, of where it had come from. Somewhere during the transit from the Joint Chiefs to his own office the card had found its way into the file.

He put the card down. "Hell, I was due for a trip to Europe, anyway."

"*Sir! You can't!*" he heard sharply from the outer office as his door began to open.

The outer office belonged to his deputy, a female officer who was also an army lieutenant-colonel.

"Don't mean to be rude, Colonel," came a familiar voice through the opening door. "But I really must see the general."

Having recognised the voice of the as yet unseen speaker, the astonished Bowmaker was already on his feet and heading for the door as it came fully open.

His apologetic and furious deputy was making a last-ditch effort to deter the forceful visitor.

"I'm sorry, sir," she apologised to Bowmaker as the Royal Air Force air commodore strode in. "This officer—"

"It's OK, Colonel. And this officer is equivalent to a one-star general."

"I realise that, sir, but—"

"Thank you, Colonel. I'll take it from here."

"Sir," she said, still furious. She glared at the newcomer before going out and shutting the door behind her.

Bowmaker stood poised, as if waiting for her to bang it shut in her fury.

"Sometimes, I wonder who's in charge here," he remarked calmly. "She has the balls and a smart way of chewing me out but somehow manages not to sound insubordinate while she's doing it. Best second-in-command I ever had." He stopped and stared at the man who had barged so unceremoniously into his office. "Is there a corner of this dangerous globe that you can't get to?"

"Not that I know of," came the easy answer.

Charles Buntline, Bowmaker vividly remembered Air Vice-Marshal Thurson saying to him once, was a well-bred thug. A member of a branch of British Intelligence that no one ever seemed to identify, the elegant Buntline was usually attired in a Savile Row suit. Bowmaker had seen him just the once in a field outfit. The change had been remarkable but Buntline, with smeared face and loaded with weaponry, had seemed just at ease. And infinitely dangerous.

His RAF uniform was as perfectly fitted as his many suits. A man who apparently had his own private funds, he was well able to indulge in his passion for stratospherically-priced clothing.

"Have you earned that uniform, Mr Buntline?" Bowmaker asked. "And those medal ribbons?"

Buntline removed his gold-braided cap, dropped it on Bowmaker's desk and smiled. "The uniform . . . alas, no; though my grade is of the equivalent rank. The medals are my own but not, of course, from the RAF; and I simply couldn't bring myself to augment the subterfuge by pinning a pair of RAF wings above them."

"Any of those for combat?"

"One or two ordinary gongs," Buntline replied with uncharacteristic modesty, omitting to mention that the Military Cross was among them. "And the odd royal favour."

"It's OK not to talk about it," Bowmaker remarked drily. "I'm almost afraid to ask," he went on, "but what brings you here?" He showed Buntline to a chair and, in a mirror image of Kurinin, leaned against his desk.

"I take it you've received our missives?" Buntline queried mildly.

"I did wonder whether they might have come from you."

"Not from me specifically. Possibly some of your own chaps."

Bowmaker gave him a world-weary look. "I'm an old warhorse, Mr Buntline—"

"Charles, please."

"I'm an old warhorse," Bowmaker repeated firmly, "and, believe it or not, I like what the wing commander and his boys are doing—"

"We know you do."

"And they will always have my support. Don't . . . jump in again. Please let me finish. As I said, I happen to agree with the wing commander's ideas, and I'll do all I can to keep that unit going. But there are times when I feel I'm being goddamned manipulated by *you* people, whoever you are."

Buntline looked back at the general silently and for so long that Bowmaker wondered whether the Englishman had listened to what had just been said.

"I have not always been the greatest fan of Wing Commander Jason's pet project," Buntline said at last, as if returning from a distance, "but I will admit that from their record so far the November boys have proved themselves to be quite proficient at carrying out their sometimes quite difficult missions. The wing commander is on to a good thing and yes, the existence of the unit has helped expand our own capabilities. We are after the same things, General. We complement each other. Our . . . let us call it support . . . ensures that continued funding for the November Programme is . . . ah . . . continued."

"So you need them again."

Buntline pulled his lips back to display gleamingly healthy teeth. "Perhaps I should give you some background."

"I'm all ears."

Buntline's lips twitched. "Very droll, General. Before we begin, you wouldn't have any tea by any chance?"

"I've got coffee," Bowmaker said.

Buntline sighed. "Of course. How silly of me. I'd be grateful for a cup of your excellent coffee."

"I'd like one myself. I'll go get them."

Buntline raised an eyebrow.

"You expect me to ask the colonel to arrange it?" Bowmaker said, knowing what the raised eyebrow meant. "She'd shoot me first. She brings me coffee when she's getting one for herself. I never ask."

"If you say so, old boy."

"I do say so," Bowmaker told him and went out.

In the outer office, Bowmaker said conspiratorially as he passed through, "Getting some coffee."

"I could have arranged that, sir," the lieutenant-colonel said with a slight frown. "The sergeant—"

"I can do it," he told her with a private smile. "Got my reasons."

"Yes, sir," she said, looking at him as if he'd just gone mad.

"And don't frown."

"I wasn't—"

"Sure you were."

Bowmaker came back through her office with the two cups of coffee, on saucers. She gave him a look of pained disapproval as she stood up to open the door to his own office.

"Don't say it," he said. Her displeasure was such, he knew, she would have brought paper cups.

She merely looked at him, shutting the door quietly as he went in.

"Ah," Buntline said as Bowmaker handed him one of the cups. "Thank you."

"Milk but no sugar. Hope you don't mind. Cutting down, you know."

"Of course."

"But I'll send for some if you're . . ."

"No. I'm quite all right. Thank you."

"Sorry we don't have those fancy cookies your government minister serves up when I'm in London."

"I'll survive." Buntline chose to ignore the hint of needle in Bowmaker's voice. "She does get the coffees for you, doesn't she, General? Your charming colonel."

"Are you kidding me? A male general officer asking a senior female staff officer who just happens to be a lieutenant-colonel to fetch him *coffee*? In the current climate, I'd be lynched."

Buntline tasted his coffee and smiled. "Good stuff. Thank you once again. As for your colonel . . . my opinion is that a lady of such balls – as you've so neatly put it before – is smart and confident enough within herself not to be bothered about something as minute as getting her favourite general a cup of coffee. I don't think she believes that she would suddenly be robbed of all dignity because of it. This is a woman who is not intimidated by an RAF air commodore – or anyone else, I'd hazard from my recent experience – and who would defend you to the death. As I've said, I just saw some of it."

"And you've come to that conclusion after that one encounter? Are you a psychologist in your spare time?"

"I have to be many things in my line of work," Buntline replied enigmatically.

Bowmaker was again leaning against his desk. "Well, you didn't come all the way up here in a fake RAF uniform—"

"Not fake, I assure you."

". . . in a non-fake RAF uniform, to talk about coffee and my colonel."

"Quite right. Absolutely not. I've come to talk about an operation we've been running for some time now . . ."

"I wonder why I'm not surprised. Just how many of these operations are your people running at any one time?"

"How many are initiated from the Pentagon," Buntline countered, "at any given time?"

"Who's counting?"

"Indeed." Buntline drank some more of his coffee.

"You were saying?"

"We've been running the operation, as I've said, for some

considerable time. It is many-faceted, requires precise handling and, most importantly, timing."

"Is Mac involved in this?"

"I'm afraid," Buntline began carefully seeming to choose his words with deliberation, "I cannot at this stage confirm—"

". . . or deny. All right. Fine. I get the message. God knows I've used those very words often enough to get out of a tight spot."

"I do realise you've got a . . . shall we say fatherly regard for her."

"Damn it, she's one of our Pentagon people!"

"I wouldn't put it quite like that. Mac is very much a free spirit."

"I know that," Bowmaker admitted. "She once told me I couldn't give her orders. Must be something about women who are lieutenant-colonels."

"I can tell you," Buntline said, relenting slightly, "that she was last heard of in Argentina. However, no longer there now, I suspect."

"Argentina? You Brits are not warming up for round two, are you?"

"Not that I know of. Though I've no doubt Jason's lads would rather enjoy some aerial fisticuffs out there, should the need subsequently arise. One would like to hope not. But one can never tell with politicians . . . of any nationality. Some of them tend to indulge in the most blatant and quite unbelieveable idiocy in desperate attempts to curry favour with their electorates. They'll do just about anything in order to hang on to the bitter end, or to get into power.

"Bosnia to Africa to the Middle East to Asia . . . examples almost too numerous to list. All too frequently, however, other people tend to pay the price for their stupidity; usually with fatal consequences."

"No political affiliations then."

"My dear General Abe, I'm what you might call a political agnostic. I exercise my vote, but not according to any party. My duty is to clean up the mess these people frequently make with as little fuss as possible. Sometimes, I like to act before they get to the stage where they may leave a mess."

"Pro-active."

"Better than being forced by circumstances to react to a *fait accompli*. That is why the November idea has now got my support. It's a pro-active unit. Think of the grief those boys up in the Grampians have already saved the taxpaying public; not that they particularly care. The public, I mean. As long as they can get on with whatever life it is they're living, it matters little how the equilibrium is maintained."

"Cynical too."

"We all are, old boy. That includes you. Perhaps you prefer not to admit it. You know what's going on out there as well as I do; all the appalling horrors that are being committed every day all over our benighted little planet. I have seen my fellow man at his very worst. I have the right to be cynical." Buntline had spoken in the mildest of voices, as if discussing the merits of a particular wine to a friend in a private club. "Unfortunately, these problems never seem to cease and one which promises particularly horrendous consequences awaits us on the immediate horizon.

"The adversaries who brought us the anti-stealth, operational prototype radar in the African desert – which was so effectively taken out by Jason's November boys – have come up with a brilliant wheeze. If they succeed – and they are very close to doing so – you can chuck out all the defensive aids currently used by aircraft, ships, vehicles and personnel. The lot. They'll be obsolete. Dead as doornails."

"What?"

"Thought that would cause some excitement. You ran an Aurora mission recently. It was tracked all the way over target, with full imagery."

"Jesus! That's not possible."

"It is only too possible, I'm afraid. If we do not neutralise this new system completely – by which I mean render it totally inoperative – every Western defensive system may as well be scrapped."

Bowmaker stared at him. "What are you telling me?"

"They have found a way," Buntline said, eyes now upon those of the air force general, "to turn whole swathes of ground, wherever there are plants and trees, into sensitive zones. They've taken what nature already possesses and augmented it.

"An aircraft like the Tornado, using terrain to hide it from radar or infrared sensors, would be exposed like a naked moth to a flame if it overflew such a patch of ground. General, they have found a way to make the plants themselves into sensors. They have created organosensors if you like, nanocomputer implants into the cellular structure of the plant itself. The computers are themselves cyberorganic; they grow within the plant. When one thinks of it, it's so simple I'm amazed it has not been done before. The ultimate in eco-warfare. The possibilities are virtually limitless. They have even talked of cyberorganic fighter aircraft in which the pilot would be truly umbilically linked."

"My God!" Bowmaker exclaimed softly. "A plane that can *feel*? A plant that can *see*?"

"And hear, and detect heat signatures, and communicate this information by naturally produced light; which makes it EMP proof too. It was only a matter of time. After all, the November Tornadoes can already change colour in flight by making crystalline paint jump through hoops."

Bowmaker said nothing for several seconds. In his mind's eye, he could see fleets of aircraft with no way of hiding, being shot out of the sky like the sitting ducks they would become.

"My God," he repeated. "And the phase-array radar?"

"A clever decoy. They wanted you to run a hot stealth aircraft to give them the opportunity to photograph it, just so they could try out the new system."

"And it worked," Bowmaker muttered bitterly.

"It most certainly did."

"So that phase-array structure is a fake?"

"We're not totally certain but, to be sure, a special operation is being proposed. If their new idea proves to be unworkable they'll have to return to standard electronics, which are themselves vulnerable to attack. And low-flying aircraft will be able to once again use mother nature for concealment, instead of finding her exposing them to enemy fire. The idea is not to attack this new sensor system. That would only prove it works, and that we fear it."

"You can say that again!"

"In such a scenario they would merely work harder to create several of these sensor areas."

"In a hot scenario, defoliants would be one way—"

"Apart from the general poisoning of square mile upon square mile of land and all the future collateral problems such an attack would bring, these systems are in any case self-repairing. They neutralise the toxins and convert them into energy."

"They certainly went to town on this," Bowmaker said grimly.

"More specifically, one person more than any other did so: Doctor Olga Vasilyeva. The woman's an absolute genius. But the entire system can be killed with a clever virus, introduced in a manner that impells the system to kill itself rather than carry out repairs. In short, it will indulge in self-cannibalism; and while it's busy eating itself it ceases to function."

"I won't ask how you came by all this."

"I can give you the basics; but only—"

"As much as I need to know?"

Buntline nodded.

"Damn it, Buntline! I'm not some enlisted man!"

"No disrespect intended, General. I'm doing this for a very good reason. People are in places of great danger. They have jobs to do and must survive to do them. We lost one not so long ago."

"How?"

"Mine explosion. But he'd already done most of his job. Pity though. We wanted to bring the doctor out."

"What happened?"

"With the mine?"

"Yes."

"He fell in love. Gets you every time."

Nine

The Special Research Unit, east of the Urals.

L irionova was back from Moscow within two days, sporting her new shoulder boards.

Milla Konstantinova stared at them. "You're a major?" she said as she got to her feet.

Lirionova gave her the smile of someone with a secret to tell. She placed a small packet on Konstantinova's desk. "I picked these up for you."

"A surprise present. I love surprises when they're good ones."

"I guarantee you'll like these."

Milla opened the packet eagerly, then stared again when she saw what was inside.

"A lieutenant's boards!" She looked up at Lirionova. "I don't understand. We're getting a new lieutenant?"

"Stop being coy, Milla. You know who's the new lieutenant."

"Really mine?"

"Really yours. You're now an officer. Colonel Abilev has already received the authorisation, which I brought with me."

Konstantinova gave one of those smiles that completely transformed her features. "This will kill Urikov, coming so soon after what we did to him. You a major, me a lieutenant. Oh how he's going to hate that! And as for that pig Melev, he'll choke."

"Now they'll think we both sleep with the general," Lirionova commented drily.

"To hell with them. Lieutenant Konstantinova," Milla went on, savouring the rank. "Sounds good, doesn't it?"

"It sounds very good."

"I'll get my new uniforms from the supply section as soon as I can."

Lirionova turned to the other personnel present who were all staring in their direction. "As you can see, we've got ourselves a new lieutenant . . ."

There was general clapping.

"And a new major!" someone said. "A celebration tonight?"
They clapped some more.

"A celebration," she agreed. "But we now require a new sergeant."
Her eyes fell upon a wiry young man with bright intelligent eyes
whose name was Yakulentov. "Ivan Ivanovitch, I am authorised to
promote you to sergeant. What do you think about that?"

Yakulentov sprang to his feet, grinning. "I think it's . . . *great*,
Major! Especially as it means more pay!"

There was laughter, and a third round of clapping to salute the
new sergeant.

"And now," Lirionova said when the noise had subsided, "I must
talk with my new lieutenant in private. Back to work!" She snapped
but without any real bite.

"Yes, Major!" they intoned like a class of children at recitation.

"They're a good bunch," she said as they entered her office.

Milla followed, carrying her new shoulder boards. "The best. As
you said, a good team." She looked down at the badges of rank in
her hand. "This is going to take some getting used to."

"You'll be surprised how quickly you'll grow into them. But you
won't be able to fraternise so openly with your violinist."

"Daminov?"

"Yes. He sometimes goes to your quarters, doesn't he?"

"Nothing happened, and nothing will. Besides, there's his girlfriend in Moscow."

"Moscow's a long way from here."

"He loves her very much."

"But does she still love him?"

"We see all letters. As women, we'd be able to tell by the
tone if she had a lover and was cheating on him. A man –
let's say Yakulentov – checking the same letter wouldn't be able
to."

Lirionova smiled knowingly. "You're right. Men. They can never
see what's going on right under their noses. So Daminov and his
Galina are true lovebirds. Which just goes to show that it works for
some people. Anyway, you'll have to move into the spare officer's
quarters and as the new sergeant Yakulentov gets yours. You know,
Milla, you deserve the promotion; and I'm really glad we're both
officers now."

Konstantinova looked pleased. "So am I. I can barely wait to see
Urikov's and Melev's faces, though."

"We'll see them soon enough."

"Now we both know nothing comes free," Konstantinova told

Lirionova seriously, "so what's really behind all this?" She leaned against an office wall and waited.

Lirionova paused for thought. "Well . . ." she began, "here's something to think about: the general wants us to keep a closer eye on Olga."

Milla raised her eyebrows in surprise. "On Olga? Are we thinking of the same person? One-legged Doctor Olga?"

Lirionova nodded.

"For God's sake!" Milla exclaimed. "Whatever for?"

The jollity went out of Lirionova's eyes. "We are allowed to call on God again in these times, but there are reasons, Milla. One of them is the fact that she can shoot so well."

"Good thing too. Otherwise that ape Urikov and his unsavoury bunch would have humiliated us. Now you tell me we must suspect her of . . . of . . . what, exactly?"

Lirionova sighed. "Look, I don't like this any more than you do but those are the general's orders and we, as his troops . . ."

". . . must obey them," Konstantinova finished. "I do know the drill. All right, so how do we carry out our little bit of treachery?"

"Milla, don't make this so difficult. You have greater responsibilities now you're an officer. We both knew that occasions like this would arise when we went into the Intelligence Service, so don't cry in my ear. It seems there are questions about the man she met in Angola."

Konstantinova snapped back into being an Intelligence officer first and everything else second. "The American?" she enquired softly.

Lirionova nodded. "Yes. I don't know all the details," she said, neatly blending truth with untruth. "We'll just have to keep a closer eye on her and wait for the general's instructions. It's important that we do not change our attitude towards her. In fact, her shooting skills have given us a genuine reason to be even friendlier. We can visit her more often . . . take a closer interest in her work. Things like that. She'll be only too glad to show us around personally. That way, we can do our job without looking like snoopers."

Konstantinova nodded slowly. "Then we can start right away. She'll be pleased to hear about our promotions."

"That's the thing about this job," Lirionova said in a world-weary tone of voice, "we can be friendly with people . . . but not really their friends at all."

Konstantinova looked at her. "Life, as the Americans like to say, is a bitch."

November base, the Moray coast. 1200 hours the same day.

The base gloried in another unseasonably warm day with visibility limited only by eyesight in all directions. High above, straggly wisps of cloud like randomly discarded cotton wool smeared themselves across the otherwise vivid blue of the sky.

A tearing thunder filled the air as two ASV Echoes, recently taken-off, shot perpendicularly heavenwards, their blue-tinged basic colour, even without Chameleon engaged, still merging astonishingly well into the background of their arena. Only the quadruple fire of their burners, blazing from expanded nozzles, marked their positions. Then the fires went out as the burners were cut and the aircraft disappeared, though their sound remained until that too faded.

In the Senior Nav Instructors' section at the OCU headquarters, Major Carlizzi had just received Ensign Brodie into his office.

"Ensign Brodie reporting as ordered, sir!" Brodie announced, saluting smartly.

"At ease, Mr Brodie," Carlizzi said, continuing as Brodie relaxed, "How would you like a flight in the ASV Echo?"

Brodie looked very pleased. "I *would*, sir!"

"I sort of had the idea that would be your answer. I've been going through the Echo's systems procedures with you in the simulator and you've done very well, as usual. It is my opinion, and that of the other instructors, that you are ready for a cross-country in the aircraft."

"I'll do good, sir."

"I expect you to. As a backseater, you are good."

"Sir, thank you, sir. May I ask the major where?"

"You and your pilot will be going across to Eggebek in northern Germany. This is a *Marineflieger* base. It belongs to the service Commander Helm and Messrs Hohendorf and Flacht come from. You've not yet met Mr Hohendorf, have you?"

"No, sir."

"Now there's a pilot's pilot. Mr Flacht is his backseater. For my money and everyone else's on this base, Mr Selby and Mr Hohendorf are *the* top pilots; and that includes both the boss himself and Commander Helm. Behind them come the other stars of Zero One squadron. Anyone getting a back seat with the top Zero One pilots is on the fast track. You hearing what I'm saying?"

"Five-by-five right there, sir."

"Mmm. I take it this means you would still like to be assigned to Zero One."

123

"You bet, sir!"

"Mmm," Carlizzi grunted once more. "You will not be landing at Eggebek but will simulate an approach, overfly the runway, then head back home. When we're done here go to the planning room, find the appropriate charts, set up your nav waypoint pattern and get it all ready to load into the aircraft's systems. Check your fuel load. The ASV Echo is very fuel efficient; far better than the birds you've been crewing during conversion training.

"There will be no air-to-air refuelling for this mission so I want no screw-ups. The *Marineflieger* boys will expect perfect timing on the waypoint when you arrive over the threshold. Having some of their buddies with us, they expect the best from November crews. Don't let the side down."

"I won't, sir!" Brodie vowed.

"What I like to hear. Briefing at Zero One is fourteen thirty hours. Take-off, fifteen thirty hours. OK, Mr Brodie. Dismissed."

"Sir!" Brodie saluted and turned to go, then paused. "Sir."

"Mr Brodie?"

"Who's my pilot?"

"Oh. Didn't I say? Flight Lieutenant Hamilton-Jones."

Brodie's mouth fell open. Then he swallowed. "S-sir?"

Carlizzi's eyes were unforgiving. "You got a problem there, Mr Brodie?"

"Er . . . er . . . no, sir."

"You are dismissed, Ensign."

"Yes, sir."

Carlizzi watched him expressionlessly as he went out.

As soon as he had finished with Brodie, Carlizzi went to see Jason.

"He's been told, to judge by your expression," the wing commander said the moment Carlizzi entered his office.

"Yes, sir," Carlizzi said.

"How did he take it?"

"My word would be shock. May I say something, sir?"

"Of course you may, Carlo."

"Should we risk Caroline with this man? He does not seem able to get past this wall in his mind about women in the front seat. He's a very good backseater. On that score alone, he's good material for Zero One squadron. On ability alone, he is fit to backseat for Caroline. The trouble is, he's Brodie; and his attitude makes a whole lot of difference."

Jason leaned back in his chair. An index finger made three slow taps on the desk; then he leaned forward, palms slapping softly as he levered himself to his feet. He moved over to his favourite window on the left side of the desk and looked out upon the airfield.

From where he stood he could see a stretch of the distant runway and a curving section of the perimeter track. Two OCU Tornadoes were taxiing along it. The sound of their engines – muted by the double-glazed panes of the window – was a relatively soft high-pitched whistle as they moved under taxi thrust. He found himself instinctively making assessments of the pilots, judging their performances by the way the aircraft travelled along the peritrack. There was no weaving from side to side, no bobbing of the nose, to betray either nervous overuse of the pedals for nosewheel steering or anxious stabbing at the toe brakes. The students were displaying good control.

He turned away from the window to face Carlizzi, feet slightly apart, hands behind his back.

Jason was a remarkable man in that the first impression of him was that he was not remarkable at all; a mistake that many had made to their eventual cost. The tenacity with which he continued to fight for the survival of the November project, despite the best efforts of opponents both within and outside the country, was proof enough of his staying power.

A man of medium build with regular clean-shaven features, his dark eyes were of such power that one could be forgiven for believing them capable of rooting to the spot anyone unfortunate enough to incur their displeasure. He was known to variously describe the area where his sandy hair receded slightly at the crown as his worry spot or bone dome polish. On occasion, when removing his cap, he tended to give his forehead a single wipe with the back of the hand that held it. It was a habit that all his crews knew well, and usually preceded the anouncement of a tough mission.

"We've got ourselves the nucleus of something very special on this station," he began to Carlizzi. "Despite the activities of those who would dearly love to shut us down, we have prevailed. Our people have carried out highly sensitive missions with virtually no publicity and certainly prevented a few nascent flashpoints from turning into full-blown international disasters.

"In other instances, we have nipped in the bud incidents that were not even given the chance to become flashpoints. That we have been able to do so with astonishingly few casualties has been due to the high calibre of the people we've got here. And I include everyone in this; aircrew and non-aircrew. The work of instructors like yourself has been invaluable. We have proved, Carlo, how working together as a truly unified command can bring spectacular results. Because our budget is truly international it can fund the very best of equipment, and the individual nations can accomplish things they would never have been able to afford by themselves. We are pointing a way forward and our responsibilities are enormous.

"To maintain our standards we can only accept people of a very high calibre. We cannot do otherwise. There are too many people waiting for us to blot our copybooks so that they can leap in and demand our closure. A badly executed mission, a high-profile crash and, like a switch being thrown, the clamour would be heard: dangerous flying, international adventurism. You know the sort of nonsense I mean."

"Only too well, sir. People do not seem able to understand why they can sleep in their beds, while in some parts of the world others never can."

Jason nodded. "Precisely. Which therefore gives me a problem with Ensign Brodie. From the assessments given by yourself and the other instructors, Brodie has all the qualities we require in a highly capable backseater. He has that rare talent, and I am loath to destroy such promise."

Jason paused and turned back to the window. The OCU Tornadoes were at the far threshold and about to take off. The characteristic roar began to swell as the pilots moved their throttles forward; then the roar sharpened into a tearing rasp as the afterburners were lit. The windows could not keep out that sound, for it travelled through the ground, and Jason could feel the familiar tremor through the soles of his shoes.

The aircraft began to accelerate, holding perfectly in station as they rushed along the runway; then they had gone out of view. He remained where he was, following them in his mind's eye, his ears attuned to every cadence and knowing at exactly which moment the pilots carried out each individual action.

He knew when the nosewheels came unstuck, when the main wheels left the ground and the aircraft were fully airborne when the gear was retracted, when the flaps began to retract, when the wings began to sweep as the speed built, when the sticks were pulled back and the aircraft went into a steep climb. He listened, and saw it all happening.

"Whose slot?" he asked Carlizzi, turning round again as the sound faded.

The major glanced at his watch. "That would be Major Gireaud with *Luitnant* Vanderkamp from the Dutch Air Force in the front seat, and Commander Helm giving a checkride to our first female backseater – coming to us from the RAF – Flying Officer Penelope Wilkinson."

"Ah, yes. Young Penny Wilkinson. Arrived two days ago. I liked the look of her when she reported to me. A friend of mine commands her old OCU and thought I should try her out before she's grabbed by an RAF squadron. He gave her a high recommendation."

"If she survives that first session with Commander Helm," Carlizzi observed "she'll at least make it to the next stage."

Jason gave one of his fleeting smiles. "She'll deserve to. I thought there were two students in the front seats. Old Dieter would be miffed to think I mistook his style for that of a student. Mark you, I couldn't see the entire take-off."

"He won't hear about it from me," Carlizzi said with a quick grin.

"And I'll hold you to that," Jason said in the same spirit. "Tell me," he went on, "how has Brodie reacted to another woman joining the aircrew? He's now got the presence of both a frontseater and a potential backseater to contend with."

Carlizzi's expression said it all. "Frankly, sir?"

"As always. You know how it works here."

"If Brodie had been a pilot, he'd be just as hard-nosed about flying with a women; except he'd be making jokes about backseat drivers."

"We do all the time at the expense of the male navs."

"Yes, sir, but just as he does with Caroline, it would be nasty stuff. The guy is good, but . . ."

"Are you worried about Caroline being with him up there?"

"Aren't you, sir?" Carlizzi countered. "You know what I think about the risk."

"I do know. But do you feel strongly enough about it to put your objections down in writing?"

Carlizzi hesitated. "In all honesty," he said after a short pause, "I cannot fail the guy without first seeing how he performs in that seat when *she* is the pilot. Yet my gut tells me he's only got to screw up once and we could be saying goodbye to Caroline, as well as to Brodie himself. You mentioned high-profile crashes. Hell, sir. The papers would go to town on this one."

"And don't I know it," Jason admitted wryly. "But you do see my problem. I trust Caroline. I have followed every stage of her career so far as a pilot. I was already impressed with her before she went into the aircrew branch. That was why I recommended her. She also knew that, to make it here, I would allow her no special considerations. Our candidates are expected to succeed on their own merit. No more, no less. She would consider it insulting if I had made exceptions for her. It would be a *de facto* admission that she was not quite up to it. What would that do to our fine principle of treating her equally?"

Jason paused to glance out of the window as a silent Tornado with canopy open and cockpit empty was towed past.

"Like many men, Carlo, I *am* worried about women in the cockpit. I worry about whether in our drive to prove we give equal opportunities to them, we are not making them dangerously exposed. In short, getting them killed or allowing them to kill themselves, to satisfy a trend. Is there any man on this station who knows how he would react if he heard a trapped woman screaming, perhaps severely wounded with the flames eating at her, as she tumbled to earth in a burning aircraft?

"Or how he would feel if he saw an enemy aircraft raking hers with cannon shells, or watching her go up in a burst of flame as a missile hit? God knows it's terrible enough watching it happen to another man. Then there's the nightmare of capture. Everyone, male or female, thinks that women are sexual targets for enemy troops. And they are. That's the reality. We are conditioned to feel protective about our women, whether we like to admit it or not. Men are tortured and abused during capture but somehow it feels worse when it happens to a woman. But I'll say this to you, Carlo: I hope that I never get so inured to this, or so fashionable, that I lose the part of my humanity that wants to protect women from suffering or death.

"We walk down the street and see two men fighting. Our first instincts are to leave them to it, unless we believe the fight to be patently one-sided. Even then, the likelihood is that many people would look the other way. But if the fight's between a man and a woman our reaction is totally different, even if the woman may be giving a good account of herself.

"These unthinking reactions control us and the conditioning works very well indeed, for example, in the favour of female agents. Those male agents who do come up against them must suppress that conditioning and treat them like any other adversary. Our male crews must be able to think like that, or the first time any of our own women get into trouble in combat, their protective instincts could seriously degrade their responses, which could in turn risk converting a recoverable situation into a disaster.

"So yes. I do have doubts, despite the fact that I rate Caroline's abilities very highly indeed, and that I am responsible for helping her into that pilot's seat in the first place. Have I done the right thing? But, more importantly, do I have the right to deprive an excellent pilot of her chosen career? Or rob this unit of her talents? Women fighter pilots are not a new idea. The Russians had many female combat pilots during the last war, although that was because of the desperate times and not a response to peacetime lobbying."

Jason paused again while Carlizzi watched him, discovering yet another facet of the man who, by sheer force of will, had brought the November idea into being.

"The choices are not easy," the wing commander went on. "We adapt to the new situation or we revert to banning women from combat aircraft altogether. In truth, as far as November is concerned, we have one choice and one yardstick. The crews on this unit must work together as a team or the whole business comes a cropper. I must therefore put both Caroline and Brodie through the hoop. I cannot afford to have anyone here who is not capable of giving of his or her best. Caroline is strong enough to cope. It really is up to Brodie."

"And if something goes badly wrong, sir? You talk of giving the women a fair shake but we both know if Caroline goes in and it goes public, the kind of people who would have crucified you if you had turned her down for being a woman will crucify you if she's hurt or killed."

"The joys of command, Carlo," Jason remarked with the air of someone who knew that score very well indeed, "and the fickle tendencies of our fellow man. As for Brodie, he is not the kind of person who can fake being good just to get through one flight. If his antipathy towards women aircrew is as strong as you believe, then he won't be able to help himself. But if he genuinely wants to be with us, he must make the effort to treat female crews fairly.

"It's either that, or he's out. There are no short cuts. Today, as McCann is fond of saying, is crunch time. I have also asked the US Navy to provide me with any relevant documents about the carrier incident that they are prepared to release to me. It will help me come to my final decision, whatever happens up there today."

"Are the documents already here, sir?"

"They're on their way. My information suggests that they will have arrived by the time Brodie and Caroline return from their cross-country. I'll be calling a meeting of the deputy commanders and the senior pilot and nav instructors, which means Gireaud and your good self." Jason went back to the window and looked out. "And then, Carlo, we'll know. One way, or the other."

Caroline was thoughtful as she monitored her displays. The ASV(E), on autopilot, turned onto the heading of the next waypoint right on time. Her check of the readouts confirmed the precision with which the manoeuvre had been executed. They were flying at 35,000 feet.

When she had met up with Brodie she had approached him in her usually open and friendly way, chating about the forthcoming flight as they prepared. His reponse had been unsettling. He had not been rude but there had been a perceptible chill in his manner; no feedback whatsoever. It had been like talking to a slab of stone.

He had gone through the sytems checks with consummate skill and speed but there had been a sense of machine-like efficiency about it. There was none of the rapport she had expected, even from someone who was flying with her for the first time. Brodie had made no attempt at ice-breaking, and his presence felt like the cold weight of permanent censure sitting behind her in the nav's cockpit.

Not having been told of Brodie's history, she was at a loss to understand it.

She scanned the air about her, keeping a watchful eye on her surroundings. Although the day's *Notices to Airmen* had detailed all known and predicted activity within the area in which they would be flying, NOTAMs were not omniscient.

It was, as always, the responsibility of the crew to ensure the safety of their aircraft, irrespective of prevailing conditions. An aircraft that was not supposed to be there could suddenly fill your windscreen – if you were not keeping a good look-out – and could introduce you to a fast and most likely terminal descent to terra firma or, in their case, the smack of a hard sea.

It had happened to at least one pilot she'd known; a soaring glider had met his jet at 20,000 feet. Both aircraft had been lost and the glider pilot had been killed. The jet pilot had ejected but had suffered substantial injuries.

"Keep an eye out, Jack," she now said easily, continuing to scan the empty sky. "Believe it or not it can get very crowded around here."

"I know my job," he told her sharply.

The nature of the response was such that it silenced her for several moments.

Shit, she thought. *What have I got up here with me?*

"I was only saying—"

"Look!" Brodie interrupted. "I know my job! I don't have to be mothered. OK, *sir*?"

"Mothered? What are you on about? I made a perfectly—"

"You need to dial ten more knots on the autothrottle if we're going to make the next waypoint on time. We've picked up a slight headwind. Unless you want me to do it on my panel."

The control panel for the AFDS – Autopilot and Flight Director System – was repeated in the back cockpit. Under standard November operating procedures, a fully qualified backseater was allowed to operate the duplicate system only under emergency conditions where the pilot was unable to do so from the front cockpit; or at the specific request of the pilot, in any circumstance.

However, crews who had worked together for some time and had learned instinctive task-sharing possessed the kind of informal understanding that could only be established with an experienced pilot and nav. A top team would develop into an operationally seamless combat crew. Zero One's combinations of Selby and McCann, Hohendorf and Flacht, Bagni and Stockmann, and Cottingham and Christiansen, had long achieved that indefinable quality. There was certainly no such empathy between Caroline and Brodie, nor could there possibly have been on a first flight.

As she had not authorised operation of the AFDS from the back seat Brodie's presumption annoyed her.

She bit back a retort she felt coming. "I'll handle it," she said as calmly as she could muster.

"Fine," he said in a barely-controlled snap and immediately fell silent.

She reached for the control panel, outboard on the left-hand console and just behind the throttle quadrant. Using the 'increase' knob at the top of the panel, she turned it until 370 knots came up in the alphanumeric window to the right of the autothrottle engage button. The throttle grips immediately moved forward of their own volition to take the aircraft to the required velocity.

The cadence of the engines swelled perceptibly then settled as 370 knots came up on the HUD. She next called up the representative page on her left-hand multi-function display, and saw the digital status read-out of the AFDS displayed there in blue-green tabular form. Time to the next waypoint was displayed and in the 'early/late' box three sets of double zeroes – separated by two dots to indicate hours, minutes and seconds – showed that they were bang on time. If late, the numerals would become red and start counting to show by how much. As adrift time was made up, they would decrease until they zeroed to show the aircraft was again running to schedule. The zero pairs would then revert to their current blue colour. If early, the count would be green.

Two of the push buttons from the twenty-four that bordered the display were marked with a plus and minus. They could also be used to increase or decrease autothrottle-commanded speeds. Additionally, the other two similarly adorned MFDs could cycle some of their comprehensively numerous functions between displays.

Having checked the system to her satisfaction, she recalled the nav page with its display of the waypoint pattern. A small elongated pulsing white cross made its way along the waypoint track, marking out the aircraft's current position. If they deviated, the cross would begin to wander away from the pattern, with digital readouts giving a continuing position update.

The entire leg to the next waypoint was made in complete silence.

Oh great, she thought grimly. *I need this sod in the back like boils on my bum.*

It was not the route to good crew co-ordination.

Ten

M ost of the flight was over water.
The initial turning point – the waypoint that would take them on the final leg to the destination waypoint one hundred feet above Eggebek's main runway threshold – was over the North Friesian island of Sylt.

In the rear cockpit, Brodie had switched the tactical air navigation system to channel 111.

"TACAN to channel one-eleven," he advised. His voice was remote, as if disconnected from his surroundings.

"Roger," she acknowledged. "TACAN to one-one-one."

She had disengaged the AFDS on reaching the initial point and was again flying the aircraft.

She reached forward with her left hand for the standby horizontal situation indicator near the base of the left-hand MFD and dialled 111 in the small window at the top right of the instrument. To the right of the window was another, which gave in red numerals the remaining distance to Eggebek. They would be doing a ground-controlled approach to the Schleswig-Holstein *Marineflieger* base before powering up and heading back for home.

"Do you want to talk to Eggebek?" Brodie asked. "Or do I?"

Caroline suppressed her irritation. It had been unnecessary for him to ask, and the superciliousness in his voice had been palpable.

"You do it," she told him. "I'll just listen in."

"Yes, *sir*."

The tone of his voice annoyed her, which was clearly his intention but she remained controlled. "What's your problem, Brodie?"

Instead of giving an explanation he ignored her completely and began talking to Eggebek.

"Eggebek, this is Hunter One. Request GCA to threshold for fly-by."

"Roger, Hunter One," came the immediate response. "GCA to threshold and fly-by. Looking forward to your visit!" the controller added with some levity.

"Hunter One," Brodie acknowledged formally, just short of being rude.

"He was being friendly," Caroline protested.

"I do something wrong, *sir*?"

She wanted to scream her frustration into the mask. "Nothing wrong," she said in a calm voice.

"Well then."

You won't needle me, you bastard, she thought determinedly.

She recalled how during the flight over she had been checking about her and, as she had checked behind, his tilted head had been turned directly towards her. In addition to the tinted visor, he had also lowered its dark shaded companion so that the helmeted head and mask had taken on an overtly malevolent aspect. She could not see his eyes but had sensed that he'd been looking back at her with cold hostility, and was certain he had lowered the dark visor just as she had turned to check the tail.

She could not fault his work in the back but was certain she never wanted to fly with him again.

They made it to the threshold precisely on time, with the blue double-zeroes confirming it on arrival at the waypoint.

"That's a beautiful ship!" came the appreciative male voice from the control tower as GCA handed them over.

"Bet you say that to all the girls," Caroline said.

"A woman!" came the astonished exclamation.

"Last time I looked," she said lightly. "Must leave you."

She pushed the throttles firmly through to combat burner. The fires belched out. The Echo began to rapidly accelerate. The wings, which had been fully spread for the simulated approach, now began to sweep as the speed continued to build relentlessly. She hauled on the stick and the advanced Tornado did its trick of standing on its tail and rocketed for altitude.

"Very, very pretty!" came from the tower.

"I know," she said.

"Eggebek to Hunter One. See you again soon."

"Who knows? Hunter One."

Brodie remained silent until they were halfway along the first leg back to November.

"You enjoyed all that shit from that guy, didn't you?" he accused.

"What do you mean?"

But he didn't reply.

The remainder of the flight back was without incident. Every waypoint was reached on time. Brodie kept his conversation to the minimum required for the efficient execution of his work in the back seat.

Caroline felt a great relief when they were at last on approach to November and decided she wanted to do something to release some of the tension she felt.

"Hunter One to November," she called.

"Go ahead, Hunter One."

"Permission for low approach and double break."

"You are clear for low approach and double break, Hunter One."

"Roger. Hunter One."

"Can we just get this thing down without the fancy flying?" Brodie said coldly.

She didn't reply. Instead, she did a fast run-in, rolled snappily twice into the break and pulled tightly into the landing pattern.

Touchdown was perfectly carried out. Brodie remained stubbornly silent right up until they had come to a stop inside the HAS and climbed out of the aircraft.

He strode away from her.

She hurried after him and caught up. "All right, Ensign Brodie. Answers."

He stopped and turned to face her. "Is that an order, *sir*?"

Throughout, he had been addressing her as "sir". Caroline knew that while the form was possibly correct in the US Navy he was employing it as an insult while remaining within the bounds of service protocol.

"No, Brodie," she replied tightly, "it's not an order. But I like to think that my backseater actually likes flying with me. I can't fault the work you did up there but there was no rapport between us. We need that if we're ever to work together in an emergency. And while we're at it, we say 'ma'am' at November when addressing a female officer. So what's the problem? I've got BO?"

"I wasn't close enough to tell."

She stared at him disbelievingly. *"What?"*

"Sir!"

"You know what I mean, Brodie! What the devil's the matter with you?"

Suddenly, he was shouting at her. "You want to know what's up with me? I'll tell you, *sir*! Some goddamned woman who got into the front seat when she was not good enough and should never have been in the fucking airplane, *and who nearly killed me*! That's what's up with me! You got that five-by-five, *sir*?"

"You're blaming me for something that happened to you? You're punishing me because a woman pilot—"

"You goddamned women don't belong in combat planes!" he interrupted with a snarl of pent-up grievance and, before she could say any more, turned his back on her and stomped off.

Caroline stood there shaking with frustration, watching as he marched, stiff-backed, away from her. She forced herself to regain her composure.

"Don't lose it, Caroline," she told herself firmly. "Don't lose it."

She took a couple of deep breaths, drawing the calmness back into her. She glanced around. No one appeared to have witnessed the little drama but it didn't mean no one had. Her eyes returned to the uptight figure striding rapidly away in the distance.

"Must have been something I said," she added drily.

Jason sat grim-faced at his desk. Sitting before him in a semicircle were the deputy commanders and the two senior instructors from the OCU, Carlizzi and Gireaud. A wallet folder with US Navy markings lay open among the papers on his desk.

"Gentlemen," he began, "this is one of the most unpleasant duties we've ever been called upon to perform. I have received certain documents today regarding the incident on the US Navy carrier in which an F-14 aircraft, piloted by Lieutenant Mary-Jane Gillibrand and crewed by Ensign John Duncan Brodie, was lost. They make sober reading.

"You will also have read the debriefing notes on the cross-country recently flown by Flight Lieutenant Hamilton-Jones and Mr Brodie. As you'll have seen, Brodie is without doubt an excellent backseater. On flight execution alone the mission was an outstanding success. They were never adrift at any waypoint, and their recovery back to base was a pinpoint exercise with fuel state well in surplus of emergency requirements. Unfortunately, the matter cannot end there. Before I continue, I will take comments from each of you. Dieter, if you please."

"My opinion is straightforward," Helm began. "I have flown with Brodie. There is absolutely no question that he is a backseater of a very high calibre. But, as we all know, we need more than that at November. We need full crew co-ordination. Brodie is perfect with a male pilot. If we are prepared to let him fly only with a man in the front cockpit, he will make a valuable addition to the unit. But doing so will have the effect of marginalising Caroline and any other female aircrew who may come to us. This will not be good for morale. I have not been always happy about women in fighter planes but Caroline is special. She *is* a fighter pilot."

Jason nodded. "Thank you, Commander. Leo?"

Da Vinci was a fully qualified backseater as well as a pilot and occupied his deputy-commander post as the most senior navigator at November.

"My feelings are the same as Commander Helm. Brodie is very good but he must be able to work with all our pilots if required to in an emergency. As in an emergency there will be great stress, it is important that he is able to perform with the skill we all know he possesses. If that is jeopardised because of his . . . feelings, we can lose a valuable crew through this. It is a great risk to take."

Jason turned to Gireaud. "Major Gireaud?"

"I must agree with the commander and the colonel about Brodie's abilities. He cannot be faulted. But I have listened to what he has had to say about women aircrew in general and pilots in particular. This attitude, for me, is disturbing. I hate to see a good man go. The question we must ask is this: who is the better person in the cockpit? Whose departure will be of the greatest loss to us? If I had to choose, I would keep Caroline. I speak as a pilot."

"And now you, Major Carlizzi."

"You know my feelings, sir," Carlizzi began. "As the senior backseat instructor, I should be taking the side of a nav who is as good as Brodie. The guy's really hot stuff. He's not quite up there with McCann, Flacht and the others; but hell, he's pretty close. Caroline needs a backseater of Zero One squadron level, and he's the perfect candidate. But the guy's a timebomb waiting for the right moment to go off; and it could happen one day, with Caroline in the front seat. I say no way. My opinion, sir: we can't risk it."

Jason again nodded. "Thank you, gentlemen. My own feelings about this entire affair run very similar to yours. However, two new factors have determined the path my decision will take. First, members of the groundcrew in HAS Omega-One witnessed an argument between Flight Lieutenant Hamilton-Jones and Ensign Brodie, soon after their flight. The argument was apparently quite heated. The groundcrew were themselves not seen, but concern on their part for Miss Hamilton-Jones led them to talk to the crew chief.

"The crew chief, unsure of whether he should allow Caroline to make her own report and therefore keep out of it, spoke to Doc Hemelsen. As the unit's counselling officer, people find it easy to take their problems to her. She was sufficiently perturbed to give me a call. I ordered Caroline to come and see me and demanded an explanation. She was naturally reluctant to make any complaint or even talk about it. She felt this would be like informing on a fellow officer, despite the fact that she admitted not wanting to fly with Brodie again.

"I ordered her to write a new report on the flight detailing everything that had occurred right up to the argument on the ground and the words used by Brodie as she remembered them. It makes interesting reading. The US Navy were also kind enough to send me a copy of their investigating board's final conclusions on the loss of the F-14. That too, makes interesting reading. It's a pity Mr Brodie does not share Caroline's reluctance to inform on a fellow officer. Brodie, incidentally, according to these documents, was already officially a junior lieutenant before he came to us."

Jason picked up two sheets of paper, stood up and walked over to his officers. He handed the papers to Helm.

"I would like you all to read these," he said. "One is Caroline's report. The other's the final page of the US Navy investigating board's conclusions. I've highlghted in blue the pertinent observations."

He went over to his favourite window and looked out. He did not turn around when he heard their soft gasps of surprise echoing each other, preferring to wait until they had all read the documents.

"We're done, sir," he heard from Carlizzi.

He turned and went over to retrieve the papers. They watched him silently as he again took his seat behind the desk.

"I believe, gentlemen," he said to them, "that it is quite obvious what our decision must be. I will expect a confidential report from each of you on Ensign Brodie. I know this will be fairly and professionally done. I want them here by O-nine hundred tomorrow morning. I'll be seeing Brodie at ten hundred hours. Thank you, gentlemen."

They all stood up, looked at him with understanding, then saluted and went out.

He got slowly up from his chair and went back to his window. Just then, there was a soft beep. He turned to look.

There were three phones on Jason's desk. One was red. This was the totally secure outside line and very few people had its number. It was the only one with a beep.

He hurried over to pick it up.

"Ah, Christopher," came the air vice-marshal's voice. "Glad you're there. Expect visitors."

"When, sir?"

"Two days, O-nine hundred hours."

"How many?"

"Five, including myself."

"Anything else, sir?"

"Time enough when we get there."

Jason's instincts told him it was a mission.

As if he could read the wing commander's mind, Thurson continued, "Whatever you're thinking, you're quite correct."

"Reading minds these days, are you, sir?"

"We know each other well enough," Thurson said.

"We do indeed, sir. I look forward to seeing you, and friends."

"Oh, Christopher . . ."

"Yes, sir?"

"Antonia would like to hear from you."

Antonia Thurson, the AVM's daughter. Jason's feelings towards her were ambivalent. He had known her since she was a child and Thurson his flying instructor. He'd been a very green young pilot then and twelve years older than her. She even used to call him uncle. She was now a strong-minded woman in her twenties determined to claim Jason as her own. He still tended to see her as a child, much to her annoyance.

Despite enjoying being with her, Jason kept a tight rein on his feelings. There were younger men she should be going after, he persuaded himself. And besides, the November project demanded all his time. He knew it was a lame excuse but it made him feel safer. His heart had been broken before.

"Christopher, why don't you simply marry the damned gel and get her out of my hair?" the AVM's voice said in his ear.

"Sir?" a startled Jason said.

"You heard me."

Then the connection was gone.

He put the receiver down slowly and stared pointedly at the red phone.

"I could have done without that."

At precisely 1000 hours the next morning, Brodie, in full uniform, was ushered into Jason's office. The wing commander was at his desk wearing his peaked cap.

Brodie came to a halt before the desk and, as he'd done for the meeting with Carlizzi, saluted smartly. "Ensign Brodie reporting as ordered, sir!"

Jason looked up, eyes giving nothing away. "At ease, Mr Brodie."

"Sir!"

Brodie stood, legs slightly apart, hands behind his back, and relaxed minimally.

Jason removed his cap, wiped at his forehead with the back of the same hand and placed the cap on the desk.

"You may remove your hat, Mr Brodie."

"Sir." Brodie tucked his cap under an arm and waited.

Jason's eyes now fastened upon the junior officer. "We run a very special unit here, Mr Brodie. We have, I believe, people of a standard that many air forces would give their eye teeth for. The November programme is about evolution. We believe what we have here is a template for the future; a fighting force that is capable of meeting the many challenges of a rapidly changing world and hopefully managing to prevent crises from turning into catastrophes.

"To do this, we need people of a very special kind. There are those who would see us closed down at the drop of a hat, for political reasons or for strategic and tactical purposes. We must give our political detractors no excuse to move against us and we can ill afford disasters in the air.

"On the international front, we must always be one step ahead of potential enemies. If called upon to carry out a mission, this must be done with the skill that has made November crews second to none. We are holding the key to the future, Mr Brodie."

"Permission to speak, sir." Brodie's eyes looked straight ahead.

"Speak, Mr Brodie."

"Sir, I am a good RIO. I believe I have much to contribute to the November squadrons, sir."

"Do you know, Mr Brodie, I agree with you."

Not quite expecting this, Brodie's eyes swivelled towards Jason. "Sir?" The eyes snapped back to straight ahead.

"I agree you have much to contribute," Jason said. "I have here your fitness reports from the instructors and the deputy commanders. As one, they agree that you are an exceptional backseater."

"Thank you, sir!"

"Early days for thanks, Mr Brodie. Now comes that part I most dislike. I find it a tragedy that someone of your quite remarkable skills should jeopardise them in the way you have."

"I do not understand, sir."

"I know all about your behaviour with Flight Lieutenant Hamilton-Jones."

"Sir, did she—" The eyes again performed their swivelling dance.

"No, Mr Brodie!" Jason interrupted in a hard voice. "She did not! She showed far more generosity of spirit than you're displaying at this very moment. There are no passengers here and there is no room for a prejudice so warped it distorts your view of the world seriously enough to make you blind to reality.

"I have plenty of respect for someone who will face up to a mistake and say 'I was wrong,' and none at all for a person who clings to a narrow view of the world irrespective of its validity."

Brodie tried to speak but Jason cut him off.

"Before you even attempt to interrupt me, Ensign, let me give you an item of reading material. Come forward."

Brodie did as he was told.

Jason handed him a sheet of paper. "You have in your hand a copy of the final conclusions of the US Navy's investigating board concerning your F-14 aircraft. Read the highlighted passages. Aloud, if you please."

Brodie stared at the paper, then looked at Jason uncertainly. "Aloud, sir?"

"Aloud, Mr Brodie."

Brodie cleared his throat and began to read, hesitantly at first then with growing astonishment.

". . . detailed examination of the recovered aircraft showed that the left engine had suffered a fuel flow malfunction due to blockage leading to an immediate loss of power in that engine and a subsequent uncommanded rolling motion. The pilot's efforts to recover the situation were seriously hampered by proximity to the deck. Faced with insufficient power for a bolter, the pilot excercised great presence of mind by retracting the landing gear to avoid fouling on obstructions and crashing into the deck, and to give clearance to get the aircraft over the side. She was also swift to secure the affected engine and pull the fuel shut-off handle, to minimise the risk of fire. There is no evidence to support the charge of mishandling. It is therefore the conclusion of this Board that Lieutenant Mary-Jane Isabelle Gillibrand showed great presence of mind in not only avoiding a disastrous crash on the deck which could have cost many lives,

but also saved the lives of her crewman and herself.
It is therefore recommended that Lieutenant Gillibrand
be returned to full flying status with all the privileges
and rights according to her rank.

The Board orders that Lieutenant Junior Grade (pend-
ing) John Duncan Brodie be recalled to reconsider his
evidence, given at the time of the original inquiry."

Brodie's mouth gulped silently as, with a visibly trembling hand, he returned the document to the wing commander.

"They fixed it," he said in a voice quivering with outrage. "She screwed up and nearly killed me and they fixed it!"

Jason got to his feet, eyes so cold it was easy to believe he was indeed capable of freezing people where they stood.

"Mr Brodie!" he barked. "Pull yourself together." He slammed a hand on the papers on the desk. "Do you know what's also in there? The deputy commanders and the chief instructors have given you assessments that by any standards are exceptional. I was even considering writing a covering assessment of my own. We are trying to salvage your career but we're getting precious little help from you. Wake up!"

Brodie drew himself to full height. "Sir, sorry, sir!"

"Sorry isn't good enough, Mr Brodie. I consider you to have the aircrew qualities we require. However, you've got a serious flaw which, unless you do something about it very quickly indeed, will cause you to wave goodbye to any hopes you may entertain of continuing a flying career."

Jason searched through the papers and picked up another sheet. His eyes speared Brodie.

"Caroline Hamilton-Jones," he said, "is a pilot worthy of your respect. She is here on her own merit. I have been in a crash with her and I'm alive today because of her exceptional flying skills. I have flown with her since, and will do so again as often as may be necessary. No one 'fixed' anything for her."

Jason stabbed at the sheet of paper with a finger. "This is something you know nothing about. It's another part of the investigating board's report. Your F-14 was one of five aircraft to have been inadvertently fuelled from a contaminated batch which created a rapid build-up of deposits in the fuel system. This eventually caused blockages."

Jason studied the sheet of paper. "The aircraft affected were flown by . . . Lieutenant-Commander Halls and Lieutenant Pyke;

Lieutenants Jerrold and Stein; Lieutenant Hendricks and Lieutenant (Junior Grade) Elkhorn; and Lieutenants Valdez and Jackson. Do you happen to know any of these people?"

"Yes, sir. They are all from my old squadron."

"Well, Mr Brodie, for your information you nearly lost Jerrold and Stein, because the very same thing happened to them: an engine out. They were doubly fortunate. They lost the engine with altitude to spare and were thus able to make a single-engine recovery to the carrier. As they were shutting down, the second engine failed. A service check disclosed the same problem as on your own aircraft. All fuel in all aircraft was then checked. The five I mentioned were fortunately the only ones to have been refuelled from the sub-standard batch. The entire stock of that fuel is itself now the subject of an inquiry. Your pilot, Lieutenant Gillibrand, has been grossly maligned, Mr Brodie.

"I would strongly suggest that when you return to your carrier you seek Lieutenant Gillibrand out, apologise to her, tell her how much you regret your previous behaviour and, to prove it, say you will fly with her for as long as she is prepared to tolerate you. There is no guarantee that she will give you the time of day after what you've put her through; but you must do it. *If* you have the courage to do so, you will be making a new start and you just might be taking the first steps to saving what is left of your career. I hate to see good talent go to waste."

Jason paused, laser eyes still probing Brodie.

"You may as well know," he continued, "that I have also received a copy of Lieutenant Gillibrand's fitness report. I'm very impressed, and I'm of a mind to poach her from the US Navy, if they're foolish enough to let me. There's an opening here for you, Mr Brodie, if you can make the required effort. You just may, at a later date, find yourself and Lieutenant Gillibrand crewing a November aircraft. It's entirely up to you.

"I'll write that assessment I intended to. Now you must return to your carrier and accept whatever medicine is meted out to you by the navy. You're a youngster with the mindset of an old man. Get rid of it, or find yourself spending the rest of your days watching other people fly. Hat on!"

"Sir!" Brodie put his cap back on.

Jason put on his own cap. "Thank you, Ensign Brodie, and good luck."

"Thank you, sir!" Brodie saluted.

Jason returned the salute.

Brodie wheeled and went out.

Jason slowly removed his cap with a sigh and sat down again. He hoped Brodie would have the guts to rescue what was left of a very promising career.

The wing commander then began to write Brodie's assessment. When he had finished he pressed a button on his intercom.

"Yes, sir?" came from his PA, Flying Officer Rose Gentry.

"Rose . . . when are Hohendorf, Selby and Bagni due back?"

She was efficiently quick with the reply. "Mr Hohendorf in five days, Flight Lieutenant Selby . . . four days and Capitano Bagni in a week. But they're all due to check in within the next forty-eight hours, in case there's an Alpha."

"We may need a recall. I'll keep you posted. Please set up a deputy commanders' meeting for one hour from now."

"An hour, sir? Are you sure?"

"Have you become an echo, Rose?" Jason enquired patiently. "Stop trying to organize me."

"That's what I'm here for, sir. You've already got an appointment for that slot."

"Oh Lord, have I?"

"Yes, sir. Major Hemelsen."

"Ah . . . Grovel to her for me, will you please? Put that back and warn the deputies."

Rose Gentry's voice hinted at a sigh. "Yes, sir."

"Thank you. And Rose?"

"Sir?"

"Sorry."

"Goes with the job, sir."

Jason allowed himself the briefest of smiles as he released the button on the intercom.

Then it was time to think about whatever mission the air vice-marshal was bringing with him.

The Special Research Unit, the Urals.

Konstantinova was in the supply section getting her new uniforms. The supply sergeant was Melev's wife, Natasha Minkova. After marrying Melev, she had insisted on keeping her own family name.

Sergeant Minkova did not fit everybody's idea of a Natasha. Big, square-shaped and with a dishpan face that hid itself in too many chins, her small sunken eyes looking as if they too wanted to hide from the world, she tallied with Daminov's description: uglier than her husband. With her black hair pulled tightly back on her round head, she could pass for a trimmer version of a sumo wrestler. Her voice was a surprise; almost melodious. Most people steered well clear of her.

But not Konstantinova.

"This one should be just right for you," she said pleasantly to the newly-promoted lieutenant. "If it's a little too big, I can do the alterations, Milla."

"Thank you, Natasha. I'll try it on, and if there's too much slack we can arrange something."

"Now that you're a lieutenant, I suppose you won't have much time for me."

"Nonsense. I'm not going to change."

"You'll have to. Captain . . . *Major* Lirionova is going places. She's fast, that one. Before you know it, she'll be a colonel and away from this dump. Then I suppose you'll be in charge."

"We can't assume that."

"I wish I was as pretty as you," Natasha said, in an abrupt swerve of subject. "Nobody will ever make *me* a lieutenant . . ."

"I'm not pretty."

"Of course you are. You've got a great body and if you smiled more—"

"I know what this is all about, Natasha," Milla said reprovingly. "I'm not going to forget you. And stop looking at yourself from the outside. You should never have married a pig like Melev, anyway. You deserve better. Besides, you're far too intelligent for him."

"Who else would have me?" Natasha Minkova asked simply.

"Anyone smart enough to look beyond what they first saw. You forget, I've seen that picture you keep hidden: you as a young girl."

"I've only showed it to you. Although my husband's seen it," Natasha added as an afterthought. There was regret in the voice.

"I saw a very beautiful young woman," Konstantinova said. "And she's still there."

"You're always so kind to me, Milla."

"I'm telling you the truth. That pig of a husband wants you like this because he knows no one would have *him*. He couldn't hold on to you if that girl came back."

"You believe that?" There was hope of a double freedom in the question.

"Of course I believe it." Konstantinova pointed to the uniforms. "Just imagine if you could get into these sizes."

"I've got big bones. I'll never be that slim."

"Perhaps, but I still say there's a slimmer woman in there waiting to come out. That girl in the picture is not from my imagination."

Abruptly Natasha smiled and, for an amazing moment, the girl in the photograph that Konstantinova had seen peeped through. "I always like our chats, Milla. You always cheer me up." She placed a podgy hand on the uniforms. "Do you want to take these with you now? Or later?"

"Later. Olga Vasilyeva has asked me to her lab. I think she wants to congratulate me. She was busy most of the night and missed our little celebration. I'll pick these up on my way back."

Sergeant Minkova nodded. "All right, Milla. I'll have to get used to calling you lieutenant," she added.

"You can still call me Milla when no one's around."

"I hoped you would win the shooting, you know," Natasha said, in another of her unexpected switches in conversation. "Captain Urikov and my husband were so angry. The captain was angry with him, he was angry with me, and both of them *hated* the three of you. When they come back from patrol tonight and hear about your promotions . . ." She let the sentence hang.

"I can just imagine what they'll say."

"They already call you and the major the general's handmaidens. You can imagine what they really mean."

"It's the right level for their minds. Back tonight, did you say?"

"Yes."

"It's too much to hope they'll shoot each other out there, I suppose . . ." Konstantinova began thoughtfully, then glanced at Natasha as if suddenly remembering she was Melev's wife. "Oh I'm sorry, Natasha . . ."

"Don't worry. Sometimes, I feel like shooting him myself."

Eleven

Olga Vasilyeva beamed at Konstantinova. "Congratulations!"

"Thanks, Olga. We missed you last night."

Vasilyeva sighed. "I'd have liked to have come but we had some problems." She tapped at Konstantinova's shoulder boards. "And you're improperly dressed. No lieutenant's boards yet?"

"I've got the boards. Liri brought them up with her from Moscow, and I've picked up the uniforms. The boards will be on before the day's over. Let me enjoy these last moments as a sergeant."

Vasilyeva made a noise like a soft snort. "If they gave me promotion with more pay, I'd grab it so fast . . ." She left the remainder of her comment unsaid, her mind clearly elsewhere as they walked.

Curious, Konstantinova said, "What sort of problems?"

"I'm taking you somewhere to show you," Olga Vasilyeva said.

Konstantinova followed her into a large room where several small pine trees were connected to various monitors. Three lab technicians in white coats were studying the monitors, going from one to the other.

"Anatoli, Yuri, Lev," Vasilyeva began, "you all know Sergeant . . . ah . . . *Lieutenant* Konstantinova as we must call her now."

The technicians nodded and smiled at her. "Congratulations, Lieutenant!" they each said.

"Thank you," Milla responded with a smile.

They gave little nods and returned to the study of their monitors.

Vasilyeva led her to one of the pines whose monitor was currently unattended.

"This is the one I wanted you to see," the doctor said. "What sort of problem? Take a look."

She tapped at the monitor's keyboard. The pine's cellular structure came onscreen, then was magnified several thousand times. As Konstantinova watched, she realised she was observing a vicious cellular war. The plant's cells were destroying each other, and taking no prisoners.

147

"What's happening?" she asked.

"The plant is dying," Vasilyeva replied. "Can you remember when we were at the shooting range I told you and Liri about a plant that had violently rejected DNA that was alien to it? I said at the time it was dying."

"Yes. I remember."

"This is not the same plant, but what you're looking at is an even more extreme form of rejection. That little pine is destroying itself from the inside. You're watching a suicide."

"A plant committing suicide? A plant's not a person . . ."

"It's life. If it wants to, the plant can end its own life."

"Oh come on, Olga. Anyway, why would it want to do that? Listen to me," Konstantinova pulled herself up short. "I'm actually talking as if that plant . . ."

"I'll answer your question in a roundabout way, to give you a better understanding of what has occurred. What do we have most of in our *taiga*?"

"The forests? Pine trees."

"Perfect for our cyber-sensor experiments. Imagine whole areas of forest being one massive sensor, far greater than the field prototype or anything we've planned so far; thousands of square kilometres. A reafforestation programme with accelerated-growth specimens would expand the sensor region virtually anywhere we chose. Nothing could fly over it without being detected. No hiding place for an intruder, no matter how low he flew. Even the smallest bird could be detected by a variety of sensor modes. Or so we thought."

"I don't quite follow you."

"Mother nature," Vasilyeva said ruefully. "Nature has a counter for everything that crosses the boundaries she has set. Our most prolific potential conduit for the sensor experiment has turned out to be the one thing that can kill it. Nature has given us the code with which to destroy the organic sensor: pine oil. The oil reacts violently when nanocomputers are introduced into its cellular structure. It modifies them and turns them into killers. It's as if the plant is saying, I can't prevent you from putting these things into me but I can make sure you get no use out of them, even if it means I must kill myself to do so. Can you imagine that? An outraged, suicidal plant!"

A bemused Konstantinova glanced from the doctor to the plant and back again, as if unsure which was the most outlandish.

"But there's more," Vasilyeva went on grimly. "We also discovered that the process by which this 'suicide' takes place can be converted into a computer programme." She reached forward to remove a slim cartridge from a zip drive. "On this little thing," she went on, holding it out for Konstantinova to inspect closely, "is a programme which, if introduced into any of the other sensor-modified plant data, will turn their own organoputers into killers.

"We've discovered – by sheer accident, in true scientific break-through manner – the one thing we were afraid of: the only defence against the system. Worse, there appears to be no counter to this defence, which is a virus of extreme potency. If I were to introduce this into the field prototype, the entire system would be dying within hours, with no hope of regeneration. It would attack even the regenerative processes.

"This cartridge, in its present configuration, can store one hundred megabytes of data; but there's not even one meg on here. The data capable of destroying years of hard work in a matter of hours is contained in a mere five hundred kilobytes. Such is the potency of the pine virus."

Konstantinova was staring at the doctor.

"Are you telling me," the new lieutenant began carefully, "that this entire project – all the money that's been spent on its development, to house and to secure it – can be turned into so much mush by that thing you've got in your hand?"

Vasilyeva nodded. "That's exactly what I'm telling you. Nature has showed us what she can really do. The experiment is safe; as long as we don't use pines."

"But now that you know there's a natural defence . . ."

"You mean the genie's out of the bottle and we can't put it back in."

"Yes. An enemy could get hold of this, duplicate the programme . . ."

Vasilyeva gave a thoughtful smile. "Where from? The enemy would need an original, and would have to insert it. This is the only one and, out here in this wilderness, your unit and Urikov's cavemen are our protectors. What enemy? And I repeat . . . where from?"

"The general always reminds us to expect anything at anytime, anywhere."

"Standard paranoia for you security people," Vasilyeva remarked, gently dismissive. "But it's your job. I can understand that. I, however, am more concerned with finding a way to neutralise this virus which uses our own cellular nanocomputers as vehicles for its destructive purposes." She slid the cartridge back into the zip drive.

"The data on here," she went on, "speaks directly to the nanos, which then react exactly as if they've been triggered by the code within the pine oil in an actual host plant. I think your general would require us to find a neutralising code to first lock out and then cancel out the killer instruction, with all the speed we can possibly manage."

"Which is what you're working on in here?"

Vasilyeva nodded once more. "We hope to find a way and, as I've said, quickly; but so far nature remains one step ahead. Every time we think we've found a door, it slams in our faces. The virus adapts more quickly than we can find doors. It's almost as if it knows what we're trying to do, and manages to ambush us long before we're even aware an ambush has been set. This prevents us from setting up an avoidance routine in time.

"Each ambush is always different and continuously evolving. To beat this process, we'd have to somehow get ahead and correctly predict the structure of the next ambush, destroy it, then make it impossible to set another. So far, *we* are the ones with the impossible task. There are literally billions, perhaps trillions, of permutations, and the virus has them all to play with. The nanos are the reason it can do this, of course. They've given it hugely accelerated capabilities. Without the nanos, we can't create the organic sensor. With them, we give the virus its killing power. I can almost enjoy the irony of it."

"Someone will have to tell the general," Konstantinova said after a while.

"Someone?"

"Major Lirionova can do it. She's the ranking officer."

"For a newly-commissioned officer, you're learning fast," Vasilyeva commented drily. "And you haven't even gone to officer school yet."

November Base, the Moray coast. 1000 hours the next day.

The subdued whistling hum of the Hercules C-130's four turbo-prop engines as it came steeply in to land sounded almost apologetic against the full-throated roar of an ASV Tornado that had just taken off. It was painted white and carried a civilian registration.

After landing, it travelled at a fast taxi to a specified location. It eventually came to a halt close to the HAS occupied by the two-seat Starfire operational prototype that Caroline and McCann hoped to fly. As its engines wound down, the loading ramp beneath the canted underbody began to lower.

Jason had received a further secure call from Thurson informing him of where the Hercules should be parked. He had also been instructed to post armed guards from the unit's special security troops at the shelter. Six of them were positioned within the perimeter of the structure. Above, one of the security squadron's MD 500 helicopter gunships carried out a low-level patrol of the airfield boundary.

Standing to one side next to two staff cars, Jason tugged at the tunic of his uniform and glanced to his left. The driver of one of the cars was inserting the pennant of an air vice-marshal into the holder on one of the front wings of the vehicle. The air force blue rectangular pennant, with its dark borders and twin horizontal red bars in the middle, fluttered in the dying slipstream of the C-130's slowly unwinding propellers.

As he watched the aircraft, Jason saw a cylindrical container with no markings secured to a low multi-wheeled trolley carefully pushed down the ramp by two of the aircraft's civilian crew. The cylinder was about the length of a central fuselage fuel tank but much slimmer, giving the impression of extra length. Another trolley, this time carrying a square container, was pushed out by a further two crew members. Bright-orange work overalls for two engineers were draped on the second container. The men wheeled the trolleys the short distance from the aircraft into the HAS. They left the equipment and returned to the C-130.

Then five more people came out: two in uniform, the others in civilian clothes. The uniformed men were Thurson and Bowmaker. One civilian was Buntline, the others total strangers to Jason. He went up to the group.

Thurson, Bowmaker and Buntline came to a stop before him while the other civilians hung slightly back.

"Christopher!" the air vice-marshal greeted him warmly. The familiar tall slim figure with the features of an aesthete held out a hand.

Jason saluted. "Good to see you, sir," he said, then shook the hand.

"Good to be here."

Jason saluted Bowmaker. "General. Nice to see you back across the pond."

Bowmaker held out his hand. "I always seem to be bringing you problems that need solving," he said cheerfully.

"That's what we're here for, sir." Jason turned to Buntline. "And Mr Buntline."

Buntline, with a smile that gave nothing away, shook Jason's hand. "Are you pleased to see *me*, Wing Commander?"

"That depends on what you've brought me, Mr Buntline."

"Interesting possibilities, Wing Commander," Buntline said mysteriously. He turned to the two civilians. "Let me introduce Mr Wilby and Mr Ländemann. Gentlemen, Wing Commander Jason, commander of the November project."

Jason went through the handshaking routine again. "Welcome to November One, gentlemen. If you'll all please follow me to the cars."

The six of them divided neatly into uniforms and non-uniforms. Jason, the AVM and Bowmaker got into the car with the pennnant, while the others followed in the second. They were driven to the building that housed Briefing Room Alpha, the unit's premier operational briefing auditorium. An Alpha briefing always meant a hot operational mission.

Briefing Room Alpha, though bigger and more comprehensively appointed, was not unlike the auditorium at Kurinin's Secret Research Unit in the Urals. The similarity between them was such that Jason or Kurinin, transferred to his adversary's base, would have found a certain degree of familiarity in his new surroundings.

A pitcher of chilled mineral water and six glasses were on a small table in the room. A sergeant was standing next to it. As she saw them, she began to fill the glasses.

"Thank you, Sarn't Huntley," Jason said to her when she had finished. "We'll take it from here."

"Sir," she acknowledged, and went out.

They all picked up a glass except Wilby, who was to talk about the equipment that had come on the C-130.

The main display computer was already running, with a large image of its basic screensaver projected onto the auditorium's huge screen. Wilby climbed the dais as the others took their seats, Ländemann at the computer itself. He placed a compact disc into the CD-Rom drive and hit a key. The auditorium lights dimmed. The screensaver changed to a logo for the company which had manufactured the as-yet-unidentified equipment. This faded out and a title faded in.

ELECTROMAGNETIC PULSE CANNON – NON-NUCLEAR
The EMPC-N^2

This then changed to the image of a slim weapon looking very much like an aircraft cannon but with significant differences. Instead of a breech section there was a smooth belling into a wider cylindrical shape which ended in a sharp cut-off. Attached to the top of this larger section was a protrusion that looked like a permanently fixed magazine. The muzzle was slightly flared. That was all there was, outwardly, to the whole weapon.

Below the illustration of the cannon was its protective case which curved smoothly outwards along its edges. In animation, it moved upwards to enclose the weapon. An image of the Starfire then came onscreen. The encased weapon was attached to the underbelly of the aircraft along its centreline, fitting neatly and aerodynamically.

To one side of the display screen, Wilby began to speak, using a remote to project a small yellow arrow upon it.

"This is a fully tested example of our EMPC-N^2," he began. "The race to create a portable and lightweight non-nuclear electromagnetic pulse weapon has been going on for some time. The main drawback to achieving this has been the size of the developmental beam generators required to produce the necessary energy for a focussed beam of substantial hitting power. By substantial power, I mean in the region of one gigawatt. A current, so-called portable generator needs a vehicle that requires an eighteen-wheeled chassis to transport it. Hardly portable or mobile and certainly out of the question for airborne use."

As Wilby spoke, the images onscreen moved and changed at synchronous pace to match each stage of his discourse.

"As we all know," he went on, "a nuclear explosion is the only 'generator' capable of totally disabling all unshielded electronic devices, military and civilian, in a vast area well beyond ground zero. A nuclear explosion, with all its resultant horrors, is thus a monstrously blunt instrument, extremely limited in feasibility. A focussed beam weapon attacks only its specific target without that by-product we all know and hate, collateral damage. It's a clean kill. Of course, our own military devices are all protected but those belonging to many potential adversaries are not, or are shielded at levels which this cannon will be able to overcome with ease.

"Our problem was to create a weapon of comparable weight to an airborne cannon – or lighter if at all possible – with its own dedicated power source. This power source had to be capable of discharging, within milliseconds, an energy beam of several megajoules. There was a single answer: storage. A battery or batteries, if you like.

"Personally, I prefer the term powercell. We were still faced with the problem of heat dissipation from the storage unit. We needed to keep the stored energy stable and at peak levels. To do this required a way of maintaining temperature integrity. We have found a way and, in doing so, not only have we kept the weapon small and light but it can fire several bursts before all energy is used up. On return to base, the weapon can be recharged by simply replacing the powercell with one taken from a static on-site generator. There is already a modified bay in the aircraft into which the powercell slots neatly."

"If I may interrupt, Mr Wilby."

"Of course, Wing Commander."

"How several are 'several' bursts?"

"Six. Think of these as an extra six, very special missiles or an extra, very powerful gun, during close combat."

"Thank you."

"You're welcome. Weapon construction," Wilby continued, "has taken a leaf out of the aircraft's own manufacture. A high percentage use of carbon fibre composites, with the minimum addition of light metals in its construction, have ensured not only light weight but high strength and durabilty. The casing is similarly constructed giving a smooth conformal fit to the aircraft, necessary to minimise drag when carried. With the weapon fitted, the aircraft retains its high thrust-to-weight ratio as well as its outstanding manoeuvrability. Any more questions, gentlemen?"

The display had reverted to the screensaver and the lights to their customary level.

"May I continue, sir?"

"Please go ahead, Christopher."

"Thank you, sir. Mr Wilby, how compatible is this weapon with the Starfire's systems?"

"It is dedicated, Wing Commander. We designed the cannon specifically for use with the Starfire. Hence the special 'ammunition' bay for the powercell. The cannon is an additional weapon, complete with its own dedicated HUD symbology. When carried, it will not affect the normal weapons fit of the aircraft. Obviously, in such a configuration, a centreline bomb or a centreline fuel tank cannot be carried. As I've indicated, it can be used both in air-to-ground and air-to-air roles."

"I'm not sure I like the idea of a beam weapon flashing all over the place during a turning fight," Jason remarked.

"In the air-to-air role, the weapon is inhibited. It will not fire unless unbreakable lock has been achieved. In short, you cannot miss with it because it won't let you. The pilot must first satisfy all the required parameters. This is a very necessary safety feature to avoid frying the systems of your own colleagues – if for any reason their own shielding has been degraded, perhaps through combat damage.

"It will also acquire an incoming missile if the pilot is in position to do so. Instead of spending precious time trying to avoid it, your beam weapon will lock-on and fry the missile's systems. The missile will then go off blindly until its fuel runs out. Acquisition of a launched enemy missile is additionally linked to the threat warning systems."

"And the host aircraft itself? How safe is it from proximity beam scatter?"

"There is no leakage from the focussed beam. It affects only targets at which it is aimed. As the aircraft is itself well shielded, the cockpit environment is, in any event, highly protected. We can fit the weapon and get the systems aligned within forty-eight hours. Then we're available to instruct your chosen crew in its use."

"Which brings me to *the* question, Mr Wilby. Why have you brought this to us?"

Instead of answering, Wilby looked at Buntline.

Buntline got to his feet. "Thank you, Mr Wilby. My turn for explanations, I think." He turned to Bowmaker. "Would you like to go first, General?"

"You know more about this than I do," Bowmaker replied mildly. "It's your ball game."

Buntline studied the general for a fleeting moment longer. "Very well." He went up to Ländemann and handed him a compact disc. "If you please, Mr Ländemann." He glanced at Jason. "This will be mainly for your benefit, Wing Commander, as the essence of this mission is already known to everyone else here. Mr Wilby, and Mr Ländemann, are fully cleared."

An expressionless Jason nodded.

Ländemann exchanged the disc in the drive as Buntline climbed onto the dais and borrowed Wilby's remote pointer.

As the lights went down once more, a large-scale map of the Baltic coast from northern Germany to Estonia came onscreen. The yellow arrow pointed to a sweeping archipelago in an indentation of the coastline, midway along.

"A Pentagon reconnaissance mission spotted an illegal phase-array construction here," Buntline said. "What was not known at the time – but known by my people – was that this site was a deliberate spoof. Oh it's real and fully functional; but it was a bait, used for an altogether different purpose. The object of the exercise was to test another system, existing quite unobtrusively within the same area. That system clearly picked up a supposedly super-stealthy aircraft, as if it were an airborne version of Blackpool Pier. In effect, as if lit up like a Christmas tree."

Buntline then proceeded to inform the astonished Jason of the existence of the cyborg plants and their sensors.

"This really happens?" he asked when Buntline had finished. "Plants that can really spot high-flying aircraft?"

"Or low-flying ones. Believe me, Wing Commander," Buntline went on grimly, "we've had people – so far undetected – in positions of extreme danger for some time. I can assure you the information is absolutely correct."

"My God," Jason remarked softly. "Flying in low, thinking you're safe from prying radars while all the time you're as naked as a babe in arms, defence systems and fighters homing in on you. Very nasty."

"And beautifully simple and clever," Buntline added. "However, there is a way to permanently disable the system. In fact, to kill it. And we've got the means. This can only be done on the ground. But we need a diversion to enable our people to get out. So we're mounting – with your help, Wing Commander – our own spoof."

"Laying out the bait, you mean."

"That too. It is in your interest and in the interests of all who fly combat aircraft that we eliminate this system as quickly and as completely as possible. Your flight will look like an incursion, and you'll be chased off—"

"They may choose to do more than just chase us off."

"Your people are quite capable of defending themselves, as we are all well aware."

"When is the mission to be flown?"

"As soon as the Starfire can be made ready. A matter of days. One week at the most, including the training of the selected crew. Our people have pressed their luck long enough and are running out of time. A full pick-up programme is already set. Taking out that phase-array will provide the necessary diversion. However, once the subterfuge has been discovered, our people will be on borrowed time unless they're already on their way to their respective pick-up points. Precise timing is thus essential."

"The Starfire will need an escort."

"I'll leave that to you. I am certain you've already got the appropriate crews in mind."

Jason nodded. "I have." Jason glanced at Thurson but read nothing in the air vice-marshal's expression.

"Well," Buntline said with the air of someone who had said as much as he wanted to. "That's about it. You'll be given dates and timings, Wing Commander, to enable you to plan the mission. You'll also be given every support facility you may require to enable you to complete it successfully. Thank you."

He left the dais, handed the remote back to Wilby and retrieved the CD from Ländemann.

"Will you be staying for lunch, sir?" Jason asked the AVM as they left Alpha.

"Very kind of you, Christopher. Then we'll be leaving. I shall have to pacify the minister, as usual. Abe will be doing his diplomatic bit with our American friends. Mr Wilby and Mr Ländemann will be your guests until it's all over, and Mr Buntline . . . Mr Buntline," Thurson said, addressing Buntline directly, "one continues to be at a loss to know exactly what you do at any given time, or how to sensibly describe it."

"Just as well, Air Marshal," Buntline responded obscurely.

He kills people, Jason thought. *And so do we.*

After lunch in the mess which Jason had also arranged for the C-130 crew, the wing commander managed to get the AVM alone while the others talked in a small group by the waiting aircraft.

"Is there anything else I should know, sir?" he began. "It isn't that I don't entirely trust Buntline . . ."

"Which means you do not."

"His line of business exists on deception. I, on the other hand, need to protect my crews as much as possible. They know the risks they take. I'm simply trying to minimise those. Every little input helps."

"In your place," the AVM said, "I'd be doing the same. What I can tell you is that your boys may get a somewhat hot reception out there from highly capable aircraft and pilots. It's almost certain that the people we're dealing with would like to teach whoever tries to stop them a salutary lesson."

"I expect they would."

"Have you decided on the crew of the Starfire?"

"Yes, sir. Caroline."

The air vice-marshal stared. "*What? Are you sure of this? If we lose her out there . . .*"

"We won't. You've seen her assessment. It takes a lot to beat Dieter Helm, even once."

"Granted. She has turned out to be an exceptional pilot, despite my reservations. But this is the deep end."

"You know as well as I do, sir, that there's no such thing as an easy introduction to a live mission. If we can't send her on one, we've no right to make her an operational pilot. Besides, the escort will be made up of my best fighter crews."

"And who's in the back seat?"

"Carlizzi. He's flown with her on several training flights and, as senior nav instructor, he'll be a steadying influence in case she becomes temporarily overwhelmed by the occasion. I also think Carlizzi's the best selection after that unfortunate affair with Brodie."

"Would Brodie have gone with her?"

"In pure backseating terms, he was certainly up to it. But his attitude was totally unacceptable on this unit."

Thurson nodded slowly. "Sorry business."

"Yes, sir. But it's out of our hands and now up to him and the US Navy." Jason's eyes looked firmly into the air vice-marshal's. "Anything else you'd like to tell me, sir?"

There was a pause as the AVM took his time about what to say. In the distance, in one of the engine running bays, a Tornado's bellow swelled and faded repeatedly like a primeval beast roaring out a challenge, as engineers carried out maintenance tests.

"Mac's out there somewhere," Thurson said at last. "And that, Christopher, is for your information only. There are no exceptions."

Jason digested this startling news. "Perfectly understood, sir. Do we have a specific location?"

"I've no doubt Charles Buntline does but he's not saying. As we're not directly involved in the operation for the pull-out, it's understandable. Remarkable young woman, that. Incredibly brave. Reminds one of the stories of the wartime agents. Young gels too, many of them were."

"Yes, sir."

"Isn't one of your pilots rather fond of her?"

"Morton, sir. Yes. He is."

"Ah yes, Morton. Too bad. Can't be easy; but there it is. Is he on this mission?"

"No, sir. I'm using the veterans. Selby, Hohendorf and so on."

Thurson nodded. His eyes studied Jason closely. "Good luck, Christopher."

Jason saluted. "Sir."

Thurson returned the salute with his customary wave in the direction of his cap. "And do call Antonia. Please. She's driving me insane."

Jason gave a sheepish smile. "I will."

The air vice-marshal went off to join the others. Jason watched as they trooped up the C-130's ramp, leaving Wilby and Ländemann behind.

Bowmaker turned to wave briefly at the wing commander. Jason raised a hand in response. He liked the American general; they were kindred spirits.

Buntline and Thurson entered the cavernous bowel of the aircraft without looking back. The ramp was rising even as the Hercules began to move.

Wilby and Ländemann came towards him, then stopped close by to watch the aircraft as it taxied away. The wash from the four propellers tugged briefly at their clothes as the Hercules turned and set off down the taxiway.

"Your rooms in the mess are all prepared, gentlemen," Jason told them. "You'll find that your bags have been brought in from the aircraft and are also in your rooms."

"Thank you, Wing Commander," Ländemann said. "We would like to begin work immediately."

"Of course."

"Can we please have some of your engineering staff to help?"

"Already done. The engineer officer has been instructed to give you all the help you require."

"Again, I thank you."

"I do have a question."

They looked at him, waiting.

"All our operational aircraft are coated with a very special paint. The fairing that contains the EMP cannon—"

"If you'll pardon the interruption, Wing Commander," Wilby put in, "I can allay your fears about that. Built into the edges of the fairing is a conductive coating we call the fusion strip. It fuses automatically with the paint, once fitted to the aeroplane. When the Chameleon is employed, the fairing will have exactly the same poly-photochromatic properties as the rest of the aircraft."

Jason gave a tight smile. "I see you've thought of everything."

"No one ever thinks of everything," Wilby said, "but we do try to come close."

"Understood. Well, gentlemen, I'll let you get on with your work. I've got my crews to prepare."

"In two days," Ländemann told him, "we shall be ready for the two who are to fly the cannon."

Jason nodded. "They'll be there."

*   *   *

As soon as Jason got back to his office, he said to Rose Gentry, "We've got an Alpha. I need those pilots back here."

"I assumed there would be, sir," she said, getting to her feet. "Their Alpha recall is activated."

Jason waved her back down. "Pre-emptive strike, Rose?"

"Something like that, sir."

He nodded approvingly. "Now get me Caroline Hamilton-Jones here in my office within the hour. Then Major Carlizzi. Hamilton-Jones first," he added.

"Yes, sir. I'll see to it." She passed him a file. "Flying Officer Wilkinson's first assessment. Seems she's doing well, according to Commander Helm."

"Young Penny. Good. Good. I'll take a close look at the *Fregattenkapitän*'s comments. And Rose . . ."

"Sir?"

"How many times have I said you don't have to leap to your feet every time I come in?"

"Er . . . several times, sir?"

"Something like that," he said drily and went into his office, taking the file with him.

Twelve

The Special Research Unit, east of the Urals. The same day, 1800 hours, local.

Konstantinova had told Lirionova of the virus discovered by Olga Vasilyeva and her team. Lirionova had thought about it overnight and had come to a decision. She now looked up from her desk at Konstantinova, properly attired as a lieutenant and leaning, arms folded, against one of the office walls.

"I think," she began, "we should take the cartridge into our custody and tell the general."

"But Olga needs it to work with," Konstantinova reminded her. "She's searching for an anti-virus."

"We could return it to her each day . . ."

"What are you saying, Liri? That you don't trust her?"

Lirionova sighed. "The truth is, I'm not sure. I never expected a virus. Not even Olga expected it, and she's the scientist. Now we have a potential scenario for sabotage."

"By the very person who invented the process?"

"Who knows? Our job is to view everything from several angles. She had an American lover who taught her to shoot even better than our own specialist troops."

"She's got one leg . . ."

"What's that got to do with it? Or perhaps it has got something to do with it. Deep down, she may be bitter. Remember she told us how the American loved her legs? I watched her face when she said that. She misses him, and that leg."

"He was a man who made her sexually happy. Of course she misses him. And of course she misses the leg. Bad enough losing any leg; but to have been told by your lover they were beautiful . . . In her place and on both counts, you would miss all that as much as she does; and so would I. It does not add up to a potential saboteur. Why would she want to destroy her own invention? All those years of hard work!"

"Are you taking her side?"

161

"I'm not taking any side, Liri. For heaven's sake! Her shooting's given us relief from Urikov's neanderthal macho posing. Perhaps I'm just playing devil's advocate. As Intelligence officers, it's up to us to to look at all the angles, as you just said."

"Don't throw my words back at me, Milla! This is awkward enough as it is. Anyway, how do we know that leg's genuine? Who has seen her completely undressed? Perhaps we should put cameras in all the sleeping quarters. It's easy enough to get a fake casing and calipers . . ."

Konstantinova was staring at her, appalled. "Liri!"

"Oh all right. So perhaps I'm groping around in the dark. Here's my decision. We tell the general; we've got to. Then, as a precaution, we also take the virus cartridge into safekeeping at the end of each working day and—"

"And if she wants to work into the small hours?"

"Then one of us stays with her."

"Oh, I'll really like that."

"We don't have a choice. This is only in place until we hear what the general has to say. From tonight, we pick up that cartridge."

"You're the boss, Major."

"Don't remind me," Lirionova said wearily. "One day, you'll be. Then you'll see what it's like."

"I can't wait," Konstantinova commented sarcastically.

November Base: 1400 hours local. The same day.

"So what do you think he wants to see you for?"

Caroline, making needless adjustments to the fit of her uniform as they walked along the mess corridor, gave a loud sigh. "That's the third time you've asked, Elmer Lee. Do you think the boss lets me in on his decisions?"

She picked at a non-existent speck on her air force blue sweater and patted the pilot's wings on her left breast. She adjusted her cap for the fifth or sixth time.

"Think it's because he washed out Brodie?" McCann, wearing his best aviator sunglasses, persisted.

Caroline stopped abruptly. "Are you giving me that lift or not?" She peered at the glasses. "Can you see in those things in here?"

"I'm giving you the lift. And sure, I can see in them."

"Good. Now shut up. You're making me nervous."

"*I'm* making you nervous?"

"Elmer Lee!" she said warningly.

"OK, OK, already. I'm shutting up. Jeez!"

"Thank God for that."

They left the mess and hurried towards McCann's stone-grey Corvette. McCann changed his Corvettes the way other people changed socks. But he remained faithful; Corvette followed Corvette. There'd been one aberration when he'd bought a fierce machine of a different make – though still American – to impress Karen Lomax; but she had flatly refused to get into it. He had got rid of it quickly and gone back to the 'vette. The 344 bhp of the aluminium V8 in this latest version brought joy to his heart. There were three loves in McCann's life: Karen Lomax, his Corvette and the Tornado ASV Echo. Sometimes it was difficult to tell which came first.

"Obey the speed limit," Caroline advised as she got into the right-hand seat of the low-slung missile.

"Hey," he said, getting in behind the wheel. "I thought I was supposed to be the back-seat driver around here."

"Sorry."

They clipped on their seatbelts and McCann started the powerful engine. The V8 burbled deeply as he moved off. A very restrained McCann kept to the station limit, which in places was as low as 15 mph.

A short while later, they stopped outside the November Operational HQ building which housed Briefing Room Alpha as well as the wing commander's office.

"I'll wait," McCann said as he pulled into a parking slot.

"You don't have to."

"It's OK. Besides, perhaps he'll tell you the real reason he busted Brodie. I've got ideas of my own, but you never know."

"The wingco's not about to explain his actions to me, Elmer Lee."

"Perhaps we've got an Alpha," McCann went on, refusing to let go of his theme. "All the brass hats came in today: General Bowmaker, the air vice-marshal and that guy Buntline. When those three are together, it usually means business . . . or trouble. Then there's that stuff in the Starfire HAS."

"Elmer Lee."

"Yup."

"Shut it."

"OK."

Caroline got out of the car and smoothed down her skirt. "How do I look?"

"Sensational. The oh-so-cool Captain Cottingham would bust his heartstrings."

"Don't you start," she warned. "We're friends; just as we're all friends on the squadron."

"Sure." McCann gave her his most impish look.

"You're impossible," she said. "And thanks for the lift."

"You're welcome." McCann followed the look with an equally impish smile and gave a little wave of a salute. "I'll be right here when you're done."

"Just don't get into any trouble."

"Me? Trouble?"

"In the air," Caroline said, "you're a genius. On the ground, it follows you like flies on a cowpat . . ."

"What's a cowpat?"

"You don't want to know." She shook her head in resignation and entered the building.

"On the ground," McCann said to himself, "I'm cute." He looked into the driver's door mirror and lowered his sunglasses a little to peer unashamedly at himself above the rims. "Yeah. Cute."

Caroline entered Rose Gentry's office.

"Is he in?" she asked in a low voice.

The wing commander's PA stood up. "Waiting for you." She went to Jason's door, knocked once, then opened it slightly. "Flight Lieutenant Hamilton-Jones is here, sir."

"Thank you, Rose. Send her in."

Rose Gentry opened the door wider and stood back for Caroline to enter.

Caroline saluted as the door was shut behind her.

"Ah, Caroline." Jason stood up. "Thanks for coming." He made it sound as if she were doing him a favour and hadn't been ordered to attend. "Take off the hat and sit down."

"Sir."

She took a chair close to the desk and waited.

Jason went over to his window, looked out for a moment, then turned to face her.

"I know I promised that you and McCann could take the two-seat Starfire up for a familiarisation flight. I'm afraid circumstances have changed. For the moment, your flight with McCann will have to wait."

"Quite all right, sir. We can always take another slot when one becomes available."

"Ah yes, but . . . how would you feel about taking her up on an operational mission?"

This was so unexpected, she felt her mouth drop open in astonishment. She closed it quickly and swallowed.

"A real mission, sir?"

"A real mission. There's an Alpha on. We intend to make it as low-key as possible but I should warn you that there's a good chance you may find missiles and other stuff flying around out there. Can you handle it?"

"I can handle it, sir."

Jason's eyes fastened calmly upon her. "I want no bravado, Caroline. No gung-ho nonsense. I'm not interested in getting my crews killed. We are not that kind of unit."

"I can do it," she insisted firmly.

"I believe you," he said after a while. "Your backseater will be Major Carlizzi. You will be escorted by four ASV Echoes. The crews are Selby and McCann, Hohendorf and Flacht, Bagni and Stockmann, and Cottingham and Christiansen. You may also be called upon to defend yourself."

"Yes, sir."

"Our version of the Starfire – which started life as the EF2000 Eurofighter – is rather like our own ASV Echoes in that it has been enhanced beyond its basic configuration. The versions we eventually do get – funding permitting – will be based upon the two that are already here. In other words, ours will be rather more advanced than those which will be going into regular squadron service both nationally and internationally.

"You'll find her extremely powerful and agile, especially with the thrust-vectoring nozzles and other enhancements you'll be introduced to during conversion training. It shouldn't be too difficult for you to keep well ahead of the power curve. She's got the wide-angle holographic HUD you're already used to on the ASV Echo and, of course, full infrared capability on HUD, helmet sight, and MFDs. Above all, she's an easy aircraft to fly. As with the ASV, *don't* fight her. Remember that always. That's about it for now. I wanted to sound you out; make sure you were ready. If you have the slightest doubt . . ."

"No doubts, boss."

"Good. You'll get the full picture at the briefing. Meanwhile, you commence getting to grips with the aircraft immediately. First, simulator sorties with Major Carlizzi; then static familiarisation with the aircraft itself and some new systems that are being added and, finally; as many flights as can be slotted in before the mission itself. It's a heavy workload in a short time but time is the one thing we haven't got."

"When is the first sim flight, sir?"

"Fifteen thirty hours today. Get into full flight gear and meet Major Carlizzi in the simulator building. He'll have the routines. And no going off the station until the mission's over," Jason added.

She got to her feet. "Yes, sir." She put on her cap.

"Do be very careful up there, Caroline," he said to her with serious concern. "I don't want to lose you."

She smiled. "Elmer Lee would never forgive me."

"Neither would any of us."

"I'll make it back, sir . . . particularly as I'll have the best escort anyone could wish for."

"See that you do. Thank you, Caroline."

"Sir." She saluted and went out.

Jason turned back to the window. He'd done it. He'd ordered his first female pilot into combat.

"Crunch time," he murmured, "as McCann would say."

McCann looked curiously at her as she returned. She got into the Corvette without saying anything.

"Thanks for waiting, Elmer Lee," McCann said. "It's a long walk back to the squadron."

"What?"

"Ah! I hear sounds coming from my right. You look like you've spent too long in a centrifuge. What gives, pretty-pretty? The boss chew you out? Been misbehaving?" He began to croon, badly, *"Ain't misbehavin' . . ."*

"I'm going on a mission," she said in quiet disbelief.

That got his attention. "You? Heyyy . . . that's something! We've got an Alpha. Right?"

She nodded, still in a daze. "I'm flying the Starfire with Major Carlizzi in the back. Four ASV Echoes as escort."

"You've got the Starfire? Wow! The gang's the escort, I hope."

Again she nodded.

"Well don't worry, pretty-pretty," McCann said. "We'll watch you like hawks. Nothing's going to get to you."

She gave him a quick nervous smile. "Thanks, Elmer Lee. I know. Despite all the training I've gone through, getting to this stage – to what it's really all about – still comes as a bit of a shock." There was a sense of wonder in her voice. "All those months of training and finally my moment of truth."

"Hey," McCann said gently. "All of us know what's at the end of the training. Sometimes you can go through a whole career

166

without going anywhere hot, unless it's for a tan on some beach. Lots of guys have done that. Others get to go in as soon as the wings are pinned on. You can hack it, kid. So how do you feel?"

"A little scared, I think."

"Scared is good. It means you're not going to do anything stupid out there. Did the boss tell you the mission?"

She shook her head. "We'll know at the briefing, whenever that is. Would you mind taking me to the squadron, and then to the sim section? I've got to suit up, then meet the major at the simulator at fifteen thirty."

McCann started the Corvette. "Your wish is my command. And don't worry, Caroline. We'll chew anything that even looks like coming your way."

She touched his shoulder briefly. "Thanks again, Elmer Lee. It's good to know."

"*Nada*," McCann said expansively. "All part of the service of the November aces."

"Modesty certainly does not become you, Elmer Lee."

He grinned at her. "Hey. Who needs modesty?"

The stone-grey car with deep red leather interior moved sedately away, its exhausts rumbling out its evocative V8 beat. The sound was soon overwhelmed by the roar of two training squadron Tornadoes on their take-off run.

Then Caroline beamed suddenly and punched her fist into the air through the Corvette's open roof. "*Yes!*"

Another grin broke through beneath the aviator sunglasses. "Now you're talking," McCann said.

Maida Vale, London.

As Caroline was getting into her flight gear, Mark Selby felt himself sink deeply into Kim Mannon and experienced the kind of pleasure that felt like bolts of electricity going through him. It seemed as if he were plunging so precipitously into her, he could go no further. Yet still he pushed.

"Aaahh. . . !" The groan was forced out of him. He strained at her, his entire body stretching until he thought he could actually feel his skin expanding with the effort.

Beneath him, Kim's arms were stretched above her head, her hands gripping his. Her thighs were spread wide, her heels digging into the bed to give leverage, her lower body pressed hard against his, holding him within her. Her head was tossing from side to side and soft mewling sounds came out of her.

Her lower body went into rapid spasms that vibrated through him as he continued to fuse himself into her. The mewling sounds turned into a long keening wail that went on and on until at last it faded in a descending cadence as their bodies slowly relaxed and they were still.

"Oh God!" she said thickly. "This just gets better each time. No! Don't come out!"

"I wasn't—"

"You moved. You moved! Meanie."

"I was only doing this."

She gasped, undulating upwards in response. "Not . . . not again?" The small neat body was a sensuous powerhouse of continuing movement, eager for more.

"That's what I . . ."

Whatever he had been about to say was soon forgotten.

"Oh yes . . . yesss . . . please . . ."

When they had relaxed once more, bodies temporarily spent, she said, "Oh, Mark. I know it sounds corny, but I want this to go on for ever."

"Speaking of which, we've not been out of this flat for . . ."

"Two whole days!" She giggled, her entire body pulsing in response. "No-no!" she went on urgently. "Don't you dare come out of there. Just lie like that. I feel cosy. Your neighbours will soon start wondering what we're up to," she added with deliberately exaggerated coyness.

"They know what we're up to."

"Or how far you've been." She gave another of her body-shaking giggles and kissed him lightly.

"Don't be crude."

"And if they don't," she went on, ignoring his words, "they must have heard this time."

"I wouldn't worry about it. This place has good insulation. Raunchy screams don't get out."

"I see. So how many women have screamed this place down, then?"

"I wouldn't know. You're the only one I've heard here."

"Just make sure it stays that way. We should have used the Chelsea house. I've got all that wonderful food specially—"

"Your father's house, you mean?"

"My house," she corrected. "He hardly uses it."

He rolled carefully so that he was still inside her. "Although this place belongs to friends, it feels like my own turf. I'm more at ease here. Just because your father has stopped giving you grief about seeing me, it doesn't mean he'll end his scheming to split us up."

"He'll have to wait a few centuries," she said in an uncompromising voice. She stroked his chest with a caressing hand. "I've told him to forget it. I've done the round-the-world bit to mollify him. And what a mistake on my part that was. You should have stopped me."

"I had to let you do what you seemed to want to."

"I *didn't* want to. We were having problems because of Father's attitude. I tried to forget you. So after we had our ludicrous disagreement—"

"Disagreement! Is that what you call it? Contrary to my beliefs, both surprising and scaring myself, I asked you to marry me ages ago . . ."

"I remember the words."

"Do you?"

"That sounds like a challenge. Are you testing me?"

"No."

"You said, 'Marry me and have my children.'"

"Spot on!"

"How could I forget?" she asked softly.

"You didn't actually say yes at the time. I took you to Holyrood Park in Edinburgh and up that craggy hill by the lake."

"You threatened to jump if I didn't say yes, and I said I thought pilots never jumped—"

"Out of perfectly good aeroplanes. I remember saying that."

"My kiss said yes."

"Then you said no, and went on your world tour. But that's all old history now."

"And I have said yes. Does Elmer Lee know he's going to be best man?"

"Not until we've got our date. He'd plague me. Can you imagine it? He'd be even more out of control than he is now. Elmer Lee gets to know at the last possible decent moment. Since his near-death experience, he thinks the angels all love him."

"Perhaps they do," she said quite seriously.

Selby gave an exaggerated sigh. "What is it with Elmer Lee? Everybody seems to think he's some kind of cherub."

"He does look like one."

"Let's get back to us," Selby told her firmly. "For all our

intentions, what your father still wants even after all this time, is that you should marry Barham-Deane, that slick City creature he calls a financial barracuda. Reggie the 'cuda's the kind of man he wants for his only child and daughter." Selby put a finger to the tip of her nose. "That means you. He doesn't want a fighter pilot who hasn't a hope in hell of becoming a millionaire."

She giggled a third time. "You could always win the lottery."

"I should be so lucky."

"Suppose you did?"

"Suppose I did what?"

"Win the lottery? Would you still be a fighter pilot?"

"I'd be a millionaire fighter pilot," he said, smiling at the thought of it.

"I may have your body sometimes," she said, licking at him with long slow strokes of her tongue, a sleek cat grooming her mate, "to do with as I please, but your plane owns your body *and* your soul; and that's what Father can't stand. He knows he can't buy you off or buy you in. You're your own man.

"He can't control you. Losing to anyone in a battle of wills is something he can't stand. Losing to you makes him livid; but if even a lottery win wouldn't entice you away from your beloved aeroplane, he hasn't a hope in hell. Thank God." She licked at him once more. "Like that?"

"Mmm," he said. "Like it."

"Here's some more then." She licked both his nipples. "How's that?"

"Mmm," he said again. "You've got an amazing little tongue."

"An amazing *long*, little tongue, sir," she corrected, dark eyes looking at him daringly. "Consider yourself privileged. You're the only person on earth who knows how amazing it is."

"I consider myself privileged. You're dangerous, do you know that?"

"That's why you love me. You knew I was dangerous the first time you saw me. But I didn't frighten you. That's when *I* knew. In fact, if I remember correctly, you were bloody rude to me at that ball."

"Hah! *You* were rude to *me*. You asked me what it was like being a paid killer."

"And you said, 'Better than being an unpaid one.' I thought that was rather good."

"You wouldn't have liked what I thought. I equated you with the sort of idiotic people who ask questions like that believing they're being clever. I also remember thinking spoilt rich bitch."

"I know you did. It was all over your face. But you wanted me. Even then."

"So what makes you so smart?"

"I could feel the heat," she said with a truimphant smile. "You were talking to me, really talking. Without words. A woman knows these things."

"So you tracked me down to this flat, after browbeating my sister's friends to tell you where we were staying for the weekend."

"And my early arrival surprised you."

"I was trying to sleep!"

"At ten thirty in the *morning*? I remember thinking fighter pilots are supposed to be up at the crack of dawn."

"Don't believe everything you hear."

The giggle came on again. "You'd dragged on your evening-wear trousers to answer the door and I could see how welcoming you were, despite your shock at seeing me."

It had not been one of his finer moments of control. His body had betrayed him.

"And *you* came here without wearing your knickers," he said defensively.

"I needed the air. But I brought them with me; and I did leave them afterwards. Marking my territory."

"You're impossible."

"But worth it."

"As far as I'm concerned, you're the one good thing your father's done."

"Thank you, kind sir. You shall reap great rewards."

"I will admit," Selby went on, "it gives me a kind of pleasure to know that people like me keep things stable so that people like him can continue to make their hundreds of millions."

The dry tone of his voice made her look closely at him. "You say that jokingly but part of you really means it."

"I'm not quite sure I can spot what's behind that little remark."

"Part of you enjoys looking down on people like him. You're up there doing things only very, very few people can. It's an exclusive club."

"He has his own exclusive clubs. Besides, he'd still be coining it, even in time of war."

She smacked his chest. "You know what I mean."

"I know we shouldn't let your father spoil our day so I'm saying no more about him."

She wriggled against him, working him more fully into her.

"Mmm!" she said. "You nearly . . . got out. Ah, that's better. Yes. Let's forget about him."

"And his many millions," Selby said.

"And his many millions," she repeated with her soft giggle.

"How many?"

"Who cares?" she said with the air of someone to whom worrying about money was something only others did. "We've got important things to do at . . . this . . . moment. Do you still carry those knickers I left that day in your flying suit pocket?"

"What knickers?"

She smacked him again. "You know what knickers!"

"Oh those red things that look like a postage stamp with strings attached?"

"Have you any idea what that postage stamp cost?"

"Working on the principle that less is more, I'd say somebody's mortgage."

She gave him a third smack.

"Hey," he protested. "What are you suddenly? A man beater?"

She bared her teeth playfully at him. "Maneater, more like."

He reached for his watch which was next to a phone on the bedside table, checked it, then put it back down. He picked up the phone.

"Well, maneater," he said, "I've got a call to make."

"Can't it wait?"

"Not this one."

He dialled an untraceable number. The double tone that sounded in his ear told him all he needed to know. An Alpha was on. He put the phone down and lay back on the bed.

As she looked at him Kim became tense. "What is it?"

There were times when remembrance of the first time he'd set eyes on her tended to return vividly. This was one of those occasions. Perhaps it was the Alpha mission waiting for him that had triggered that particular memory.

It had been at the corporate ball she'd mentioned. He had gone only under duress, doing service as a stand-in escort for his sister Morven. Escaping from the crowd and seeking refuge, he'd seen the neat body, the short black hair, the thickish eyebrows and wide-apart dark eyes that had been so full of mischief as they studied him challengingly. Her small sharp nose had accentuated the generosity of a mouth that, even at that early stage, he'd wanted to kiss. But he'd held off. She had looked fiendishly expensive; not the sort of person who would have had the time for him, or so he'd thought.

The black gown with the gold highlights; the intricately designed

172

gold necklace at her throat; the golden sandals on her feet; the black earrings that hung from small lobes; the black-dialled wristwatch with its golden band had all spoken of painfully rich tastes. Too rich for him, and probably dangerous with it.

But he had reckoned without Sir Julius Mannon's only offspring. She had selected and hunted him out with a single-mindedness that had stunned as well as excited him. She had excited him that first night and the following morning when she had appeared so unexpectedly at his door; and she was still exciting him.

"I've got to go," he now told her regretfully.

"Now?"

"I'm afraid so. I'd better grab a shower and get dressed."

"Can you tell me?" she asked, not really expecting that he would.

"No," he answered gently.

She had moved again, and was now lying fully on top of him. "Will you be all right?"

"Of course I will."

"I love you so much, Mark."

"And I," he said, kissing the tip of the small sharp nose, "love you."

"And my red knickers?"

"And your red knickers."

"Don't you ever go up with anyone else's in your flying suit pocket. Do you hear me?"

"I hear you. That's never going to happen."

"That's all right then," she whispered, moving some more against him.

"Are you ever still?"

"Not while you're in there, I'm not," came another whisper, punctuated by soft intakes of breath. The tremor in her voice was not from fear for his safety. An opaque look had come into the dark eyes and the tip of her tongue flicked out once, twice, to lick at her lips. "One more for the road? One . . . more? And . . . and I can tell . . . just like that morning . . . *oooh* . . . in there . . . you think so . . . too. *Oh-my-oh-my-oh-my . . . ooh yesss!* Oh Mark! Mark! I love . . . I love . . . *I love youuu!"*

As he felt himself falling deeply into her, Mark Selby realised he could not imagine making love to anyone but Kim Mannon, for the rest of his life.

Thirteen

C aroline, in full flight gear but minus her ASV helmet, entered the airlock to one of the full-mission, air combat simulator domes. She shut the outer door to maintain sealing then opened the second, shutting it as she stepped into the dome itself with its exact, fully functional replica of the two-seat Starfire cockpit.

Carlizzi, also in full gear, was waiting by the mobile access steps with one of the sim section staff, a non-aircrew flight lieutenant with whom he'd been in conversation. Carlizzi was holding a helmet that looked appreciably different from the one he normally used. The man with him held another in one hand.

"Hi, Caroline. Feeling fit?"

"Fit as I'll ever be."

"OK. This is Archie Haxton. Next to Wilby and Ländemann, he's our main man on the Starfire systems. He and his staff will be running the control room for us. And that helmet he's carrying so tenderly is for you."

She shook hands with Haxton. "Hullo, Archie. Haven't seen you in the mess."

"Married quarters," he explained. "So you're going to take our star into the blue yonder."

She smiled. "Yep."

"You're looking happy about it." He tapped at the helmet. "You'll find this bone dome's a good fit. If you're satisfied, you can hang on to it for actual flying of the aircaft as well. When you get aboard, I'll give you a basic brief and Major Carlo will guide you in the specifics once he's installed. So it's up the steps and into the front pocket. I'll hand the dome to you once you're in and secured."

"Right."

She climbed up the steps to the narrow landing that was just beneath the rim of the spacious cockpit, and got in. Haxton followed, waiting until she had secured her harness before handing her the

174

helmet. She placed it on the windscreen rim while she waited for him to continue.

"First," he began, "this is a faithful cockpit replica of the aircraft you'll be flying. It's got six degrees of initial motion cues – pitch up and down, roll left and right, yaw left and right – then the visual system takes over. Instead of the long-travel, full motion set-up of non-static sims in general, this system commences a short-travel motion cue which the visuals then smoothly follow through.

"Without looking at the cockpit movements from the outside, you'd never guess the entire thing wasn't moving in great arcs; rather like the big jobs on stilts. Our system's neatly enclosed, moves slightly but is greatly augmented when the visuals kick in. You'll never detect the stage at which this occurs. A full roll is precisely that.

"This system is exactly like those of the ASV simulators with which you're already familiar and which include infinitely variable weather conditions, day or night. However, there are further enhancements. The visuals, as you'll see when they come on, are even more photo-realistic, and much smoother when they take over from the initial motion cues. Although the ASV sims are excellent in their own right and far superior in general to simulators at other units belonging to countries in NATO, you'll be fooled even more by this particular kit into believing you're flying in the real blue. The only thing this work of technological art can't do—"

"Is leave the ground," she finished for him. "All you sim people say that."

He grinned. "Can't blame a man for trying. However, with this piece of kit, it's even more so. The helmet system has extra functions beyond those you use with your ASV version. Threat warnings are now three-dimensional. In effect, you'll know the precise direction of the threat when the warning tone sounds: ahead, at an angle off your six, below, above, anywhere at all . . . just as nature intended. Your direct voice input is more instinctive and less limited in understanding commands. I know you ASV pilots hate your version of the DVI and seldom use it, if ever. But this is different. I promise you."

"It doesn't argue, does it?"

"Not quite. But it does suggest alternatives."

"What? It makes operational decisions?"

"It *suggests* alternatives," Haxton repeated, stressing the important word. "Your ASV already prioritises its targets. So does this aeroplane, and threats as well. The only difference is that it also vocalises what its got on the MFD. Instead of relying on a normally quick scan of a given page, you've got this little beastie in your ear to remind you."

"Vocalises," she repeated. "I'm going to have to listen to a backseater *and* this thing? I thought all these wonderful systems were supposed to ease workload."

"You can't believe everything you hear," he remarked drily. "People once said computers would do away with paperwork. But seriously, you'll find your workload has been reduced. Considerably."

"I'll take your word for it. So what do I call it? We've aready got Bitchin' Betty, Nagging Nora . . . I think I'll give this one a man's name."

"It's a woman's voice. Tests have shown that artificial intelligence vocals in the cockpit gain more attention if the voice is female." The dryness in his voice was palpable. "Don't blame me. That's what rigorous testing has proved."

"I'll call this one Sodding Sid, and sod his gender."

"He's not smart enough to have a complex about that, but one day who knows? Mark you, I once knew a woman called Sid. A man she certainly wasn't."

"I wouldn't let your wife hear you say that in that tone of voice."

"That's all right. I married her."

"Oops!"

Haxton gave another grin. "You can call your DVI Sodding Sid, if you want to. But don't forget to register your voice with the aircraft or it won't listen to you."

"A kite with attitude. It had to happen."

Caroline looked about her, feeling her way around the cockpit. Though the office of the Echo was itself highly advanced, the Starfire's was even more so. Three main MFDs straddled the cockpit, with the central display stepped down slightly. As on the ASV, they were bordered by several softkeys which could call up a vast number of displays.

Above the central MFD and set in the base of a smaller MFD beneath the HUD, were the two engine power indicators. These were in the form of green digital circles formed by short hatchmarks that increased or decreased round the clockface, according to power setting. A triple-numeric window, giving the power state readout, was at each centre. There were only two ordinary instruments: an artificial horizon and a compass. Both were at the top of the instrument panel on the right side of the HUD. Standby, get-you-home aids. There was also a hidden panel containing more get-you-home instruments.

Haxton was watching as her hands moved round the cockpit. "You seem pleased," he said.

"I am. This feels good."

"Just you wait till the system's fully powered up. At first you won't believe what you're seeing and feeling. You'll be on oxygen as if in the real aircraft, and your pressure suit will squeeze at you according to the Gs you pull. There are bladders in the ejection seat to simulate buffet and add to the sense of movement, say in a tight turn. The entire cockpit will also buffet if you approach the stall in any attitude during flight. She won't let you spin but, if you somehow lose control, you've got the panic button on the stick. Press that and the aircraft takes control and returns to flying integrity."

"That's okay for MiG-29 and Su-27 pilots," she said. "They've got their panic buttons. I won't use mine."

Haxton looked at her. "A little bit of hubris? Is that what I'm hearing?"

"No. I'm simply saying I won't allow myself to get into such a situation."

Haxton raised an eyebrow. "Now I understand how you came to beat Commander Helm."

"You know about that?"

"If there's someone on this station who's been to another galaxy, *he* might not know. Now I think I'll leave you to the tender mercies of Major Carlizzi. I'll go and start the ball rolling. The lights will go out and the show will commence. We'll skip the pre-flight procedures for now, just to get you into the air. So you'll be on the runway, ready for take-off. See how she feels."

Caroline nodded. "All right."

"Fine. Helmet on. Get connected." Haxton went back down the steps.

Caroline put the helmet on as Carlizzi came up and climbed into the back seat. Haxton was right, she thought. The helmet was a perfect fit. It was exactly her size. Someone had been doing their homework.

Haxton pulled the steps free then left the dome.

"Okay, Caroline," came the major's voice. "I've got almost the same equipment fit in the back pocket, including duplicate flying controls, plus the usual backseater stuff. As Archie said, we'll be at the runway threshold at start. When everything's online, engines will be running and standard HUD activated. You can turn on the helmet sight if you want to, but I'd suggest you wait on that for now. Plenty of time to take you through the sighting system. Just to give you the feel of things, do a take-off and fly around for a while."

"Right."

The lights went out, and she gasped. It was as if they were actually outside. She looked about her, then up at the sky. It was a bright day with wisps of cloud high above.

"My God!" she said. "This is the November area for real!"

Carlizzi chuckled. "Not quite real but pretty close. Detailed photo-mapping. The system's got a world coverage you wouldn't believe. Beats even the ASV sims, and they're hot stuff already. Pretty good, huh?"

"*Good?* The ASV sims are more than excellent but you're right. This . . ." She paused, searching for the right words to correctly express her reactions. "That runway's so real. And as for the sky . . ." She looked over each shoulder. She could see behind her as if in a real aircraft.

"Well, Caroline?" came Haxton's voice. "What do you think?"

"I think . . . wow!"

"Sounds like a McCannism to me." Everyone knew about McCann.

"For once, it's appropriate."

Then Carlizzi was talking, brisk and professional. "Checks complete. Voiceprint registration. I'll do the entry from here. Get ready."

"I'm ready."

"Say anything. Voiceprint channel is open."

"This gives me a hard-on," she said.

There was silence.

"Anything wrong?" she asked.

"Thank you for that unusual entry, Flight Lieutenant Hamilton-Jones," Carlizzi said in a tone of voice that wasn't quite sure how to pitch itself. "Nothing's wrong. You gave it a nice long sentence with enough modulation. Listen."

"Voiceprint accepted," she heard as Sodding Sid spoke to her with the sensuous tones of a woman. Then, "'This gives me a hard-on.'"

"That's my voice! It repeated it at me!"

"Naturally. This is standard with the upgraded system. When all ASVs are up to Echo standard, this will be part of the upgrade. It's letting you know it's heard every word."

"Can that be erased?"

"I've entered it into all the voice recognition command systems. You'll have to wait until after the flight. I'd suggest not using that in the real aircraft, unless you don't mind having it listened to by the engineers when they do a routine check. It stays in memory and can only be erased with your own voice."

"Lesson number one," Caroline said ruefully.

"There you go," said the New York-accented AMI major. "Any pilot who flies it for the first time has to do the voiceprint register. They're working on an upgrade that will give access to the aircraft only if your voice is already in memory. Someone can't fake your voice, or try to fool it with a DVI disc in the slot. It checks the voice frequencies; minutely. Unless that person has exactly the same vocal cords as you and speaks in precisely the same way, it just won't start."

"Not so good for someone trying to steal one."

"No good at all. In addition to standard manual access, DVI enhancements let you do the following: data entry, HUD/MFD moding, radio channel selection, weapons selection, autopilot engage/disengage. That's just the beginning. There are plans for a lot more. All November aircraft will receive these upgrades. I'll take you through the voice routines as your conversion progresses. You OK so far?"

"I'm fine."

"OK. Just a routine flight for the first hop. Let's go. Canopy down."

"Roger," Caroline responded, selecting canopy shut. "Canopy coming down."

The warning tone sounded and the clamshell began to lower. It sealed shut, further increasing the sense of reality. The warner stopped.

The engines were running and the hatchmarks were moving round the circles, then they stopped as power setting stabilised at idle thrust. The numerals showed 061 each. The HUD was online and the artificial horizon and compass operational. The MFDs all showed basic displays. On the left was the artificial horizon page with the HUD pitch ladder repeated.

The central display showed the navigational moving map display of the local area, with the aircraft's current position marked by a pulsing red circle midway along a line that marked both heading and reciprocal. The right MFD showed a graphic of the aircraft, with its weapons and fuel load.

The tremors and sounds going through the cockpit were as real as on any aircraft and, in this case, exactly like a fully airworthy Starfire.

"Open her easily," Carlizzi advised. "She's lighter than the ASV Echo. Fast as your own aircraft accelerates, this one's like a lightning bolt. So watch it for the first time. Stay ahead of the curve. Then it's a walk in the park."

"Got it."

"Starfire One for take-off," Carlizzi called.

"Starfire One, you are cleared for take-off," Haxton responded. "QFE 1013. Wind is zero knots."

"Roger November," Carlizzi acknowledged. "QFE is 1013, wind zero. All yours now, Caroline."

The Starfire, unlike other "electric" jets such as the F-16, the Rafale or fly-by-wire prototypes of the Su-27, did not have a sidestick. But Caroline found she liked the solid feel of the central stubby control of the Starfire. She had counted nearly twenty-four function switches and buttons on the throttles and the stick, which would enable her to operate various systems without taking her hands off these primary controls.

"Here goes," she said.

She'd noticed that the Starfire rode perceptibly higher than the ASV. The view was superb.

She held the aircraft on the brakes and smoothly moved the throttles forward. She could feel the powerful tremor going through the aircraft; then she released the brakes and shoved the throttles into full afterburner simultaneously. Carlizzi was right. She *felt* it as the Starfire hurled itself forwards at a rate which, despite her experience with the ASV Echo, still caught her a little by surprise. But she recovered quickly.

In the blink of an eye, it seemed, the aircraft was airborne.

"Wheels," she heard Carlizzi say.

She quickly reached for the lever with the small white wheel which she was pleased to note was in the familiar place. She moved it to the "up" position.

"Gear travelling . . ." Carlizzi announced, ". . . and locked. She's already got plenty of speed. Take her up."

Caroline gave an easy but firm pull on the stick. The travel was minimal but the Starfire kicked its nose up steeply and rushed upwards, accelerating in the climb.

"Oh my God!" Caroline uttered softly. She glanced behind. Far below, the runway pattern was receding at an astonishing rate. It was all so realistic. "It's . . . it's—"

"Quite something?" Carlizzi suggested.

"Yes!"

"You wait until we get to the real bird. That will be something else again. And that was a neat take-off, by the way. I think you're going to do good."

"And *I* think . . . I'm going to love this!"

The Special Research Unit, the Urals: 2100 hours local.

Konstantinova entered the main monitor room of the viral research lab. Olga Vasilyeva was alone.

The doctor looked up from her microscope, her expression neutral. "Come to watch over me?"

"Olga . . ."

"It's all right. Major Lirionova has explained the situation."

"She's Liri," Konstantinova corrected, "and I'm Milla. Remember? We're still your friends."

"Are you?" Vasilyeva retorted.

"What do you mean?"

"Are security people ever anyone's friends? Even your own?"

"Olga . . ."

"It's all right. Doing your job."

"The general feels it's for the best."

"I thought you were going to wait before telling him."

"I told my superior officer—"

"Who seems, in these matters, to be superior to Colonel Abilev himself. So she told her superior officer, the general. Yes, yes. I know how that goes. Everybody has to compete for funding from limited resources, so I suppose I should be grateful. After all, without the kind of money that built this place I could never have done the type of research I'm doing.

"And at a time when even our memorial statues are being stolen for the copper to turn into hard cash, I ought to consider myself privileged. Well, if you're going to be around, you might as well make yourself useful. Take the cartridge out of that machine over there and bring it to me, please. There. That one by the pile of books."

Konstantinova looked around until she saw the computer Olga Vasilyeva was talking about. She went over and removed the cartridge from the zip drive, then carried it over to the doctor.

"Crazy, isn't it?" Vasilyeva said as she took the cartridge. "Thanks. The only one in existence, and it can kill everything we've ever done.

It's always the way. All it ever takes is one little bug." She snapped the cartridge into the new drive, then peered into the microscope. "Take a look at the monitor."

Konstantinova looked. A cell with a reddish border was challenging one with a green edge. Green-edge absorbed the red-brimmed interloper. It simply vanished.

The doctor sighed. "That's the ninety-ninth attempt so far and the ninety-ninth failure." She leaned back, away from the instrument.

"The reddish one was an anti-virus?"

"Tried to be. As you saw, it had no chance. This thing is beginning to look invulnerable. But as long as it exists, our work will be at risk until we can find a way to stop it. I suppose I can almost sympathise with your general. All right, Milla. Your people can have the cartridge at the end of each working day. But if I'm working late, like tonight, I'm afraid you'll just have to babysit."

"Don't remind me," Konstantinova said.

"By the way, the news is Urikov and Melev are livid about your promotions."

"That's a surprise."

"Watch out for those two, Milla. I've seen their kind in places like Angola: soldiers on the edge of discipline. They're nursing big grudges. In their minds, it almost seems as if you got your promotions for beating them. Liri now outranks Urikov, and you outrank Melev. A bad combination. Just watch your step with them. Melev is Belorussian. When a Belarus is good, he can be the best human being in the world. When he's bad like Melev, he can be a total, unredeemable shite . . ."

"Shite?"

"Shite. I got that from an English botanist I met abroad. A woman. I couldn't put into Russian some of her other swear words. Just don't turn your backs on Urikov and Melev."

Konstantinova looked at her. "Thanks for the warning. Sounds like the sort of thing you'd do for a friend."

"We women should stick together. And a dead American lover does not mean I'm a traitor," Vasilyeva added with a ghost of a smile.

Two hours later, she was still working. From time to time, she had asked Konstantinova to type in precise instructions on the keyboard while she continued to peer into the microscope. Every so often she would raise her head to study the monitor.

Still later, she sighed and leaned away from the instrument.

"Nothing," she said wearily. "Not a damned thing! It just keeps devouring anything in its way. It has successfully converted all the nano functions into one: killing. In the world of the mutated nano it is king, emperor, warlord. Nothing must exist beside it, even if it means eventually killing its own host. I've created a monster. Microscopic, but still a monster." She rubbed at her eyes. "And I've had enough for today. You can take the cartridge." Then she gave a quick smile. "Shall I get you a special portable safe?"

"A cartridge box will do; then I'll put the whole thing in our safe. To tell you the truth, I'd rather not have it with me."

"Don't look at me," Olga Vasilyeva said, giving in to a little *schadenfreude*. "Your general's orders. Stay down here long enough and you'll know as much about it as any of us."

"No thanks. Typing in your instructions parrot fashion does not make me a lab genius."

The doctor looked at the Intelligence lieutenant and smiled.

The A1 Autobahn between Hamburg and Bremen, Germany: 0930 hours local, the next morning.

Heading south, *Korvettenkapitän* Axel Maximillian Baron von Wietze-Hohendorf, one of Jason's top poachings from Germany's *Marineflieger*, drove the metallic blue Porsche 911 Carrera 4 coupe at high speed on the unrestricted stretch of motorway. The 285 bhp propelling its relatively light gross weight made for astonishing velocity. His control of the car was absolute.

There was no gripping of the steering wheel, no fidgety side-to-side movement; just a sensitive interfacing with the superb wizardry of the vehicle. He drove the way he flew: always in control, but also in empathy with the machine. There was no darting from lane to lane as he overtook slower cars. It was all done with such timing he had very little need to touch the brakes or to slow down appreciably. The smoothness of his driving ensured that his passenger remained undisturbed.

Noting his crop of fine blond hair, someone had once rashly told Hohendorf that he looked like Hollywood's idea of a Roman. The palest of blue eyes had surveyed this rash person with a distant coolness. Hohendorf had made no response, embarrassing the man – a fellow *Marineflieger* pilot who was not on Tornadoes – far more than if he'd said something. But the unfortunate airman could be forgiven his apparent mistake. Though perhaps taller than the average Roman soldier from the north might have been, Hohendorf's general appearance did sometimes give credence to the idea.

He was exactly six feet tall. Legend had it that on first joining the service, he had informed the examining medical staff that, at a height of 1.8288 metres, he had been constructed with precision. He had meant it as a joke to enliven the solemnity of the occasion. They had not appreciated it. He was slim but looked tough and very fit. His unlined face could at times fool one into thinking him barely out of his teens; until you looked into the eyes which, by contrast, seemed far older.

He took a quick glance at the right-hand seat. Morven Selby had reclined the backrest and was dozing, a dreamy smile on her lips. He was crazy about her.

She had breathed new life into him. When he'd still been with the *Marineflieger* his wife Anne-Marie had walked out on him, leaving him in the depths of despair. Alone in the marital home, he had focussed all his energies on his flying, refusing to allow what she'd done to him to destroy his career as well. Already a highly-skilled instinctive pilot, he had become so finely honed that it was almost as if her departure had forced him to find even more from within himself. But deep inside, she had left an oppressive emptiness.

Anne-Marie, a tall elegant blonde of patrician coolness, was a countess in her own right with lands and a castle in the south of the country to rival the Hohendorf *Schloss* in the Teutoburger Wald.

She had never really wanted to be a service wife, though the cachet of landing a fighter pilot had induced her to make a desultory stab at it. She had been fully aware of Hohendorf's love of flying combat aircraft but had expected that he would soon tire of his toy and take a real job as a senior flying executive with the family airline, of which her father was president and owner. It had been her plan. But she had missed her old jet-setting lifestyle, and Hohendorf hadn't played his part. He'd had no intention of leaving the service. It was thus not long before she left and began an affair with the senior pilot of the airline, leaving Hohendorf to his devices.

Then had come the selection for the November programme.

And then too, had come Morven.

Unable to resist her territorial instincts, Anne-Marie had suddenly rediscovered she had a husband and wanted him back. Hohendorf well knew this had nothing to do with a new flush of love but all to do with saving face. The thought that she was no longer being pined-for had been hard for her to swallow and, considering herself far superior to Morven Selby, she continued to express outrage at Hohendorf loving someone she looked upon as of lower status.

Hohendorf stole another glance at Morven, loving every part of her. Anne-Marie had no idea what true class was. As far as he was concerned, it had nothing to do with castles, lands or wealth. Morven had none of those but she was everything he ever wanted in a woman: her humanity, her warmth, her love . . . He felt a warm glow as he remembered their love-making.

"I can see you," she murmured. "You're having those thoughts again. In the car too."

"You're awake! How long?"

"I saw when you looked the last time. You've been thinking about all those times you've ravished me. I know that look."

"Are you complaining?" he teased.

She made a sound that came from deep within her, stretched in her seat, then pressed one of the buttons at the side of the seat squab to raise the backrest. Her thighs swelled provocatively in her tight jeans. With seeming absentmindedness, she stroked the front of her jeans.

"No complaints," she replied softly. "Can I lean over to kiss you?"

"Let me pass this car first. Then the road is clear."

The Porsche shot past a Mercedes saloon, its engine wailing.

"OK," he said. "Time for a fast one."

Careful not to touch the gear lever, she leaned across to kiss him quickly on the cheek.

"Thank you," he said with a smile.

"My pleasure."

"Ah yes. Your pleasure. I love your pleasures."

"And I know what you mean."

He grinned but said nothing.

"What speed are we doing?" she asked as the road surface appeared to stream beneath their wheels.

"Two hundred and forty-five kilometres an hour . . . about one fifty mph. I have plenty of power still in reserve."

"A hundred and fifty miles an hour?" Her words ended in a squeak.

"Just a cruise. At this speed, my Tornado is already taking off."

"This is not your Tornado."

The Porsche, seemingly glued to the road, entered a wide sweeping bend. It did not budge from its directed path.

"You are afraid?" he asked. "I will slow down."

She stared at the streaming road and shook her head. "I'm never afraid with you. You really do enjoy this car, don't you?"

Hohendorf had only recently replaced his much-loved 968 with the newer car.

He nodded. "I like the way it handles. It is precise, like my plane. And I enjoy the sound of the engine."

"It's getting to me too," she said.

"Normally, people think only men can appreciate this."

"Don't you believe it! I can only afford my creaky old 2CV, but I can still love something like this."

"Would you like to drive it?"

"You'd turn me loose in this? Where I come from, a man never lets a woman near his pride and joy."

"I don't come from where you come from. In a few kilometres, we will be at the autobahn service station Ostetal-Sud. We can stop for gas and have a proper breakfast. You can try the car there. See how you feel with it. It is not like other cars, but I will help you to understand how to drive it. Plenty of room to do so, and we have got a lot of time before we take the ferry from Amsterdam. As we have our tickets, we can board without having to wait in a ticket line. So? You will drive?"

Having received the Alpha warning the night before, he had decided to set off early, cutting short their stay. After spending some time with his parents at the family *Schloss,* they had gone north to Schleswig-Holstein for a quick visit to his former squadron. Then had come the Alpha. So it had been an early departure with just coffee and rolls for a snack breakfast.

Normally, he would have gone the Hamburg route but late April into early May was still too early. The Hamburg ferry didn't start till early June. The Amsterdam route would take fourteen hours to Newcastle. From there he would drive north into Scotland, first to Aberdeen where she lived and worked as a marine biologist then across country to the Moray coast and November One.

She was shaking her head. "I'd rather not, but I appreciate the offer. You have no idea what this means to me."

"My car is your car," he told her simply. "Any time you wish to drive it, just tell me."

She placed a hand on his shoulder and left it there.

He smiled contendedly as they drove on towards the service station, the warmth of her hand coursing through him.

It had been so typically unexpected of him, Morven thought. She knew how much the car meant to him yet he had offered her the chance to share the driving pleasure with him. She felt as if they were children and he had offered to let her play with the most precious toy of his collection which he kept hidden, saving it to share with someone really special.

The time they'd had together at the *Schloss* had been blissful. She had vowed never to return there after the first time he'd invited her. Anne-Marie had turned up unexpectedly but perhaps not surprisingly, given what she now knew about Hohendorf's estranged wife. Morven still recalled the incident with considerable embarrassment.

Axel's mother had been very good to her, standing up for her against Anne-Marie. The Baroness had never forgiven her erstwhile daughter-in-law for what she'd done to her son.

But it had been a different story with Mark. His antagonism towards the relationship had at times been intense and she had only belatedly appreciated the dangerous rivalry in the air it had created between the two pilots. One particular ocurrence had almost led to Mark crashing into the sea during a ferocious training exercise in air combat.

Neither Axel nor Mark himself had told her of it. But Elmer Lee McCann had spoken to Kim, convinced that Mark would one day take things too far and kill all four crew members in the two aircraft. For Elmer Lee to express worry to anyone outside the cockpit about anything his pilot did was a unique phenomenon in itself. Kim had taken it very seriously indeed and had subsequently relayed the entire story to her.

She didn't know that Selby had been bawled out by the wing commander, for Jason had seen it recorded in all its ignominious glory in the Ops Centre.

But things had changed now. Her brother had long since given a sort of blessing to the relationship. But she knew he was still unhappy about the fact that Anne-Marie still hovered around. Axel wanted a divorce. Anne-Marie was still spitefully refusing. That particular battle seemed set to continue.

Morven understood her brother's protectiveness. When she was still barely into her teens their mother had died, knocked down by a lorry not far from their home one dreadful winter. Their father had died a year later both of a broken heart and a heart attack. It had fallen to Mark to become the protector. He still tended to continue the role, even though she was now a grown woman and despite the fact she'd told him often enough that the time for him to let go was long overdue.

She was pleased that he had found Kim Mannon – though it was more like Kim having hunted him out. She liked Kim and already looked upon her as a sister.

You are very thoughtful," Hohendorf said into her reverie.

"Oh, just remembering a few things."

"Nice ones?"

"Most are."

"And the others?"

"Not serious enough to worry about."

"OK." He would not press her. A large blue sign with white lettering flashed past. "Ostetal-Sud in five kilometres. We will get the gas, eat and have a little walk around. When we are finished here we go on to Osnabruck, then we take the A30 which will take us into Holland. After that, it will not be far to Amsterdam-Ijmuiden."

"Osnabruck, did you say? That's near Tecklenburg, isn't it? Near your family."

"Yes, but we do not have time to stop again. I have booked us a fine cabin like the last one," he continued, "for the return trip. We can have a very nice long rest on the boat."

"Oh yes? And what will we do there?"

He smiled. "Sleep?"

"You must be joking," she said.

She was so refreshing. It was one of the many things he loved about her. With Anne-Marie, he would almost have had to make an appointment.

"Hey," she said, tapping at his shoulder.

"What?"

"You've got that look again."

His smile widened.

Thank you, God, he said to himself, *for bringing this beautiful woman to me.*

He had not thought that one day he'd allow himself to sufficiently drop his emotional guard to fall in love again but Morven proved him wrong from the moment he saw her. He was quite unaware that she was Selby's sister. It wasn't long, however, before he also realised it would not have made the slightest difference, had he known at the time.

At first, while appreciating Selby's natural anxiety for his sister, Hohendorf could not quite understand the other pilot's overt hostility. Selby had insisted it was because Hohendorf was still married, despite the fact that the marriage had been effectively over well before Morven arrived on the scene. The incident with Anne-Marie at the *Schloss* had only exacerbated matters; but when the hostility culminated in the near-fatal incident over the North Sea, Hohendorf was forced to confront Selby over his attitude.

Obsessed with besting Hohendorf that day, Selby had lost his situation awareness and in a high-energy tight turn had almost dipped a wing into the water. Had that happened, the result would have been catastrophic; Selby and McCann would have died instantly. Luckily, Selby had recovered in time but it had been unpardonably reckless flying.

It would have been a poor enough display by a baby pilot but from someone of Selby's calibre it had been astonishing. Having given himself the fright of his life, Selby had been shocked into seeing things differently and his attitude seemed to change overnight. The fact that the wing commander had severely carpeted him might also have had something to do with it.

Yet the strangest of things was that on operational missions Selby the consummate professional never put a foot wrong. In combat, Selby always unquestioningly backed him up and Hohendorf knew that Selby had a high respect for him as a pilot; a respect that was mutual. It was as if a switch was thrown and all hostilities paused for the duration.

Some time ago, Caroline Hamilton-Jones had told him that Neil Ferris had once described them as twins, so alike were they in their flying skills yet so very different to someone who knew what to look for. Ferris had even claimed to be able to spot them in the air by their flying styles, even if he had no prior knowledge of who was flying which aircraft.

On occasion, Hohendorf had even considered the thought that despite the concept behind the November programme Selby still harboured deep anti-German feelings. He'd once asked Morven and had instantly regretted doing so. She had been shocked and angry. Hohendorf had killed the subject fast, seeing how unhappy the question made her. They never spoke of it again.

He gave her another quick glance out of the corner of his eye. He would never tire of her. She had the strong frame and clear complexion of someone who spent much of her time working out of doors. As a marine biologist and a fully qualified diver, that came with the job. Her hair, dark and richly lustrous, was long enough to fall well past her shoulders. Her eyes were a luminous green, her face heart-shaped with a firm chin. A high curving forehead and a strong nose that contrasted sharply with a vulnerable mouth gave her a striking beauty. As for her legs . . .

Hohendorf paused his thoughts, realising where they were leading.

"There you go again." Her voice broke into his daydream. "It's becoming a habit."

"There I go where?"

"That look of yours is back. You'll have to wait till we get on the boat, Axel."

"I am so obvious?"

"I caught that last look you gave me. Your eyes were taking my clothes off."

"You do these things to me."

"I should hope so too."

He had cut speed and moved into the inside lane. He now moved smoothly into the exit that led to the service station.

"Ostetal-Sud," he said.

Fourteen

November base, 10.01 hours local. The same day.

Jason's office intercom beeped.

"Yes, Rose," he said into it.

"All Alpha pilots have checked in, sir. I've just received Capitano Bagni's. His was the last. Squadron Leader Selby arrived last night. The others are on their way."

"Excellent. When they're all on the station, arrange an Alpha briefing for one hour after the last man has arrived, if this is before twenty-two hundred hours. If later, O-eight hundred hours the next day."

"Yes, sir."

"By the way, does Mark Selby know he's now a squadron leader?"

"Not yet, sir. I thought I'd let you drop the bombshell."

"Thank you, Rose," Jason said drily, "but yes . . . I'll drop it at the briefing."

"Mr Hohendorf's double K has also come through. There's a letter in your pile from the *Marineflieger* confirming it and another from his old unit to say they took the opportunity while he was over in Germany to present the new rank to him. They hoped you wouldn't mind."

"Don't mind at all."

"I think they're rather proud of him over there."

"So they jolly well should be. And ask Doc Hemelsen to meet me at the Starfire simulator section in . . . thirty minutes."

"Right away, sir."

"Thank you, Rose."

Half an hour later, Jason drove into his parking slot outside the vast simulator building. There were parking spaces bearing the legend WG CDR JASON all over the huge spread of the November base. No one ever parked in them, even by mistake and even when some might not have been used for weeks. Nobody wanted to be caught out if Jason made a surprise visit.

Helle Hemelsen was already waiting, standing by her car. The day was bright but there was a smell of rain in the air. A stiffish breeze came off the Firth, strong enough to play at her clothing.

Hemelsen was one of those women whose beauty was so well hidden that if you managed to spot it its sheer power left you breathless. She always dressed in a manner which though smart was also somehow frumpy. Her long fine hair, which could gleam almost white in the sunshine, she always wore tightly coiled whether she was wearing her cap or not. Her spectacles magnified eyes that carried an indefinable power and appeared to hide many secrets. Her smile was always warm, and her ability to make people feel at ease was perfect for the job that Jason had poached her from the Danes to do.

There were many on the unit who thought her incredibly sexy. Some fantasised about what it would be like to see her with that magnificent head of hair let down and the glasses removed. They would always remain fantasies.

"Thanks for coming, Helle," Jason said as he climbed out of his car.

The Danish major saluted, then smiled at him. "The boss calls, I appear."

"I'm never sure who's boss around you," he said.

"Don't even trying playing mind games with me," she said with easy familiarity. "You're talking to the expert."

"Don't I know it! But this morning, I want the expert to listen in on Caroline."

She nodded. "OK." She looked about her, glancing at the parked cars as they walked towards the entrance. "You can learn plenty from watching the cars people drive."

"Oh do come off it, Helle. That's glossy magazine stuff. I don't expect my resident soothsayer to believe such nonsense."

"Some of it's padded out by the magazines, of course. But there is an element of truth. Take Caroline. She has bought herself a new MG sports car to celebrate returning here as a fighter pilot. Knowing the person she is, it is what I would have expected. Some of the aircrews, and non-aircrew, tend to buy according to nationality. Others don't.

"Hohendorf has always owned Porsches, but Flacht, his fellow-German and a family man, came over from Germany with a humble Datsun saloon. Now he drives a Volvo. It fits the profile, but not quite. Hohendorf didn't buy his Porsches because they're German but because they're Porsches.

"Selby still uses the all-wheel-drive Ford Cosworth he's had for a long time now; and it's in perfect condition. Better than some brand new cars. McCann always buys American and, with the exception of one hiccup, always the Corvette. Bagni, Italian cars every time. He started with a little Fiat sports car and now has a Barchetta – another Fiat. Stockmann, our US Marine, also buys American. For him, it's the Firebird. But Cottingham buys British: a Jaguar. My fellow Dane, Christiansen, has a Saab. As expected . . ."

"And you?"

"Oh, I fit the stereotype," she said cheerfully. "Typical Scandinavian." She pointed to her own Saab.

"Anyone less typical, I've yet to meet," Jason said as they approached the entrance to the building. "I wouldn't put it past you to have bought that car deliberately, to appear to fit the stereotype."

"Careful, sir," she said drily. "You'll start learning all my secrets."

He looked at her warily. "Oh no you don't. You always try a sneak analysis on me. Is that what this business about the cars was all about?"

"No. I was merely making an observation."

"That my crews are predictable?"

"In the case of your crews, certainly not. Their skills in the air prove it. They're very individualistic, despite their apparent predictability, and are very reliable. They bought the cars they wanted. Cottingham, for example, has always wanted to own a Jaguar. It was a long-held dream. Bagni's cars are Italian, for sure, but always the same make, and so on."

"Why do I still feel this is more about me than it is about them?"

"Are you ever going to put Antonia Thurson out of her misery?" Helle Hemelsen was looking at him with a sideways tilt of her head, the tiniest of smiles at the corners of her mouth.

The unexpected question almost threw him. "Are you ever going to stop testing me?"

"It's what I'm here for. You command all this expanse of military real estate."

"Time to stop testing the boss," he said firmly. "You're here to listen to Flight Lieutenant Hamilton-Jones."

"Yes, sir," she said as they entered.

He still felt he'd lost that round. Par for the course.

Caroline marvelled at the agility of the Starfire in the virtual environment in which she was currently fighting. The world about her looked so real, she believed it. There were even vortices streaming from the opposing aircraft as they flashed past. There had been no weapons exchanges. The current exercise was intended to get her accustomed to using the aircraft in a fight and making the maximum use of the astonishing manoeuvrability afforded by the thrust-vectoring nozzles. So far, she had not been tapped by the opposing aircraft.

Compared to the formidable ASV Echo, the Starfire was a twinkling demon. The aircraft complemented each other, she felt. The Starfire was a light-bladed stiletto to the ASV Echo's razor-sharp flick knife.

"I'm going to request a pause, Caroline," Carlizzi said. "You're doing so well, I think we can got hot on this. Pause the simulation, Control," he added to simulator controllers.

"Roger," came Archie Haxton's voice. "Simulation paused."

They came to a halt in mid-air.

"We couldn't have done that for real," Caroline quipped. "Hey, I don't like this war. I'm stopping it."

"If only," Carlizzi said seriously. "OK. As I said, we're going to use the hot stuff. So one more check of the DVI commands. Once we're back in, you've got to use them instinctively. The intention is to give yourself an extra window in the time available. Parts of a second can make the difference between a kill for you or for the other guy. You don't have to use the DVI if you feel manual input is faster in the situation facing you. This thing's here to help, not command you. Got that?"

"Got it."

"OK. Here's a reminder of the weapons commands. Check out your left MFD."

Carlizzi had called up the weapons command page and had patched it over to the front cockpit. She scanned the list.

Command	Weapon	
ALPHA ONE	Skyray Beta	X LNG RNG
ALPHA TWO	Skyray Alpha	LNG/MED RNG
ALPHA THREE	Krait	MED/SHORT RNG
GAMMA ONE	Gun	HI SPEED
GAMMA TWO	Gun	MED SPEED
GAMMA THREE	Gun	LO SPEED
GAMMA FOUR	Pulse Cannon	

"That's all you require for now, and for the mission," Carlizzi went on. "There are others for bombs and air-to-ground missiles but for this mission they're not in our ball park. Remember, you do this instinctively. It must become second nature; but it's always good to know that page is there if you need it. Are you OK for restart?"

"I'm ready."

"Fine. One other thing: you won't be flying against the computers. Although they've been programmed with the moves from some of the hottest fighter jocks internationally from World War One to the present, it's still best to have a human opponent. Fighter combat is never absolute. There are always all kinds of variations on the theme. So two of the other domes are linked to this one for the fight."

"You mean there are two blokes out there waiting to take me on?"

"Sure are."

"Thanks for nothing, Major!" Caroline said.

"You can hack it."

"I'm glad you think so. Will you tell me who they are?"

"Now that would really spoil the fun."

"Thanks again for nothing."

"Any time." Carlizzi grinned in his mask. "When we resume, things are gonna happen fast, real fast. So heads up. Ready?"

"I'm ready," she repeated.

"OK. Resume, Control."

"Roger," Haxton acknowledged. "Resuming."

Carlizzi had not been wrong. Almost immediately, warnings sounded in her helmet: one behind and below, the other high at eleven o'clock.

She went for DVI. "Weapons!" she snapped.

"Weapons mode selected," came Sodding Sid's voice immediately. "Armed."

"Helmet sight on," she advised Carlizzi. "OK you sods," she said to her unknown opponents, "you're not going to get me in a sandwich." The sighting arrow had confirmed the location of the high bandit.

"Alpha Two," she told the DVI.

"Alpha Two selected," Sodding Sid confirmed.

Almost immediately she got the tone from the missile, but it had not yet achieved lock. Whoever was up there was spoofing but, like all November missiles, the Skyray could autonomously burn through jamming and dodge spoofs.

She hauled the Starfire into a climb, staying out of afterburners to avoid giving an unnecessarily hot infrared signature to whoever was waiting below. She broke the climb suddenly by pulling onto her back, rolled ninety degrees almost immediately, pulled into a tight G-intensive turn, rolled upright and again climbed steeply, hitting the burners very briefly as she did so.

There was an immediate warning from the bandit below. The 3D location of the sound told her precisely where he was. She flicked onto her back and pulled into a steep dive. The arrow on the helmet found the quarry and instantly the hunting target box solidified and pulsed. The surprise move had given her what she'd hoped for.

IN RNG appeared on the helmet. SHOOT.

She fired. The simulator's computers sent a missile streaking off towards target, marking the virtual sky with its passage. In the distance below there was a sudden bloom of flame. A faint rolling sound was heard on her headphones. Sound effects courtesy of the simulator.

"Alpha Three!" she bawled to Sid, ordering a Krait to be armed as she hauled the Starfire round.

"Alpha Three selected," came the soft-toned acknowledgement.

Carlizzi, who had deliberately remained silent, now said, "That was a shit-hot move." He sounded impressed. "In air fighting the quick unexpected move is always better than fighting like two cats after the same fish, or looking fancy. That gives the bandit's buddies time to come in and zap your head off while you're thinking up all those hot manoeuvres. Surprise was complete. What made you do it?"

"I wanted him to think I was going after the high boy. While high boy was getting ready to counter me, I went after the real shooter who was so busy trying to sneak up he never expected me to turn on him."

"You fight mean, Caroline." Carlizzi sounded as if he were enjoying a private joke. He checked behind. "High boy's coming down, turning hard to stay on our six. He's reeling you in. Looks like he wants to gun you down. Go to guns."

She didn't waste time confirming. "Gamma One!" she ordered on the DVI.

"Gamma One selected."

"All right," she muttered to her unknown adversary. "You want a gunfight? You've got one."

The artificial world tumbled about her as she continued to deny the bandit a gun solution; but whoever was in the other dome was drawing inexorably closer. Although he could not get on her six she was not shaking him off either.

Suddenly she had an inspired thought. "Who the hell's behind me? Commander Helm?"

"No. Even if I would tell."

"Definitely not him?"

"Definitely not."

"Who . . . is . . . it? Mark Selby? Is he back? Nico? Major Gireaud?"

"If you waste time trying to work out who's coming up your tail, you're going to get your ass reamed. Come on, Caroline! Enough of the questions. The fight is all."

Another sixty seconds of hard manoeuvring passed. Even the super agile Starfire seemed unable to shake off her pursuer.

Jesus, she thought. *Who the hell is this? Axel Hohendorf! It must be him. He got back early and . . .*

Reason told her it could not be Hohendorf.

The aircraft she was fighting were representations of the Mig-29 and the Su-27. The computers had endowed the representative models with exactly the same flight characteristics as the real aircraft and the modular design of the simulator cockpits had enabled the engineers to kit out the adversary cockpits in the other domes with equipment very close to emulating the two bandit aircraft.

Many other aircraft could be represented in the domes with corresponding flight performances. Any pilot getting into the cockpit fitted out as an aircraft with which he was familiar would find no serious differences.

She had put the MiG out of the game with her lucky shot but the Sukhoi was still giving her a hard time.

"What are you doing wrong?" Carlizzi queried calmly.

"I'm doing every bloody thing I can!"

"Think."

She thought. Suddenly she rolled left, continued through but instead of breaking right fell into a dive. Immediately, she hauled on the stick. The additional pressure caused the vectoring nozzles to kick the tail further down. The nose pitched up, abruptly cutting the dive and sending the Starfire into a climb. She had the throttles at combat burner though speed was relatively low. She kept up the backward pressure.

The Starfire was almost pivoting about its axis.

Looking up through the canopy, she saw the bandit aircraft hanging nicely above her. The targeting arrow had found it and the box was moving nicely towards it.

I've got you! she almost yelled.

But no. He was no longer there.

"Shit!" she swore. "I've lost him!"

"Don't be hard on yourself. That was an inspired move. Better than going round in those goddam circles you were describing before, no matter how small. You caught him out. You're beginning to think. And remember, *he* hasn't been able to get you yet."

She didn't get him but he didn't succeed either. When "Knock it off" was called, she brought the simulated Starfire back to a perfect landing.

She raised the canopy thankfully. Her entire body felt damp within her flight gear.

The dome lights came on as the visuals were switched off. The cockpit continued its background electronic humming.

"That was good stuff, Caroline," Carlizzi said. "You're getting to know the aircraft pretty well, and fast. I think you're nearly ready for a real flight."

"Thank you, Carlo. So tell me, who were my opponents?"

"Why don't you wait and see?"

As they were releasing their harnesses, the door to the dome opened. More than one person entered.

She turned in her seat to look, and saw Haxton moving the steps towards the cockpit. Then three other people came into view. Her eyes widened in astonishment.

Jason and Helm, in flight overalls, were looking up at her with barely perceptible smiles. Behind them was Helle Hemelsen, who seemed amused.

"Shit, Major," she hissed at Carlizzi, "you told me it wasn't Commander Helm!"

"It wasn't. You'd already shot him down."

"Shit!" she said again. "That's twice now I've done that to him. So that was the boss in the Su-27?"

"Aren't you glad I didn't tell you?"

"Well, Caroline?" Jason called up. "If you're quite finished whispering to your backseater, care to come down?"

"Yes, sir! On my way."

She made her way down to the floor and looked at Jason and Helm awkwardly.

"Didn't know you two were in the domes, sir. Hullo, Doc."

Hemelsen nodded at her.

"And why should you?" Jason demanded. "You would not have known the identities of your adversaries in a real fight."

"No, sir."

"That's twice now, Miss Hamilton-Jones," Helm said, but he seemed to be actually smiling. "Is it personal?"

"Er . . . no, sir! I just did . . . something unexpected."

"Good move. Always the unexpected. It is the way to fight in the air."

"Yes, sir."

"And you gave me a very difficult time," Jason said. "I was never able to get a gun solution. And I did try. A good show, Caroline. But never forget this: something that worked once in a particular situation may be lethal in the next. If we were to re-fly that fight and you tried the same manoeuvre, I'd be waiting for you. *Never* repeat yourself. Remain fluid at all times and keep your opponent permanently guessing if you can possibly manage it."

"Yes, boss."

"You did very well."

"Thank you, sir!"

Jason, once again in uniform, was slowly walking the short distance back to the cars with Helle Hemelsen. The *Fregattenkapitän*, still in overalls but wearing his white *Marineflieger* cap with gold braid on black peak, followed them out.

"She's getting quite good. I'd better watch my reputation. People will start thinking I'm getting soft."

"Somehow, Dieter, I don't think that's likely to happen. And thanks for coming to help me spring the surprise."

Helm chuckled. "She surprised *us*. That was a top move."

"Yes it was, wasn't it?"

"She's turning into a good fighter jock, that one . . . if we can call women pilots jocks."

"As long as no one calls them jockesses," Helle Hemelsen said with the tiniest of smiles.

"Major," Helm said to her gravely, "I would not dare. Now I'd better go off and see if I can find a baby pilot to scare." He saluted. "Sir."

Jason returned the salute and watched his deputy leave.

"Comments?" he said to the doctor as Helm started his car and drove off.

"About Caroline? She's coping exceptionally well. The pressure of the coming mission does not seem to be getting to her. She's focussing all her energies on doing the job properly. Like all your people here, she doesn't want to let you down."

"*Me?*"

"Of course you. I have said this to you before. This entire place runs on an energy that comes from you. Your crews are proud to have been chosen, proud of the concept of this place, and have the highest regard for you. This includes Commander Helm and Colonel da Vinci. Commanders in their own right, their respect for you is total. You're even able to have the senior officers at your beck and call . . ."

"Never my beck and call. Lowly wing commanders do not have air vice-marshals and American air force generals at their beck and call."

"Perhaps not in those precise terms, but they certainly fight hard for you. The air vice-marshal is your champion out there. General Bowmaker sees in you what he was as a younger man and probably wishes he had done something like this. Even that great cynic, Charles Buntline, likes you. Of course, he would never admit it . . . at least not to your face."

"I would certainly not expect *that*, not from the Charles Buntline I know." They had reached her car. "Better let you get back to your office." He held out a hand. "Thanks for coming."

She shook it. "You're welcome. When I first got here you shook hands only as a polite necessity. It was all very British and correct. You're getting dangerously continental. There are so many of us around now."

"I pick up some of your bad habits," he said easily, "you pick up some of ours."

She smiled and saluted. "If you say so, sir."

He returned her salute and waited until she got into her car. She gave him a little wave as she drove away.

There were those on November One who were of the opinion that the Danish major was secretly in love with the wing commander.

Very wisely, they kept those opinions to themselves.

Moscow, the same moment in time.

The immaculate Colonel Gregor Levchuk knocked once on the door to Kurinin's office, and entered. He carried a single sheet of paper, a computer printout.

Kurinin looked up expectantly. "Gregor?"

"I've received an intriguing report from the communications surveillance department, General."

"How old?"

"It's just come in. But the eavesdrop itself was over a period of days. Three encrypted bursts, very brief, from within western Europe."

"That's not news. It goes on all the time. We pick up theirs, they pick up ours. Then we all have fun trying to decipher each others' messages."

"Ah yes, but I feel this is different. One came from northern Italy, one from northern Germany and one from London."

"Isn't there a better pinpoint? Source and destination?"

Levchuk shook his head. "London is the closest pinpoint; but there's so much going out of there anyway, it was nearly swamped by other traffic."

"Most of which was probably ours," Kurinin said with dry humour.

Levchuk paused. "Yes, General."

"Smile a little, Gregor!" Kurinin chided. "If we didn't, we'd all go mad on this insane planet."

"Er . . ."

"Never mind. So, what makes these bursts of code any more interesting than the thousands we trawl through? You have no source and no destination."

"That is, in itself, of interest. Someone's trying hard to avoid being identified."

"Perhaps. We do that. They do that. I need more."

"The ultimate destination, as I've said, remains hidden. There's an elaborate routing system. There was no trace after one reached America."

"One of the many American Intelligence agencies?"

"No way of telling so far. As I've said, our attempted tracer came up against a brick wall. If you'll take a look, General."

"The 'shadow' organisation?"

"As with the American agencies, we have nothing to go on."

Levchuk laid the printout on the desk, spreading it open for Kurinin's scrutiny. It was a diagram that looked like a drummer's brush, but double-headed. A single bright yellow horizontal line joined two verticals, depicted in black. Beyond each vertical a multitude of yellow dashed lines radiated.

"The horizontal line is the burst of code," Levchuk explained, "and the vertical bars the blocks placed in the paths of our trace attempts. Beyond the bars are the possible sources and destinations of the messages. Not only are we currently unable to break the encrypted bursts themselves, we can't even breach the blocking codes."

"All of which is most intriguing, Gregor. But you still haven't given me anything concrete. I want a prognosis."

"My instincts."

Kurinin stared at him. "What?"

"We've known each other a long time, General. You know what my instincts are like. I feel there's something to these bursts of code that should interest us. The bars on that diagram – which I call gates – represent the cut-off points in each of the three locations mentioned.

"In Germany, the lower gate begins just south of Bonn. The upper is the Danish border. In Italy, the lower gate is south of Rome and the upper on the Italian/Swiss frontier. For London, the lower gate is in Kent, the upper in Hertfordshire." Levchuk pronounced the county the English way. "That's as close as we can pinpoint in each case."

"And your prognosis?"

"Important enough to warrant further investigation. My instincts are almost shouting. These three were highlighted by the computers as meriting a closer look. I'd like to watch for more. We've introduced a programme that will automatically piggy-back the burst next time it comes, then travel to both source and destination."

"What if those 'gates' of yours detect the intruder? There may be a retaliatory strike in their programming. We could lose entire chunks of memory and files. Are you suggesting we take that risk?"

"There is something else," Levchuk said, instead of making a direct reply.

"Which is?"

"We've never picked these up before. Their protection means they're not normal traffic. I suggest we set up a special team whose task it will be to maintain a permanent covering watch for the next transmissions."

"Very well, Gregor. Do it. I trust your instincts."

"Thank you, General."

Airline flight to Aberdeen, Scotland. 2000 hours local.

Niccolo Bagni, in black jeans, buttoned-up blue Oxford shirt and subtly co-ordinating Armani jacket, relaxed in his seat. He possessed a high forehead, a face of strong planes and a proud nose. His dark hair was trimmed close and his dark brown eyes tended to gleam in certain types of lighting. Bagni was not a big man, a good five inches under six feet. His body was compact yet there was an elegance about him that belonged to someone much taller.

He glanced out of the aircraft window, hoping the notorious Haar, the fast-moving and unpredictable sea fog that could sometimes affect the airport, would not be present to delay or divert the landing. So far, there had been no announcements from the flight deck to the passengers about any poor weather conditions up ahead.

His route had been Florence – Dusseldorf – Aberdeen and this was the final leg of his flight. Fifteen minutes to landing. Once through Customs, he'd get his car from the car park for the journey back to November One.

He'd received the Alpha warning in Florence the day before after a particularly enjoyable time with Bianca. She had still not yet agreed to marry him. Despite having been lovers for years she had not changed her mind about marriage while he continued to be a fighter pilot. A highly successful clothes designer with boutiques in Paris and New York, as well as in Milan, her earnings far outstripped his.

But money was not the problem. She was almost pathologically terrified of being made a widow and seemed to believe that the day she married him the countdown would begin to a fatal ending of his career. For his part, he could not imagine giving up the job he loved so much to become the accessory husband of a star of the fashion world. He didn't want to be known as "Mr Bianca Mazzarini".

"Why should we marry?" she'd said to him. "We love each other and our lovemaking is wonderful. We are happy as we are. Let us not do anything to spoil it. Before you went to that place in England—"

"Scotland."

"Scotland, England, it is the same."

"Don't let the Scots hear you."

"You know what I am saying, Niccolo. Before you went over there, you were not so bothered about marriage."

"Many things have changed. I see life differently. Do not misunderstand me. I don't want you to think I want to own you . . ." No one could "own" Bianca.

"I know you don't want to own me. But think of this: as long as you are still flying where would we live? What would be different? I would still not live at your base. We would be doing exactly the same as now. I am already faithful to you, Nico. Marriage would not make me more faithful."

Even before he'd put the question – as he'd done on a previous occasion – he'd known her reply. But he was beginning to wish she was there to be embraced at the end of a particularly trying day, or mission. Surely, he'd thought, she must have the same feelings at the end of her day?

"Of course I feel that way," she'd said when he'd asked about it. "Shall I close my boutiques to be with you all the time? Would I be the same Bianca then?"

He knew she would not be.

"And I," he'd told her, coming honestly to terms with it, "would not be the same Nico if I stopped flying fighters."

"I know," she'd told him, her voice soft and warm. She wanted the fighter pilot, but not a fighter pilot husband.

"But time can be so short sometimes," he'd said unexpectedly, surprising even himself.

Her eyes had widened at him. For the briefest of moments, a very real fear had come into them. "*Never* say this to me again, Nico! Promise!"

Her reaction had startled him. "Bianca, it was just a comment."

"Never say that again. Promise me!"

"All right, all right. I promise."

Thinking back on the exchange, Bagni recalled the look on her face. It had been close to panic. He'd never seen her like that before and even now could not quite understand it.

The familiar ping as the seat-belt lights came on interrupted his thoughts. He clipped on the belt and, like every pilot he knew, began to listen to every cadence of the aircraft as the flight crew prepared for the landing.

Landings. Once, they had been his own secret nightmare.

Bagni's artistry in the air had earned him the nickname of "El Greco" from his former colleagues in the *Aeronautica Militare Italiana*. Though he was Florence born, his family had originally come from Syracuse in Sicily, which might have had something to do with the name. He was proud of the fact that he was in part descended from the ancient Phoenician traders who had once plied the Mediterranean.

Despite being a brilliant flyer Bagni had been terrified of landings, certain each one was going to be his last. Although he always landed perfectly, it made little difference to his private fear. When he'd been selected for the November programme, that fear had doubled. Flying two-seat aircraft, he had reasoned, would mean he'd have to worry about killing his backseater as well.

But flying at November One had progressed so well that he

had begun to push this very special nightmare to the back of his mind. Then something quite appalling had happened, bringing it screaming back at him. Always deadly in air combat – whether in training or during a real fight – his to-the-limit flying had caused the relatively inexperienced Richard Palmer to suffer the G-induced loss of consciousness that in turn led to the crash that had killed both Palmer and Neil Ferris.

Bagni had then performed the worst landing of his entire career; after two very shaky tries. Sergeant Gail Graham, then Jason's secretary/PA and about to be commissioned, had been Palmer's girlfriend. Bagni had never forgotten how devasted she had been. Sometimes, he still saw her face.

Going straight to the mess after a ghastly debrief, Bagni had shut himself in his room and had sat staring at his violently shaking hands for hours. He'd felt he had killed four people that day. Gail Graham had left the unit, but Caroline had returned in style.

The next morning Bagni had gone to Jason to request being grounded. It had all been his fault, he'd told his CO. He'd also confessed his fear of landings. Jason's response had been to order Bagni into flight gear to carry out ten consecutive landings, with Jason himself in the back seat. Each landing had been flawless. The wing commander had sent him away after saying there would be no more talk of grounding. He had never looked back.

The airliner slammed onto the runway with a force that jolted Bagni back to his surroundings.

A young businesswoman who had joined the flight at Dusseldorf was sitting in the aisle seat next to him.

"That was a rough one," she said. "I saw by your expression you didn't think much of it, either. Do you fly then?"

"A little."

"Oh well. You know about these things. You should tell him off." She smiled at him nervously.

"We're safely on the ground now. It's all over."

"Thank God for that!"

He didn't see her again once they'd got off the aircraft. He was relieved to find that his car was safe and that no one had tampered with it. He put his case into the boot, slung his jacket into the back and climbed in behind the wheel.

It was still fifteen or so minutes to sunset, which meant at least forty-five minutes of reasonable light before dark.

He started the engine and drove off.

Thoughts of marriage to Bianca, the nervous businesswoman,

vanished like the shedding of a temporary skin. A subtle change came over him. He was back on November turf. He was focussed on the Alpha mission.

He was once more a November pilot.

Fifteen

November base the following day. 0900 hours.

Jason was in Rose Gentry's office, on his way to his own.

"What's the status on Bagni and Hohendorf?" he asked.

"Mr Bagni got in last night, sir," she replied.

"Good. And Hohendorf?"

"He'll be on the Amsterdam ferry. When he left, he said he'd be taking that route across and back. The eighteen hundred from Amsterdam yesterday was the first since his receipt of the Alpha. He'll definitely be on it. That takes about fourteen hours. According to the ferry people, it should arrive in Newcastle by O-nine hundred today. He'll be dropping Miss Selby off in Aberdeen, then come straight here.

"It's two hundred and thirty-four miles to Aberdeen. In that car of his, allowing for traffic and hopefully escaping the attentions of any traffic police, I'd give him well under five hours to make it there if he sticks to the speed limit. Less if he doesn't; particularly if he takes the A1 all the way from Newcastle to Edinburgh, then continues the journey via Glenrothes and Dundee. Thirty minutes or so in Aberdeen for tea or coffee and perhaps a warm goodbye . . ."

"I don't think we need that part, Rose," Jason said quickly.

"No, sir," she said, unabashed. "Leaving Aberdeen and again allowing for slow-moving traffic and traffic police, I'd put him here by sixteen thirty hours at the very latest; well before your one-hour deadline for the last man in, sir. He'll be here for the Alpha briefing at twenty-two hundred. If he is here by sixteen thirty you'll be able to call it earlier, sir, if you wanted to."

Jason raised his eyebrows fleetingly at her. "Quite Remarkable. Well . . . you do seem to have everything under control, Rose. Warn the guardroom to tell Mr Hohendorf when he arrives that he's got an Alpha briefing at . . . perhaps we'll make it eighteen hundred hours, if he does arrive by sixteen thirty."

"I'll get right on to it, sir."

"Thank you, Rose."

207

"Sir."

"Remarkable," Jason repeated to himself as he went into his office. "Quite remarkable."

Rose Gentry smiled and picked up the phone. When she'd finished relaying the wing commander's orders to the guardroom, her intercom beeped.

"Yes, sir?"

"As you seem to be so much in control, Rose, no doubt you can give me a status report on the mission crews?"

"Yes, sir. Selby and McCann, Cottingham and Christiansen, Bagni and Stockmann, and Morton and Flacht are all up; air combat on the ACMI range. Flight Lieutenant Hamilton-Jones and Major Carlizzi are in the Starfire simulator. Mr Flacht and Major Morton have a second slot: a low-level cross-country to Wales. But they'll be back down in plenty of time for Mr Flacht to make the Alpha briefing."

"Comprehensive as ever. Thank you, Rose."

"Sir."

McCann sang, "Oh, we've been rumblin' and a-tumblin' and a-ramblin' and a-scramblin' . . ."

"McCann!"

"Yope."

"Yope?"

"Sure. Yo and yep together." McCann made it sound as if the thing was so simple it needed no explanation.

"Give me strength," Selby said. "Anyway, no singing."

"I've got a great voice," McCann reasoned cheerfully.

"If you believe that, sing to yourself."

"And so it came to pass . . ." McCann intoned as if Selby had not spoken, ". . . it was seven for us guys, and one for the other guys. That should have been a zero, goddammit," he finished, sounding aggrieved.

"Don't be hard on him. He did well."

They were returning from a friendly tussle with seven French Mirages on the ACMI range. Friendly was perhaps a misleading way of describing it as the fight had been ferocious with no holds barred. Three of the ASV Echoes had got two kills each, with Morton scoring one. Unfortunately, he had been so relieved to have at last snagged the brilliantly-flown Mirage that he'd relaxed and had reacted to Flacht's warning far too late. The Mirage pilot's wingman, quickly exploiting the heaven-sent opportunity, had nailed them. It had been a close-quarter agile

208

missile shot *within* gun range. Unorthodox but effective. A kill was a kill. In a real match you'd be heading earthwards and in no position to debate which weapon had done the deed. Cottingham and Christiansen had then scored their second kill by nailing the opportunist wingman.

Flacht was not a happy man. Morton was not too pleased with himself either, knowing exactly why he had fallen victim to the Mirage that had so effectively ruined his day.

The four aircraft, in tight echelon formation, were now tearing along the main runway at ultra-low altitude, Selby leading. They went snappily into the break, fanning out in a smartly executed choreography.

McCann watched as the runway pattern appeared to rise on the left wingtip as the wings spread for landing. He glanced behind and to his right. The other three were moving neatly into station in a slightly off-set line astern. Morton had performed the break as sharply as the others.

"Guess a guy can sometimes make the mistake of relaxing too soon," he said, taking Selby's advice and going easy on Morton.

"He's feeling bad enough as it is," Selby said. "It will all be there on the recording. Let's not give him more grief."

Remembering the day when they had themselves nearly gone into the drink, McCann wondered whether Selby's sympathy for Morton may have had something to do with that.

"OK," McCann agreed.

The four aircraft landed with synchronised precision.

"So I'm not invited on the mission," Morton said. "The boss is that pissed off with me?"

The Tornado was on a wingtip, threading its way between two mountain peaks in Wales. It rolled upright and went scooting up a mountainside that suddenly appeared at the end of the narrowing gap.

Morton held the stick lightly as the hungry rocks flashed beneath them, seemingly close enough to touch. He then went into a left bank beyond ninety degrees and pulled into another valley. He rolled upright a second time, then settled down for a straight dash along the deep trough of the valley. A snaking river streaked past, a hundred feet below.

They were on their second flight of the day.

"The boss is not angry with you," Flacht said carefully. "Did he ask you in for a private reprimand?"

"No. But I don't know which is worse: being bawled out, or getting the silent treatment."

"The boss understands you know what happened and does not feel he must also tell you. It serves no purpose."

They sneaked past a jagged vertical cliff, canopy to rock-face, a ghostly skirt of vapour fluttering off the trailing edges of the mid-swept wings.

"Hell, I know I screwed up out there. I should have listened to your call."

They were upright again, rolling steeply in the opposite direction to enter a third valley. Morton had been flying the entire route manually.

"It happens," Flacht said, calmly watching a razor-edged peak hurtle past above them. *Not bad*, he thought. "Do you imagine Axel listens to me every time?"

"It's different with you guys. You're a team."

"You will get a permanent backseater soon, Chuck. Look, my friend, if the boss did not think you were good enough, you would not be on the squadron. You would not be at November at all."

"I suppose," Morton said thoughtfully. "I still wish he'd asked me on the mission, though."

"I do not think we shall be running out of missions," Flacht said in his careful English. "You'll get plenty of opportunities. And anyway, I am sure he has his reasons. Quite certainly, not any you might think of."

"I suppose," Morton repeated.

The Tornado tilted steeply once more onto its wing.

Morton, Flacht thought, was really getting to grips with low-flying in the ASV Echo.

Hohendorf proved Rose Gentry absolutely correct. At exactly 1630 hours, the Porsche stopped at the guardroom. He got out and went up to the duty corporal at the window, to sign in. He recognised the NCO.

"Ah, Corporal Hogarth. I'm back like a bad penny, as you can see."

Hogarth's severe features broke into a smile. "Welcome back, Mr Hohendorf. You've got an Alpha briefing at eighteen hundred."

"No rest for the wicked, eh?" Hohendorf said as he signed in on the NCO's clipboard.

"So they tell me, sir." Hogarth's eyes strayed to the Porsche. "How's she doing, sir?"

"What? Oh!" Hohendorf saw where the corporal's eyes were focussed. "Beautifully, Corporal Hogarth. Beautifully."

"Yes, sir. I bet." Hogarth retrieved the clipboard. "Thank you, sir."

"Thank you, Corporal. Good afternoon."

"Afternoon, sir."

Hogarth watched as Hohendorf got back into the car and drove away.

"Just listen to that sound," he murmured in admiration.

He noted down the time of Hohendorf's arrival and counter-signed it.

Briefing Room Alpha, 1800 hours.

No one was late. The four Tornado crews, plus Caroline and Carlizzi, were waiting in the auditorium for Jason's arrival. All were in flying overalls, Hohendorf included, and the leather flying jackets exclusive to November aircrew.

The participating nations were not yet quite ready to sanction a distinct uniform for November personnel, both air and ground. However, the international nature of the project was acknowledged by unique shoulder patches, but national uniforms and ranks had so far been retained. The patches were shield-shaped, incorporating the national flag of the individual and the NATO insignia, one on each shoulder.

The single gesture towards a unified form of dress was the special jacket. This was in a deep gleaming stone-grey that was almost black, with NATO-blue lining. In certain light conditions, the jacket appeared to shift colour. The crews liked this chameleon-like effect which they considered rather appropriate.

As they waited for the wing commander, their collective attention was fixed upon the three golden bands on the leather of each of Hohendorf's epaulettes. They all shook his hand to congratulate him on his promotion.

McCann sat down on his left. He tapped at the closest epaulette with a probing finger. "Nice and new. So what's it mean? Commander, or something?"

Hohendorf favoured him with an amused smile. "Don't you know your NATO ranks, Elmer Lee?"

"Hey . . . I count up to my rank, and that's it. Anything above that, I salute. Anything under, I bawl at. So, do I salute you?"

"Strictly speaking, yes. I'm now a *Korvettenkapitän*. But I won't keep asking you to salute me. I promise."

Everyone chuckled at McCann.

"Well?" he asked. "What's that for real?"

"In your air force, I would be a major."

"Oh hell. Another major. Sorry, Major Carlizzi."

"That is quite all right, Captain McCann. I—"

Just then Jason entered, carrying a box file which he placed on the table next to the dais. They all sprang to their feet.

"Do sit down, please," he told them. When they had done so, he went on, "Before I commence the briefing, I'd like to congratulate you on your recent promotion, Mr Hohendorf."

"Thank you, sir."

Jason went over to shake Hohendorf's hand. "Had a good leave?"

"Yes, sir."

"Sorry we had to drag you back early."

"No problem, sir."

"Mr Bagni, how was my favourite part of Italy?"

"As beautiful as ever, sir."

"And Mr Selby . . . I won't bother to ask whether you enjoyed London. You clearly did."

"I tried my best, sir."

They laughed with Selby.

"However," Jason went on, "may I ask why you choose to come before me improperly dressed?"

Selby was astonished. "Sir?"

He hastily inspected his clothing to see if any item had been left out. His name patch was in place, as were his pilot's wings. The two blue rings of a flight lieutenant were in place on each shoulder. Everyone peered at him.

"Sorry, sir," he said to Jason, "I don't quite understand."

"I know you don't," Jason told him mildly, going back to the table. The wing commander opened the box file and took out a small square box. He returned, and handed it to the bemused Selby. "These came for you."

Selby looked at the box.

"Don't stare at the thing, man. Open it."

"Yes, sir." Selby gingerly opened the box and stared some more. "Oh my God," he said. He got to his feet. "Er . . . thank you, sir!"

"Squadron Leader Selby." Jason shook Selby's hand. "Congratulations."

"Thank you, sir!"

As Selby sat down again, they all crowded round to peer into the little box. A pair of loops, each with the blue rings now separated by a third, thinner one, rested there. They all congratulated him.

"Wow!" McCann said, shaking Selby's hand vigorously.

"*Wow*, Mr McCann?" Jason asked.

"Yes, sir. Kind of neat. Mark's now a . . ." He paused. ". . . major?"

"Equivalent of. Yes."

"Sir, I'm surrounded by majors."

"We all know your history with majors, Mr McCann. You'll just have to grin and bear it. Things could be worse."

"Not possible, sir."

"*You* could be a major one day, if you stay out of trouble long enough."

McCann grinned.

"Mercifully," Jason said, "that's some distance away. Mr Selby and Mr Hohendorf."

"Sir?" they responded together.

"You're both buying the drinks in the mess tonight."

"Yeayy!" everyone chorused.

"But only one round," Jason went on. "Starting tomorrow, you've all got seventy-two hours of hard flying ahead of you. However, your mess bills won't be getting off that lightly. On completion of the mission, you'll continue buying the drinks so that we can properly celebrate your promotions."

"Now you're talking!" McCann said.

"Thank you, Captain," Jason said sternly. "And now that we've all congratulated our newest majors, let's get on with the briefing."

Jason removed his cap, wiped at his forehead in the familiar manner, then put the cap down on the table. Taking some papers and a remote out of the box file, he climbed the dais and went up to the lectern. A tiny microphone and a shaded lamp were attached to it. He placed the papers on the lectern.

"I'll be laying out the basics," he continued as they returned to their seats and gave him their full attention. "But various people will follow me with details of weather, communications, refuelling and so forth, at further briefings.

"The mission is condenamed STARFIRE. The Starfire aircraft – crewed by Flight Lieutenant Hamilton-Jones as pilot and Major Carlizzi as navigator – is tasked with permanently disabling an illegal phase-array radar. The four ASV Echoes are to be its escort. If you're wondering about possible response, there may well be fighters sent aloft to interfere with the mission. However, the event won't be made public by the other side. After all, how can there be an attack on something that does not exist?"

There were smiles, but even McCann prudently chose not to interrupt.

"Which brings me to the rules of engagement. You are to make no offensive move unless attacked yourselves but you will protect the Starfire. You all have the right to defend yourselves but unless forced to, you are to get out of there without engaging in air combat, if at all possible.

"I cannot stress this too strongly. Any pilot who breaks these rules of engagement will need a very good reason. Note I said reason. I will not tolerate an excuse. The offending crew will almost certainly be jeopardising their careers here at November One, unless that reason is fully justified. I want you all to take this very seriously on board. I will make no allowances for rank or experience."

Their expressions told him they had.

"The Starfire," the wing commander went on, "although fully armed air-to-air, will not be carrying an additional load of conventional air-to-ground ordnance. This is to be an electronic disabling of the phase-array and its relevant communications systems. The aircraft has been fitted with a special weapon – a pulse cannon – which is currently being integrated into the weapons fire control system. There will be complete data fusion, enabling the weapon to be selected at will, with its attendant symbology linked to the helmet sights, the HUD and the MFD repeater.

"You may have seen a pair of unfamiliar civilian guests in the mess. These two gentlemen are Mr Wilby and Mr Ländemann, the systems experts for the new weapon. The official terminology is ElectroMagnetic Pulse Cannon – Non-Nuclear. To avoid that mouthful, and recognising that aircrew hate words with too many syllables, you'll be pleased to know it's been designated the EMPC-N^2, or more simply for those of you who can't even make it that far, EMPC."

Soft chuckles followed this.

"Our civilian friends have been working – with a little help from our own November engineers – to integrate the system as rapidly as possible so as to have it fully operational in time for the mission. They will be briefing you all at some stage in the proceedings. Caroline, you and Major Carlizzi will be making a first flight tomorrow."

She nodded. "Sir."

"You will still be required to make more simulator flights. The only way to test the performance of the cannon in the time available will be as a simulated excercise, with all the necessary parameters programmed into the sim computers by Mr Ländemann. You will actually be flying the attack in the simulator, with full target presence in the visuals. This will be as close as you can possibly get to the real event."

Again she nodded. "Understood, boss."

Jason shifted some papers. "During the next seventy-two hours, both Starfire and escort will be flying prearranged slots on the ACMI range. Be on the alert! You will be attacked from any direction without warning by a mixed force of German Air Force MiG-29s and US Air Force F-15 Eagles.

"They will be simulating hostile MiG-29s and Su-27s. I don't expect any kills against you. It does not matter whether you get any kills. If you do, so much the better; but the object of the exercise is to take no casualties yourselves. In the real scenario, this is the minimum result I shall expect. I want none of our people left out there.

"The timing of the mission has been carefully planned over a number of months. It has been chosen to coincide with several NATO and allied forces manoeuvres which have been taking place from the North Cape to the Baltic, the Mediterranean, the Black Sea and the Gulf. One more flight of aircraft will not be of particular interest. I can tell you that our mission is in fact itself a cover for *another mission*; but I cannot tell you more about that."

Hohendorf raised a hand.

"Yes, Mr Hohendorf?"

"Is the Starfire target real, sir?"

"It's very real, I assure you. Expect to see fighters, though how they will eventually react is open to question. To continue. Your route will be one thousand nautical miles each way. You will not be carrying exterior tanks. Refuelling aircraft will be on station at specified waypoints. You will make a high-speed dash to the target, at low level. You'll be subsonic at Mach 0.81 at ingress. Accelerate to target, then go supersonic on egress. This should give them very little response time.

"You'll make the approach as low as you dare, on autopilot if you wish. Your new passive referencing system can take you to fifty feet even over water, if you choose to engage it. Restrict radar emissions from your aircraft, as this may alert interested parties. Do bear that in mind. Fifty miles from target, resume manual control if you've been on full autopilot. There'll be just enough time left to take up position and fire the EMPC, and then you can concentrate on getting home. Escort aircraft will also fly in low. Once the attack is complete, use whatever tactical formation is most appropriate for a safe recovery to base.

"You'll no doubt have been alerted by my mention of water," Jason continued drily. "Time, I think, to tell you where you're going. Lights, please," he said into the microphone on the lectern.

The auditorium lights dimmed and the main screen flashed into life. A large-scale aerial map, showing a spread from the UK to the Baltic Sea and Lithuania, Latvia and Estonia appeared.

"Shit," someone said.

"As well you might," Jason said. He did not seek out the speaker. "Yes, lady and gentlemen. You're going on a Baltic excursion." The remote placed its lighted arrow on the target. "The primary objective is on that strip of land. We all know where that is, don't we?"

"Oh we do. We do!" came the unmistakeable tones of McCann.

In the relative gloom, they did not see the briefest of smiles that flitted across Jason's lips. Again, he chose not to comment on the interruption.

"Not so long ago," he said, "a nose-around in that area would excite every SAM and radar unit from Lubeck to Gdansk to Ventspils. The radar warning and attention getters on your aircraft would go beserk and, if you were lucky, you might even get a SAM launch." He sounded as if he spoke from experience. "Mr Hohendorf, you might have some idea of what I'm talking about. I believe early in your career, you used to run what was generally described as the chicken gauntlet; checking to see how awake they were over there, just in case."

Hohendorf cleared his throat. "I didn't realise you knew my little secret, sir."

"I know everything."

"I was very young and impressionable, sir," Hohendorf said in his defence.

A roar of laughter followed this.

"Young and impressionable. Weren't we all, once? Any luck?"

"We got a few SAMs thrown our way but, as you can see, they didn't score."

There was more laughter.

"And how did you avoid them?"

"We went very very low. Johann Ecker, my backseater at the time, used to call it our waterski dance. Sometimes, we did this at night."

"We remember Mr Ecker with great fondness," Jason said. "He did us a good turn on the Pale Flyer mission. Clearly, he needs to be mad as well. Pity we couldn't keep him with us, but the *Marineflieger* would have none of it. They felt we'd stolen enough from them already. We could have paired such an experienced nav with Chuck Morton.

"Well, Mr Hohendorf," Jason continued, "you'll be paying another visit to your former playground. This time round however, it won't be so hostile. Times have changed, and most of that coast is now friendly . . . except, of course, for that strip of land here." The remote arrow blinked a few times. "Note your waypoint pattern, including refuelling points."

As Jason spoke, a blue line, starting from November One, began to trace itself across the map. Each time it came to a waypoint, a small bright yellow circle came into being. It changed course from each circle and moved on to another. At two locations, a green square appeared. These were the two rendezvous points with the tankers. At the target itself, a bright red triangle appeared. The blue trace turned tightly from there and headed back along the same waypoints.

"This route can be modified in flight," Jason said, "should the situation warrant it. Any such changes can be sent via secure datalink to an AWACS which will be on station, well away from your route and deep in friendly airspace. Because of the recent changes in world affairs, you'll now be flying in relatively friendly airspace for most of the way. I do mean relatively. Take nothing for granted.

"However, once you're off the Gdynia claw – that strip of land there . . ." the illuminated arrow moved to a thin stretch of land that probed inwards, as if pointing towards Gdansk itself ". . . expect high interest from anywhere within 045 to 110; virtually dead ahead. Do not be complacent. They could also be coming at you from the north, or even on your six having been lying in wait to spring an ambush.

"At that point, you will be forty nautical miles from target. I was originally told that the airborne EMPC would have sufficient portable charge for six bursts at a ten-mile range. I have since been informed that this initial range erred somewhat on the conservative side. Performance has been found to be for five bursts at twenty miles, giving the Starfire a better escape margin.

"The bursts will be fully automatic if you keep your finger on the trigger, Caroline. They'll be streamed in one second. You can vary the speed by firing single bursts. I would suggest, however, you stick to the former and get yourself out of there. You have no time to mess about with spaced bursts. Acquisition is fully automatic. That cannon knows what it's looking for.

"It has been calculated that your presence in the area will not create undue interest until you're relatively close in, as it may be interpreted as just another exercise with prospective new allies. However, don't bank on it; use that cover for as long as you can. The mission is timed to get you there at twilight when lighting conditions most favour the Chameleon; but try to restrict the use of afterburners as much as you can. You don't want to give any infrared missiles that may be coming your way too much of an enticement to dinner. Now . . ." Jason added, ". . . airfields from which you are likely to expect trouble if the situation deteriorates."

The arrow pointed to no less than six in the vicinity, with three the most likely to be first to send fighters looking. The arrow indicated one on the strip itself, close to the target area; one on the cape to the north of it; and the third just inland of this. Each of the three airfields was highlighted. A caption in red appeared next to them.

WARNING: AIRCRAFT INFRINGING THIS AIR-SPACE ARE LIKELY TO BE FIRED UPON WITH-OUT WARNING.

"Take that warning very seriously indeed," Jason told them.
No one said anything.
Another caption appeared in the general area.

WARNING: UNLISTED RADIO EMISSIONS MAY CONSTITUTE A NAVIGATIONAL HAZARD.

"Your systems are hardened," Jason went on, "so high-intensity emissions will not affect them. However, keep a careful watch. We want no uncommanded overflights because instruments have gone off beam.

"Callsigns. The mission callsign will be, as I indicated earlier, STARFIRE. This will also be the callsign of the aircraft itself. The escorts will be: Starfire Zero-One – Hohendorf and Flacht; Zero-Two – Selby and McCann; Zero-Three – Bagni and Stockmann; and Zero-Four – Cottingham and Christiansen. Escort pair leaders: Zero-One leads Zero-Three and Zero-Two leads Zero-Four. Zero-One has command of the mission. Zero-Two takes over if Zero-One goes down. Zero-Three and Zero-Four follow in that order; although if matters come to such a pass, we'll be staring into the face of a major disaster. Bring me no disasters. I expect to see you all back here.

"Finally, diversion airfields in case you get into trouble." The arrow pointed. "One here, north of Rostock, the other in Schleswig-Holstein. Mr Hohendorf and Mr Flacht will know both of these well, and Caroline has done a cross-country to Schleswig-Holstein.

"Whatever you do, do not attempt to land at any airfields in Poland, despite the fact that the country is a prospective NATO member. The resulting international embarrassment would be a worse nightmare than you could imagine. It could also permanently jeorpardise the continuing existence of the November programme. This would be a gift to our adversaries, both national and international.

"And that's it from me. You'll be brought up to date with more details during the further briefings. Both Commander Helm and Colonel da Vinci will also be briefing you from time to time. Now if there are any questions? No? Remarkable. My briefing skills must be improving. Lights, please."

"We're just eager to get to the bar, sir," McCann said as the lights came up.

Everyone stood up, wondering for the umpteenth time whether McCann had yet again badly misjudged the situation. But McCann's guardian angel was continuing to work overtime.

Jason seemed unperturbed. The wing commander collected his papers, placed them in the box file and stepped off the dais.

Then he paused. "I mentioned Chuck Morton earlier. Today, he received a harsh lesson because he allowed his concentration to slip. Had this been a real fight, he would now be dead – you too, Mr Flacht – and I would be trying to think of the proper things to say to your families. You are never so good that you can't learn a lesson. Major Morton was fortunate today. Learn from his mistake."

The wing commander picked up his cap and put it on.

"As you're so keen to get to the mess bar, Captain McCann," he said, expression giving nothing away, "perhaps you could ensure everyone is there in thirty minutes, in civilian attire. Post-nineteen hundred hours dress code."

The November dress code after 1900 hours in the mess required that jackets be worn. Ties were compulsory.

"One of these days, McCann," Selby warned when the wing commander had gone. "One of these days . . ."

"Hey . . . the boss was cool."

"Freezing, more like."

219

"Nah." McCann stared pointedly at the small box in Selby's hand. "Sir."

"Don't push it, McCann."

The mess bar was heaving. Both Helm and da Vinci had accompanied Jason to the festivities, and a lot of people seemed to have heard of the celebration.

Selby found himself in a crush that included Caroline, Hohendorf and McCann.

"Our mess bills will be screaming with pain after this lot," he said to Hohendorf ruefully. "I never knew we knew so many people. They can drink as much as they like, almost . . . while we're restricted to our one glass of tipple."

Hohendorf looked amused. "Amazing how popular we are."

"Oh well, we don't get promoted every day." Selby raised his glass. "To you, old son. Well done."

"And to you," Hohendorf said as they clinked glasses.

"Morven would probably die of shock if she saw us."

"She would say it's the euphoria of the promotions."

"Tell you what," Selby said. "After the mission, let's all go to dinner. You, me, Kim and Morven."

Hohendorf gaped at him. "You are serious?"

Selby nodded. "The one glass we're allowed tonight has not made me drunk. So I must be."

Hohendorf nodded slowly. "That's a date."

McCann looked at them critically. "Now I've seen everything." His eyes searched the room. "Where's Karen, anyway?"

"Over there by the picture of the Hurricane," Selby told him with sharp glee. "She's being chatted up by one of the new baby pilots."

The arrival of Helm saved a riposte from McCann.

"So, Axel," the commander said to Hohendorf, beaming. *"Herr Fregattenkapitän."*

"Let us have a talk about old times in Schleswig. I am certain your friends will excuse you."

"Of course, sir," Selby said. "See you later, Axel."

"OK," Hohendorf said as he moved away with the still-beaming Helm. The commander appeared to be unbending a little now that Hohendorf was a lieutenant-commander.

McCann had his own ideas about the change of attitude. "I think the commander's had more than one—"

Selby clamped a firm hand over McCann's mouth.

The Kansas City imp's eyes looked at him furiously. "Whh-hh-hh-hh!"

"Can't hear you," Selby told him in a fierce whisper. "Whatever you were going to say, shut it. The commander can still hear your loud voice."

"Let me," Caroline said.

She put an arm about McCann's neck and held on tightly. Being a little taller than he was, she had a good purchase. She whispered something in his ear. McCann did not quite turn a bright shade of beetroot, but he came close.

Selby removed his hand slowly, staring at the remarkable change. Caroline still held McCann in her fond necklock.

"You wouldn't!" McCann said.

"Try me."

"OK. I'll be good."

"So sweet," Caroline said, releasing him. She kissed him on the cheek.

Selby was looking at her in wonder. "How did you do that? You've actually shut him up. What's the secret?"

McCann looked stricken as he waited for Caroline to speak.

"A lady never tells," she said, with a smile at McCann who took a quick drink to cover his confusion.

By the large oil painting of the Hurricane which had a similarly-sized painting of a Messerchmitt Bf-109 next to it, Karen Lomax had spotted the little drama. She did not believe her territory was being encroached upon but nevertheless made a hasty excuse to the eager pilot who was indeed chatting her up, and left to join Selby's group.

"Anything I should know?" she said brightly, looking at McCann as she came up to them.

McCann blushed again.

"Elmer Lee!" she said. "You can't be drunk on one glass."

Caroline was trying hard not to break into peals of laughter.

"Um," McCann said to Karen, "can we find ourselves a quiet corner?" He dragged her away before she could say anything.

Selby looked at Caroline. "You've got tears coming out of your eyes. Can I share the joke?"

She shook her head firmly. "Sorry, Mark." She gave his shoulder a brief pat. "No can do. It really wouldn't be fair to him." She wiped away the tears. "Life's so crazy sometimes. Here we are, about to go on a mission in a few days, and all I can think of is Elmer Lee's little secret."

Sixteen

C aroline and Carlizzi, in full flying gear, got off the crew minibus and entered the HAS where the Starfire awaited them. As they walked, the air pounded with the thunder of eight engines as the four escort ASV Echoes began their take-off run.

Caroline paused and turned to watch. Without looking to check, she sensed that Carlizzi had also stopped.

The first pair of Tornadoes were already wheels up. Keeping tight formation, they reefed their sleek noses upwards and climbed vertically on the fire of their afterburners, wings sweeping as they went. Moments later, they were followed in the same manner by the second pair.

The four aircraft climbed in precise formation until they suddenly disappeared. The sound of their engines could still be heard until that too faded.

Caroline turned to face Carlizzi. "It's eerie watching them change appearance from the ground."

"Yeah. Now you see them, now you don't. Spooky, isn't it? Imagine what it's like for the guy who's trying to fight you when all he's got is a lot less than a second to visually acquire." Carlizzi paused, listening. "Nope. They're gone all right. Well, that's the escort on its way to do battle on the ACMI range. Our job today is nothing so glamorous. We're just doing a very careful fam hop. OK?"

She nodded. The familiarisation flight was to get her attuned to the aircraft.

"Now remember," Carlizzi went on, "everything will be exactly as in the simulator. Don't try to readjust. All you've got to keep remembering is that this one moves for real. Just go easy and it will all fall into place."

"Got it."

Wilby and Ländemann were waiting for them.

"She is all ready for you," Ländemann said to her. "The weapon

222

is fully integrated. When you are in the cockpit, I will give you some details."

She nodded at him. "All right."

"Now I will walk you through the pre-flight."

The two-seat Starfire, with its characteristic cockpit hump, had a pair of extendable boarding steps, but the step ladder that had been used by the engineers had been left in place. While Ländemann walked with Caroline around the aircraft, doing the pre-flight checks, Carlizzi climbed up to the step ladder's boarding shelf and got into the rear cockpit. Wilby followed and stood on the shelf to check whether he needed help.

The systems had already been put online, and a faint sibilance hummed softly through the rear office. He began working through the test procedures.

On the ground, Caroline scrutinised the EMPC. It had been mounted on the underbelly of the aircraft, slightly offset in its blended housing so that it did not foul the landing gear doors.

"Strange beast," she said to Ländemann. "What do I get out of there? Plasma bursts?"

"One day," he replied seriously, "it could happen. Who knows? But this is devastating enough for our times."

"Can I really fry their circuits with this from twenty miles out?"

"Certainly. If you think about it, it is quite a distance for an airborne weapon of this kind. Theoretically, if you were twenty miles straight up and in a dive on target, it would work just as well. We are preparing a version for retractable vertical mounting on larger, full-stealth technology aircraft.

"The burst will first go round a concentric chamber, building energy as it goes, before exiting through a variable nozzle. All the carrier aircraft has to do is fly level, electro-magnetically cooking any susceptible equipment on its flight path. Eventually, horizontally mounted weapons like yours – when we have made the charge units smaller and more powerful – will have ranges of possibly well over a hundred miles."

"The ray gun is really here."

"You've got one on your aeroplane, Miss Hamilton-Jones."

They finished the walk-round, then Caroline climbed up to the front cockpit and got in. She was pleased to see how familiar it was after the simulator. Everything was where she expected it to be. Ländemann had followed, and now went down on one knee to lean slightly into the cockpit.

"Of course," he began, "you will not practise with the cannon, except in the simulator. I shall be there to go through the procedures with you. But we can show you how the system works on the aircraft itself. Please put on your helmet."

She did so, and connected herself to the aircraft.

"Do your voice check."

"Voiceprint register, please, Carlo," she requested, briefly holding the unsecured mask to her face as she spoke.

"Roger," he acknowledged. "Speak any time you want to. Secure your mask so that the DVI registers you properly."

She secured the oxygen mask as Carlizzi had advised. "I never have bacon for breakfast."

"Voiceprint accepted," announced Sodding Sid's twin sister. "'I never have bacon for breakfast.'"

Caroline felt herself smile as her words, in her voice, were repeated back to her.

"There you go," Carlizzi said. "From now until the mission's over, the DVI's at your command. You can unclip the mask until we're ready to roll."

She did so, letting it hang away from her face.

"All right," Ländemann said to Caroline. "Activate the cockpit systems check. That way you can run through the weapons checks without arming them. When it's running, call up the DVI and run through the weapons list. The HUD and helmet sight symbology will change as appropriate."

She reached for the right-hand console and depressed the start button on the test panel.

"Weapons," she told the DVI, again holding the mask to her face.

"Weapons mode selected."

She ran through all the weapons until she came to the EMPC.

"Gamma Four."

"Gamma four selected."

The HUD and helmet sight symbology was like nothing she'd seen before. Instead of the normal green, this was a glowing blue. No mistaking which weapon was in use.

A thickly drawn circle was at the centre. This was fixed. A pulsing equilateral triangle of the same colour but brighter, oscillated, filling the entire viewing area then reducing in size until it was within the circle. This motion was continuous, with the triangle slowly spinning about its axis. Below the circle was a set of zeroes next to the RNG symbology. That was all. Then the mobile triangle vanished.

"What happened?" Caroline asked. "The triangle's gone."

"It is still there," Ländemann said to her. "It is in wait mode. First, it comes on to let you know the weapon has been activated; then it disappears, to wait until a target has been acquired. You wouldn't want to have it pulsing in your face all the time, especially at night.

"When it has acquired, it reappears and enters the circle, but not permanently. It no longer spins. The circle is on the aircraft's centreline. Entering the circle means it has achieved full acquisition of the target. The triangle remains that size and hunts out electro-targets. It will pause on each target found, then move on to the next in priority. This happens rapidly. When the EMPC is discharged, the bursts will go where the triangle has marked. You have no aiming to do once you have activated it and are in range. It will say 'in range' and give the command to shoot. The cannon will do the rest automatically. You have understood?"

She nodded.

"Good. Now I will leave you to fly the aircraft. Good luck."

"Thank you."

Ländemann and Wilby went down. The ladder was moved away.

"All on our own now," Carlizzi said. "You OK?"

"I'm fine."

"OK. Start engines."

Jason was in the control tower to watch the take-off. Helm and da Vinci were with him. The three senior officers stood in a small group at a vantage point that allowed them a clear view of the entire runway but kept them out of the way of the tower personnel.

They watched as the the nose of the Starfire dipped slightly as Caroline made a final test of the brakes, then the engine nozzle flared wide as she pushed the throttles into afterburner.

The Starfire accelerated rapidly, holding a steady line down the runway. Then it was lifting gently, wheels coming up and tucking in. The gentle climb was held as it went out to sea.

Jason was nodding approvingly. "That's it," he said softly. "Nice and easy. No fancy footwork on your first time out."

As if she had heard him, Caroline maintained her steady climb and the aircraft rapidly went out of view.

Jason turned to his companions. "She'll be fine."

"We know you're worried about her," Helm said. "We all are. But yes . . . we also believe she will be fine. She's an excellent pilot and with Carlizzi she is in good hands."

"She needs to be," Jason told them, "for the mission."

*　　*　　*

"All right," Carlizzi said when they had reached 25,000 feet above the water. "We've got the altitude and the airspace to ourselves. Get yourself at ease with the airplane. Fly around doing gentle things, then, when you reckon you've got the hang of it, let rip. See how you go. I'm just gonna sit back here and enjoy the ride."

"OK," she said.

Gently at first, she began to put the Starfire through its paces; then with growing confidence, she began to chuck it around. She went into searing climbs, fleeing through streamers of cloud; tight loops that turned the world upside down; rapid flick rolls that whirled the horizon; G-intensive turns that crushed at her – all the manoeuvres flowing seamlessly from one to the other – high speed, low speed, full burner thrust-vectoring manoeuvres, low-speed thrust-vectoring manoeuvres. On and on she flew, the supreme agility of the Starfire making her feel she commanded the very air itself.

It was half an hour before she was once again flying straight and level.

"I could stay up here for ever."

"That was very impressive," Carlizzi said, "but I'm afraid I'm going to have to bring you back to earth. Even the birds need to refuel to stay up, and so does this high-tech bird. All your fancy dancing means we've got to head back to base, or we lose one pricey ship, and we swim. You'll be up again this afternoon. So what's say we head on back?"

"Roger," she said reluctantly.

The Special Research Unit, east of the Urals. 1500 hours local.

"Why can't Ivan Ivanovitch do it tonight?" Konstantinova asked Lirionova.

"He's a sergeant. The general wants only the officers to have custody of the cartridge at the end of the working day. You know that, Milla."

"But there's just the two of us," Konstantinova protested. "If we're going to have to babysit that thing until Olga finds her anti-virus, that could take for ever. We're not here for this, Liri."

"Would you like to tell that to the general?"

Konstantinova said nothing.

"I thought not."

"You can ask him to allow Sergeant Yakulentov onto the roster, given the circumstances. No one expected to be dealing with a virus.

This gives us an extra responsibility. We should spread this duty."

"I'll try," Lirionova said, "but don't expect much. Anyway, Olga seems to like having you around."

"No more than you."

"Oh, I don't know. She seems more open with you."

"Perhaps your being a major inhibits her."

"Olga? Nothing inhibits Olga. She had that affair with an American . . ."

"Don't tell me you've never fancied any of the Americans you've seen in Moscow, at embassies and such like; and not just because you might have been there to shadow them either."

Lirionova smiled suddenly. "Perhaps one . . ."

"Ah ha!"

"He was a marine captain."

"Ah ha!" Konstantinova said again. "And? Did you? You know."

"We never got the chance. One of his security people spotted him having coffee with me and had him posted out."

"Don't tell me. You were on duty."

"Half and half. He did have a great body," Lirionova added wistfully. She sighed at what might have been. "So what's this about you going out on a patrol?"

"Another challenge from Urikov."

"Be careful . . ."

"He came up to me when I was having something to eat and started going on and on about how the real work was being done out there on patrol and not sitting in here day after day in cosy comfort. The man's an idiot. He's got a real problem; but he annoyed me. I'm afraid I said I'd go out with one of the APCs just to show him we're not just soft desk merchants."

"Milla," Lirionova said wearily. "He set you up!"

"Of course he did. But what can he do to me? If he tried anything, he'd be looking at a posting at the end of nowhere. He knows that."

"I still think you should be careful. I could always order you not to go."

"And prove his point? Don't forget, you took up his challenge for the shooting contest."

"Don't remind me," Lirionova said. "All right. I suppose if you're determined to accept Urikov's ludicrous challenge and go on that patrol, I'll need an extra person on the roster. I'll ask the general about Ivan Ivanovitch, but only for when you go out on that patrol. It's a compromise. Take it or leave it."

"I'll take it."

Half an hour later, Moscow time.

Levchuk entered Kurinin's office with the day's updates.

"Anything on those transmissions?" the general asked as he scanned through them.

"Nothing as yet, General. They've covered their tracks very well. Which leads me to think I was correct in my original assessment of the situation. Something important is going on. I know the evidence is tenuous at best, but I feel it. If I had corns, they'd be itching."

"The state of your feet does not interest me, Gregor, but your instincts do. Are our NATO friends planning new mischief?"

"Nothing that we can as yet detect. There are, of course, the usual manoeuvres we discussed earlier. They've got their usual series going on all over the place—"

"Which we'll watch in our usual manner," Kurinin interrupted.

"But it's all routine."

"What isn't routine," the general said in a hard voice, "is the fact that they'll be encroaching into areas they could not have used before without risking a bloody nose. The Black Sea, the Baltics . . . They come far these days, on their so-called manoeuvres. We've rotated the fighter units in the Baltic area recently, haven't we?"

Levchuk nodded. "We've got two new squadrons up there, commanded by people who think our way: one of MiG-29SKs commanded by Lieutenant-Colonel Sergei Tikhoniev and one of Su-35s with Lieutenant-Colonel Aleksandr Pedrov in command. Pedrov's squadron is incomplete, however. His aircraft are brand new and are being supplied slowly. I believe he's currently got only six, and has more pilots than aircraft. Not all of his pilots are fully operational. Two have gone straight to the aircraft from training and are quite young lieutenants. The area's commanding general is also sympathetic to us."

"Tell both colonels to mount standing patrols. But they must not engage any NATO planes they spot, unless specifically ordered to do so. They are there to observe and to report. I'm not ready to countenance any trigger-happy pilots. Sympathetic or not, I'll hold that general and those colonels responsible if there's an incident we can't hush up."

"Yes, General."

"See to it, Gregor."

Levchuk inclined his head slightly. "I'll have it done." He paused in the act of leaving. "One last item. We have a rather amusing request, General." Levchuk appeared to be smiling thinly.

"Amusing?"

"From the research facility. It would seem that Captain Urikov's up to his tricks again. This time, he has challenged the female officers to go on a patrol. He claims they're so soft they couldn't stay out, even for a short patrol."

"And?"

"Lieutenant Konstantinova took up the challenge."

"Good for her!"

"Which brings me to the request from Major Lirionova. She wants permission to temporarily assign Sergeant Yakulentov to the duty roster for end-of-day custody of the virus cartridge, this to last only until Konstantinova returns from the patrol."

"Which patrol will she be on?"

"One that leaves in two days. Three days in the field."

"She's got guts, as I would expect of all my people. The weather's still not settled out there yet. It's easy to get lost in a sudden blizzard. Siberia at its most elemental can still neutralise the most modern of communications systems. But the experience will do her good. Tell Lirionova she has my authority for the temporary roster change. Tell her also that if Urikov gets up to any tricks with Konstantinova, I'll ensure he lives to regret it."

"I'll see to it."

November base. 2000 hours local.

Both the Starfire and the escort aircraft had flown an intensive programme, interspersed with briefings and debriefings related to the coming mission.

The ASV Echoes had scored against their friendly opponents without getting tapped themselves.

At the end of a high-pressure day's flying, Jason pronounced himself satisfied with the results from both Starfire and escorts. Their crews were high on adrenalin but they grabbed themselves an early night. Even McCann decided against seeing Karen Lomax that evening.

A remarkable thing in itself.

By 0700 next morning, all five mission aircraft were back in the air; the escorts on their way to the first of two air combat slots on the range, the Starfire on a long hop into Icelandic airspace on a programme that would include extensive low-level flight over water and a refuelling rendezvous at 20,000 feet.

For Caroline, the day was a packed one. On her return, there was to be a simulated flight of the mission itself which included simulated use of the pulse cannon. Following this was another real flight, this time the second slot on the ACMI range with the escorts, for a full-blown air combat exercise against a mixed bag of F-16s and F-15s.

"How do you feel?" Carlizzi said to her.

"I'm OK."

She was flying the Starfire manually, as low over the water as she dared, at high speed. The sea looked close enough to touch.

Carlizzi looked about him calmly. "We're entering Reykjavik/Faroe sector. Hell," he went on coolly, "I can get out and walk! Good thing there are no fifty-foot waves around here!"

She smiled in her mask. She knew she was not low enough for that but appreciated the compliment. It was low enough to impress him.

Carlizzi had an electro-optical view ahead on one of his multi-function displays. He could see a ship. This low down, the range was close: twenty miles. He called up several degrees of magnification until he could identify the flag on the stern.

"Looks like we got ourselves a British ship on the nose. Royal Navy frigate. You want wake them up?"

The idea appealed. "They might not like it."

"Hell, they should be awake. We're in the twenty-mile zone and not a peep from their radar watch."

"We're almost in the sea. They can't see us."

"Better pull up some, unless you like eating naval radar masts."

She left the pull-up until the very last moment. They roared over the ship, then dropped almost to sea level once more.

"Stylish," Carlizzi said. "I like it. You're flying this bird like you've been doing it for years."

"A penny for what you think they're saying on that ship we just flew over."

"As they have no idea it was a woman who just gave them their early morning call, they're probably calling you all kinds of bastard while they try to identify you so they can file a complaint."

She laughed.

"OK," Carlizzi went on. "Go to two thousand feet, go left to two fifty, then make a gentle climb to twenty thousand. We're going to find ourselves a gas station. You've done tanking before so this should be a walk in the park. Tanker in fifteen minutes. Take a look at the nav page on your central MFD. Tanker position is in, and nav steering bug's been reset on the HUD. Follow that or the arrow on the helmet sight."

She followed Carlizzi's instructions and was soon in the climb towards the tanker. In fifteen minutes exactly, they had a visual on the big aircraft.

"Starfire to Tango One-Five," Carlizzi called. "Is the bar open?"

"We never close, Starfire! Tequila, Pina Colada, Marguerita, even pure malt . . . name your poison."

"Some nice jet juice will do."

"Then come to the bar, Starfire!"

Caroline made her approach from behind the massive Tri Star K.1, easing towards the already unrolled fuel line with the drogue basket at its end. She had already extended the refuelling probe on the right side of the cockpit, and now guided it towards the circle of lights within the rim of the basket, making infinitestimal adjustments with the throttles as the Starfire inched forward and the probe snicked into the drogue. The connect light came on, then the fuel transfer light. They were drinking.

"Sweet work," Carlizzi said to her.

When they'd taken on all the fuel they needed she disconnected and retracted the probe, slowing slightly and moving left to clear the tanker.

"Thanks for the drink," she said.

"Hey! You're a girl!"

"Just a minute. Er . . . yes. I just looked. I am."

She could see a face peering at them from one of the tanker aircraft's windows. She did a flashy roll, showing the tanker the Starfire's belly as they plunged for lower altitudes.

"Very nice!" a voice called.

"Me, or the flying?"

"Both."

She laughed.

"I think," Carlizzi said with dry humour, "you've kinda got the hang of this thing."

"I think so too," she said.

The Special Research Unit, east of the Urals. 1200 hours local.

Lirionova and Konstantinova were having lunch.

"So you're still going on this mad patrol, Milla?" Lirionova asked.

"Why not? The general's approved. And he was nice enough to promise to have Urikov's balls if that neanderthal throwback got funny with me. And tonight, we've got Ivan Ivanovitch on lab duty. So everything's worked out perfectly."

At a far table, Melev was sitting with three other soldiers. The sergeant had spotted them and was leering in their direction.

Lirionova glanced up by chance at that moment, and saw it. She looked away quickly.

"Melev's going too, isn't he?"

Konstantinova nodded. "Yes. He's Urikov's bosom pal, as you know. They always patrol together."

"Just be careful. I still think you're crazy to do it. Three days out there with those—"

"Come on, Liri. Even they wouldn't be mad enough. What do you think will happen? The other soldiers will just stand around while those two abuse an officer?"

"Those are Urikov's men. Their first allegiance is to him. Melev still considers you a sergeant because you've not yet been to officers' college, even though the commanding general himself gave you the field promotion. There are so many factions in our army these days, it's hard to know who to trust. Will even the thought of what the general might do have any effect?"

"And if I didn't go? We'd not hear the last of it. We hold the primary authority here, even above the colonel in an emergency. It's a man–woman thing with those two. They still don't want to believe we beat them at the shooting contest. If one embarrassment isn't enough for them, that's their hard luck. I'm not prepared to put up with their crap. Are you?"

"No. But it's too late now, even if I wanted to. So when do you set off?"

"O-six hundred tomorrow. I think they're testing me to see if I'll get out of my warm bed to make it in time for three days of fun and adventure."

"Don't joke."

"Don't worry, Liri. I'll shoot the first bastard who gets funny. I'm going armed like any soldier on patrol. I won't be able to miss at point-blank range. How would they explain *that*?"

Whatever Lirionova had been about to say was interrupted by movement on the periphery of her vision. Melev was approaching their table.

"Well, *Lieutenant*?" he said to Konstantinova as he came up. He stared balefully down at her. "Still think you're a soldier? Or are you going to chicken out, come morning? We don't play at being soldiers."

"I am a soldier, Sergeant. I'll be there in the morning, kitted out for patrol. And watch how you talk to me, *Sergeant*."

Melev's eyes narrowed. "Get a nice long sleep tonight, Lieutenant," he said. "You won't get much cosy comfort out there in the wasteland. No one's going to give you extra space in the APC." He studied her for a few moments, then abruptly turned away to return to his table.

"I can see you like living dangerously," Lirionova said.

November base, 2000 hours.

The remainder of the day had been a success. Caroline had "fried" the target on her simulated mission and, during the air combat exercise on the ACMI range, got an Eagle by dragging him low and turning into his circle, using thrust-vectoring to great effect. But her primary concern had been to stay out of trouble, which she did. No one had been able to tap her.

The escorting ASV Echoes had successfully fended off all attacks on the Starfire, scoring three kills in the process. No ASV was caught.

They were now returning to November One in tight line abreast formation, with Caroline leading from the left. When they were close to the airfield they moved smoothly into line astern, leaving the Starfire in the lead as they roared low over the main runway to peel in an expanding fan into the fighter break.

They gave Caroline plenty of room to land first, so that she could deploy her braking 'chute on touchdown.

They landed in pairs and, with thrust reversers, came to a halt well before half the runway had been used.

After the debrief, Jason announced he was well pleased with the day's results.

They were mission-ready.

The Special Research Unit, 2300 hours local.

Sergeant Ivan Yakulentov walked along the deserted corridor on his way back to the Documents Section to put the virus cartridge safely away for the night. The doctor had worked late, and he was looking forward to getting rid of the thing and getting off to bed. He began to yawn as he turned a corner.

Then the lights went out.

Yakulentov came to, half-sitting, half-lying on the floor.

His first thoughts were for the safety of the cartridge. Then he felt a huge relief. He still had it.

So what had happened? Had he simply passed out? He wasn't the kind of person who did. He began to worry. Was there something wrong with him? Was he seriously ill? He was a healthy young man. Had he simply fainted? If so, why? Healthy young men shouldn't faint just strolling along a corridor.

How long had he been out? He glanced at his watch. Thirty minutes since he'd left the doctor. But no one had come this way to find him lying there. They couldn't have, or he'd have woken up in the onsite hospital.

He sat up, rubbing the back of his neck absentmindedly. He must have landed awkwardly, somehow bruising his neck; but it didn't feel bruised.

He looked around. No one. The corridor was totally empty. In a way, he was pleased.

He looked guiltily up at the ceiling, then again felt relief. This corridor was far enough from the lab to be free of surveillance cameras. It wouldn't have done to have been caught collapsing on camera.

He stood up slowly, feeling slightly groggy but otherwise OK. He'd just go to the section, he decided, place the cartridge in the safe and go off to bed. No point telling anyone about this. It wouldn't look so good for him.

A newly-promoted sergeant falling down on the job the first time he was given the responsibility was not the sort of thing that would make the general happy. The cartridge was safe.

No harm done.

Seventeen

At 0600 the next morning, Konstantinova, in winter camouflage combat clothing and carrying an AK105 Kalashnikov assault rifle with a KLIN machine pistol slung across her chest, entered the building that housed the APCs. Hanging from the belt about her waist were ammunition pouches for both weapons. A sizeable fieldpack was on her back. She wore a fur hat, the security service badge prominently displayed at its centre.

Three armoured personnel carriers, twin engines already warmed up, were getting ready to leave. The noise reverberated through the hangar-like buiding. These specialised versions of the BTR-80, soft-terrain eight-wheeled armoured vehicles which were really AFVs – armoured fighting vehicles – carried a turreted gun assembly of twin 23mm cannon, mounted on top. They had boat-shaped hulls with high-mounted exhausts, clearly indicating their amphibious capabilities. Inclusion of the turret meant capacity was down to six, including commander and driver. However, this also meant more space inside and, on stops in the field, allowed at least four people room to sleep lying down.

By one of them, Melev stood watching as Konstantinova approached. His gaze was a blend of male appraisal and finely restrained insolence.

"So you made it, Lieutenant," he began. "We didn't think you'd have the guts, or be foolish enough." He looked her up and down, inspecting her as he would a strange creature. "Well, you look the part. Although I don't know which. Who do you think you'll be meeting out there? American marines?" He gave the field pack a smack that made her stagger slightly, and smirked. "What's in there? Your make-up? At least, you're not wearing a helmet as well."

Without waiting for a reply, he jerked a thumb at the BTR. "You're travelling with me, Lieutenant. Isn't that nice? And guess what? Your violin-playing friend Daminov is with us today. Sweet and cosy. The captain decided he was having too soft a life and should do a patrol now and then to roughen those pretty hands of

235

his. I'm going to enjoy this." He placed his hands on his hips and shook his head in exaggerated despair. "Women."

Konstantinova glared at him. "Sergeant, just you keep remembering I'm not one of your soldiers to push around, and we'll get on fine for the duration of this patrol. OK?"

He glared right back at her. "A sergeant one day, an officer the next." He looked as if he was about to spit at her feet. "I only take orders from the captain."

He turned away from her and began shouting at the troopers to board the APCs.

Urikov entered the building, ignored her completely, and boarded his command vehicle.

Konstantinova walked round the back of the vehicle Melev had indicated, and boarded it via the short watertight armoured ramp. Daminov was already inside. There were two other troopers. One was from the pair that had been beaten at the shooting match. Both men looked back at her impassively.

There was a seat next to Daminov. "Lieutenant," he said.

"Thank you," she said, taking the seat. Like the other soldiers, she did not remove her pack.

"It's going to be noisy in here," Daminov said. "But it's not too bad, really; and light comes in through the driver's windows."

The ramp began to rise, and there was a scrambling noise outside as Melev entered the turret hatch from above. The ramp sealed itself shut.

"Let's go!" Melev shouted, although with his headphones and mike on there'd been no need to yell at the driver.

The BTR began to move.

An hour and a half later, Sergeant Yakulentov knocked on the door to Lirionova's office.

"Come in."

"I'm taking the cartridge back, Major," he said as he entered. He gingerly rubbed at his neck.

"All right." She glanced at the spot he had touched. "Something wrong with your neck?"

"I think I slept awkwardly last night," he replied sheepishly. "Probably a strained muscle."

"Get the medical people to look at it if it continues to give you trouble."

"I will, Major. Now I'd better get that cartridge back to Doctor Vasilyeva, or she'll be after my guts."

Lirionova smiled. "She can be rough where her work is concerned. Off you go."

"Oh, by the way, Major, did Lieutenant Konstantinova really go off on that patrol? She wasn't at breakfast when I went in. I just wondered . . ."

"She's gone. Personally, I think she's crazy. But a challenge is a challenge."

"Yes, Major."

Yakulentov went off to return the cartridge.

The Siberian wilderness, 0910 hours patrol time.

Two of the BTRs had stopped close together. The third, commanded by Urikov, had continued on ahead. The crews were out. They stood in a rough semicircle around Melev, who had a section of a map flattened against the sloping front quarter of the snout of his vehicle.

In this part of the *taiga*, the thaw was well under way; but there were plenty of snow-speckled patches of ground, and the shallow pools of summer were still being held in abeyance by the hard layer of permafrost below ground. Even the trees still bore small loads of snow on their branches.

Everyone was wearing gloves, Konstantinova noted, glad she had also chosen to do so. She was pleased there was no wind. The fierce Siberian blows, she knew, could send the windchill factor into double figures within seconds, despite the time of year.

"You all know the drill," Melev began, "but for the benefit of our guest the lieutenant, I'll go over it again."

There were loud groans.

Melev took it in good heart and grinned. "Yes, yes, I know. But there it is." He smirked at Konstantinova. "Follow closely, Lieutenant."

She looked stonily back at him.

"From this point," Melev continued unperturbed, "we sweep in three directions. The captain has gone on ahead on his sweep. Our BTR will sweep Sector Green One-Five . . . here." A blunt finger jabbed at the map. "And Junior Sergeant Katuschenko's to the left, Sector Red One-Five. The captain has Blue Sector.

"We'll be using sweep pattern Omega, which means we will not meet up again at rendevous point Yellow until the third day but will remain in radio contact at regular four-hour intervals until the last one at nightfall. Emergencies, as usual, have priority.

Julian Jay Savarin

"All BTRs make their individual bivouacs for the night. This routine will continue for the three days of the patrol, as we sweep our designated sectors. Sometimes we will travel across swampy ground or shallow water. Don't worry, Lieutenant, we won't let you drown. The BTR engines can be switched to drive waterjets. So you'll be quite safe. Have you got all that, Lieutenant?"

"I've got it, Sergeant."

"Good. I was afraid I might have to repeat myself."

There were loud sniggers from the others, but Daminov did not join in.

Konstantinova said nothing.

"All right," Melev said. "Let's move!"

Konstantinova listened as the BTR's engines changed cadence. The waterjets were in use. There was a gentle rocking of the vehicle as it swam across what seemed like a large lake. She could just see it through the armoured glass of the driver's windows.

Then the BTR changed course and seemed to be going left. Soon, it was rolling up a gentle slope as the engines again reverted to land drive. It rocked slightly, then the ground was level again. It drove for a while longer, then stopped.

"Everybody out!" Melev ordered.

The ramp was lowered and they piled out of the dripping vehicle. Konstantinova was pleased to find that there was still no wind to speak of. She was lucky with the weather. She hoped it would remain like that.

"There's a remote unmanned listening post three kilometres from here," Melev said as he jumped down from the turret. "The captain wants it checked out to make sure undesirable elements have not come out here to commit sabotage."

Konstantinova looked about her. This was not the time for her to admire nature's wild beauty. The bleak landscape, with its patches of forest and open ground still hard from the permafrost, might have looked beautiful to a lover of nature but, to anyone else, it was singularly uninviting.

"Out here?" she said sceptically.

Melev looked at her with his baleful eyes. "Since when did you become a tactician, Lieutenant?" As usual, he did not wait for a reply. "Three kilometres there and three kilometres back is a nice easy walk to stretch your legs," he continued to the troopers. "Daminov, you stay to guard the vehicle. You three," he said to the other men, "go on ahead. You've been here before so you

238

know the location of the listening post. I will be following with the lieutenant."

"Yes, Sergeant," they said together and looked expressionlessly back at him, but their eyes showed a lively expectation. Daminov looked from them to Melev, to Konstantinova, and back to Melev.

"Sergeant," Daminov said, "I've never been. Perhaps I could go on the patrol to the listening post with you and the lieutenant."

"And who will guard the vehicle?" Melev's mild, reasonable question belied the fact that he had no intention of changing his mind.

"One of the others?"

"Daminov."

"Sergeant?"

"You've got your orders. Now shut up!"

"Yes, Sergeant." Daminov glanced at Konstantinova as if to say sorry.

"All right, you lazy pigs," Melev said to the troopers, "move out! And I'd better not get there before you."

The troopers set off at a trot.

Melev waited a good fifteen minutes before saying, "Our turn, Lieutenant. Daminov!"

"Sergeant?"

"Make sure you're always on the radio. I don't want to have to call you twice. I'll be checking to make sure you're not asleep."

"Yes, Sergeant."

"All right, Lieutenant. If you please." Melev grinned at Konstantinova. "Ladies first."

"We'll walk together, Sergeant," she said, "Or you go first."

Melev's eyes were calculating. "Together then. For now."

As they moved off, Konstantinova was aware of Daminov's worried eyes upon her.

They had been walking for about ten minutes and were in among some pine trees, well out of sight of Daminov, when Melev made the move she'd been long expecting. He suddenly grabbed at her, and hauled her roughly to shove her against the trunk of a big pine. Her fur hat tilted with the force of the shove, nearly covering one eye. She felt her boots sink into the soft detritus of the forest floor.

"You think you're so smart, *Lieutenant*," he snarled. He had his pistol out, its muzzle touching the tip of her nose. "What are you trying to prove, eh? That you women can soldier with the best of us? You were stupid to come on this patrol, and you deserve what you're going to get. And don't think that ponce Daminov would have been any help to you. We would have chewed him to pieces. Accident, we would have said. He fell into a lake and drowned. They would find him perhaps in a thousand years, frozen in the ice like those things the scientists dig up.

"Or perhaps you think your fellow officer the captain will back you afterwards, when you make your complaint. Forget it. The captain's one of us. A hard man who came up the hard way. He *always* backs his troops. You're on your own, *Lieutenant* . . . really on your own, kilometres and kilometres from anywhere. The men up front won't expect us for a while. Without me, you don't get back; so be nice. Now drop your weapons and the pack."

She did as she was told, watching him carefully.

"Open your combat smock."

"I'll freeze."

"Fucking open it!"

She began to obey, but was too slow for his liking.

"Come on!" he said roughly, staying close to her. "I haven't got all fucking day!" He reached for the smock to do it himself.

A sudden gasping wheeze came out of him. The gun fell out of his hand. His foul breath fanned at her as his mouth opened wide in astonishment. His eyes seemed to be popping in slow motion and a strange squeaking sound now followed the wheeze.

She stood where she was, looking straight into the popping eyes.

Melev looked slowly and painfully down to where her gloved right hand was jammed against his stomach. It held a knife, buried to the hilt.

The knife moved and he jerked in response, wheezing louder. It moved again, wrecking his insides.

"Someone," she said tightly, "tried this with me once. He got what you're getting."

He fell slowly away from the knife, the blade coming out of him with reluctance. There was remarkably little blood on it. As he hit the ground, his combat helmet bounced off his head. Both Melev's hands were grabbing at his stomach now, as if to quell the pain that was still preventing him from speaking.

"A present from Natasha," she added coldly.

His mouth moved several times, like a beached fish panting to return to the water. A violent tremor went through his entire frame.

At last he seemed able to speak. His eyes were staring at her with an unreal intensity.

"Your . . . your voice. You sound . . . different. Who . . . who are you?"

"Wouldn't you like to know."

She wiped the knife against his clothes and he watched with surreal interest as she returned the knife to its sheath beneath her combat smock.

"I never . . . spotted that," he said.

She made no comment. With a swift economy of motion she set her hat firmly back upon her head, secured her smock, picked up the fieldpack and put that back on, then picked up her weapons.

"Don't leave . . . me here like this," he pleaded. "I know . . . this is a bad wound. I . . . won't make it. Shoot me. Let me die . . . like a soldier. You're a . . . soldier."

"I thought you said I wasn't."

"The . . . way you move. Very different . . . now. You are . . . soldier. Shoot me. Afraid . . . the others will hear . . . the shot? The captain . . . the captain will get you. You'll never . . . get away from here."

"If only you knew, Sergeant."

There was an authority in her voice that brought a frown to his forehead. He sensed he was listening to someone who was more than a newly-promoted lieutenant.

"Who are . . ." Then he died.

It happened so unobtrusively it was like a pause tagged on to his last words, the question still incomplete.

She looked down at the body. "I can't feel regret," she said. "Sorry."

She stooped to do some swift rearranging of the dead sergeant's clothes, then set off after the others.

She knew just how she was going to trap them.

From a distance, the listening post looked like a mound of stunted grass. Closer inspection showed it to be a small blockhouse, just big enough for two people to squeeze inside to check the equipment.

From the air, it looked like just another clump of vegetation. Its antennae were superbly camouflaged, looking like shrub branches even at close range. The post, and others like it, were sophisticated remote eavesdropping stations which formed part of a network that served Kurinin's clandestine organisation.

They had never been sabotaged, for the very good reason that only one agency outside Kurinin's group knew of their existence; but Kurinin knew nothing of this. It was not in the unknown agency's interest to sabotage them; although it could have done so at any time, had it so wished.

The three troopers that Melev had sent on ahead were still more than a kilometre from their destination. They walked bunched together, not expecting anything to interrupt the routine of their journey. They looked as if they were on a morning stroll.

"Think he's giving it to her?" the one who had been beaten at the shooting contest asked.

"By now? Bound to. You know what he's like. He always wanted to fuck an officer."

"Of either sex?"

They laughed bawdily at that.

"To me she's still a sergeant," another said.

"She's an officer," the third insisted. "Get used to it. It doesn't matter how she got the promotion. I think it's a bad thing the sergeant's doing. When she gets back—"

"Who says she's getting back, Baliniev?"

The one called Baliniev stared at the speaker. "Have you all gone crazy? She's Intelligence! The general will not stand for it! Do you all want to get shot on some lonely night?"

"What's the matter? Guts turned to water?"

"You're both mad," Baliniev insisted. "Melev will destroy you. He was always borderline—"

"Crazy or not, he's a good soldier."

"He's gone over the edge," Baliniev said firmly. "You can't just take a woman officer out here – an Intelligence officer especially – screw her, kill her, and then hope to get away with it. I'm telling you, he'll get you all shot."

"She came of her own free will. She'll have an accident."

"I want nothing to do with this," Baliniev said.

"We're a team. We always support the team. Melev and the captain will see we're clean."

"Clean? I'm a soldier. I don't fuck and then murder female officers." Baliniev strode on ahead.

The other two looked at each other. "Trouble."

"Melev will sort him out."

She knew exactly where the listening post was.

She had made good time, easily catching up with the slowly moving soldiers. She could see them up ahead as she shadowed them from cover. They had stuck to open ground in order to make rapid progress; but they weren't really doing so.

When she thought she was close enough she removed her pack and unslung the rifle. She kept the KLIN.

She quickly unfastened a small compartment on the pack and removed three small items which she put into a side pocket on her smock. Securing the fieldpack again, she hid pack and rifle, and marked the position with short lengths of small dead branches, placed in a manner that made it seem as if they'd been there all winter.

Then she pointed the KLIN into the air and fired two deliberately spaced shots.

They seem to echo through the entire forest and beyond.

Baliniev stopped. "Shots."

The others had also stopped.

"Hunters?" one suggested. "Aren't there supposed to be wolves around here?" He looked about him as if expecting to see a pack of wolves coming at them.

"Don't be stupid," Baliniev snapped. "Hunters? Out here? Wolves?"

"Why not wolves?"

Then the shots came again, effectively putting an end to the bickering.

"The sergeant! He's in trouble! Come on!"

"We don't know that," Baliniev insisted. "He gave us our orders. You know what he's like . . ."

"He's in trouble, I tell you! Come on! Let's go!"

They started back, disobeying their orders. Baliniev followed reluctantly.

She now lay in cover, watching as they came closer, arguing among themselves weapons at the ready. She had positioned herself so that they would pass close by. Despite having been alerted by the shots, they had still not sufficiently increased their situation awareness. In any potential combat arena, such laxity could easily prove fatal. Today they would be luckier than most.

"Stop right there!"

They were so shocked to hear her voice they came to an abrupt halt.

"What the hell's going on, Lieutenant?" the more truculent one shouted. "Where's the sergeant?"

They peered towards the forest, trying to work out where she was.

"Drop your weapons!"

"What?"

Two rapid shots barked into the cold silence. All three jumped; they couldn't help themselves.

"Hey! OK, OK! We're dropping them. Keep your panties on!"

Two more shots followed.

"All right! It was a joke!"

"Jokes like that can get you killed."

They dropped their weapons and raised their hands without being asked.

"Look," the one who had elected to speak began, "it was the sergeant's idea."

She smiled to herself. They quite obviously could not even begin to work out what had happened, and had latched on to the one idea that would fit the way they were thinking. Even though they could not work out how a supposedly inept brand new female officer had managed to get away from Melev after being raped, it was the only thing they could imagine.

"Share and share alike was it? It that what it was going to be?"

"No!" Panic. "It was not like that at all. Look, where's the sergeant?"

"Dead, with a knife in his gut."

That got them. It was clear what they were thinking. A raped woman bent on revenge . . . with a gun and a knife!

"Look," Baliniev began, reason in his voice. "I was not going to be in on this—"

"Easy for you to say."

"It's true!"

"Baliniev, you shit!" the truculent one snarled.

"Quiet all of you!" she snapped. "If you don't want to be like your sergeant, do exactly as I say. Turn around!"

They obeyed.

"Remove your helmets."

"Wha—"

"Remove them!"

The helmets dropped to the ground.

"Anyone who turns round is a dead man."

"You sound different—"

"Shut up! I mean it about your turning round. You'd never make it."

They never knew when she got behind them. Each felt something thinly sharp enter his neck. As rapid unconsciousness hit, they fell raggedly to the ground. Working quickly, she dragged each man and his weapon to the edge of the patch of forest. She put their helmets back on. They'd be out long enough for her purposes. In her pocket were the three now-empty ampoules with which she had punctured their necks.

She went back to collect her gear and headed out for the listening post at a pace that would have surprised the soldiers, had they been awake to observe it.

She reached the listening post in half the time it would have taken Melev's troopers. She made no attempt to get inside. Instead, she put down her rifle, removed the fieldpack and took something out of it that looked like a large mobile phone. It was in fact a combined communication unit and computer. She reached again into the pack and took out the virus cartridge. She slotted it into the zipdrive of the comm unit and, standing deliberately near the post, pressed the SEND button.

A satellite passing overhead picked up the coded burst and relayed it to another satellite which in turn relayed it to a terrestrial receiving station somewhere in Alaska. The same message, newly encoded, went back to the second satellite which then relayed it to an AWACS flying a racecourse track near Iceland. The AWACS sent the signal on to a receiving unit in the Baltics. The entire automatic transmission took less than a second. Her single touch of the SEND button had initiated it all.

She removed the zip cartridge. It had no further use. Like the fieldpack and the firearms, it would find a resting place in a freezing lake somewhere. She had just picked up the fieldpack and the rifle, when she heard the sound of engines.

"Right on time," she said with satisfaction.

She stood by the listening post as the APC came to a halt, almost touching her. The turret hatch opened. Urikov's head poked through, then he climbed out.

He scrambled off the vehicle and approached her, face impassive. They stood watching each other for a few moments. Then suddenly he grinned and embraced her tightly, strong arms going about her own arms which hung down, weighted by the pack and the rifle.

He let go and stood back. "So you did it."

"Hello, Max. Yes, I did it."

"You always were the computer genius. Still are, obviously. You were good even as a pimply teenager. You taught the old hands a thing or two."

"I was never a pimply teenager."

"No. You weren't."

She stared at him. "You bastard," she said cheerfully. "Nobody warned me you had come back in. And up here, of all places! I nearly died of shock when I realised who 'Urikov' really was."

"You're good at what you do," the man she'd called Max said unrepentantly. "You gave nothing away. I knew you could handle it, even when surprised."

"So you *were* told I'd be slotted in?"

He nodded. "One of us had to know. As I was already on site, it made sense."

"The change in you!" she said wonderingly. "Last time I saw you, you were trying to drink yourself to death on a beach in Portugal. What changed your mind?"

"You. You gave me a roasting, if you remember. You were hard that day, Mac, almost nasty. But you did me a favour. You made me see myself as I was. Self-pitying."

"I was watching a good man go down. I couldn't just stand there and do nothing. So . . . you've gotten over her?"

"Oh no," he told her soberly. "That's going to take years. But getting back into the business helps take my mind off her. Back then in the bad old times, I was navel-gazing with the grape; and the slope was going one way. Downhill."

"Now that you're back, be careful, Max. I know you're using the danger as a pain barrier but remember, Kurinin is very dangerous and very clever. Never forget it."

"I've been commanding his security troops for a while now. I can handle it."

She smiled. "You're still very good at planning multi-level strategies. That shooting contest, this patrol—"

"And Melev. Let's not forget Melev. His predictability made the whole thing work."

"Where on earth did you find him?"

"Moscow. I saved his life in a brawl, then offered him the job at the research unit."

"Saved him? I don't suppose you managed to start the brawl yourself?"

"There were people around who wanted a fight," he replied obliquely.

"So Melev had been picked out ages ago, at some other unit?"

"You know how things work, Mac. Plans are made well ahead. What happend to him?"

"Dead."

Max did not seem surprised. "And the others?"

"Dozing in the forest back there. I gave them stronger shots than the one I gave Yakulentov. We'll be well away by the time they wake up. They'll concoct their own story, blaming Melev for what happened while keeping themselves out of it."

"As we expected."

She nodded. "I feel sorry for Olga; her entire work is going to be destroyed."

"You've sent the virus on?"

She nodded. "Yes. I copied the original onto a zip cartridge from the Section stock, then coded some new instructions for the virus itself before putting it back into Yakulentov's pocket. The clean copy, which I've got with me, I used for the transmission. I wish I could have bought Olga out though."

"She'll be brought out."

Mac looked hopeful. "You're sure?"

He nodded. "Contingencies have been made. Let's say her talents are needed elsewhere."

"Does she know?"

He shook his head. "She has no idea and never will. I'm still the super-macho brute she believes I am. And now, we'd better get *you* out. Kurinin will be after your blood with a vengeance when he finally works out what has really happened. You must be out of the country well before that occurs."

"And you?"

"I told you. I can handle it."

He scrambled back up the APC and climbed through the turret. Soon, she heard the sound of the ramp being lowered. She hurried round the rear and got in. "Max" Urikov was the only other person inside. He was now in the driver's seat.

"Your men!" she called. "Where are they?"

"Waiting two kilometres from here. There are only two of them. I made a habit of varying the number I took on patrol so that it became a familiar thing. The two out there are handpicked."

"You mean they're—"

"Yes. But they will only see you when you have changed."

"So how many people do we have in that research unit?"

"Enough. Now you had better get changed. We'll dispose of your gear later."

As she began to get things out of the fieldpack, she thought drily how right Melev had been when he'd sarcastically asked if she had her make-up in there.

She began to change quickly as the vehicle moved off. By the time the APC had stopped to pick up Urikov's men, a fat woman nearing sixty who could have been anyone's grandmother and who looked beaten by life, was sitting in place of the lithe young woman. The men climbed into the hull of the vehicle, nodded at her, but did not engage in conversation. One of them replaced Urikov in the driver's seat.

The APC travelled for several more kilometres before coming to a halt. Urikov climbed out of the turret. Mac got out, now carrying a rough bag. The two men remained inside. A civilian vehicle that looked like a Jeep Cherokee was waiting. The driver did not get out.

Urikov came to stand next to her. "This car will take you to your next stop. Someone else will pick you up—"

"I do know the route out, Max."

"Yes. Of course you do. I won't wish you luck."

"No. We never used to." She studied his face. "You look very different to when I saw you out there in Portugal."

He grinned. "How do you like the brutish look? Bit old for a captain, but it fits the role."

"Still very young for a general," she said. "That's what you are now, I suppose?"

"Perhaps," he said. He, in turn, studied her new persona. "You were always very good at this too. You're still the best pupil I ever had. Watch yourself, Colonel."

"And you, General. Try to forget her, Max," she went on softly. "Time to let go. I know it's the boring old thing everyone says in situations like this but—"

"Easier said than done," he told her quietly. "When someone gets under your skin the way she did mine . . ." Abruptly, he turned and climbed back onto the APC.

He disappeared through the hatch. The APC moved off.

She walked towards the waiting vehicle with the slow steps of an aging woman who had experienced a tough life. She opened the door and climbed with apparent difficulty into the Cherokee clone.

The driver said nothing to her as he put it into gear.

Baliniev and his comrades came to, feeling stiff and cold. They jumped up and down to renew circulation, then decided to look for the sergeant. When they eventually found him, they looked down in shock, uncertain of what to do. They stared at his clothing and came to the conclusion they were supposed to.

"We ought to look for her," Baliniev said.

"Are you crazy? Look at the sergeant!"

"She's out there, wandering about, probably going crazy. She'll freeze to death tonight."

"So what?"

"He tried to rape her!" Baliniev said. "So she killed him. It's happened before, you know. Any night in Moscow, or Leningrad, or—"

"Forget it, Baliniev! The wolves can have her. I'm not going after any madwoman with a knife. Go ahead, if you want to get castrated."

"She could have done that before if she'd wanted to. We were out of it, or have you forgotten? And what wolves?"

"Fuck off! Let's get the sergeant back to the APC. The captain will have somebody's balls for this."

"Not mine," Baliniev said. "I tried to stop it."

"Of course you did, you whining shit! Make yourself useful. Here. Help me move him. Take the feet. Then go find a fucking dead branch strong enough to carry his weight."

"Who are you to give me orders?"

"I'm senior to you, Baliniev. Go on then!"

It took the reluctant Baliniev about five minutes to find a suitable length of wood that had not rotted over the winter. He tested it by putting one end on the trunk of a fallen tree and jumping on it a few times. The log withstood the onslaught.

"This should do," he said, hauling the log back to them. "I still say we should try and find her," he added, returning to his theme.

"*You* go and find her, bleeding heart. The wolves can have the both of you. Now help us tie the sergeant round this, if you're going to hang around."

Using ropes from their packs, the three soldiers trussed Melev's body by its hands and feet, suspending him beneath the log as they would an animal kill. Then they began to make their way back to their APC, two of them carrying the log on their shoulders.

Baliniev got the end with the feet.

Daminov was sitting on the opened ramp when they came into view about an hour later. He sprang to his feet and stared dumbstruck as they approached with the sergeant's body.

"What the hell happened?" he demanded. "Where's the lieutenant? Where's the lieutenant, Vladimirov?" he asked the senior trooper. He grabbed Vladimirov by the shoulders. *"What have you done to her?"*

Vladimirov poked his assault rifle into Daminov's stomach with a force that made Daminov stagger.

"Touch me again," Vladimirov snarled, "and I'll blow your fucking guts out, you violin-playing ponce!"

"Oh that's it," Baliniev said. "We shoot each other now."

Vladimirov rounded on him. "Shut the fuck up! Let's get the sergeant in the vehicle."

Daminov said, "I'm going to make contact with the captain's APC."

The rifle pointed. "You wait till I tell you to."

"What? Are you mad? The sergeant's dead and the lieutenant's missing! We've got to tell the captain! Baliniev!" Daminov appealed to the one person he felt would understand.

"Don't look at me. Vladimirov seems to think he's the sergeant now."

"Let me think!" Vladimirov said. "Put the sergeant down."

They put Melev's body in the APC, then freed it from the pole.

As he dragged the length of wood back out, Baliniev said, "What's there to think about? Melev raped the lieutenant. She killed him. Now she's wandering about out there, probably out of her skull."

He said nothing about being ambushed by her. The others chose not to correct his story. Collective guilt was working just as Mac had thought it would.

Daminov looked from one to the other. "I still think we should call the captain. If we don't, can you imagine what he'll do when he does find out?"

"All right," Vladimirov said at last. "Here's the story. Melev raped her. She killed him. We tried to find her but couldn't. We brought the sergeant back. Now we're reporting her as lost. The captain can then get all three APCs to carry out a co-ordinated search and bring out helicopters as well. I still think she'll be dead by the time they find her. But go ahead."

Daminov went to the radio.

"Shit," he said after a few seconds.

"What's wrong?" Baliniev asked.

"The radio's dead. Completely. Not a peep."

Eighteen

H elm was on the podium. Behind him, the large map with the mission waypoints to target was displayed. In addition to the mission crews, both Jason and da Vinci were in attendance.

"You have all had as many briefings as you're likely to need," he began, "and as you will have heard from the met people, the weather is in your favour for tonight: good, but with doubtful visibility on the way back. Not so good for any pursuing bogeys, unless they go to missiles. Cloud cover and moist air should degrade their infrared rounds. If you're out of there fast enough, they shouldn't even see you."

"They could be waiting," McCann suggested.

Helm looked at him. "You would like an easy life, Mr McCann?"

"So boring, sir, an easy life."

"*If* there are bogeys waiting," Helm continued, after a hard stare at McCann, "the escorts will tie them up while the Starfire completes the mission. However, remember the rules of engagement. No use of weapons unless fired upon first."

McCann looked as if he wanted to say something about that but wisely kept his mouth shut.

Helm then switched on the remote and placed the illuminated arrow on a point fifty nautical miles north-east of November One.

"Waypoint Alpha. After take-off, you'll be at Flight Level four fifty for a fast transit to your first refuelling rendezvous. You will note that this has now been changed. At the end of the briefing, navs will download the new data for systems update."

The arrow moved from Waypoint Alpha at 45,000 feet to a point almost directly west of the Friesian Islands off Wittmundhafen. STARFIRE AARA 1 FL 290, was captioned on the map.

"Descend to Flight Level two ninety for your first rendezvous with a tanker. Take on fuel and continue descent until you cross northern Germany at one thousand feet. Notify Eggebek on Channel one eleven as you overfly. Once over the sea again, descend to lo-lo

251

for your high-speed dash – naturally *without* burners – to target. You should still have enough fuel left to mix it with bogeys, should they put in an appearance.

"Don't make a party of it. Be quick. Any such engagement must be offensive defence. In short, you will drag them away from base, making them fuel conscious and getting worried about fighting out of their own airspace. As you will be just on the edge, it won't take long to drag them there.

"If you meet Su-27s, despite the fact that they possess a high internal fuel capacity it is unlikely they will be fully topped up. If they have been on combat air patrol, they may even be running short by the time you arrive. On egress, your next refueller will be at Flight Level three hundred, here."

Another caption had taken up position on the screen: STARFIRE AARA 2 FL 300.

The lighted arrow was pointing to a Baltic island.

"Thirty nautical miles southwest of Bornholm," Helm said, "at thirty thousand feet. Take on all the fuel you can carry and make a high-speed high-altitude dash for home. To make life easier there will be two refuellers with a one thousand-foot altitude separation and five miles apart. One pair of escorts to one tanker, the other pair will accompany the Starfire to the second tanker.

"The target is two hours ahead of us. You are timed to arrive at twenty hundred hours local time, eighteen hundred mission time. This allows for two hours of flight, including refuelling during ingress. The twilight should be perfect. Time of discharge of the EMPC *must* be twenty hundred hours local time. Take-off is at sixteen hundred hours. Any questions?"

There were none. The map on the screen vanished and the lights came back up.

"Then I thank you. I wish you all good luck. Come back in one piece." He tightened his lips in one of his well-known near-invisible smiles. "Besides, Mr Selby and Mr Hohendorf, I have not yet finished giving pain to your mess bills." He gave a brisk little nod and stepped off the podium.

"That should make you guys hurry back," McCann whispered to Selby.

"I heard that!" Helm said. But he didn't look too mean.

Mark Selby favoured McCann with a glance that could best be described as dagger-tipped.

McCann held his counsel as Jason left his seat to stand before them in front of the podium.

"I've not much more to add. You've all worked very hard to get yourselves up to speed in the very little time available. You're as familiar with the details of the mission as you're ever likely to be and I have every faith you'll carry it out successfully. What you do this evening will make a vital difference to the way the international climate develops in the near and not-so-distant future.

"The Starfire mission is being launched to cope with exactly the kind of situation we are in existence to deal with. The disappearance of the old certainties, terrifying as they were, has brought in its wake something even more terrifying: out-of-control uncertainties. Our job is to neutralise these as effectively as possible, whenever they occur. I'll simply echo Commander Helm. See that you're all back here, in one piece."

At exactly 1600 hours November time, the Starfire lifted its nose and climbed towards the first waypoint. It was followed by the two pairs of ASV Echoes. Soon, Starfire and escort had disappeared into the high blue.

An eerie expectancy settled upon the station. Everyone knew this was the first mission ever launched by the unit with a female pilot going into possible combat. Everyone was hoping she would make it back.

Jason stood by his window, still hearing in his mind the thunder of the ten engines as the five aircraft raced down the runway. He hoped he would be watching all five returning to land at base.

A knock made him turn. "Come in."

Rose Gentry appeared. "Major Morton, sir."

"Ah yes. Send him in, please."

She stood to one side outside the door. "The wing commander will see you now, Major."

"Thank you."

Morton entered and saluted. Rose Gentry closed the door quietly behind him.

"At ease, Major. You may remove the cap."

"Sir." Morton took off his peaked cap.

"I'm certain you're wondering," Jason began, "why I did not include you in the mission. You may speak frankly, Mr Morton."

"Well yes, sir. I've been wondering about that. Why wasn't I selected?"

"To begin with," Jason said, "we needed just the four escorts. Secondly, I needed the most combat-experienced ASV crews. I know you've been in combat with the ASV and you've got a kill, but Major Carlizzi was your backseater that day. However, we needed him for the Starfire. We have still not found you the permanent backseater we feel you deserve but many suitable ones are coming through. You won't have a long wait."

"I'm glad to hear that, sir."

"Chuck, I do appreciate your keenness. I want only the keen ones here and I can promise you there'll be more missions coming your way than you will believe possible."

Jason glanced briefly out of his window as two training aircraft taxied past.

"The world's on a knife edge, Major," he continued. "Unfortunately, there are not as many people trying to prevent it from tipping over as there are doing the pushing. You'll get all the combat flying you're likely to want but sometimes, *not* getting into a combat situation can be even more important. Tonight, my hope is that there won't be one."

"Understood, sir."

"And now tell me; the envelope that came for you not so long ago . . . Was it good news?"

"It was, sir," Morton answered.

Just three words written upon it. As usual, there had been no indication of originating location.

I love you, Mac had written.

He wondered where she now was and hoped she was safe.

"Good show," Jason said.

Five hours east of where Morton was standing, the aging woman, now wearing thick glasses, was sitting on one of the cheaper seats of the Trans-Siberian Railway, heading westwards. She was trying to sleep but was clearly not being successful and was having a difficult time getting comfortable. A young man, sitting opposite, had been regarding her sympathetically.

"You look tired," he said, making conversation.

"I am," she admitted. She gave a loud sigh. "This is such a long journey. And at my age . . ." She sighed again. Her accent marked her from eastern Siberia.

"How far are you going?"

"To Leningrad to see my daughter and my grandchildren. She lives there with her husband. He is from Leningrad." She sounded as if she did not approve of a son-in-law from the distant Baltic city on the edge of western Russia.

"Leningrad? You mean St Petersburg."

"I mean Leningrad," she said firmly, weak eyes looking at him sternly from behind the glasses. "My daughter is very good, even if she lives so far away. I am now alone, but she won't get me going to live out there with her and that man of hers. Do you know he even has clothes from the Western capitalist countries? But she sends me some money, and these glasses are from her. She also sends my ticket when I go to visit her."

The young man's expression clearly showed he thought he was dealing with a diehard communist. The old ones refused to accept change. Leningrad indeed. But he was prepared to humour her.

"It is a very long journey for you," he agreed. "I am going to Moscow. My first time. I have a job with a hotel. I want to be a chef."

"To cook for foreigners," she said dismissively. "A cook is a cook. Ordinary Russians cannot afford hotels where *chefs* cook." She heaved a sigh and began to nod off.

"Would you like my coat?" he asked solicitously, still prepared to humour her. "I can fold it and you can use it as a pillow. Perhaps that will help you sleep better."

"You are a kind boy," she said, relenting slightly. "Thank you. But I'll be all right. When you get to my age sleeping is like losing valuable time, so perhaps I shouldn't do too much of it." She clasped her gloved hands on her stomach and tried to doze again.

He smiled tolerantly and left her to it.

But she was going a lot further than St Petersburg, and not all of it by train. She would eventually be flying from Tallinn in Estonia to Helsinki in Finland. That would not be the end of her journey either.

And she would no longer be a middle-aged grandmother.

The Special Research Unit, 2106 hours local.

Olga Vasilyeva stared at the monitor, then peered through the microscope once more. She couldn't understand it. The virus appeared to have mutated. She studied the monitor again and tapped at the keyboard. A series of codes she did not recognise scrolled at reading pace.

She stared. What the hell was going on?

"Sergeant!" she called to Yakulentov who, again on duty, was standing nearby. She was still staring at the monitor.

"Yes, Doctor?"

"You haven't been playing around with the equipment in here, have you?"

"Me?"

"No, no. Of course not. It's a crazy idea. Never mind. Forget the question."

A bemused Yakulentov looked at her as she continued to divide her attention between the monitor and the microscope.

"Yes, Doctor," he said.

Scientists, he thought. Didn't know one day from the next.

Waypoint Alpha, 1606 hours mission time.

"And here we are at forty-five thousand feet," McCann said as he looked about him. The five aircraft, with the two escort pairs in combat spread on either side of the Starfire, were almost translucent in the bright sun. "Don't we look beautiful."

He glanced down at the nav display. Time for course change counting down. Six zeroes appeared. As one, the five aircraft turned onto the new heading. Communication between them had been unnecessary.

"One thing about what Commander Helm said," McCann went on as they settled onto the new heading.

"I know you're going to tell me," Selby remarked wearily.

"Yeah well . . . what makes him think the bogey pilots have read the same book that he has? They may not be out of fuel. They may follow us well out of their airspace. They may be mad as hell and won't give a shit about how far they chase us—"

"And they may all have bad colds and go home. Scared?"

"Sure I am," McCann replied with disarming candour. "But it doesn't mean I'll lose it if things get hot."

"You never lose it up here, Elmer Lee. Down on the ground, now that's another story."

"Never lose it, huh? Hey. That's a nice thing to say. I guess you really do like me after all."

"Don't push it," Selby growled at him.

But Selby was smiling in his mask.

The first refuelling rendezvous was made on time and from 29,000 feet they began the descent that would take them across the top of Germany near the Danish border at 1,000 feet.

They carried out their notification on Channel 111 as they overflew, heading eastwards and back out to sea.

"Roger, Starfire," came the acknowledgement.

Then they were dashing at high speed across the Baltic, as low as they dared.

The Special Research Unit, east of the Urals.

"Better get ready for a long night, Sergeant," Olga Vasilyeva warned Yakulentov. "I'm going to be here for some time. There is a problem I must try to correct."

She couldn't understand it. The virus had not only mutated but appeared to have created its own set of instructions, defying all attempts by her to find a way of countering it.

"If you want to go off to bed, Sergeant, you can. I won't tell anyone."

Very mindful of what had occurred the night before, Yakulentov had no intention of leaving without the zip cartridge.

"I'll stay as long as is necessary," he said.

"All very commendable, I'm sure. Oh well, suit yourself. I'll probably be here till morning. We've got the coffee machine and the samovar in the rest room. Help yourself to tea or coffee. No alcohol, I'm afraid. But there may be some chocolate bars as well."

"I'll have the coffee, thanks. Can I get you something?"

"No. Thank you. I'm all right. And don't come back in here with your coffee. I don't want an accidental spill on the equipment."

"Yes, Doctor."

When the sergeant had gone to the rest room, she studied the virus's antics on the monitor.

"So what got into you?" she asked the screen.

If she made no progress by morning she would have to inform Lirionova, who would then immediately inform the general.

It was not a prospect she was looking forward to.

Melev's patrol APC, the Siberian wilderness.

They had pitched their one-man tents near the BTR-80 APC. A chemical lightstick picked out the BTR with a subdued glow. No one had wanted to stay in the vehicle with the dead body.

Vladimirov had put Daminov and Baliniev on first watch; Daminov because he chose to blame him for the unserviceable radio and Baliniev because he was paying him back just for the hell of it.

"The captain's bound to come and check why we haven't made our call," Baliniev said to Daminov as they paced a short distance from the BTR. "He'll pick up the emergency beacon."

"I feel sick," Daminov said. "The lieutenant's out there all on her own. We should have tried to look for her. There's nothing wrong with the APC; our navigation systems are working; we know where we are and you three roughly know her last position. We could have searched for her. She could be wandering anywhere by now. There are pools and swamps she could stumble into. We're in big trouble for leaving her like this."

"Would you like to say all that to Vladimirov? He'd shoot us, and the APC would still remain here. The captain will come looking, then we'll see."

"She'll be dead by then of cold, if nothing else."

"She's got her pack. She can pitch her tent and wait. She's also got her personal beacon. She's not completely helpless."

"Who knows what state her mind's in? She's killed a man who was raping her."

Vladimirov poked his head out of his tent. "Are you two old women going to shut up?" he yelled savagely. "I'm trying to catch some sleep! You'd better let me, if you want to be relieved later. Or you can both stand guard all fucking night!"

"What about the wolves, Vladimirov?" Baliniev sneered. "You're more afraid of Melev's body than the wolves?"

"You're asking for it, Baliniev!" Vladimirov, ghostly in the dim light, withdrew his head angrily.

"See what I mean?" Baliniev said to Daminov in a low voice.

"I see what you mean."

Experimental CybOrganoSensor (ECOS) Field Unit, Baltic region.

The person who had supplied the access code had been at station at the precise time to monitor the download of Mac's transmission, and had watched as the virus had been incorporated into the system. The infected codes had been transmitted at light speed along conduits, transforming the cellular nanos into self-cannibals.

The unit was already dying as the infection spread rapidly but it would take some considerable time before this would be spotted. By then, it would already be far too late, even for neutralising action. Besides, no counter-action could be taken.

There was no cure.

At the Special Research Unit in the Urals, Olga Vasilyeva was still working away, trying to discover how the already cannibalistic nanos in her sample had become what could only be described as clinically insane.

1729 hours, mission time.

Caroline held the Starfire steady at one hundred feet above the water. She had programmed the autothrottle for 600 knots. She left the throttle leavers alone while she concentrated on maintaining the aircraft's altitude. None of the aircraft were using their radars for height referencing in order to reduce the risk of early detection. At current speed, there would be no tell-tale sonic booms trailing in their wake.

She glanced to her left and saw a pair of ASVs slightly below her, one even lower than the other: Hohendorf and Flacht, and Bagni and Stockmann.

"If he goes much lower," Carlizzi was saying, "there'll be plumes of steamed water marking out a trail. See it for miles." He'd obviously been checking them out from time to time. "The low guy's in the lead. Must be Hohendorf. He's the low-level hotshot around here."

But Hohendorf's aircraft was just above the point at which watersteaming would begin.

"He's balancing it finely," Carlizzi said.

"And *I* know my limits," she said. "I'm not going any lower."

"Hey, this is good stuff. You're doing fine. We're nearly there and it looks like we haven't excited anybody yet. Malmo FIR's over to our left but we're ten miles outside the boundary, so we shouldn't be getting any interrogation from our Swedish pals." Carlizzi searched the sky above. "And I don't see any friendly Viggens or Gripens coming round for a peep. Three-zero minutes to target."

Three hundred miles to go in just thirty minutes.

She glanced at the nav display page on one of her MFDs. The time to target read 00:30:00. It moved to 00:29:59, counting down.

The Malmo flight information region extended round Bornholm, she knew, then up towards the Gulf of Bothnia to join Stockholm FIR. Not where they were going.

"Is Bornholm Swedish?"

"Danish, but closer to Sweden."

"Like the Channel Islands are closer to France."

"I guess. Before you know it," Carlizzi went on, "things are gonna start happening real fast. Suddenly, you'll begin to wonder where the time's gone. So here's the sequence. At thirty miles out and three minutes to target, you arm the weapon. That will save you time. You know the routine. At twenty-five miles and thirty seconds to range, accelerating now, you do a pitch up to one thousand feet for the weapon to acquire.

"Once in range, your pitch-up will send all the alarm bells haywire, if we're still clean by then. They'll then sure know we're around. Just like in the simulator, the weapon will do its own acquisition and ranging, and will fire when ready. All you do at the pitch-up is hold on to that trigger. The discharges will go off like greased lightning and we'll be getting the hell out of there. Hopefully, we won't have any hostile company as we hightail it home."

"But we might."

"We surely might. Do I repeat that stuff again? Or you're OK?"

"I'm OK."

In Starfire Zero-One, Flacht had been keeping a sharp eye on an MFD infrared display, searching out any shipping along their flight path.

He knew the other backseaters would be doing the same. So far, though they had flown past a mix of vessels of various sizes including ferries, fishing boats and a couple of cruise ships, no warships of any nation had been spotted. Their route had been devised to make such encounters as unlikely as possible.

However, an image that had appeared onscreen was now exciting his interest.

"Take a look at this," he said to Hohendorf in German, repeating it to the front cockpit. "ID coming up."

He raised the magnification of the rounded twin-masted shape with the interesting superstructure. Distance and bearing were constantly updating. Then the ID was blinking for attention: TRAWLER – INTELLIGENCE GATHERING. CODE 329A.

Flacht knew that if he called up the code, full ID including name or number of the ship would follow. But there was little need. They knew it was the kind of ship stationed to report NATO aircraft movements. As its presence in the area had not been in the Intelligence notes, this could only mean its deployment was very recent, a matter of hours.

"Think he's spotted us?" Hohendorf asked, as the ship, which had been off their left wing, disappeared rapidly behind them.

Flacht kept the historical image on the MFD for a while longer. He then replaced it with new real-time images of other ships.

"Five aircraft flying very low heading east," Flacht said. "I'm certain he will. Too late to worry about it. The other Starfire aircraft will have picked it up too."

"Perhaps he will think we're on a routine exercise."

"Perhaps."

But they didn't really think so.

As Flacht had said, the other backseaters had indeed spotted the trawler.

In the Starfire, Carlizzi, knowing the trawler for what it really was, said to Caroline, "That trawler could be trouble."

"How bad?"

"Time will tell. We're nearly there so reaction time may not be quick enough to be a problem."

"On the other hand . . ."

"Yeah," Carlizzi said. "Could be an interesting ball game."

Lieutenant-Colonel Pedrov had taken his entire complement of six brand-new Su-35s aloft for a general training flight cum combat air patrol.

The Su-35 – an advanced version of the Su-27 – while it did not have the vectoring nozzles of the experimental Su-37, was fitted with the canard foreplanes that gave the big and powerful machine exceptional agility. However, trials of the Su-35 were still going one and, despite the Kurinin-initiated deployment of the six examples to Pedrov's unit, they were really operational prototypes.

Pedrov's further problem was that two of his pilots, good as they were, were still too inexperienced to be turned loose in such potent machines. Left to him, he would not have had them on the squadron at all. He could think of many other, more experienced pilots he would have chosen, given a free hand. Moreover, much as he personally loved the new aircraft with its advanced displays and its sidestick controller, he would have been happier with the earlier, central-stick Su-27K which had been through its thorough testing programme and was fully integrated into the service. Some 35s had the central stick, but none were on his unit.

He was particularly worried about his youngest pilot, Lieutenant Pyotr Grachev. Though a good pilot, even an aggressive one, and better than many others of a similar level of experience, Grachev at times still seemed afraid of the aeroplane. Pedrov had been putting all his pilots – of whom he had more than aircraft – through as rigorous a flying programme as he could with limited resources; and one of the most limited was fuel. This inevitably meant the same aircraft were up more often than he would have liked, in an ideal situation.

But these were not ideal times for the nation. There was confusion, uncertainty and growing chaos. Stability was urgently needed. Like Kurinin, he wanted the nation to once again be respected and even feared, and be backed by powerful armed forces.

"All pilots," he called. "There are no reports of NATO aircraft near our patrol area; but if you spot any, do not engage. I repeat. *Do not engage*, unless I specifically order it. We are here to shadow. No more. These are not the old days. Pay particular attention, Blue Three."

"Blue Three."

Blue Three was Grachev.

All aircraft were fully armed.

Moscow, the same moment in time.

There were three people in the duty section: two sergeants – one junior – and a lieutenant. The duty officer for the evening should have been a captain; but he had swapped with the lieutenant to spend a steamy evening with his girlfriend. It was an error both officers would eventually live to regret.

The senior sergeant, young for the rank, stared at the transcripts coming in. He collected them, studied them closely and felt certain some were connected, but couldn't quite understand how. Nevertheless, going entirely on instinct, he chose five apparently disparate items to show to the lieutenant, feeling they were of the greatest prority.

He went into the lieutenant's office. "Sir, I think you should look at these."

The lieutenant had been promoted through the ranks, believed he'd seen everything the world had to offer and suspected that the sergeant was too ambitious for his own good.

"Why?" he asked, taking them indifferently.

"Look at them, sir. Please."

The lieutenant looked, shifting the sheets of paper with the same indifference. "A burst of code from one of our own listening posts somewhere in Siberia; a distress beacon from a BTR-80—"

"In the same general area."

The lieutenant looked up at the sergeant. "Don't interrupt me again."

The sergeant swallowed. "No, sir."

"The BTR crew are probably drunk and couldn't find their way out of their own backsides," the lieutenant went on with open contempt. "Aren't there other BTRs out there?"

"Yes, sir. Two more on regular patrol."

"Then they'll find them. You're disturbing me for *this*?"

"Please go on, sir."

"A trawler spots five NATO aircraft flying very low, going east . . ." The lieutenant paused.

The sergeant waited eagerly.

The lieutenant moved to the next sheet of paper. "Probably one more of their stupid manoeuvres. A burst of code," he read on, "to the ECOS field unit in the Baltics." He placed the last sheet with the others and sighed. "I know you think you're the brains around here, Sergeant Shelenkov, but what's the connection?"

Shelenov, who was surprisingly well-read, took his courage in both hands. "Pearl Harbour, sir."

The lieutenant stared. "What?"

"Pearl Harbour, sir," Shelenkov repeated. "1941. The Americans received plenty of apparently unconnected intelligence reports and were slow to put it all together. Some of the officers wouldn't listen."

The lieutenant's eyes seemed to go red as they narrowed. "Be very careful with me, Sergeant. Don't cross the boundary into insubordination."

Shelenkov persisted. "I would inform the general and Lieutenant-Colonel Levchuk—"

"You would, would you?" the lieutenant shouted, causing the other sergeant in the outer office to turn to look. "Who the hell do you think you are, Shelenkov? Do you know where the general and the colonel are right now?"

"Yes, sir. At a reception."

"Yes, sir! At a reception for foreign dignitaries. And you expect me to drag them out of there, on the strength of these?" The lieutenant slammed his hand on the sheets of paper. "What the hell do you take me for? These can wait till morning." A nasty grin appeared on his face. "Unless you think the West is suddenly about to invade."

"No sir, but—"

"Get out of my office!"

Shelenkov went back to his desk and made copies of the reports he'd passed to the lieutenant.

"I'm going to take them to the general," he whispered to his colleague.

The junior sergeant cast a wary eye in the direction of the lieutenant's office. "Are you crazy?" he whispered back.

Shelenkov stood up. "Perhaps." And began to leave.

The lieutenant spotted him. The officer rose from his desk and hurried to the door of his office.

"Shelenkov!" he bawled. "You come back here or you're facing a court martial! *Shelenkov!*"

Shelenkov left the office without a backward glance.

End Moves

The time to target was now reading 00:03:00.

"Showtime!" Carlizzi said. "Arm the weapon."

"Weapons!" Caroline told the DVI.

"Weapons mode selected," came the warm tones of Sodding Sid. "Armed."

"Gamma Four," Caroline ordered.

"Gamma Four selected. Auto-acquisition ON."

The EMPC blue HUD symbology went into its routine, with the pulsing rotating triangle doing its fancy dance.

"Pretty," Caroline said.

Then the triangle did its vanishing trick.

"Accelerate," Carlizzi advised.

She disengaged autothrottle and eased the levers forward, but stayed out of afterburner. The Starfire seemed to unleash itself. Over to her right and left, the escort ASVs kept perfect station. She knew they'd also be accelerating.

She felt a slight tightening in her stomach. There was no going back now. It was time.

"Time for pitch-up approaching . . ." Carlizzi said, ". . . now!"

"Going up!" she ackowledged.

She eased the stick back for the shallowest of climbs, finger on the gun trigger, holding it down. The Starfire seemed to float upwards. The thousand feet came in a blink. The Gamma HUD was alive again, the blue triangle going into an incredible darting sequence across the HUD as it acquired and marked its targets. Then nothing happened. The Gamma HUD vanished.

"Target destroyed," Sodding Sid intoned.

"What do you know?" Caroline said as she broke away, going into afterburner as she headed fast for altitude.

The escorts, right on cue, fanned out in a protective screen and followed.

"A lot," Carlizzi said. "Sid knows a lot."

"I heard nothing, felt nothing, saw nothing. Did we do anything? Or have we trekked to this hornets' nest just to screw up? Suppose the whole mission is a fake and there's no such thing as an EMPC? I mean . . . nothing bloody happened, Carlo!"

"Why do you think nothing happened?" he asked quietly, checking the twilit sky for unwelcome companions.

"I know we were told to expect this. And I know the blue-white lightning flashes in the simulator—"

"Were just graphic emulations to give you a kind of visual reference. But this is the real gun. The pulse is invisible. We're not talking ray guns like in a movie. You heard Sid."

"But it's so eerie. Nothing came out of the bloody gun! I expected a cue of some kind, despite the forewarning."

"But something did come out of the gun. And you did see something. You got your cue. You saw the Gamma HUD."

"Do you mean to say we actually did fry their circuits?"

"We surely did. If anyone was watching, it would look like we carried out some manoeuvres. No hostile action."

"But—"

"When did you last see a radio wave with the unaided eye?"

"Eerie," Caroline said again. "And that gizmo cannon really does work?"

"Mission accomplished. The gizmo cannon works. Back there, a lot of circuits have suddenly gone down and some guys are scratching their heads wondering how come all they can get is static, or nothing at all. With luck, they may not even be able to talk to any fighters they've got upstairs; assuming they've got anyone up top."

"So we're home and dry."

Ping!

"Not yet," Carlizzi said gravely. "We've got company."

"They've seen us?"

"Not yet," he repeated. "Cut the burners. I'm going into Chameleon. We spotted them first on fused electro-optic infrared. That was our friendly Sid's non-vocal warning. They're way upstairs and haven't yet acquired us against the water. But it won't be long. We won't talk to the escorts. Hohendorf will be carrying out his tactics. He'll call when he needs to. A secure datalink transmission is still a transmission, even if the other guy doesn't know what the hell you're talking about; but he'll know you're out there somewhere. Stay put on this heading."

"Roger."

Staying out of afterburners, the Starfire and its escorts headed at high speed for more friendly airspace.

Weapons systems were fully online and armed.

It was Grachev who made the first contact.

"I've got something!" he called, excitement in his voice.

His infrared tracking ball had picked up a heat trace but it was not stabilising. Nonetheless, he had a bearing of sorts.

"Calm down, Blue Three!" Petrov commanded. "All aircraft, ladder formation. Let's see what's going on. And do *not* engage without my permission." He wondered why he hadn't heard anything from the ground radar.

The six aircraft went into a ladder formation from 40,000 feet down to 10,000, with a vertical separation of 6,000 feet between each.

Grachev was at 28,000 feet, and felt a hot flush go through him. *NATO fighters!*

"Starfire aircraft," Caroline heard Hohendorf's voice say in her headphones. "We've got a ladder heading our way. We're out of their airspace. Keep going. I repeat. Do not turn to engage. Keep going."

She knew he had used voice deliberately on an open channel, instead of secure datalink. If the bogeys were listening in, he clearly wanted the leader to know he was not looking for a fight.

Petrov was indeed listening in. He had set up a frequency scan and caught the last half of the message.

"Keep going," he heard. "I repeat. Do not turn to engage. Keep going."

I'll chase them for a bit, he thought, *then turn back.*

It was a way of breaking the monotony of the training flight. But they were streaking away.

"Full burners, everybody!" he called. "Let's give them a chase. Show them we're awake out here. But watch the fuel!"

The six Su-35s lit their burners and gave chase.

"There're still coming, Carlo!" Caroline said, watching her threat display.

"Yeah. I got them. But they don't look belligerent. They would have tried a few lock-ons, just to rile us. I think they just want to play. But we'll watch 'em, just in case."

"OK."

*　　*　　*

In Zero-One, Flacht watched the warning display closely.

"What do you think they're up to?" he asked Hohendorf. He had identified the six incoming aircraft as Su-35s.

"Muscle-flexing. Nobody's told them we've done anything hostile so they're just playing watchdog. If they've got no one who's nervous, it's OK. They're pros."

"And if they've got a nervous baby?"

"It could get dangerous if the leader doesn't keep control."

"Let's hope he can. But just in case . . ."

"We can hurt them."

"I've got a lock!" Grachev shouted, and fired a medium-range missile.

It was a Vympel R27TE with infrared seeker and a range of close on seventy nautical miles. It was headed for Starfire Zero-Three, Bagni and Stockmann's aircraft.

Petrov was horrified.

"Blue Three!" he barked. "I warned you! Disarm your weapons!" He hoped the NATO pilot was skilled enough to avoid the missile. This was not a situation he wanted on his plate.

But Grachev's blood was up. He didn't even hear his commander. He fired another R27, at the same target.

"Jesus!" Stockmann exclaimed. "I've got two rounds heading our way! I'm spoofing! Better go into shit-hot pilot mode, Nico. We got some serious avoiding to do!"

"I'm into shit-hot mode!" Bagni said and broke combat formation in order to deny the locks of the incoming missiles.

"We've got hard company," Stockmann called in a calm voice. "Avoiding."

Hohendorf watched as Zero-Three shot skywards, leaving a hot sunburst flare behind to entice the hungry R27. He knew that Stockmann would also be jamming the missiles' seekers.

"All Starfires," he called as he hauled the ASV Echo tightly round to face the oncoming fighters, "go hot but stay restrained. This may be someone who has panicked. I'll take care of it. Okay, Wolfie," he said to Flacht. "We must end this now before it gets worse and turns into a circus. They are well out of their airspace. Arming Skyray Beta. Have you got the launch aircraft?"

"Got him, and locked. On your sights."

Hohendorf saw the seeker diamond pulse and lock on the HUD and on the helmet sight. The designating arrow pointed almost straight ahead and slightly down. The Skyray had its prey in a firm grip and was getting excited, its lock-on tone building to a high crescendo.

"You must have read my mind, Wolfie," Hohendorf said grimly, and squeezed the release.

The Skyray hurled itself off the rail and streaked eastwards into the darkening sky, leaving a brilliant comet-like wake.

In Zero-Three, Stockmann watched with relief as the first missile curved away, looking for the meal it had somehow lost.

"Doing good there, Nico," he said between grunts as Bagni hauled the ASV into punishing gyrations. "Now for number two. This one looks mean and determined as hell. That is one hungry flying pencil."

A deep grunt came from Bagni in reply as the Tornado flipped onto its back, then began to haul itself tightly into a curving dive that merged into a hard climbing turn.

"Still there," Stockmann said. "God*damn*". This shit's got a tight hold on our butt. I'm spoofing some more."

The missile began to veer.

"Hey! We're looking good! I think we beat him! Good going, Nico. Good—"

The missile exploded.

What sounded like hailstones peppered the aircraft. But it flew on without a tremor.

"Nico! You OK!"

"I am fine. That was close."

"Yeah. Too goddamned close. Some dying bits came our way, but I've got no lights up on the CWP. You?"

"Mine is quiet. No lights."

The central warning panels in both cockpits carried an array of warning lights that would tell them the bad news if any system went down. So far, it remained happily unlit.

Stockmann felt a huge relief. No lights on any of the warning panels meant the missile's dying gasp, though close, had not caused damage.

"Axel's popped at him," Stockmann said. "Hope he got that bastard, but good."

*   *   *

At that very moment, the Skyray exploded against Grachev's aircraft, ripping it to pieces and consuming him in a fiery hell. Not sufficiently alert to possible retaliation, Grachev had no idea what hit him. He'd made a fundamental error in air combat, and had become fixated by his target.

Petrov saw the violent explosion below at Grachev's altitude, and felt despair. He had warned the hot-headed lieutenant. Now the price was paid. The other pilot had been astonishingly quick; a professional who didn't waste time.

Then Petrov was startled to hear a voice: in English but tinged with an accent that sounded American, but which was clearly not the speaker's native intonation.

"Sukhoi leader. Enough. We do not want a fight. Sorry about your man but he fired first. Weapons are now disarmed and we are going home. Sukhoi leader. Do you copy?"

"I copy," Petrov replied. "Weapons are down. We are also going home. Let us hope we do not meet again like this. We may decide not to turn away next time."

"Understood. Out."

"Return to base," Petrov ordered his remaining aircraft.

They reversed heading and set off at high speed.

Petrov was sombre as he thought how Grachev had suffered the ultimate penalty for disobeying orders. It was symptomatic of the current state of the nation, he thought, feeling angry at the waste of a young life. Why had they sent him someone who was clearly not yet ready for such high-risk gamesmanship?

The world had changed. Demarcation lines were fluid. To cope, fluidity of action had to be the new way. There was no longer a fixed line in the sand. Both line and sand were shifting continuously. At least there was a man in Moscow who seemed to hold the key to a return to stability. But when that key was eventually turned it would be too late for those like Grachev.

As he flew back to base, Petrov still could not understand why the radar had made no contact with them.

He called the base on the approach frequency. "Why have we heard nothing from the radar?"

"The radar's down," he was told.

"What?"

"It suddenly stopped operating."

"When did this happen?"

They told him.

He felt a tingle go through him. *The NATO aircraft.*

270

He shook his head. They had done nothing; they had simply turned away. No weapons had been launched.

And yet.

Petrov was pensive. His instincts were telling him something, but there was no evidence to back them up. The rules, he decided, were definitely changing.

And Grachev, by his impetuousity, had fallen foul of them.

STARFIRE AARA 2.

Zero-Two and Zero-Four had taken on fuel and returned to a stand-off position, waiting for the other three aircraft to complete refuelling. The Starfire and Zero-One had completed. Bagni and Stockmann in Zero-Three were now at the tap.

Datalink confirmation of mission success and the downing of the Sukhoi had already been transmitted to November One. It was all over bar the final leg home.

From his position just off the tanker's left wing, McCann had a clear view of Zero-Three. As he watched the aircraft, plugged into the drogue basket and seeming to float on the end of the fuel hose, something strange happened to it.

"Hey! Mark!"

"What now?"

"Take a look at Nico and Hank. What the hell's going on?"

Selby looked.

Zero-Three seemed to be rapidly changing colour, rather like an airborne relative of the octopus.

"Their ship looks like something on heat," McCann suggested.

"Thanks for the typically graphic description, McCann. Their Chameleon must be on the blink. Perhaps that missile did hit something after all."

"Hey guys," McCann called on the secure channel. "Displaying for a mate?"

It was Stockmann who answered. "Can it, you cornfed Kansas City gargoyle."

"Gargoyle?"

"We took a hit in the Chameleon sensors," Stockmann said in exasperation. "I'm trying to stabilise to one colour. Happy now?"

"Hey. I just thought you guys were giving us a show."

"Zero-Two, can you put something in that guy's mouth?" Stockmann pleaded.

"Oh that I could," Selby replied. "But he's trussed up in the back."

"What's your status?" Hohendorf said to Stockmann

"Fuelling nearly complete and there seems to be no other system malfunction."

"It seemed that way earlier," Hohendorf reminded him. "Better stay alert, just in case something else goes." He was well aware that Stockmann didn't really need reminding. The marine would already be doing just that. "If serious, head for one of the diversion airfields."

"Roger."

Zero-Three completed refuelling without further drama. The formation peeled away from the tanker and headed for high altitude, for the transit back to base.

Moscow, the same moment in time.

Sergeant Shelenkov had driven to the ambassadorial building where the reception was being held. The place was ringed by diplomatic protection troops in smart uniforms and he was stopped by two of them, one holding up an imperious hand.

He got out of the staff car he had borrowed without the lieutenant's authority. One of the troopers shone a light in his face and on his uniform.

The man's attitude changed. "Security," he said.

"That's right, soldier. I'm here for General Kurinin and Lieutenant-Colonel Levchuk."

A lieutenant came up. "What's going on here?"

"The sergeant's here for General Kurinin, sir," the trooper with the light said.

"Is he supposed to be leaving so soon?" the lieutenant asked. "People are still arriving, as you can see."

"I'm not here to pick him up, Lieutenant . . . at least, not unless he wants to come back with me. I've brought something of great urgency he must see right away."

The lieutenant held out a hand. "I'll see that he gets it."

"Sorry, Lieutenant. I only give it to the general himself."

The officer's eyes were hooded in the gloom. "Are you refusing to obey me, Sergeant? And while you're at it, let's see some identification."

Shelenkov took his ID out of a breast pocket. "I'm with the general's staff, sir. I must see him."

The lieutenant took his time inspecting the ID. "Must? You could be anybody, in spite of this thing."

Fed up with the time-wasting, Shelenkov took out a small clipboard from a side pocket of his tunic. There was a sheet of headed paper on it. He held it out to the lieutenant as the man returned his ID.

"And what's this?"

"An official document, sir. If you'll sign it, please. It says you refused me entry to see the general with papers of great importance."

The lieutenant seemed to rock on his heels. He glared at Shelenkov, then finally gave in with bad grace. "Let him through," he ordered.

Shelenkov drove through the high open gates of the entrance and pulled up next to a British ambassadorial car.

A captain came up to him. "Yes, Sergeant?"

Shelenkov saluted. "I'm here to see General Kurinin and Lieutenant-Colonel Levchuk, Captain. Urgent papers."

"Are they expecting you? I would have to interrupt—"

"I'm sorry to cut in, Captain, but I just had to ask the lieutenant if he would sign an official document refusing me entry."

"Are you threatening me?"

"No, sir," Shelenkov said patiently, "but the general might—"

"The general might do what?"

The captain snapped to attention. "General!"

Shelenkov stood erect.

"I saw the car," Kurinin said. "What might the general do, Sergeant? I assume you've got a very good reason for gatecrashing an official function?" He did not dismiss the captain but drew Shelenkov to one side. "Did your superior officer send you?"

"No, General."

"No? You did this on your own authority?"

Kurinin looked very dangerous, Shelenkov thought, but he stood his ground. "Yes, General. There are papers I felt you should see right away."

"You what? You *felt*? You, a sergeant, disturb me at an official function because you *felt*?"

"Send me to a penal battalion if I'm wrong, General, but please look at the papers I've brought."

Kurinin looked at his underling. "Bold gamble. Where are they?"

"In my tunic, General."

"Resourceful too. All right. Come with me." As they went past the captain, Kurinin said, "Find me a quiet room, Captain, then find Colonel Levchuk and ask him to join me and Sergeant . . ." He looked at Shelenkov.

"Shelenkov, General."

". . . and Sergeant Shelenkov."

The captain stared at Shelenkov, then with a fraught "Immediately, General," set off on his errands.

The captain was quick with both the room and a curious Levchuk. As they entered the high-ceilinged ornate room, Kurinin turned to Shelenkov.

"All right, Sergeant Shelenkov, show me why you should not go to a penal battalion for interrupting my evening."

"Pearl Harbour, General," Shelenko said as he pulled the papers out of his tunic. "That's what I told the lieutenant."

"Pearl Harbour?" Kurinin frowned as he took the papers. "What are you going on about, man?"

He stiffened as he read. He passed the papers wordlessly to Levchuk whose stance visibly changed as he too read them. No one realised that two of the sheets of paper remained stuck together by friction.

Kurinin looked at Shelenkov. "Is this what you meant by Pearl Harbour? Apparently unconnected pieces of information forming part of a bigger picture?"

"Yes, sir. I told the lieutenant, but . . ."

Kurinin nodded. "Pearl Harbour," he said grimly.

"General, I'm in trouble with the lieutenant. I left without his authorisation."

"He's in trouble with *me*. You're smarter than he is . . ." Kurinin paused. "You keep saying 'lieutenant'. I thought Captain Leonidov was duty officer tonight."

Shelenkov remained silent.

"I see," Kurinin said in grim tones. "I won't get you into more trouble, Sergeant. Drive me back. I want to see what else this lieutenant has decided I should not look at." He turned to Levchuk. "Gregor, I suppose you'd better stay—"

"If I may interrupt, General. I hate these functions."

"So do I. Let's go."

The lieutenant could not believe it: the general in dress uniform followed by a similarly attired Levchuk followed by the sergeant. He knew he was in trouble.

Kurinin marched straight up to him. "Where is Captain Leonidov?"

274

"General, I . . ."

"Sergeant Shelenkov!" Kurinin kept his eyes on the lieutenant.

"General?"

"Take two armed men, find out where Captain Leonidov's whore lives, go there and arrest him on my authority!"

"Arrest him, General?"

"I'm beginning to like the way you think, Sergeant. Don't give me cause to change my mind. Get moving!"

"Yes, General!"

Shelenkov hurried out.

"And as for you, Lieutenant, in the old days you'd have been shot on the spot! Or sent to a Siberian hell-hole! Put youself under arrest until I decide what to do with you. Get out!"

As the lieutenant scuttled away, Kurinin glared after him. "Pearl Harbour," he muttered.

Later in his own office Kurinin, still in dress uniform, looked at Levchuk.

"Your instincts, Gregor, were correct. An intelligence-gathering ship spots five ultra-low-flying NATO aircraft; encrypted transmissions are intercepted, apparently from one of our own isolated listening posts, going who knows where; a seemingly lost APC . . . I have a feeling we have not yet heard the worst of it."

"I agree."

A knock sounded. "Come!"

A captain that Levchuk had dragooned into replacing the disgraced lieutenant entered. He carried more transcripts, and one sheet of paper that he held out first.

"The junior sergeant found this on the floor, General, and thought it might be important. It's one of the sheets that Sergeant Shelenkov brought you. We weren't certain if you had already seen it."

"I'll have those," Levchuk said. "Thank you, Captain."

"Sir."

The captain left and Levchuk handed Kurinin the single sheet.

As the intelligence general read it, a burst of swearing filled the room. "It must have been stuck to one of the others." He handed it to Levchuk. "Another transmission, this time to the ECOS unit!"

As Levchuk read silently, Kurinin leafed through the recent transcripts.

A sharp intake of breath came from him. "The radar was mysteriously disabled while those NATO aircraft were in the vicinity, but no weapons were used. A feint, perhaps, for something else? One of

Pedrov's pilots gets over-excited and shoots two missiles at them, then gets shot down himself . . ." He smacked the papers down on his desk. "We're going up to the Research Unit," he said tightly.

"When?"

"Tonight!"

November Base, 2010 hours local.

Having flown westwards, there was still plenty of daylight left when they charged low over the main runway. They landed one by one, giving Caroline and Carlizzi in the Starfire first slot. Bagni and Stockmann in Zero-Three, landed last.

Which was just as well.

Jason and his deputies were again in the tower to watch all their pigeons return to the roost.

Then a sharp call came from Stockmann.

"We're having a problem here," he said. "Standby one."

Zero-Three had moved to the far end of the runway and had stopped. Several sets of binoculars were trained on the aircraft.

Helm picked up a pair to pass to Jason. The wing commander shook his head and continued to look impassively out at the stricken ASV Echo. Helm put the glasses to his own eyes.

"Starfire Zero-Three," the duty air traffic controller called. "Your status?"

"Engine fire. We're taking care of it."

Jason's face was impassive as he watched the aircraft.

Emergency procedures were put into immediate action. Scant moments later, fire and medical crash crews were on their way.

The other four aircraft taxied on to their respective hardened shelters.

McCann turned his head to follow the speeding vehicles. They'd all heard Stockmann's conversation with the tower. There was nothing they could do, and could only hope their fellow aircrew would get out unhurt.

"Looks like that missile did some damage after all," he said to Selby as they taxied on.

"Yes," Selby agreed soberly. "At least they're home. That fire could have happened over the North Sea. They might have had to eject."

"Yeah. It would have been a cold bath."

"They'll make it."

"Sure hope so."

In Zero-Three, Bagni and Stockmann had rapidly gone through the fire on ground procedures.

The attention getters kept coming back on each time Bagni pressed one of the flashing red buttons to let the system know he had been alerted. They were telling him that more systems were failing.

The throttles were closed and the high-pressure cocks shut. Low-pressure cocks had also been shut down. The fire extinguisher button for the right engine had been pressed and the auxilliary power unit turned off. Several lights now showed on the CWPs, denoting that many functions dependent upon the right engine had failed or were about to. But the one that grabbed attention most was R FIRE – fire or overheating in the right engine bay.

Only fleeting seconds had passed since the problem had made itself known; but it seemed like years. The moment was fast approaching to abandon the aircraft. They might have to do a zero-zero ejection and were not looking forward to it.

Then, even as they watched, the R FIRE light winked out.

Bagni again pressed one of the hooting attention-getter buttons. This time, it remained silent. Other systems were going offline, but the R FIRE light did not come back on.

"I think we should leave before it changes its mind," a relieved Stockmann advised.

"I think you're right. Canopy coming up."

They unclipped their masks as the great clamshell raised itself, both relieved that it worked, doing away with the need for a possible jettison had it had jammed shut. They gulped at the fresh air and had disconnected themselves from the aircraft by the time the canopy was fully open.

"Pins in," Bagni said.

They rapidly re-inserted the red-tipped safety keys into the slots of the ejection seats and canopy firing mechanisms to prevent uncommanded ejection, just as the first vehicle with an attached step ladder reached them.

They exited the aircraft quickly and moved some distance away as the fire safety crews arrived.

Then the medical team arrived.

"Thanks for coming, guys," Stockmann said, grinning, "but you don't get your hands on us today. We're fine. We'll just walk a while."

As he and Bagni walked slowly away, helmets in hand, Bagni said, "This has happened to me before."

"What do you mean?"

"When I was with the AMI, on the 104S, I had a fire warning. I put her down OK. There was no fire. But later an inspection showed a crack in the fuel pipe. A little longer in the air and I would have had a very bad fire. Maybe an explosion."

"She got us home," Stockmann said after a pause. "Nico, I like flying with you."

"Yes?"

"Yes, old buddy; and I like your guardian angel even more."

In the tower, Jason received the news expressionlessly.

"Well, gentlemen," he said to Helm and da Vinci, "it appears we'll be inflicting some serious pain on Hohendorf's and Selby's mess bills tonight. Perhaps Bagni's too, for good measure."

"It would be even more of a party," Helm suggested smoothly, "if we attacked all ten mess bills. Successful mission, damaged aircraft returned, crew safe and well. Ten celebrations."

"You have got a point," Jason said, warming to the idea. "That ought to please McCann."

Helm's face cracked open into a smile of malevolent glee.

In the Siberian wilderness, Urikov found his missing APC – whose radio he had himself disabled the night before the patrol – the next morning.

They secured Melev's body on top of the BTR to keep it cold and because no one wanted to travel inside with it. He sent the vehicle back with the body to the research unit, remaining in command of the other two to carry out a search for the missing Konstantinova.

Helicopters were sent out to aid him. Two days later, the search was called off. It was assumed she had fallen into a lake somewhere and had drowned in the freezing water, perhaps after being trapped beneath an underwater outcrop.

Kurinin spent several days at the unit, setting in motion a thorough investigation into the entire affair.

The soldiers accused Melev of raping the female officer and stuck to their story. Yakulentov never admitted he had been unconscious. Olga Vasilyeva was still failing to counter the rampaging virus and, at the ECOS field unit, the disease was still some way from being detected.

A frustrated Kurinin returned to Moscow with Levchuk.

Back in his office, he pored through the huge pile of statements and reports. He was not satisfied. Something was very wrong. Something kept calling to him.

Levchuk, on one of his visits to the office, said, "Step back from it for a while. You'll get a fresh perspective."

"Anything in your own copies to excite your interest?"

"Many strands, but I've not yet found the key that links them all."

"What about that famous instinct of yours?"

"Still dormant."

"That's it!"

Levchuk stared. "That's what, General?"

"The knife. The damned knife!"

"I don't follow."

"Melev was killed with a knife. You saw that wound; you've read the autopsy report. That was a professional killing. A woman being raped would have stabbed in a frenzy. This was clinical execution. Melev was taken with surgical precision and that takes a very special kind of training. It's so damned obvious we missed it completely. We were all occupied with the rape . . . As, I'm quite certain, was intended."

Kurinin had almost been speaking to himself. He stood up, began to pace, then stopped.

"So tell me, Gregor, where would a sergeant, who *I* made up to lieutenant and who could barely shoot straight, learn to use a knife in that manner? I don't think she's dead at all."

"What?"

"And I want those soldiers grilled until they beg for mercy! They're lying about something. I think Melev did set out to rape her and the soldiers were in on it; but Melev got the shock of his life, a terminal one. I also think Melev was himself set up. From the statements we've so far recorded, he was after her. She used that, cleverly. And did you note how his widow, the rather large supply sergeant, looked more relieved than grief-stricken? Konstantinova was her friend, when no one else would be.

"I also find it intriguing that the area where she was lost is not covered by any of our own high-resolution surveillance satellites. And the listening post, which has hidden cameras and acoustic devices triggered by the opening of the door, was never touched. She knew what she was about."

Kurinin's eyes seemed to blaze as he looked at Levchuk.

"She was right under very our noses," he uttered softly. "Somehow, her organisation got her in. Whatever else she may be, she's certainly bold and dangerous. We can only imagine the damage she has been able to do; much of which, I'm very much afraid, we shall only discover over time. Who *are* these people?"

"You *believe* all this, General? How did she survive in the middle of nowhere on her own, and be missed by the search parties?"

"I'd like to know that too. But don't worry, my friend. I have not yet taken leave of my senses. You were right. You suggested I look at it from another perspective. I have; even if it seems like an apparently crazy one. Use this perspective and see how different the picture looks.

"Many things then begin to take on a new logic of their own. When we check deeper into Konstantinova's relationships with the other personnel at the unit, we may discover some intriguing factors. We must search obliquely. She will not have been obvious. For example, there's the sudden increase in potency of the virus which so defeats Dr Vasilyeva's best efforts. Konstantinova – or whatever her real name is – also made a point of befriending the doctor."

"No more so than anyone else."

"She would have been careful to ensure that."

"You're giving her a lot of credit for all this," Levchuk said calmly, "assuming she's who you think her to be."

"This is a very resourceful woman," Kurinin told him. "I think the time has come to train Lirionova. She has been made to look foolish. When I tell her what I believe about her friend Konstantinova, she will have a powerful motive to hunt her down. Like everyone else, Konstantinova must have a vulnerable spot somewhere. We'll just have to find hers."

Kurinin looked at Levchuk, seeing the uncertainty in his subordinate's eyes.

"I am right about this, Gregor."

November base, one week after the mission.

Rose Gentry knocked on the door to Jason's office, opened it and popped her head through. "The major's here, sir."

"Thank you, Rose. Come in, Mr Morton!"

She stood back as Morton entered, then shut the door softly.

Morton looked at Jason uncertainly, wondering why he had been called in to see the wing commander.

"Don't look so worried, Major. You haven't done anything wrong.

Why do my crews always seem to think I'm about to carpet them?"
Jason asked rhetorically in a dry voice.

"Boot camp, sir. It stays with you."

"We call it square-bashing. But I get the drift. Well, you're not
here to be carpeted, Major. You're off to Granada."

"Grenada, sir?" Morton said, misunderstanding.

"Granada," Jason corrected. "Andalucia. Spain."

"Why, sir?"

"Seems the Pentagon want you there."

Morton looked chagrined. "Oh no! They're not hauling me out
of here! With respect, sir, I'm enjoying my return to flying."

"Fear not, Major. You're not being grounded. But the Pentagon
insists." Jason passed him an address. "You'll be there at ten hundred
hours Granada time, in two days. Travel arrangements have been
made. Get your civvies. Don't miss your flight. Enjoy the Alhambra
while you're at it. And the warmth."

A thoroughly confused Morton saluted. "Sir."

Something that might have been a smile appeared briefly on
Jason's features as he watched Morton leave.

Loja, Granada, Spain. Two days later, 1000 hours local.

Morton, still unsure of what was happening, stared out of the window
of his room in the rather splendid hotel, in the countryside some thirty
kilometres from the city. No one had been in touch since he'd arrived
the night before.

He glanced at his watch yet again. One minute past ten.

A knock sounded.

"Yes?" he called tentatively.

"Room service," a voice muffled by the solid door replied.

"I didn't—"

There was another knock, insistent this time.

He went to the door, pulling it open. "I said . . ." He stared. "Oh
my God!"

"Well?" Mac said. "Do I get to come in?"

Anderson County Library
300 North McDuffie Street
Anderson, South Carolina 29622
(864) 260-4500

Belton, Honea Path, Iva,
Lander Regional, Pendleton,
Piedmont, Powdersville,
Westside, Bookmobile